MW01673692

FREE BIRD RISING

BOOK SEVEN OF THE FOUR HORSEMEN TALES

Ian J. Malone

Seventh Seal Press
Virginia Beach, VA

Chris Kennedy/Seventh Seal Press
2052 Bierce Dr.
Virginia Beach, VA 23454
http://chriskennedypublishing.com/

Ordering Information:
Quantity sales. Special discounts are available on quantity purchases by corporations, associations, and others. For details, contact the "Special Sales Department" at the address above.

Free Bird Rising/Ian J. Malone -- 1st ed.
ISBN 978-1948485913

Dedication

This story was written in loving memory of the legendary Denny Crane. I will miss you, my little man. More than you could ever know. Denny Crane: October 25, 2006 – August 8, 2018

* * * * *

Part One

Chapter 1:
Fires and Frying Pans

Taylor settled into the command chair of the Earth Mercenary Ship *Valiente* and glanced back to the tactical station. "Talk to me, Billy. What do we have?"

"Sensors count three Dutya ships on an intercept course," Billy said, his broad face and square jaw bathed in the glow of his console.

"Make and model?" Taylor asked.

"Two laser frigates, *Syn* class, and one heavy cruiser," Billy said. "Long range scans indicate stock ordnance across all platforms."

Taylor hoped that meant there'd be no surprises. "Time to intercept?"

"Nine minutes at current speed," Billy said.

Taylor turned to his navigator down front. "How far to the stargate from our current position?"

The navigator ran a series of checks on her console. "Looks like three-point-eight light seconds, give or take."

"Could the *Valiente* clear that before those ships arrive if we maxed her out?" Taylor asked.

The navigator shook her head. "Sorry, Chief, but I wouldn't recommend it. We'd have to push our engines way past safety regs to make that kind of speed, and even then it'd still be tight."

"How tight?" Taylor asked.

"Under sixty seconds, and that's being generous." The navigator swiveled her seat to face her commander. "Best case scenario, we'd risk cracking something under the stress of acceleration. Worst case, we'd compromise her reactor and blow ourselves to hell."

Taylor wasn't a fan of either option. *Come on, T. Think.* He rubbed his forehead as a trio of blips drew closer to their position on the large, three-dimensional Tri-V projection down front. This was supposed to have been a textbook private security job. Pick up the client—in this instance, a Trade Guild arbiter bound for the Galactic Union world of Sakall—then deposit said client at his destination, upon which time Taylor's company, Swamp Eagle Security, would receive the balance of their contract fee. The whole Sakall voyage was scheduled to take over a month, with four separate jumps through hyperspace, known as transitions. The *Valiente* had wrapped three of those sans incident. The fourth, it seemed, was destined to be more interesting.

Why can't these things ever go to fargin plan? Taylor knew the answer to that. He returned his attention to tactical. "Well, crap. We can't run, but I ain't exactly in a fightin' mood today, either."

"Glad to hear that," Billy said.

"So, we got a third option here or what?" Taylor asked.

Billy pursed his lips. "Honestly, Chief, I don't know that we do. The Dutya and the Jivool have been locked in this trade dispute for more than a year, hence the importance of these talks. Don't get me wrong, there are a lot of folks who want peace to succeed. However, there are just as many who prefer the status quo, and they'll do anything they can to maintain it."

"Even attack an Earth ship?" Taylor asked.

Billy snorted. "Are you kidding? The only species the Dutya hate more than the Jivool is us."

"So that's a yes, then."

Billy gave a somber nod.

Wonderful. Taylor toggled up the mirror feature on his console then accessed Billy's screen. Thankfully, the laser frigates were of the Dutya's *Syn* class. That meant they were older and wouldn't pose much of a threat so long as they were kept at a distance. The cruiser, on the other hand, presented a problem.

"Think these fellas will talk to us?" Taylor asked.

Billy shrugged in his seat. "Worth a shot."

Taylor glanced across the bridge to his communications officer. "Open a channel, Priority One."

"You got it, Chief." The officer buzzed a series of commands into his terminal. "Broadcasting on the emergency frequency…now."

"Incomin' Dutya vessels," Taylor said. "This is Chief Taylor Van Zant, commander of the EMS *Valiente*, flagship of the Earth mercenary company, Swamp Eagle Security. Please identify yourselves and state your intentions."

The Dutya were a rodent-like race whose dialect consisted mostly of chirps, clucks, and hisses. Thus, the ship's reply came in the form of digitized English, courtesy of the *Valiente*'s translation matrix.

"This is Dyshone, commander of the Dutya cruiser *Setour*. There have been reports of pirate activity in these territories. As such, we have come to ensure the arbiter's safe passage through the region."

"Pirates, you say?" Taylor caught a "knock it off" look from Billy for his sarcasm. "Well, that's real generous of you to hold the arbiter's wellbeing in such high regard. Tell me, what do these safety precautions of yours entail?"

"My crew has prepared a shuttle," the Dutya said. "Please allow it to connect with your ship's docking collar, then place the arbiter aboard. We will take him the remainder of the way."

Taylor clicked his tongue. "Yeah, that ain't gonna work for us at all."

The navigator and the comm officer traded looks. "See, my company has a signed contract for this operation, and that contract clearly stipulates that we don't get paid unless your arbiter debarks from our ship onto his planet." Taylor paused. "I like gettin' paid, Commander, and I'm pretty sure you do, too. Now, if there's been some sort of mix-up here, you're welcome to take that up with the Mercenary Guild. Otherwise, I'd kindly ask that y'all stand aside so we can do our jobs."

The digital voice hissed an angry spat of gibberish that even the computer didn't recognize.

"Oh, that doesn't sound good," Billy muttered.

C'mon, pal. You bowed up and showed us all you've got danglies. Now it's time to let cooler heads prevail and move on down the line.

More static crackled the line.

"If you are not prepared to relinquish the arbiter by choice," the Dutya said, "then we are prepared to take him by force."

Damnit.

"Enemy weapons are coming online!" Billy announced.

Taylor made a slashing motion at his throat, and the comm officer killed the channel. "These little fargin jerkwads wanna play, fine. Set Condition Red."

"Condition Red established." The overhead alert lighting glared red as the comm officer sprang into action.

"Tactical," Taylor continued, "spin up all tubes and particle batteries, then get the anti-missile systems online. I want a firin' solution on these sombitches as soon as you can get me one."

"Yes, sir," Billy said.

Taylor sat up in his seat and tightened his belts as all three aggressors loomed larger on the Tri-V.

"Frigates One and Two are forming up ahead of the cruiser," Billy said.

"Range?" Taylor asked.

"Point-eight light seconds and closing," Billy said.

Per Taylor's recollection of *Syn* tactics, they typically wouldn't fire laser batteries until they'd closed to within fifty thousand miles of the target.

"Frigate One is firing!" Billy shouted.

Crap. "Skew turn ten degrees off axis to starboard!" Taylor barked. "Execute!"

The *Valiente*'s engines groaned in protest under the sudden exertion as the entire bridge pitched to starboard. Seconds later, a mild shudder rattled the deck under Taylor's boots as laser fire grazed the ship's exterior.

"Impact to sections four, five, and six of the forward hull," Billy said. "Reflective armor is holding; damage is minimal."

Taylor shot a wounded look to tactical. "Anytime you're ready to play with those buttons of yours, Billy, feel free."

Billy's fingers were like lightning at his console. He glanced up and grinned. "Firing solution acquired on Frigate One."

"Kick her ass!" Taylor ordered.

A swarm of dots sprayed from the *Valiente*'s portside missile tubes on the Tri-V, then rushed toward the lead frigate. They struck in seconds, igniting in a massive plume of light against her hull.

"Contact!" Billy announced. "Frigate One is breaking off!"

"Yeah, but Frigate Two isn't," the navigator said.

Taylor wasn't about to get behind the eight ball this time. "Helm, skew turn thirty-two degrees off axis and prepare to open fire on frigate two."

"Acknowledged," the navigator said.

Another groan roared from the engines as the ship complied with the command. A moment later, another swarm of lights poured from the *Valiente*'s tubes.

"Frigate is releasing counter measures!" Billy shouted. "Impact in three…two…one."

A splash of light engulfed the Tri-V screen. This time, though, it didn't consume the enemy's ship, but rather the vacuum in front of it.

"Any hits?" Taylor asked.

Billy shook his head. "Minimal. We nicked her, that's about it."

Taylor chewed his lip as Frigate One re-entered the fray. Together they assumed a flanking formation in a clear setup for an attack run. *Enough screwin' around.* "Spin up the particle accelerator spinal mount. Let's end this now."

"Heads up, Chief!" the navigator shrieked. "Enemy cruiser has closed to weapons range!"

"Billy?" Taylor snapped his head around.

"Enemy cruiser has a lock!" Billy shouted. "She's firing!"

"Helm!" Taylor screamed. "Skew turn forty degrees to—"

"Brace for impact!"

A massive explosion rocked the hull, sending every member of the *Valiente*'s bridge crew smashing into their seatbelts. A klaxon sounded throughout the ship.

*Son of a…*Taylor scrambled to collect his thoughts. "Helm, I want—"

"Laser frigates are flanking us from the other side," Billy cut in. "They have a lock…firing!"

Another explosion rocked the ship. This one, however, was followed by another sound, one no commander ever wanted to hear.

"Fusion reactor breach," the system said in a voice so calm it was eerie. "Reactor failure in five…four…three…"

Taylor closed his eyes as chaos reigned supreme and waited for the inevitable…again.

"Session terminated," the simulator said once the entire *Valiente* crew had perished. "You may exit when ready."

Taylor just hung his head. *Wait for it.*

"So," Billy's voice chirped in Taylor's earpiece. "If you had to guess, what would you say went wrong there?"

Taylor winced. "I got outgunned three to one?"

"That's part of it," Billy said. "That's not all of it, by any stretch, but it's part of it. Come on down, and we'll talk about it over some lunch."

Taylor sighed and removed his helmet, allowing his sandy blonde hair to tumble past his shoulders. Then he removed his gloves and body sensors and dismounted from the training platform, where a

Latino sergeant in a black battle dress uniform, or BDUs, emblazoned with the Iron Conquistadors logo handed him a water bottle.

"Thanks, Dez," Taylor said. "I owe you one."

"Not to worry, Chief Van Zant." Fernandez pointed to the sweat, pouring in buckets down Taylor's cheeks. "You want one of my troopers to bring you a towel?"

"Nah, I'll make do." Taylor used the sleeve of his flannel overshirt instead. "I've always had a nasty tendency to sweat like a whore in church when I'm under stress. I guess the command chair qualifies."

"Apparently so." Dez chuckled.

Taylor pulled his hair into a loose ponytail, then reached back and removed the wireless pinlink that had connected his mind to the simulation via the tiny ports behind his ears. "I swear, Dez," he said, touching the protrusions with his fingers. "I've had these pinplant things almost a year now, and I don't think I'll ever get used to them. No Human bein' oughta have a computer hardwired into his brain this way. It ain't natural."

Dez laughed and took back the pinlink. "I hear you, amigo. For what it's worth, I felt the same way when I first got my pinplants. It's confusing as hell, having all that data swimming around in your head like that. Still, trust me when I say they're damn handy in a scuffle."

Taylor huffed and threw on his overshirt, then fished his keys from his jeans. Could he see where being able to mentally connect to his hardware in a firefight might be useful? *Sure.* That still didn't change the fact that the whole process—at least, what little Taylor understood of it—was downright creepy.

The door across the hangar swung open, causing both men to turn.

"Captain Dawson." Fernandez threw up a salute as Taylor's executive officer walked toward them.

"Dez," Billy said.

Dressed in hunter-green BDUs and a snug t-shirt bearing the vibrant eagle, crossed muskets, and fanned palmetto leaf of their company's logo, Captain William R. Dawson was just north of fourteen years Taylor's senior, with the rugged features of a corn-fed Nebraskan and the close-cropped haircut of a man whose entire being screamed ex-Navy.

Billy also possessed one of the driest wits Taylor had ever seen. *When he relaxes long enough to show it, anyway.*

"Tell your boss we really appreciate his letting us commandeer his training room for a few days," Billy said. "Be sure to let him know we'll pay for the time as soon as our next contract rolls in."

Dez waved off the suggestion. "It's no bother, I can assure you. The comandante told me as much. He also said to get you whatever you need, and to let you know the Eagles are more than welcome in our house. They always have been."

Taylor offered his host a grateful smile. In truth, he looked forward to the day when his people could afford a simulator of their own, rather than having to rent one from their neighbors.

"And how is old Marcus Cortes these days?" Billy asked.

"You know the comandante." Dez chuckled. "Ornery as ever and always on the go. Speaking of, he's off-world right now, which is why he's not here to greet you in person. He sends his regards, though, and says you should stay to train as long as you need."

"Nah, that's okay." Billy slapped a hand to Taylor's back. "I think three days is enough for old Captain Starkiller, here. We'll grab our things and be on our way."

Once outside the Conquistadors' training hangar, Taylor and Billy crossed the compound toward their vehicles, the North Florida sun warm on their faces as a mild, salty breeze rolled in from the Atlantic Ocean two blocks away.

"I'm sorry for what happened back there," Taylor said. "You know, for bombin' the mission the way I did."

"Oh, you bombed it all right." Billy chuckled. "You had *one* job, and that was to get your crew to the stargate. All you had to do was fend off that cruiser and make a run, but instead, you let yourself be goaded into a conflict with the two smaller ships, and it cost you."

Taylor sighed, and he slid on his Jacksonville Generals cap, then adjusted the bill.

"Don't be too hard on yourself," Billy said. "At this point last year, you were tending bar in Cocktail Junction, not commanding a starship. These things take time, believe me. Don't rush it."

"Yeah, well," Taylor scoffed. "Something tells me 'master strategist' ain't ever gonna be a descriptive on my resume, no matter how much time I practice."

"Maybe, maybe not." Billy shrugged. "Good strategy doesn't always have to be complicated. To the contrary, it typically just requires some good old common sense."

Taylor looked up.

"Stay cool," Billy said. "Know your strengths, your weaknesses, your opportunities, and your threats, then leverage that information for best possible success. If you can remember all that, then execute it in combat, you'll come out ahead more days than not."

Taylor appreciated the pep talk. All things being equal, though, he still preferred ground-pounding with a rifle in his hands to warming a command chair with his butt out in the cosmos. That reminded him. "Any word from Smitty?"

"You realize that's the fifth time this morning you've hit me with that question, right?" Billy asked. "It's not like she can communicate with us from hyperspace."

"I know." Taylor grinned. "I also know how much our newest company commander is missed by some of the crew when she's away."

Billy answered with a smirk. "No, there's been no new word from Commander Smith. Per her last check-in, the contract appears solid, as does the client, though I expect she'll have more to say on the matter when her ship re-enters our system in…" he checked his watch, "about three hours."

Taylor snapped his fingers. "Speaking of starships, where do we stand on ours?"

Billy frowned and looked away.

"What?" Taylor asked.

"It's nothing," Billy said.

"Oh, it's clearly something. I'm pretty sure I know what it is, too, so out with it. That's an order."

Billy ran a palm over his dark, burr-cut hair. "Why that one?"

"Why which one?"

"All due respect, Chief, I've known you since you were a toddler who couldn't resist taking a dump in the bathtub. Don't be coy. It's not your style."

Taylor figured the man had a point. "All right, fine. I presume the 'one' you're referrin' to is our brand-new flagship?"

"Ha!" Billy guffawed. "'Brand-new' are hardly the words I'd use when describing that bucket. She's beyond obsolete and a step above scrap on her best day. Hell, I'd feel safer crossing hyperspace in a wheelbarrow than I would in that thing."

"Easy," Taylor said.

"You know what I mean," Billy said.

Taylor rolled his eyes. "I get it. The ship's a fixer upper. Believe me, Keeto hasn't shut up about all the work she'll need once she's ours. Still, it's the *ours* part that matter. Ownin' our own flagship will save us a bundle in subcontracting fees because we'll no longer have to outsource for transportation to go off-world. That's huge for us."

"I understand that," Billy said. "But why this ship?"

Taylor veered onto a new sidewalk. "Because this ship—beater though she may be—is all we can afford in cash. Will she ever be the EMS *Pegasus*? No. But she'll perform well enough to get us by until we can land some more contracts, amass some more capital, then cash flow an upgrade down the road."

"Ah, come on, Chief," Billy said. "It doesn't have to be that way and you know it. Look around. You've got friends in this town, powerful friends, with lots of resources. Friends who would happily float us the credits we need to buy something decent, then we could pay them back with the profits from future jobs."

"Not happenin'."

"Why not?" Billy pressed. "Hell, it doesn't even have to be a *nice* ship. Just one that, you know, flies."

Taylor halted and faced his XO. "You of all people oughta know the answer to that."

Billy broke off and looked away.

"My brother financed this entire operation into a mountain of fargin debt because he wanted to be seen as the Deep South's equivalent to a Horseman. Did he succeed? Yeah, for a while. Then he wasn't around to pay the bills anymore, and that's when the creditors came and took a wreckin' ball to everything he'd built." Taylor pursed his lips. "Our family lost everything in that mess, Billy. Our money, our pride, even our homes. We'd have stayed chained to that poverty, too, had it not been for the MCA deal."

"Now there's an idea." Billy brightened. "You could ask the MCA folks for more credits. Tell them you need the extra capital to stay competitive in the marketplace. That'd be true, by the way."

Taylor shook his head. "I sold MCA Creative forty-nine percent of the pie in exchange for what I needed to pay off Terry's last debts and resurrect the Eagles, clean. I will *not* jeopardize this company's future with the same mistakes Terry made, nor will I forfeit my family's majority stake for more investor cash. I don't care how many starships it'd buy." Taylor returned his focus to the XO. "I may have a lot to learn about command, Billy, and I'm glad you're here to help me with that. But when it comes to runnin' the books to keep an operation afloat—be that a merc outfit of sixty-one, or a family of four—I know what I'm doin'. I've had to for a while now."

Billy raised his hands. "You're the Chief. If you wanna buy the beater then buy the beater. You have my word that Keeto and his engineers will make her all she can be."

"Thanks, brother." Taylor patted the other's arm and kept walking. A minute later, the duo stepped out into the parking area where Taylor waved goodbye to the checkpoint guard en route to his Harley Davidson Fat Boy, which slumbered under a palm tree across the lot.

"Hey, guys," a new voice said.

Taylor glanced up to see the Eagles' lead medical officer, Paul Wright, approach from his flyer wearing loose-fit slacks and a casual shirt.

"How'd it go?" Paul asked.

"Not bad," Taylor said. "I made it a whole five minutes this time before I got Cortes's entire crew blown up."

Paul opened his mouth, closed it, then opened it again. "Well, that's…reassuring."

"What brings you out, Doc?" Billy asked.

Paul adjusted his glasses. "I was on my way over to startown to meet a colleague coming in from Piquaw. That put me in the neighborhood. So, I thought I'd drop by."

Jacksonville Startown—formerly the areas of Mayport, Neptune, and Atlantic Beach—was the section of Jax that housed the city's starport. This made it home to tons of businesses, from temporary storage and mechanics to payday lenders and arms merchants, none of which seemed to jive with a socially-challenged geek from Maryland.

Taylor tilted his head.

"Okay, fine," Paul said. "I met a girl on the GalNet, and we're having coffee in an hour."

"And there's that other shoe I've been missin'." Taylor snickered.

"Yeah, yeah. Yuck it up." Paul frowned. "Seriously, though, I did want to catch up with you guys. There's something brewing back at the Clubhouse, and I thought you'd want to know before you got back."

Taylor and Billy traded looks.

"There's a woman hanging around our facility," Paul said. "She's been there all morning."

Billy scratched his chin. "Can you be a little more specific? Between staff, contractors, spouses, and girlfriends, there are lots of women around our shop."

"Not like this." Paul raised a finger. "This one carries press credentials."

"Ah, crap," Taylor grumbled. "Let me guess. She's about five-foot-two and a hundred ten pounds, with brown hair, tan skin, and a morphogenic tattoo of a bear cub on her right forearm."

Paul blinked. "How'd you know?"

"Her name is Lisa Kouvaris," Taylor said. "She's a beat reporter with the *Jacksonville Times Union*. She's been pokin' around the Clubhouse for a few weeks now."

"What does she want?" Billy asked.

"You got me." Taylor pulled off his cap and tucked it away then retrieved his riding helmet. "All I know is she's interested in writin' some sort of story about us."

Billy glanced at Paul, then back to his boss. "So, what's the problem? Good press is good press. You take it where you can and run with it."

"That's always been my thinking," Paul agreed.

Taylor rocked his bike off its kickstand and climbed on. "Sorry, boys. I'm here to run the business and get us all paid. My job description don't say nothin' about interviews."

"You're also the new face of Swamp Eagle Security," Paul added.

"The doc's right," Billy said. "Like it not, you're the majority owner of one of the most well-known mercenary outfits in the world that doesn't have a horse in its logo. At least, we used to be. You've gotta know a little facetime comes with the territory."

"Exactly!" Paul exclaimed. "Come on, Chief. It's just one interview. Heck, your brother used to thrive in this kind of limelight. It landed him a ton of play, too." He winked. "Especially with the ladies."

Taylor sighed. *You know, Paul. For a guy with an M.D. plus dual Ph.D.'s in nanotechnology and xenobiology, you really are a fargin dumbass sometimes.*

The Atlantic surf crashed in the distance.

"I'll grab lunch back at the Clubhouse and deal with this reporter," Billy said, glancing at Taylor while Paul just stood there, looking awkward. "Come in through the back gate when you reach campus. That way she won't see you if she opts to be a pain and squat out front."

"Ayew," Taylor said. That was Eagles' slang for Acknowledged and Understood, or AU.

"Where are you headed?" Paul asked.

Taylor rose on a toe and fired up his bike, sending the vintage Big Twin engine chugging to life. "I've got some business of my own to handle in Jax Startown. FYI, that's probably gonna put me a tad late, so don't wait up."

Billy raised an eyebrow. "What sort of business?"

"Nothin' big," Taylor said. "It's just an errand I've gotta run."

Now Billy really looked suspicious. "Might I inquire as to the nature of that errand?"

"Sorry, Hoss." Taylor grinned and slid his sunglasses on. "That information is classified."

* * * * *

Chapter 2: Beers, Brothers, and Brawls

"I'll be damned!" Rex O'Malley bellowed from behind the bar, his New England accent as thick as ever. "The Prodigal Son returns! What's up, Hillbilly T?"

Taylor strolled in through the ragged wooden door of the Hell House and threw an arm around his former coworker. "You see it, brother. How's life back here in the service industry?"

"Eh, par for the course, I'd say." Rex tipped the brim of his Boston Red Sox cap. "We're all just livin' the dream and killin' time until the next high-rolling customer rides in with a hard thirst for Jax's finest brew and a fat account for tipping."

Taylor chuckled, remembering his friend's plight. The Hell House was one of the few watering holes left on the startown strip—Cocktail Junction, as it was called—that still employed flesh-and-blood bartenders. Everyone else had gone automated to cut costs. Couple that with the place's dumpy roadhouse charm, affordable prices, and old-world style, and the Hell House had always been a haven for those craving a touch of nostalgia with their booze.

"Speaking of brews." Rex aimed a thumb at Taps' Row. "What can I getcha?"

"Gimme my standard," Taylor said.

"Good grief, Hillbilly." Rex cringed. "You do realize you ain't broke no more, right? You don't have to drink like it."

Taylor grabbed a stool and sat down. "A man's brand is his brand, bud. You know that. Those things typically don't change once they're set, money or no money. Besides, Long Branch Light is a local brew, and we natives like to support our own."

Rex shook his head and pulled a frozen mug from the cooler. "All the quality beer we got in this place, and my boy still drinks like a backwoods farmhand fresh off a tobacco crop. Go friggin' figure."

Taylor laughed. Meanwhile, the digital pop of faux-vinyl crackled from the jukebox, then rolled into the opening guitar riff of *Learning to Fly* from Tom Petty and the Heartbreakers.

Somebody's got good taste. Taylor searched the room for the song's player. There were two older men shooting billiards in the corner, while a trio of other folks had ensconced themselves in a booth toward the back.

"Here ya go." Rex salted a bar napkin, then set Taylor's mug down. "One ice-cold glass of Jax-brewed piss water, made to order, just for you."

Taylor saluted with his glass. "So, down to business. Were you able to get it or what?"

Rex looked wounded. "That's harsh, man. Seriously, when have I ever *not* come through for you on these kinds of things?"

Taylor answered that with a smirk.

"Fine." Rex reached under the bar and came back with a lone object. Small, rectangular, and solid to the touch, the plastic case glistened under the bar lights in its original factory-sealed shrink wrap.

Now that's what I'm talkin' about. Taylor cradled the old-timey cassette in his fingers. "I honestly didn't think I'd ever get my hands on this. Do you know how rare it is to find one of these in this condition?"

"Very, if the price you paid my starport guy is any indication," Rex said. "Don't expect any change back, either. It took your whole wad and my finest negotiating skills to get him to part with that."

Taylor didn't care. He sat there, staring in wonder at the plastic case with four men in western-style clothes on the cover. "My dad was huge into the oldies when we were kids, so stuff like this played in our house all the time. I'll tell you right now, Rex. For all the music America put out in the late-twentieth century—especially country music—nobody did it better than these guys. They called them The Highwaymen." He looked up. "This right here is what you call timeless, my friend."

"I know," Rex said. "I've been forced to endure their twangy charms on more than one occasion by a certain former coworker of mine. Only back then, we listened to it via the Net. You know, that magical place in the sky where all music lives forever in a crisp, clean digital format?"

"Ain't the same as hearin' it on the original medium." Taylor brandished his cassette. "Back in 1985, that was this."

Rex waved off his friend while the latter tucked away his prize.

"So," Taylor said. "Outside of work and antique music devices, what else is new?"

"Eh, same old." Rex shrugged. "Sky's blue. Water's wet. My Sox promise to suck again this season. Pretty much just the usual."

"Move the club to North Florida, and maybe one day you'll sniff a pennant again."

Rex fished a dirty sponge from the bar's sink and smacked his guest in the face with it.

"*Dude!*" Taylor protested through the stench.

"Maybe next time you'll think twice before you blow that kind of trash out of your word hole," Rex said. "The Sox are of Boston, by Boston, and will always reside *in* Boston, period. Nothing's gonna change that, either. Not some slick arms billionaire with a shiny new stadium, or even a cockamamie tax law that lets us pillage the league's free agents. We stand by our team, just like they stand by us."

Taylor rolled his eyes. "If you wanna die on Purist's Hill, then be my guest. But remember this." He pointed to his Jax Generals hat. "Eight World Series titles in two and a half decades say the Rays were smart to leave Tampa."

Rex flipped him the bird. "What's up lately in merc land?"

"Ah, not much." Taylor sipped his Long Branch Light. "We just wrapped our fourth contract since re-openin' shop, and I've got one of my company commanders runnin' down number five as we speak."

"Can I ask what kinda contracts we're talkin' about?"

"Mostly low-risk, small-time stuff," Taylor said. "Executive security, private escorts. That sort of thing."

Rex heaved a sigh. "Man oh man, how the mighty have fallen. I can remember a time when Swamp Eagle Security got the crème de la crème of jobs around this town. Garrison, training, high-end cadre, you name it."

Taylor's gaze met the bar top.

"I mean, your friggin' brother, man!" Rex continued. "Now there was a cat who knew how to make an entrance. I kid you not. Terry

Van Zant would strut in here like the cock of the walk after a gig, then cover every tab in the house for grins, giggles, and gonads, plus a forty percent gratuity right off the top for the staff—busboys included! People loved that guy! Seriously, T, he was like a…" Rex trailed off, doubtless at the sight of Taylor's cap pulled low over his eyes. "Ah shit, Taylor, I'm sorry. I didn't mean—"

"Don't sweat it." Taylor raised a palm. "Trust me, I'm used to it. Comp me next round, and we'll call it square."

A shade of color returned to Rex's cheeks. "I'll do you one better. How about I throw in a burger, too, seein' as how that so-called beer of yours costs less than the pop in my soda gun?"

Taylor nodded his thanks then watched his friend vanish into the kitchen with the burger order.

You'd forgotten how much you missed this place, huh? Glancing around the room, it dawned on Taylor just how true that was. Life back then had seemed so much simpler. For one, there'd been no combat, not that the Eagles had seen much of that recently. There'd also been no real responsibilities to mind—no checks to write, no meetings to attend, no decisions to make that, under the right circumstances, could determine whether people lived or died under Taylor's command.

On a personal note, there'd also been no legacy here. On the contrary, Taylor's time at the Hell House had marked perhaps the only point of his twenty-three-year-old life when the name Van Zant hadn't followed him around like a specter. Here, he was just Hillbilly T, the long-haired hippie bartender from Riverside with a love of cheap domestic booze, Major League Baseball, and fishing.

If only Shands Hospital took pickle jar tips for nanite treatments. Taylor checked his watch. He needed another beer, badly.

"Hey, Donnie, look who it is," a voice said.

Ah, crap. Taylor turned to see three men enter the bar. The first was a tall fellow, wearing dirty jeans and a plum-colored work shirt that reminded Taylor of that goofy dinosaur from his nephew's favorite cartoon. The second man sported heavy coveralls with a nasty skid mark down the front. The third wore a rumpled mechanic's shirt and a snaggletooth grin, which he aimed at Taylor.

Roughnecks from the starport.

"If it ain't the boy wonder himself," Snaggletooth said. "Tell me, *Chief*, what brings you back down here to fraternize with us mere mortals?"

Taylor presented his mug. "Good drinks and good company, mostly."

Snaggletooth traded sour looks with Skidmark.

"Is that right?" the latter said.

"Yep," Taylor said.

Snaggletooth folded his arms. "Well then. Seein' as how you're feelin' so communal today, how's about you buy me and my boys here a few rounds?"

Taylor rubbed his forehead as a waitress wearing denim shorts and a tank top emerged from the kitchen.

"Whoa, wait a second." She halted at once, eyes wide. "Y'all boys can't just come in here and—"

"Shut it, Peaches." Snaggletooth cut her off. "This don't concern you. It's just a friendly conversation between me and Wonder Boy."

The trio took a step forward, and Taylor briefly considered pulling the sidearm concealed under his flannel. *Not yet.*

"Sure don't look friendly to me," a throaty voice said from the corner.

All eyes shifted to the two men shooting billiards as they paused their game and approached the bar, still holding their cues.

"What do ya say, Stan?" the voice's owner asked. He was a short man with a silver beard and leathered skin, wearing denim overalls and a straw cowboy hat. "This here encounter look even remotely friendly to you?"

The second man—a tall gent with grizzled features, wearing a brown duster and matching fedora—shook his head. "No, Jack, it most certainly does not. To the contrary, I'd dare say these men mean to do this youngster harm if left to their devices."

"This don't concern you, old timers." Snaggletooth grunted.

"That there'd be true," Jack said. "Even still, I must confess. I abhor with every fiber of my bein' an unfair fight. And three against one?" He clicked his tongue. "Well, that strikes me as all sorts of unfair."

Stan tapped his shoulder with the end of his pool cue. "Yep."

Taylor took a final pull of his beer, exhaled, and climbed off his stool. "Listen, fellas. How about we all just take a minute and—"

"Look out!" the waitress shrieked.

A glass bottle whizzed past Taylor's ear and shattered against the bar with a crash.

"Let's dance!" Jack launched forward as if shot from a cannon and drilled the dinosaur with a hard right. The big man hit the floor, wailing, amid a geyser of nose blood.

"Don't mind if I do!" Stan whooped, slamming a cross to Skid-mark's jaw.

That left Taylor alone with Snaggletooth. *Great.*

The greasy mechanic charged in, swinging wildly and chasing any strike he could get. Most of his blows caught air as Taylor dodged aside. One, however, made contact, sending a white-hot jolt of pain tearing through Taylor's ribcage.

Okay, so maybe you ain't a total flunky after all. Taylor staggered back to regroup. He then lunged in for an offensive run of his own, baiting Snaggletooth with a series of jabs and body shots, only to set the man up for a full-force uppercut to the jaw.

The mechanic howled and fell back, clutching his face as a steady stream of red poured from his lip. "You'll pay for that, you little shit."

"Stand and deliver, Hoss," Taylor said.

This time when Snaggletooth stormed in, Taylor had a plan. He juked left, then right, then left again. Then, seeing the mechanic's fist sail past his head, Taylor seized on the opening and caught the man's wrist in a joint lock.

Snaggletooth jerked and snatched, but it was no use. He'd been had, and the panicked look in his eye said he knew it.

His dominance firmly established, Taylor flexed the mechanic's arm until he felt a pop, eliciting a scream. He then pinned Snaggletooth's wrist to his back, spun him forward, and face-planted the roughneck into the bar top.

Thwack! Snaggletooth fell to the floor, joining the other roughnecks.

"Woo, Nelly! That was fun!" Jack hollered. "What do ya say, boys? Was it good for you?"

The men on the floor had no answer save for a faint set of groans.

"Stan, I don't think they heard me." Jack retrieved his beer for a quick swig then landed a boot-first mule-kick to the side of Skidmark's head. "Now listen outta your good ear!"

Taylor could've sworn he'd heard that line before.

"I do not," Jack said. "Repeat, do not *ever* wanna see you ugly sons of bitches in here again. We savvy? Now pick your sorry fargin asses up off that floor and get." He feigned another kick. "I said *get!*"

The roughnecks stumbled to their feet, grumbling all the way, and departed the premises sans any further objections.

"Holy crap." Rex exited the kitchen and glanced at Taylor. "I leave you alone to watch my bar for five minutes, and this is the reward I get?"

Taylor shrugged.

"You gentlemen all right?" Rex asked the old men.

"Eh, that depends." Jack brushed a speck of lint from his overalls. "I personally like to do my fightin' first thing in the mornin', given the chance. You know, when I'm fresh. Alas, a wise Englishman once said, we can't always get what we want. But, sometimes we get what we need."

"And you needed a bar fight?" the waitress asked, incredulous.

Jack tipped up his cowboy hat, blue eyes twinkling at the girl thirty years his junior. "Exercise is a vital part of a man's daily regimen, ma'am. It helps keep him spry, alert, and virile."

The waitress blushed.

"Thank you, fellas." Taylor offered the strangers a hand.

"Pardon, son, but you, uh..." Stan touched a finger to his own cheek.

"Oh, right." Taylor reached up and plucked a glass shard from his face, courtesy of Snaggletooth's smashed beer bottle. "Not to worry. I got nanites in my bloodstream that'll patch that up in a jiffy."

"Ah," Stan said. "Good deal, then."

Taylor lobbed the bloody shard into the trash can behind the bar and blotted his face with a napkin. "Like I was sayin', I really appreciate you fellas jumpin' in like that. It was damn neighborly of you."

Jack waved off the comment. "No worries, son. To be honest, it's been a bit too long since we've been in a scuffle, so we're obliged for the refresher."

Taylor cocked his head. "Why do I sense that 'a bit too long' ain't exactly that long?"

Jack flashed a smile.

"Who are you guys, anyway?" Rex asked.

"The name's Bowyer," Jack said, "Jack Bowyer, from Stillwater, Oklahoma. This here's my partner, Jedidiah Stan."

Taylor wrinkled his nose, recognizing the names but not quite able to place them. Then he caught sight of the U.S. Special Forces tattoo on the underside of Jack's forearm. "Wait, are you…Blackjack Bowyer and Mississippi Stan?"

Stan tipped his fedora. "At your service."

Taylor's jaw would've hit the floor had it not been hinged to his face.

"Look, Stan. He's heard of us," Jack quipped.

"You guys rode with Asbaran Solutions twenty years ago on the Medford contract," Taylor said. "My brother used to tell stories about the two of you. He said you once took on a full horde of Oogar with nothin' but a burned-out Mk 5 CASPer and a chem pistol with three magazines. He said you had no support."

Stan made a face. "It was more like a company of Oogar with a Mk 4 and five mags. Still, the no support part is true."

"What brings you to Jacksonville?" Taylor asked.

"A little of this and that," Jack said. "Mostly we just come lookin' for a new adventure."

"And jobs," Stan added. "Jobs are good, too."

"Several of our old merc buddies have long since migrated down here to North Florida on account of the taxes," Jack said. "They say the work is good, and the pay is even better. So, given that we've been off-world a while, we figured it was time to come back south and give the old Liberty State a whirl."

Taylor fished his Generals hat from the ground and dusted it against his jeans. "Well, gentlemen, you've come to the right place. My name's Taylor, Taylor Van Zant."

This time it was Jack's turn to look surprised.

"I'll be damned." Stan chuckled. "How did I not pick up on that?"

"Ain't that the truth," Jack agreed. "Now that you mention it, son, you even look like Terry." He pointed to Taylor's ponytail. "Except for the hippie hair. That's new."

"I get that a lot." Taylor grabbed a fresh napkin from the bar and jotted down the Eagles' contact info. "You say you're here to find work? Well, I can make that happen. Give this number a ring anytime and ask for Captain Billy Dawson. He's my XO. He'll handle all the arrangements from there."

Jack studied the napkin, then extended a hand. "Well, all right then, Mr. Van Zant. I reckon we'll be in touch. How's tomorrow sound?"

"Fine by me." Taylor jumped slightly when the name Ron Carnegie began flashing in his lower-right field of vision. *What the hell?* Then he remembered. *Damn pinplants.* "Listen, fellas. Speakin' of calls, I got one here I have to take. If you'll excuse me?"

Jack shoed him off with a hand. "Go, do your thing."

Once outside of the bar for privacy, Taylor cut right into the nearest alley and keyed the *accept call* option via thought command. "Hey Ron," he said aloud. "What's goin' on?"

"I could ask you the same question," Ron aid. "What in the blue blazes are you thinking, kid?"

Taylor raised an eyebrow. "Come again?"

"Rumor has it you're about to spend a boatload of your company's hard-earned credits for a piece-of-crap frigate that hasn't been good since the Jaguars left town for London."

Taylor muttered a curse in his mind. "Did Billy put you up to this?"

"No, he did not," Ron said. "This call is all me."

"This call got a point or did you just wake up this mornin' in a mood to bust my chops over business?"

"A little of both, actually," Ron said. "I'm calling to save your butt from making this horrible decision, and to give you an alternative."

Taylor wrinkled his nose. "What kind of alternative?"

"Not over comms," Ron said. "Come out to my place, and I'll show you."

*****

Chapter 3: Echoes of the Past

His call with Ron concluded, Taylor ducked back into the Hell House long enough to power down his burger and say goodbye to Rex. After that, he boarded his Harley and headed out for the Steeldriver Defense Group main campus, located forty miles southwest in the old Orange Park.

The route Taylor chose out of startown was the same one he always took, straight down 295 South. Granted, there were better, shorter ways to reach the Steeldriver's campus. However, this one netted Taylor a solid fifteen extra minutes of road time, plus a pristine view of his hometown's skyline.

Taylor had been lucky. He'd grown up at a time when Jacksonville had ranked among the top cities in America for places to live. Prior to his generation, that hadn't always been the case.

Toward the end of the twenty-first century, after decades of political feuding with the so-called "Panhandle Rednecks" up north, the citizens of Florida's southern half had petitioned the U.S. government for the right to independent statehood. The request was granted, and in 2085 the American flag saw a fifty-second star added to its pattern.

Naturally, most of Florida's powerhouse tourism drivers—Disney, the cruise industry, and so forth—had supported the move, as had many others who'd fled south to join them in the new South

Florida capital of Orlando. This left North Florida, and cities like Jax, with nothing on which to hang their commercial hats. Soon, empty shopping parks, rotting factories, and decimated property values were commonplace from Daytona Beach to the Alabama line. By 2096, everyone including the state's lawmakers knew something had to change.

In a stunning break from tradition, the North Florida Congress passed sweeping legislation that scrapped the state's tax code and replaced it with a one percent consumption tax on goods and services. In effect, this took North Florida from being among the nation's elite taxers to rivaling Texas as the cheapest place in the country to do business.

The response was instantaneous. Almost overnight, companies from across the American landscape flocked to cities like Pensacola, Tallahassee, and Gainesville to seize on the new incentives. Every industry was represented, from tech brands like Mozilla and EXT to automotive companies like Ford and Sierra Motors.

Still, no trade was more represented in the new North Florida than the mercenary field, an industry which by then had become the backbone of the global economy. Now, whereas a Galactic Union contract worth eighty million credits would've netted an outfit forty million post-tax in New York, that figure ballooned to sixty million in North Florida. Pair that with the abundance of land cities like Jax offered on the cheap, and while the South Florida economy languished under bloated deficits, North Florida's economy was vibrant and alive—flush with billions in mercenary cash.

Spotting the exit for Tebow Drive, Taylor hooked right off the interstate and headed north up Coughlin Avenue until the expansive compound that was the Steeldriver's main campus crested the horizon. The place was impressive, especially considering that the man who'd built it had scarcely owned two nickels to rub together when he'd arrived in Jax thirty years ago from Pittsburgh. Ron Carnegie was nothing if not hardworking, and over time he'd grown Steeldriver from a three-person outfit working training and support contracts to one of the largest merc firms in the southeast, employing more than six hundred people.

Taylor hoped to one day return his own company to that kind of status. In their prime, the Eagles had employed almost twice that amount.

Easing up to the chain-link entrance, Taylor signaled to the checkpoint guard that he was there to see the owner. Once inside, Taylor taxied his Harley up the path to the main administrative complex, then turned right toward the airfield per his host's instructions.

As promised, Ron was waiting outside a hangar cluster when Taylor entered the parking lot. A thin man of smallish stature, Carnegie had just turned sixty-two, and he had short, silver hair, a matching mustache, and prominent lines across his sun-bronzed features. He was also, as many noted, one of the more eccentric dressers in Duval County. That was evidenced by the day's wardrobe of knee-length Bermuda shorts, flip flops, and a camo-patterned Hawaiian shirt.

Now there's one snowbird who embraced his new environment.

"Hail to the Chief!" Ron grinned and adjusted his sunglasses as Taylor parked his bike.

"Hey, old man," the latter answered. Once he'd dismounted, the two men shared a hug then stood outside a massive hangar, talking.

"How's the retired life these days?" Taylor asked.

"Meh." Ron raised a shoulder. "I fish a lot, play a lot of golf, hang out with my grandkids. That sort of stuff."

"Sounds like Heaven," Taylor said.

"Oh, it is," Ron said seriously. "I'd be lying, though, if I said I didn't miss the action some days."

Ron had retired from active merc field duty a few years earlier to stay closer to family. While he remained heavily involved in Steeldriver's day-to-day operations, most of the company's dealings off-world were now conducted by Ron's XO.

"How are things across the tracks?" Ron asked.

"Not bad," Taylor said. "We just wrapped an executive security contract over in the Jesc Arm that paid fairly well. I've got Smitty on her way back now from Karma with something new."

Ron stabbed a finger into his guest's chest. "I could kick your ass for poaching that girl out from under me. She was one of my best."

"Hey, don't get testy with me, old man," Taylor defended. "Smitty saw a chance to jump ship and move straight to senior command on my staff. It ain't my fault she wanted to advance her career."

"Please," Ron scoffed. "As if career advancement was the real reason she left."

"It's the only one on record I know of," Taylor said slyly.

"Uh huh." Ron seemed less than convinced. "How's the family?"

Taylor smirked and slid on his Generals cap. "They're good, all things considered. Rita just wrapped her third semester of medical school at Georgia and is well on her way to an M.D."

"Bright girl, your sister," Ron said.

"Yes, she is," Taylor said proudly. "Given the choice, I still wish she'd gone to Florida State and stuck close to home. But that's just me bein' selfish."

"And a Seminoles fan," Ron shot back.

"True story," Taylor said.

Ron pocketed his hands. "How's Jolene?"

"Believe it or not, Jo's fantastic," Taylor said of his other sister. "She's been clean almost eight months now. She's got a job. She's steady in rehab. Hell, she's even talkin' about goin' back to school for a social work degree so she can help other—"

Ron's gaze hit the pavement as if attached to an anvil.

Now who's the ragin' dumbass? Taylor looked away.

Ron's middle son, Samuel, had graduated eight years ago from the Duval Mercenary Service Track program as one of the brightest coding minds in the state. He was a real whiz kid, so much so that his accomplishments had earned him an apprenticeship with one of the big-timers in Houston. Problem was, computer programming wasn't the only thing Sammy had studied while in Texas. As the story went, he'd also become quite the frequent flyer of Space City's drug scene, a misstep that eventually cost him his ride.

Sammy returned to Jax a total disgrace, to himself and the entire Carnegie family. To his credit, the boy had managed to stay clean for a while. But then, being the resourceful kid he was, Sammy had found a way to score some cash and had used it to fund a New Orleans bender with friends.

Ron was off-world on contract when he'd gotten the call. NOLA Police had found Sammy's corpse in a Bourbon Street hotel room, the needle still in his arm.

Ron had announced his retirement after the funeral.

"I, um." Taylor cleared his throat.

"How's your mom?" Ron changed the subject.

Taylor didn't answer.

"That good, huh?"

Taylor shrugged. "At least she's talkin' to me again. Granted, our conversations center mostly on the weather, local news, and baseball. But I reckon that's a start."

"You listen to me, son." Ron leaned in to catch Taylor's full attention. "You did what was necessary to take care of your family. End of story. I know your mom didn't want any more of her kids entering the merc business after Terry's accident, but she didn't want a terminal illness, either. Your decision to take MCA's money and reopen the Eagles saved her life. Don't you *ever* forget that."

Taylor nodded, grateful. "So, this alternative of yours. What's it all about?"

Ron's smile returned. "Better to show than tell. Follow me."

Taylor trailed his host across the blacktop to the hangar where two mercs in gray BDUs slid the entrance open. Once inside, Taylor let out a gasp. *No friggin' way.*

The ship on the docking platform before him measured roughly four hundred feet in overall length with a seventy-foot beam and a streamlined frame that gave her a visibly sleeker look than others of her class.

"Is this a Navarro?" Taylor asked in awe.

"Good eye." Ron folded his arms. "The Navarro Starship Company's famous—or infamous, depending on whom you ask—Model 12 cruiser, at your service."

Taylor couldn't believe what he was seeing.

Even though mankind had spent almost a century traveling the stars of the Galactic Union, they still hadn't perfected the process of building their own ships. Many companies had tried, including offshoots of Binnig and Lockheed Martin, but most had found only nominal success. The lone exception, to some degree, had been a Michigan native named John Navarro.

Navarro had devoted years of his life to studying alien engineering, and had even spent five of those years abroad, analyzing the tech in person. When he returned to Detroit, he did so with what he deemed a revolutionary new design and ambitions of starting his own shipyard. He'd almost succeeded, too. Then one day, the authorities showed up at his home with handcuffs and a federal warrant for embezzlement charges.

As for Navarro's ship—a modified take on an Izlian warship—most hailed it as the first real success story of Human starship engineering. Sadly, only a handful had made it to market before its designer had gone to prison. Now, they were more or less a novelty.

"What is this?" Taylor asked.

"This, kid, is the alternative I mentioned." Ron stood up straight. "Or, as I like to call it, Swamp Eagle Security's new flagship."

Taylor stepped forward, appraising the vessel from the tip of its sleek, copperhead nose, down the hull of its tapered body, to the bulbous, circular housings of its fusion torch and primary thrusters. "I appreciate the gesture, Ron. I do. Fact is, though, this ship belongs in a collection. Not with me."

"Oh, stop with the judging already." Ron looked offended. "She may be older, but she's by no means ready for the shelf. She's just…"' He paused, searching for the word. "Seasoned, like the rest of us."

"That may be," Taylor said. "It still don't change the reality that I can't afford her price tag."

"Who said anything about a sale?"

Taylor faced his host. "Wait, are you…givin' this ship to me?"

Ron nodded.

"But…why?"

"Because she's yours," Ron said. "Well, technically she belonged to your brother, but you catch my drift."

Taylor stood there, dumbfounded.

"Terry purchased this ship on a whim from a guy in Houston looking to liquidate some assets off the books," Ron said. "I told your brother the whole thing sounded shady, but he assured me it was fine. Besides, we all know how Terry loved his toys."

Taylor frowned, recalling the ocean of debt he'd inherited with the Eagles.

"Anyway," Ron continued, "it took Terry some time to have the vessel moved back to Jax. However, once that happened, he sent her straight here to me for storage, and she's been here ever since."

"Terry had his own service crew with the Eagles." Taylor wrinkled his nose. "Why would he send the Navarro here instead of back to his own shop?"

"You got me, kid." Ron shrugged. "This arrangement was supposed to be temporary. Terry asked me as a personal favor to stow this thing so his people could tweak her systems, then she was supposed to go home. That was the deal."

"What kind of tweaks are we talkin' about?"

"Again, no idea." Ron faced the Navarro. "All I know is that Terry's engineers would stop by after hours, work on her until sunup, then lock the door on their way out."

"And that didn't strike you as the least bit odd?" Taylor asked.

"Terry was a lot of stupid things," Ron said. "Untrustworthy wasn't one of them. I knew your brother had his reasons. I also knew he wouldn't put me or my organization in a tough spot. So, I took him at his word that all was fine and stayed out of it."

Taylor stroked his chin whiskers. "And this was when exactly?"

Ron pursed his lips. "About a month before the Hammerhead trip."

Taylor cringed.

In addition to a species of shark defined by its hammer-shaped nose, Hammerhead had also been the name of Terry's final contract as head of the Eagles. At least, folks had assumed it was a contract. No one knew for sure, since Terry hadn't kept anything on the books, save for a name. Some had suggested Hammerhead was an unsigned training contract, others a handshake agreement to provide garrison work somewhere.

But for who? Taylor had scoured the Union's GalNet for an answer to that question. He'd come up empty, just like everyone else.

Whatever Hammerhead was, Terry had thought it enough of a priority that he'd fast-tracked a recruiting trip to Karma Station as soon as he'd returned home from his previous deployment. He'd made it to Karma without incident. It wasn't until his ship, the EMS *Bogrider*, had entered hyperspace back to Earth that things had gone horribly wrong.

"You okay?" Ron asked.

"Yeah, fine." Taylor's mind snapped back to the present. "If this ship has been here in your hangar for the last six years, why am I only hearin' about it now?"

Ron shifted his stance. "Taylor, this cruiser is all that remains of Terry Van Zant's legacy. Had I breathed a word of its existence to anyone, even you, odds are better than decent that the creditors would've swooped in and claimed it along with the rest of Terry's estate. I didn't want that. So, out of respect for your brother, and on the off-chance that the Eagles ever returned one day, I filed the title change under Steeldriver, then kept both my mouth and this hangar shut until I had another option."

Taylor furrowed his eyebrows. "You do realize we've been back open a year now, right?"

"Kid, you've run four contracts in twelve months, three of those off-world. Let's face it." Ron huffed. "You're not the easiest cat in town to catch up with these days."

Taylor laughed.

"Oh, I almost forgot." Ron snapped his fingers. "We do know one change Terry made to this ship."

Taylor perked up. "Which is?"

Ron led his guest around the hangar and halted near the front of the Navarro. There, stenciled in a thick red font on her bow, was the vessel's name.

EMS *Ryley Osyrys.* Taylor sounded the words out, trying to wrap his head around their meaning. "Ry-Lee O-Sy-Ris." His eyes bulged. "Oh, my brother is a world-class dick!"

"I know, right?" Ron snickered. "What I wouldn't give to be a fly on the wall when your blockhead XO catches sight of this."

Taylor tried in vain to stifle a snicker of his own.

"Excuse me, Colonel Carnegie?" One of the mercs approached from the entrance with a handheld comm unit. "I've got the captain on the line. He needs to speak with you right away."

Taylor motioned to the handheld. "You couldn't take that yourself?"

"Are you kidding? The first thing I did after retiring was have them take all that electronic, pinplant crap out of my skull." Ron winced. "That shit ain't natural, man."

Taylor extended a hand. "Thanks, old man. I mean it, thank you. I really do owe you for this."

Ron knocked the hand aside. "You owe me squat, kid. Truth is, every merc in this town owes a debt of gratitude to your brother. Steeldriver, the Conquistadors, Stonewall Solutions. None of that would have happened without Terry. He was the original Duval County Madman. We're just a bunch of posers, following his lead."

Taylor gave his new flagship a parting glance.

"Now go," Ron said. "Get out of here before your idiot logistics guy cashes the Eagles in on that rust bucket you've been eyeing. I'll have the *Osyrys* transferred to your campus first thing in the morning."

Exiting the hangar, Taylor returned to his Harley in time to see his XO's name flash in his field of vision. "Hey, Billy. What's up?"

"Smitty's transport just emerged from hyperspace. I thought you'd want to know."

"And?"

"And she reports the contract is solid," Billy said. "She's prepped to make the pitch as soon as she lands."

Looks like we're gonna get to kick the tires on our new ride sooner rather than later. Taylor chuckled, recalling the Navarro's name.

"What?" Billy asked.

"Oh, nothin'." Taylor smiled and strapped on his helmet. "Call up the crew and tell 'em we got church in an hour. I'm headed back now."

"Ayew," Billy said.

* * * * *

Chapter 4: Church

In stark contrast to the sweeping asphalt and sprawling industrial landscape that was the Steeldriver Defense Group's main campus, the Eagles' complex was scarcely considered habitable by most who visited. The facility had been erected from the bones of the old Castillo Airfield, located thirty miles south of downtown Jax in St. Johns County. Formerly a private airstrip for the local research community, the place had been ravaged by a hurricane some forty years earlier and subsequently abandoned. That, coupled with the property's location in the heart of swamp country, had made it taboo to most city mercs, which in turn had made it a bargain real estate buy, even by North Florida standards.

These pansies swing some of the biggest guns known to man, yet they're freaked out by some water snakes and an oversized lizard with teeth. Taylor had never understood that. Then again, he'd grown up with this country—predatory species and all. The latter didn't change the fact that this land was also home to some of the most striking natural beauty either Floridian state had to offer, from its thick plumes of palmettos and Spanish moss to its dense pockets of wetlands covered in cypress trees, red cedars, and cabbage palms.

"Welcome to God's Country, boys," Taylor's late father had said upon bringing his sons out here on their first-ever hunting trip. "You respect it, and it'll respect you. That's how this whole deal works."

Taylor remembered that speech like he'd heard it yesterday. Crossing through the complex's rickety back gate, he taxied his Harley up the sun-bleached pavement—past the admin shack, the two remaining hangars, and the tarmac—then brought the bike to rest out front of the old air-traffic control tower. The latter now served as the Eagles' command post, aka the Clubhouse.

"Excuse me, Mr. Van Zant?" a female voice called once he'd killed the engine.

Taylor hung his head. *For a company that specializes in security we sure do suck at it some days.*

"Mr. Van Zant," the voice repeated. "Can I please have a word?"

A brunette in her late-twenties trotted over, wearing faded jeans which were frayed at the knees and a green blouse with the sleeves rolled past her elbows.

"Ms. Kouvaris, I presume," Taylor said.

"That's right." The reporter halted and produced a small device the size of a pencil, clicking it active. "And it's Lisa, by the way. I was hoping maybe we could chat."

Taylor glowered at the device. *I hate bein' recorded.* "About what?"

"About being back in business," Lisa said. "As of this Friday, Swamp Eagle Security will have been back in mercenary action for exactly one year. My editor seems to think that's a newsworthy event around here."

"Well good for him." Taylor dismounted from his bike and spun to go.

"Ah, come on!" Lisa protested.

Taylor ignored her and kept walking.

"So much for Southern hospitality!"

"Hey, lady, you're the one who ambushed me, remember?" Taylor said. "Maybe it's different up north, or wherever you come from. But down here, that ain't how you start a conversation."

"Maybe I wouldn't have to resort to such tactics if you'd man up and take my call."

Taylor chuckled at her attempt to bait him with the "man up" line and kept walking.

"I'll bet your brother would've talked to me."

Taylor froze in his tracks.

"I just got here six weeks ago, so I didn't know him myself," Lisa added. "From what I hear, though, Terry Van Zant never missed an opportunity to put the Eagles' name in lights, especially here at home."

Taylor kept his eyes on the orange and red horizon. "That was certainly part of his charm."

"But it's not yours," Lisa surmised.

Taylor sighed and returned to face her. "Listen, Ms. Kouvaris."

"Lisa."

"Lisa, fine. Whatever. Let's get somethin' straight, right here and now. I didn't re-open my brother's company to become some sort of fargin celebrity. I did it because a lot of people dear to me really, really needed me to."

"So you didn't want to be a mercenary then?" Lisa stepped forward, her recorder still out and on.

"No, I've actually wanted to be a merc since I was little," Taylor said. "Most kids from around these parts do when they come out of school. Fact is, things change, and sometimes our priorities need to change with them. It just so happens that, later in life, my priorities shifted again, and that brought me back to the Eagles."

Lisa nodded, seeming to get his meaning. She turned off her recorder and tucked it back into her shoulder bag. "I'm sorry I played the brother card on you. That was probably out of bounds. It's just that…well, I wasn't here at the time of Terry's accident. I guess that means I lack perspective."

Taylor appreciated her candor. "It was a hard time for a lot of folks, ma'am. Not just me."

"Which is precisely why I'm here to write this story. Your brother—and by extension, Swamp Eagle Security—meant a lot to the Jacksonville community. At a time when outsiders were flocking to their city to milk it for all they could, Terry gave them one of their own to cheer for." Lisa chewed her lip. "Listen, I get it. Your brother was a camera flower, and you're not. That's fair. But, if I could offer you some unsolicited advice?"

Taylor gave a reluctant nod.

"Terry recognized that by putting the Eagles in the limelight, he could use that platform to direct attention to other causes that mattered." Lisa paused. "With all due respect, Mr. Van Zant, that's a skill you'd be wise to learn."

Taylor stared off into the sunset and considered her point. "You said you've only been in town a few weeks. Where'd you come from?"

"Houston," Lisa said. "I've got a lot of experience covering mercs out that way for the *Chronicle*, so my company sent me down here to work with the *Times*."

"Your accent doesn't strike me as native Texan," Taylor said.

"That's because I'm not one," Lisa said. "I grew up in Chicago."

Taylor found that interesting. "Chi-Town, huh? Good ballclub."

"Yeah. They do okay." Lisa raised her forearm and presented her Cub tattoo, her sea-green eyes seeming to shimmer in the sun. "Not the same since they moved out of Wrigley, though. I grew up with that ivy."

Taylor laughed and keyed his comm via pinplant. "Post, this is Van Zant. You got a twenty on Doctor Wright?"

"Affirmative, Chief," a woman's voice returned. "He's on the firing range with Commander Furlong."

Crap, it had to be Quint. Taylor frowned up at the decades-old water stain running down the side of his Clubhouse.

"Shall I have the doctor come find you?" the voice asked.

"Nah, that's okay. I'm headed there now. I'll find him. Van Zant out." Taylor killed the call and motioned for Lisa to follow.

"Where are we headed?" she asked.

"To find you an escort," Taylor said. "Kudos to you for gettin' by security on your own. If you're to stay here, though, and not get booted out on your ass, you're gonna need campus credentials."

After passing the Clubhouse, Taylor cut right past the engineering hangars, then proceeded ahead to the open-air firing range on the backside of the property. There, he spotted Paul on one of the far lanes.

"Hey, Chief, what's—" The doctor did a double-take upon seeing Lisa.

"Paul," Taylor said. "You remember Lisa Kouvaris from the *Times*?"

"Um, of course." Paul checked his pistol was safed, then laid it aside and extended a hand. "It's good to see you again, ma'am."

"Doctor," Lisa greeted.

Taylor looked around. "Where's Quint?"

"He ran back to storage to score us some more targets," Paul said. "We've been out here an hour, and we're pretty much out."

Lisa inspected the stack of tattered paper on the bench beside the doctor. "I thought most merc outfits used virtual sims these days for all their training."

"Most do," Taylor said. "The ones who can afford to build proper training rooms, that is."

Lisa wrinkled her nose.

"We're working up to it," Paul added.

"Chief!" a deep voice bellowed from across the lawn.

The group turned to see a tall, dark-skinned man with a shaved head and neatly trimmed goatee marching toward him. He wore dark jeans with combat boots and a sleeveless black t-shirt, exposing his brawny arms covered in tattoos.

"Quint," Taylor said. "How goes the session?"

Quint presented a paper target with a man's silhouette, its face and chest peppered with tight clusters of holes. "Aces, baby. Aces."

A sheepish Paul didn't bother showing his target.

"Who's our guest?" Quint smiled at the reporter.

And here we go. "Quint, I'd like you to meet Lisa Kouvaris." Taylor raised a hand to gesture an introduction. "She's gonna be spending some time with us."

"Is that a fact?" Quint's grin widened.

"Lisa, this is Commander Quinton L. Furlong," Taylor said. "He's presently the commanding officer for Atlantic Company, one of two such trooper units employed by Swamp Eagle Security. The other is Riverside Company, as led by Commander Smith. You'll meet her shortly."

"It's nice to meet you, Commander Furlong," Lisa said.

"Please." Quint gave an exaggerated bow then took her hand in his. "Call me Quint."

You're such a jerk, Paul said to Taylor via look.

Taylor stifled a cough with his fist. "Ms. Kouvaris is a reporter with the *Jacksonville Times Union.*"

Quint dropped the woman's hand. "A reporter?"

"That's right," Taylor said. "She's here to write a story on the Eagles' one-year anniversary of bein' back in business."

Quint's brown eyes narrowed. "Huh. Well then, welcome aboard."

Lisa seemed to ponder something as the commander returned to his targets. "Wait a second. You're Quint Furlong, the Fury of Fulton County."

Quint gave a mutter but not much else.

"You were a five-time All Star for the Atlanta Braves," Lisa continued. "First base, if memory serves. You won Rookie of the Year by an almost unanimous vote, then went on to claim three Silver Slugger Awards, two Gold Gloves, and a runner-up for league MVP. Most think you'd have won it the next season, too, had you not been banned from the game on gambling charges."

"Okay, first off, they were allegations, not charges. Secondly, they were total horse shit." Quint spun back to face his accuser. "Hear this, and hear it good, lady. I never *once* bet on baseball. Understand? Basketball, martial arts, stock cars, sure. I even placed a few wagers on the old NFL before it finally went under. But I never—*never*—bet on baseball. I loved the game way too much to dishonor it like that."

Lisa raised her palms as an uneasy silence fell over the group.

"So." Paul adjusted his glasses. "Now that we have that bit of awkwardness is behind us, what can we do for you, Chief?"

"Quint, you're with me." Taylor aimed a thumb at the Clubhouse. "Smitty's back with a proposal, and we got church in five minutes."

"Ayew." Quint ducked out of the conversation as if his pants were on fire.

"Paul," Taylor shifted. "I need you to show Ms. Kouvaris here to admin and get her some access credentials. After that, I'd like you to show her around the campus."

"Wait, me?" Paul did another double-take. "But I was about to—"

"Thanks, brother." Taylor patted his doctor's shoulder. "I knew I could count on you."

* * *

As one of only three structures on the entire Eagles campus with functional air conditioning, the Clubhouse was something of a multipurpose facility, serving as one part command center, one part domicile, and one part hangout spot for the crew. Parts one and three were housed in the old tower control room upstairs. The apartment where Taylor slept most of his nights on a secondhand bunk from a thrift shop was housed on the ground level.

Taylor and Quint entered the structure through the side, then climbed the stairwell to the control room on level two. From there, they crossed the open floor—past the bar, the Tri-V, the shag couch, and the dart boards—then headed for the lounge turned conference room where Billy waited with the others.

"Welcome back." The XO rose from his chair at the long wooden table with the company crest carved into its center. "How was Ron Carnegie today?"

"Feelin' charitable, as it happens," Taylor said.

"Really?" Billy cocked his head. "How so?"

"We'll get to that." Taylor greeted the rest of his senior staff on his way down the table. In addition to Billy and Quint, that consisted of Commander Dinah Smith, or Smitty, and the Eagles' lead engineer, Keeto. The former wore the same hunter-green BDUs and ex-military aura as the XO. The latter wore nothing at all. That was typical of most Athal, since their insectoid bodies possessed more than enough fur to do the trick.

"Okie dokie." Taylor found his seat at the head of the table. "Church is officially in session. Smitty, what do we got?"

The blonde commander in her early-thirties swiped at her slate to access an image, which she then mirrored to the Tri-V beside the Long Branch Light sign across the room. It depicted a three-dimensional portrait of a Zuparti male adorned in elegant gold robing.

"What am I lookin' at?" Taylor asked.

"A bloody sweet opportunity, that's what." The Australian native laid her slate down and clasped her fingers. "Meet Ushavo. He's the prince elect of the Ytara, a small clan of Zuparti residing on the northernmost continent of Sakall."

"Sakall." Taylor remembered the name from his earlier training session. "That's the Union trade world almost all the way out to the galaxy's Fourth Arm, ain't it?"

"Correct," Smitty said.

Quint whistled. "Talk about a hike. That's gotta be, what? Six, seven transitions from Earth?"

"At least." Keeto's species had multiple rows of teeth. This gave their speech an inherent hiss. "A voyage to Sakall would require us to cross two full arms of the galaxy. By my calculations, that's a minimum of eight weeks hyperspace transit time—each way."

Taylor stroked his whiskers. "That's one helluva deep space run."

"It's a helluva lot of supplies, too," Billy added. "A job like this would suck up nearly all our current resources, especially if we're looking to deploy both companies, which I'm assuming we'd have to."

Taylor nodded.

"The Ytara are presently locked in a mineral dispute with the neighboring clan to the east," Smitty said. "The prince is concerned his rivals could attack while he and his family make their annual pilgrimage to the Zuparti holy land next month."

"So the prince wants security," Taylor said.

"Precisely." Smitty toggled something on her slate. A second later, the Tri-V image shifted from their client's portrait to a topographical map of Sakall.

Damn, that's a lot of mountains.

"The prince estimates the pilgrimage will take roughly two weeks total." Smitty pointed to a section of the map. "That's five days through this range, plus a four-day stay in the valley, then five days back to his province."

Quint put up a hand. "Hold on a second. Are you saying this whole trip requires zero off-world travel once we get to Sakall?"

Smitty nodded.

"Why does this guy need a specialized escort for that?" Quint asked. "I mean, from what I can see here, we're only talking about a few hundred miles. Pack up your family, roll up your fasting kit and your knee-mat thingy, then hop a maglev train and go."

Smitty shook her head. "Per Zuparti customs, anyone who voyages to the holy land via any means other than on poneevy risks banishment from the afterlife."

"I thought a Panini was a sandwich," Quint said.

"A poneevy," Smitty corrected, "is a species of land animal indigenous to the region. The Ytara have been domesticating them as beasts of burden for centuries."

Quint slid back in his seat and tugged at his goatee. "Wonderful. So when all is said and done, we get to spend two months cooped up on a dank-ass starship, only to touch down on a distant planet in the butt-crack of the galaxy for a two-week mountain excursion astride a stank-ass alien camel." He huffed. "I hear Panama City's nice this time of year. I wonder if the Stormriders are hiring."

Smitty shot her colleague a sideways look. "On the upside, the prince wants us specifically for this job, and he's prepared to pay handsomely for our services."

"How handsomely are we talkin'?" Taylor asked.

"Our usual fee plus an additional thirty percent, with two-thirds paid in advance and the balance coming upon contract fulfillment."

"Bring on the stank-ass camels!" Quint sat up straight.

"That's a generous offer, all right," Billy noted.

Taylor drummed his fingers on the table. "Did this prince of yours say why he wants us so badly?"

Smitty shrugged. "He just said that he'd heard of the Eagles' reputation in security circles, and he wanted that class of company protecting his family on their journey."

Taylor stifled a frown. *Wonder if he knows these ain't the same Eagles?*

"There is a catch." Smitty raised a finger. "All of this is set to take place during the Zuparti month of fasting. By their calendar, that's only two seasons from now—ten weeks, by ours."

"Wow, that doesn't give us much margin for error," Billy said.

"No, it doesn't," Keeto agreed.

"Can it be done?" Taylor asked.

Billy rested his chin on his fist. "Traversing that kind of terrain on animals leaves us vulnerable to attack from a lot of different angles, not the least of which is from on high. I'd feel a whole lot better if we had a few scout drones lying around to watch our backs from the sky."

"What about our Hemming guy?" Taylor asked. "Think he'd hook us up?"

Billy rocked his head from side to side. "We'd have to put in a rush order. That won't come cheap."

"We can mod the contract to write in the extra expense." Taylor shifted in his seat. "What else?"

"Some extra ground ordnance would be nice," Billy continued, "not to mention a squad or two of CASPers that don't belong in a museum."

Gee whiz, Billy, I've never heard that one before.

The XO hunched forward onto his elbows. "At the end of the day, all of this is gonna hinge on our ability to find a transport that, A, can leave in the next seventy-two hours, and B, has enough cargo space to tote all of our gear. You've gotta know that's no small order on this sort of timetable."

Taylor studied the faces of his staff and readied his words. "We don't need to contract out with another company for transport, not anymore. As of this afternoon, Swamp Eagle Security now has its very own flagship."

Stunned looks rocketed around the table.

"Are we talking about the wheelbarrow here?" Billy asked.

Taylor shook his head.

Billy blinked then widened his gaze. "Wait…Ron Carnegie gave us a ship?"

"In a manner of speakin', yeah." Taylor motioned to Smitty for permission to commandeer her slate. She slid the device over, and Taylor used it to key up the tech specs Ron had sent during the drive back. A moment later, a 3D render of the vessel floated on the Tri-V for all to see.

"Is that a Navarro Model 12 cruiser?" Keeto moved closer to the projection.

"How in the world did Old Man Carnegie come by one of those?" Quint asked.

"He didn't," Taylor said. "Terry did."

Billy's eyebrows pulled together.

"So this is your brother's ship?" Smitty asked.

Taylor leaned back and steepled his hands.

"How is this possible?" Billy asked. "I thought the bank seized all of Terry's assets after the accident."

Taylor recounted Ron's story of the Navarro's less-than-above-board purchase, and how it had come to be docked in a Steeldriver storage hangar.

"I'll be damned…" Billy trailed off, clearly immersed in thought.

"What of these modifications you spoke of?" Keeto pointed to the image. "Do we know of their nature, or what systems were altered?"

Taylor shook his head. "As of now, y'all know everything I do. All other questions will have to wait until tomorrow when we take possession."

"She got a name?" Smitty asked. "This new flagship of ours?"

Taylor took in a breath, eyes flicking back to his XO. "She does, actually. She's the Earth Mercenary Ship *Ryley Osyrys*."

Billy's head snapped around. "You're joking."

Taylor shielded a snicker with his palm.

"That sneaky little ball-busting punk," Billy muttered, a twinge of embarrassment reddening his cheeks.

"I don't get it," Smitty said. "What's a Ryley Osyrys?"

"Ryley Osyrys ain't a what," Taylor said. "It's a person. As for who he was or his significance to the Van Zant family…well, I'll leave that for the XO to explain, if and when he elects to do so."

Billy's disdainful look said that wasn't happening anytime soon.

"All right, so it's settled," Taylor said. "We take the contract and get this prince fella to his holy land, then back home to his constituents."

Heads bobbed around the table.

"Good deal." Taylor checked his watch and found the hour well past six. "Smitty, send a message to our new client and tell him we accept his terms if he'll accept the modification. After that, I want you to coordinate with Quint first thing tomorrow to get our new recruits up to speed on Eagle operations."

"Ayew," Smitty said.

"Oh, and speakin' of recruits." Taylor returned to his XO. "Billy, I want you to be on the lookout for two more by the names of Bowyer and Stan. We met earlier over in the Junction, and they said they'd be in touch in the mornin'."

"Bowyer and Stan?" Billy tilted his head. "As in Blackjack and Mississippi?"

"The very same," Taylor said. "I want them brought up to speed as soon as they're on campus. I figure we can use their experience right about now."

Billy raised a shoulder. "Okay, but that won't leave me any time to go see the Elephant Man."

Taylor's expression twisted into a smirk. "What do we need to talk to him for?"

"This is the first time we'll be taking our own ship through the stargate," Billy said. "She'll need to be registered first with the guilds. Under normal circumstances, we'd do that through the Commerce Guild, who'd then pass those credentials on to the Cartography Guild for gate access. In this case, however, given our time crunch, it's probably best that we notify the gate master ourselves to expedite the process."

"I'll handle that," Smitty said. "I've met the master before. I know how to handle him."

Taylor stayed her with a hand. "I need both of my company commanders here, workin' with our new batch of troopers. I'll deal with the Elephant Man myself."

Billy lowered his voice. "Chief, you don't have to do this. One of us can—"

"I'll be fine," Taylor said with all the reassurance he could muster. "After all, this had to happen at some point, right? Best to get it out of the way now."

No one answered that.

"Y'all good on your assignments?" Taylor asked.

Everyone nodded.

"Good." Taylor rose from his seat. "Then let's get to it."

*****

Chapter 5: Facing Giants

Rising from his bunk at oh-five-thirty the next morning, Taylor hauled himself upright on the first alarm, then managed the ten-step zombie walk to his shower without incident. He'd slept like crap the night before, despite all precautions. He'd downed an herbal tea. He'd gone to bed early. He'd even taken a shot of whiskey around midnight when the other stuff hadn't worked.

Still no dice. Taylor hadn't been surprised. Not on this day. Not with what he had to do.

Once out of the shower, Taylor slicked his hair back with his fingers, then pulled on his usual wardrobe of jeans, boots, and a flannel overshirt. After that, he retrieved his personal carry weapon, a nickel-plated JX-45 compact, from its lockbox and keyed the weapon into active-safe mode.

Dubbed the Firestorm in homage to Jacksonville's Great Fire of 1901, the JX-45 was a handheld laser-pistol driven by a chemical magazine, or chem mag, as opposed to a power cell. This gave the weapon a lighter all-around weight, while also creating a more sustained rate of fire per mag load. The Firestorm was produced by Hemming Arms, a local manufacturer founded in 2095 by twin brothers from Alabama known for their innovative design work with Springfield Armory.

You can do this. Taylor shoved his Firestorm into the concealed carry rig under his shirt and reached for his Generals cap, its familiar navy-blue fabric soft in his grasp. *You've got to do this.* The door to his apartment all but slammed from its hinges when he stormed out.

As was customary for anyone seeking to leave the solar system, the Eagles would need to book hyperspace passage through Earth's stargate if they meant to fulfill the Sakall contract. That meant a trip to meet the gate master—the Elephant Man, as he was known around the Clubhouse.

Taylor's jaw clenched as he boarded the shuttle to go off-world. He hated dealing with gate masters, in part for their legendary aura of xenophobia—*a fancy word for arrogance*—though mostly because he just didn't trust them.

When Terry's ship had failed to emerge from hyperspace after leaving Karma, Taylor's family had petitioned both the Cartography Guild—the masters' employer and lords of the gate network—as well as the Science Guild—makers of the navigational drives which guide ships through hyperspace—for a full enquiry into the accident. Each had initially declined, citing in not so many words that "shit happens" in hyperspace. That was true, for the most part. In the century since mankind had joined the Galactic Union and begun utilizing the gate system, multiple ships had gone missing, each one presumed lost in transition. Still, like Humans who swam in the ocean despite the threat of sharks, the number of ships lost paled in comparison to the legion who used the gates without issue every day. Couple that with the sheer volume of drives the Science Guild produced—each one costing a small fortune—and the Van Zants had been lucky to get a cursory glance at their case, much less a legit investigation.

'Likely engine failure,' my ass. Taylor grunted as he boarded the shuttle the Eagles' chartered from Steeldriver for the stargate trek. From there, he stopped by the cockpit to greet the pilot before proceeding to the crew cabin, where he found Lisa Kouvaris already buckled in for launch.

"Early start this morning, huh?" she asked.

Taylor yawned and cinched up his safety belts.

"Thanks for letting me tag along on this," Lisa said. "Normally I've gotta fight for this kind of access, so I really appreciate it."

"It's no problem," Taylor said. In truth, he still wasn't sure why he'd signed off on her coming, except that when one was entering the domain of a group as shady as the gate masters, it paid to have a member of the press in one's entourage.

Several minutes of thunderous G forces and bone-jarring turbulence later, the shuttle broke free of Earth's atmosphere and blasted toward the stargate near the system's LaGrange point.

"Hey, can I ask you something?" Lisa brushed back a strand of her hair which hung suspended in null gravity before her eyes. "I've covered a ton of merc outfits over the years, from Cartwright's Cavaliers in Houston to Virgil Caine's Danville Express in Virginia. They all have their own way of doing things. Even still, the one commonality they share is that every single one of them seem to be a lot more…" she searched for the word, "formal than Swamp Eagle Security."

Taylor shrugged. "How do you mean?"

"Well, for starters." Lisa pointed to his hair. "Your dress code isn't exactly regulation, nor is the first-name basis most of your people seem to keep with each other, regardless of rank. Your senior staff meetings are called 'church,' your command post is a full-blown party shack complete with bar, and, lest we forget, you drive a Harley to campus each day." She cocked her head. "Maybe it's me, but you guys feel more like a biker gang than a paramilitary merc outfit."

Taylor chuckled. "What can I say? I like to promote a family-like work environment for my employees."

"Yeah, about that." Lisa fished a slate from her shoulder bag and keyed it on. "Why does everyone call you 'chief?'"

Taylor made a face. "The phrase chief executive officer comes to mind."

"You know what I mean," Lisa said. "Most merc company owners I know have adopted a rank of some sort to signify their command status. Something like admiral or commandant. Hell, even your brother took the title of colonel. But you didn't. You went with chief. Why?"

Taylor blew out a sigh. "Rank oughta be earned, not adopted. I realize some folks don't see it that way, and that's their prerogative. But I do. Everybody on my team who wears stripes came by them honest, be it Billy and Smitty in the Navy, or Quint with the three outfits he served in prior to ours. But me? The only placed I ever served before this was behind a bar in Cocktail Junction."

Lisa flashed a wry smile. "The redneck bartender turned merc owner. Only in America, right?"

"Damn straight," Taylor said. "Still the greatest country in the world, if you ask me."

Lisa swiped open a fresh page on her screen. "You mentioned your XO, Captain Dawson, a second ago. He was one of the original Eagles, wasn't he?"

"Yes, ma'am, he was. Billy founded this company as a minority owner right alongside my brother after they'd both done time in the Navy."

"So they met in the military?"

"No, no," Taylor said. "Billy and Terry met during sophomore year at Lee High School, when Billy's family moved to Jax from Lincoln, Nebraska. They graduated in the same class, then made a pact to start their own merc outfit and strike it rich. Problem was, they had neither the training nor the capital to get started."

"And enlisting was the answer to that?" Lisa asked.

"Joinin' the Navy is the answer to a lot of things for a lot of kids in Duval County." Taylor shifted in his seat. "In Terry and Billy's case, that meant eight years of service while they squirreled away all the experience and cash they could. After that, they returned home to Jax, finalized their business plan, and began courtin' investors. Swamp Eagle Security was born eight months later."

Lisa whistled. "Wow, they didn't waste any time."

"No ma'am, they did not," Taylor said. "But that was Terry and Billy. Apart, they were both solid troopers. Together, they were a force of nature, be that on the battlefield or the high school baseball diamond."

"Sounds like they were pretty tight," Lisa said.

Taylor adjusted his cap. "Put it to you this way. The first time Terry got busted by our old man drinkin' beer underage, it'd been Billy who'd stolen the six-pack from the food mart down the street."

"Nice." Lisa started to say something else but paused. "Hold on a second. Captain Dawson is your XO."

"That's right."

"Sooo…not an owner anymore?"

Taylor dropped his gaze. "No, ma'am. Captain Dawson no longer holds any ownership stake whatsoever in Swamp Eagle Security. He's purely an employee."

Lisa's sea-green eyes cut left then right then back to her host. "Can I ask why?"

Taylor exhaled. "I'm sorry, Lisa, but that's a private matter. Suffice it to say, Billy sold out and left the Eagles for a job with the Iron Conquistadors about a year before Terry's passing. He bolted town after the news broke and spent the next five years abroad."

"But he came back," Lisa said. "He came back to work for you."

Taylor nodded as his guest waited for him to elaborate. He didn't oblige.

"Okay then." Lisa coughed into her fist. "Moving on to Commander Smith. She served with Captain Dawson in the terrestrial navy, correct?"

"Yes, ma'am," Taylor said. "You'd have to ask Smitty if you wanted to know any more about her," Taylor said. "She's only been with us a short while, so I haven't had a chance to really get to know her. I do know her folks moved her from Australia to North Carolina when she was a teenager, so she is a dual citizen. I also know Steeldriver offered her a job straight off her discharge, which is how she landed in Jax."

"Steeldriver, huh?" Lisa pursed her lips. "I read about them, too. It's a shame what happened to the owner's kid. Sounds like he had some real potential."

"He really did," Taylor agreed.

"What about." Lisa paused, presumably to sound out the name in her head. "Jisawa Dimune Mokeeto?"

"Keeto," Taylor said.

"Right, Keeto. How in the world did you manage to land an Athal engineer on a Human merc team?"

Taylor dropped his gaze again. "Keeto is the lone survivor from the Athal colony on Xentu."

Lisa snapped her head up. "The one wiped out by the Zuul? I thought all the colonists were killed."

"They were," Taylor said. "All but one. The Eagles were called in on a relief contract after the Zuul cleared out. That was our maiden gig back, actually, and the first under my command. Anyway, a squad of our troopers found Keeto buried in the rubble of what had formerly been his barracks. His family was there, too, only they didn't make it."

Lisa's words trailed off into a murmur. "Dear Lord in Heaven. And he's been with you ever since?"

"Yes ma'am. Our people gave Keeto food and medical attention, then offered to take him home. He wouldn't go."

Lisa looked away as a cloud of awkwardness fell over the cabin.

"For what it's worth?" Taylor cleared his throat. "Keeto ain't the down-and-outer you'd expect. To the contrary, he's quite the chatterbox when you put a few shots of tequila in him."

Lisa laughed, albeit weakly. "An ex-owner and Naval commander, an Australian operator from Tobacco Road, an exiled ballplayer turned mercenary, and an Athal outcast turned EMS engineer. I must say, Chief Van Zant. That's one interesting crew of characters you've assembled."

"Yes ma'am, they are that," Taylor said. "They're also the best damn command staff in the business as far as I'm concerned."

"You sound pretty confident of that," Lisa said.

"I better be." Taylor grunted. "I lean on them every day to keep from lookin' like an idiot as their leader."

The duo continued swapping stories until eventually their conversation was interrupted by the crackle of static through the cabin's intercom speakers.

"Excuse me, Chief?" the pilot asked. "It's Morris up front. I thought you and Ms. Kouvaris might wanna know we're entering visual range of the stargate."

Taylor tapped his fist to the comm button on his chair arm. "Copy that, Morris. Thanks."

Staring through the porthole ahead, Taylor watched the massive, cable-connected ring come into view. As best he could understand it, a stargate functioned as a sort of solar-powered conduit, or shunt, that allowed ships entrance into hyperspace. Some ships possessed shunts of their own. However, those were rare, to say the least.

Most gates were activated once per day on schedule, then occasionally by request when needed. That was provided, of course, that the gate had amassed the requisite charge for an unscheduled opening, and that the requesting company could pay the Cartography Guild's fee, which was nothing shy of exorbitant.

Greedy fargin bastards.

Once the shuttle had docked alongside the stargate's admin station, Taylor unfastened his belts and allowed himself to float out into the open. He then braced himself against one of the other seats and pushed off, soaring in zero G down the corridor toward the debarkation hatch.

"You ready?" Morris was already waiting, his magnetic boots holding him upright.

Taylor found his footing and engaged his own boots then waited for Lisa to the same. "Go for it."

A gust of air rushed into the cabin from the docking collar's jetway outside.

"One small step for mankind," Lisa muttered.

Taylor shot her a grin, then strode into the tunnel as the hatch ahead spiraled open. Once through it, the trio trudged down into a dimly lit corridor of steel panels and exposed ventilation ducts, where a squat robot on treads waited to greet them.

"Chief Van Zant," the robot said in a modulated voice. "Gate Master Haju is expecting you."

"Thanks, but we'll—" Taylor frowned in mid-sentence as the robot turned its back to lead them out. *Rude much?*

Grudgingly, the group fell in line behind their guide, mag boots clanking against metal-grated decks as they navigated the series of tunnels that would take them up to the gate master's chamber.

And here I thought my apartment was spartan. Taylor studied the chamber's industrial decor and found it equally as dank as the rest of the station. Cramped and cold, the lobby featured a small seating area with two sets of doors on opposing sides of the room. The first, to Taylor's left, was a single door made of the same slate gray material as everything else on the station. The double doors to his right, however, were something very different. Comprised of rugged stone, the doors when closed featured an elaborate carving across most of the top section, depicting twin suns rising over what appeared to be a ruined landscape.

Taylor wasn't sure what the depiction meant, just that it was old.

"Master Haju will see you now," the machine said.

Morris stepped forward.

"It's all right." Taylor stayed him with a hand. "I've got it from here."

Morris furrowed his eyebrows. "With respect, Chief, your XO was real clear that I'm not to leave your side."

Taylor patted the pilot's arm. "I'll be fine. You wait here with Ms. Kouvaris. I don't expect this to take long."

Morris was clearly uneasy with the order, but he didn't argue.

"Good luck," Lisa said.

Taylor nodded his thanks, then took his cue from the robot to head for door one on the left. Once through it, he waited while the lights flickered active, though only to about half the brightness of those in the lobby.

"Communications offline," read the words in his lower-right field of vision.

Dammit. Taylor had forgotten that part. The gate masters were nothing if not paranoid about privacy, so much so that some of them opted to have their stargate chambers fitted with signal dampeners that blocked all non-sanctioned communications from going in or out.

Whatever. Taylor shot a sardonic look to the ceiling, then surveyed his surroundings. The office before him wasn't much larger than the room he'd just departed. On one side lay a desk space, complete with seating stools and an access terminal. On the other lay a small common area with a wall-mounted Tri-V unit.

"Chief Van Zant," a baritone voice said. "I must confess, I was beginning to wonder if this meeting would ever truly happen, or if you'd be content sending your XO in your stead."

Sorry, Hoss, but my douchebag tolerance hit zero when I quit tendin' bar. Taylor kept that to himself as the massive alien emerged from the shadows.

Like most of the others in its occupation, Earth's gate master was a member of the Sumatozou, a race of aliens that resembled in many ways small elephants who walked erect. Same wrinkled features. Same pitch-black eyes. Same mountainous gray frame. The major difference in the species came in the form of their trunks. Earth elephants had one, while the Sumatozou had two smaller trunks, each sporting green stripes down the center with red trim along the edges.

"Are you incapable of speech?" The gate master sauntered forward, embroidered robes swooshing at his ankles.

"No, Master Haju, I speak perfectly fine." Taylor crossed his arms. "I just prefer to consider my words before lettin' them spew out of my mouth."

Haju's trunks flopped with his snort. "How very…unexpected. If your brother was any indication, such a quality for temperance is far from normal within your line."

"What can I say? I'm full of surprises."

Both beings stared at each other for a long moment.

"So." Taylor tipped up his Generals cap. "Are we gonna stand around here waxin' nostalgic all mornin' or are we actually gonna do some business?"

Haju motioned his guest to a stool opposite the desk. "I understand you mean to make use of my stargate with a new ship. Is this correct?"

"It is." Taylor produced a slate containing the *Osyrys*'s credentials and slid it over.

The Sumatozou studied the device's contents. "Impressive. By Human standards, that is."

"Thanks. We like her."

Haju toggled via swipe from image to image. "Curious. In the decade since my assignment to this system by the Cartography Guild, I've never actually cleared one of John Navarro's creations through my stargate. Intriguing ships, these cruisers. Tell me, where did you find this one?"

"Neighborhood garage sale," Taylor said. "Turns out, folks really will throw anything out these days."

The gate master glowered at his guest.

If this prick screws you out of gate access, you don't get paid, genius. Taylor decided it best that he resume his *think first* strategy from earlier. "Terry bought her on a whim at an auction in Houston just before his last trip to Karma. Apparently she needed a lot of work. So he parked her off rotation until his crews could get her up to speed. She fell off the books during all the creditor stuff, which is why we're just now learnin' about her."

"Interesting." Haju drummed his sausage-like fingers on the desk. "I presume then, given the timing of these events, that your brother was unable to finish said repairs before his unexpected demise?"

Taylor was suddenly very cognizant of the loaded Firestorm under his shirt. "That's right."

"And you have?"

Taylor nodded.

Haju reclined his seat, his twitchy expression seeming to suggest that at least one question was hanging on the tip of his tongue. He didn't ask it. Instead, the gate master resumed his study of the Navarro. "Perhaps the only thing more intriguing than the nature and history of your new ship is her name. Might I inquire as to the significance of…" He paused to sound out the words. "Ry-lee O-sy-ris?"

Taylor laced his fingers. "It belonged to a friend of the family."

"Indeed?" Haju said. "How delightfully native."

"Sure, whatever."

Haju keyed off the slate and handed it over. "Very well. I think I have everything I need to process your new vessel and clear her for gate access as early as tomorrow. Will that suffice for your purposes?"

Taylor rose and pushed in his stool. "Yep. Much obliged for the—"

"There is, however, the matter of the one-time expedience fee."

Taylor froze. "The what?"

"All mercenaries, Human or otherwise, are required to register their ships through the Commerce and Information Guilds, at which time those credentials are relayed to the Cartography Guild, then to us, the gate masters." Haju shifted on his seat. "Since you are opting to navigate the process in reverse, you are in effect creating additional work for the Cartography Guild. Naturally, there is a fee for that."

Taylor blinked. "You're shittin' me."

"No, Chief Van Zant." Haju smirked. "I can assure you that I am most certainly *not* shitting you. That would imply that I am being dishonest, and as you well know, such behavior is beneath my kind."

Taylor slumped back onto his stool, beyond annoyed, and reminded himself that his grievance was with the Cartography Guild, not the gate master. If Haju said the fee wasn't his call, then that was the reality. For all the Sumatozou's faults, of which there were plenty, honesty issues weren't on the list. If a member of the species gave their word, then that was that. To violate such a pact was to dishonor one's family.

Floppy-eared putz sure seems happy to play messenger, though. Taylor stared at the grinning alien and rubbed his own temples. "How much?"

"Ten thousand Union credits."

"Ten thou—" Taylor guffawed. "That's half my company's retainer!"

"So it would seem." Haju steepled his massive hands at his chest. "Alas, business is business, and the Cartography Guild has its own financial obligations to meet. So, now that we understand each other, how would you prefer to pay?"

Taylor allowed himself a brief fantasy involving alien strangulation then presented his yack and flipped it skittering across the desk.

"Many thanks," Haju said. He then plugged the card into a device and waited for the latter's indicator to flash red to green, signaling a finished transaction. The whole process took seconds.

"It's been a pleasure doing business with you, Chief Van Zant." Haju returned the yack to its owner. "I do sincerely hope this won't be our only encounter."

Taylor didn't dignify that with a response. He snatched up his card, tipped his cap, and whirled for the door.

*****

Chapter 6: Launch Day

The next four days were a whirlwind of preparations as Taylor's crews worked overtime to get the Eagles ready for Sakall. The first order of business was to get Keeto and the engineering staff up to speed with the *Osyrys*. Luckily, that process proved relatively straightforward, thanks to Ron and the Steeldriver folks who'd taken exquisite care of her the last six years. Of course, that hadn't stopped Earth's most obsessive-compulsive Athal from going over the cruiser's systems with a fine-toothed comb. But such was the hallmark of a good engineer.

On the morning of launch, Taylor said goodbye to his jeans and flannels for something more businesslike—hunter-green BDUs with all the usual accessories—then locked up his Firestorm compact in favor of his duty weapon, a full-sized version of the same model. Finally, he traded in his Generals cap for a black one with his company's insignia, then fed his ponytail through the back and headed for the door.

In many respects, the *Ryley Osyrys*'s interior wasn't unlike the stargate station, in that both carried an overwhelmingly industrial aesthetic. Steel-paneled walls, exposed ventilation, metal-grated floors. The difference, however, came in the design. Whereas the stargates had clearly been constructed with large species like the Sumatozou in mind, the *Osyrys* had been built by a Human for Humans. That meant eight-foot ceilings instead of fifteen in the corridors, plus tighter quarters and a more confined all-around vibe in the common areas to maximize space.

Boarding the cruiser on E Deck, which housed the main cargo bay and debarkation hatch, Taylor rounded a series of junctions en route to the lift that would take him to the *Osyrys'* bridge on C Deck. When the door opened, Taylor emerged onto a catwalk overlooking the bi-leveled room that, for all intents and purposes, served as the central hub for all ship's operations.

"Ten-hut!" Quint announced in his best formal voice. "Commanding officer on the bridge."

"Knock that fargin crap off, man," Taylor said with a smirk.

Quint snickered and returned to his terminal.

Stepping to the guardrail beneath the soft glow of the overhead lighting, Taylor took a moment to refamiliarize himself with the bridge's layout. A horseshoe-shaped chamber with officer posts on each side, the center featured a massive Tri-V unit in front with the navigation post staggered slightly right behind it.

"Where's Smitty?" Taylor looked around, finding only Quint and Billy, plus a newcomer he guessed to be their new navigator. Everyone was in uniform.

"She's down on D Deck with the platoon sergeants," Quint said. "They needed some help getting the troopers organized into crew quarters before launch. Smitty went to help out."

Taylor nodded. "How about our reporter friend? She aboard yet?"

Quint's grin pulled abruptly downward with his tone. "Ms. Kouvaris is settled into crew quarters on B Deck. I told her you'd have to sign off on her bridge access."

"Good man." Taylor's gaze lingered on the lush green scene in the Tri-V as he descended the steps to join the others. "I reckon this is the new navigator I've heard so much about."

The three-foot-tall alien with owl-like features snapped out a salute.

"Relax, dude," Taylor said. "The only time we get that formal around here is when we've got a diplomat aboard. Which, you know, is never."

The Buma exhaled and dropped his arm. "Oh, thank the gods."

Taylor arched an eyebrow at the alien's accent. *New York?*

"I kid you not," the Buma continued. "During all my time in the Brooklyn MST program, I never could get my digits right for those Human salutations." He waggled his fingers. "Besquith? Sure. Oogar, no problem. Although between us, I'd just as soon have my feathers plucked out than spend six weeks trapped in deep space with those big moody bastards."

Taylor spotted his XO chuckling from the corner of his eye.

"What?" The Buma looked around, clearly confused.

"Oh, it's nothin'," Taylor said. "You're just…not what I expected."

The Buma scratched his head. "You may find this hard to believe, but I get that a lot."

"Ya don't say," Taylor remarked.

"I do say," the Buma answered. "My great grandfather was on the Galactic Union welcome wagon that made first contact with humanity last century. He liked the place, so much so that he took a post at the first embassy in Manhattan after Earth signed its charter with the Mercenary Guild. Fast-forward a few generations, and you get yours truly."

Taylor pocketed his hands. "Does yours truly have a name?"

"Tuzana Ibansk Phrankolith," The Buma took a bow. "Or Frank, as they call me back in the neighborhood."

"Word has it The Golden Horde called you a coveted nav recruit," Taylor said. "Them and about two dozen other outfits."

"That's the rumor," Frank said.

"So why us?" Taylor asked. "Why come to Jax instead of headin' for the bigtime in Houston?"

Frank gave a sideways tilt of his beak. "Honestly? I got eight older siblings, all turned merc straight out of school like me, and all now in Houston. Don't get me wrong, I dig Space City. It's a great town. I just wanted to go someplace where I could make *my* mark on the business. Know what I mean? That, and well." He shrugged. "*Taste of*

Home rated Jacksonville as one of the top five cities in the South for food."

Taylor blinked. "You're a foodie?"

"Damn skippy," Frank said. "You like Italian, yeah? Gimme your galley for an afternoon. I'll whip up some linguine with a white wine clam sauce that'll have you pissin' your Wranglers before you leave my table."

Taylor got the distinct impression he was gonna like having this alien around. "All right then, Frank. Take your post and get us clear with orbital control to move out."

"You got it, boss." The Buma spun back to his post, where a set of plugs waited for insertion into his pinplants.

"Billy?" Taylor turned to the tactical station on the bridge's right side. "Is the *Osyrys* packed up for our trip?"

Billy rolled his eyes, clearly still sour over the lack of a name change. "We're packed and ready."

"Did Hemming come through with our order?" Taylor asked.

"It took them an extra day, but yeah," Billy said. "The shipment came in last night. You'll also be happy to know that I pulled some strings through a logistics buddy of mine with Harvick's Hurricanes to get us a few of their old CASPers. They're stowed with the others down below."

"Sweet." Taylor did love a CASPer. Then again, who didn't love a nine-foot-tall, powered armor suit that was strapped to the hilt with four hundred pounds of onboard weaponry? "Which model did we get? The Mk 6 or Mk 7?"

"Two sevens and four sixes," Billy said. "That gives us one seven for every member of the command staff, plus platoon sergeants and most of the trooper threes. The T1s and T2s will have to stick with Mk 6s until I can find us another deal to upgrade."

Taylor nodded. "Good lookin' out. I appreciate that."

Billy's uninspired look said he'd have preferred to get with the times via the CASPer Mk 8.

Taylor would've, too. *If only they weren't four times the cost.* He turned to astrometrics on his left. "Quint? We good on your end?"

"Gold as gold can be," the ex-slugger said. "I'll have to recalibrate once we're in orbit, of course. But for now, all scopes read us in the clear."

The lift doors opened and the last member of Taylor's command staff emerged onto the bridge.

"Hey Smitty," Taylor said. "How are the kiddos? Tucked in good and tight?"

"They seem to be for now," the Aussie said en route to her post next to Quint at communications. "Call me in an hour, though, when the probies are floating through globules of their own puke in zero G."

"I'm *so* not cleaning that up," Quint muttered.

Smitty sat down and keyed her ident code into her terminal. "I've gotta hand it to you, Chief. You really do know how to pick your recruits."

"How do you figure?" Taylor asked.

"Those two old farts you signed?" Smitty turned to face him. "They came aboard, all right. The one called Jack bloody well made a pass at me outside the mess hall."

Taylor snickered on his way to the command chair at center-deck. Once there, he buckled in for launch, then swiped open a channel using the display console on his chair arm. "Engineerin', this is the bridge. You copy?"

"Ayew," Keeto's voice said. "We read you loud and clear. What do you require?"

"Best I can tell, we're all set for launch up here," Taylor said. "What's your status?"

"Reactors One and Two are active and engaged," Keeto said. "Reactor Three is online and standing by. F11 reserves are fully charged and primed for core injection."

Per Taylor's schooling, fusion power was the mainstay of power generation in the galaxy, be it for propelling ships like the *Osyrys* through the cosmos or powering cities like Jax through the night. This was made possible by way of a neutron-dampening element known as F11. A rare isotope of fluorine, F11 served as a stabilizing agent for the fusion process. Without it, there was no space travel.

"The *Ryley Osyrys* is as ready as I can make her," Keeto concluded. "You may launch when ready."

"Copy that. Bridge out." Taylor killed the channel and considered his next words. He'd stood on a starship bridge for more launches than he could count with Terry, events which were always preceded by some rousing speech that inevitably brought the crew to their feet in applause.

Taylor cleared his throat and thumbed open a ship-wide channel. "All crew, this is the bridge. EMS *Ryley Osyrys* shows green across the board. Stand by at your stations. We're a go for launch."

A brief silence filled the room.

"Well done, Chief," Billy said. "Really."

Taylor appreciated his friend's sentiment, even if it was crap. "Okay, Frank, she's all yours. Just do us all a favor and don't ding the paint on the way out of the garage."

"Wouldn't dream of it, Chief." Frank keyed a series of commands into his nav console before taking over with his pinplants. A second later, a low rumble reverberated through the deck, followed by a series of tremors as the waking thrusters outside built to crescendo.

"Liftoff in three..." Frank called over the roar, "two...one...mark."

The entire crew braced as an explosion of force rocked the *Osyrys'* hull, lurching her from her docking platform and prompting her skyward.

"Acceleration altitude achieved," Frank called over the cacophony. "Throttling up; main engines for orbital boost...*now*."

Taylor's fingers became a claw at his chair arm, his teeth chattering in his head, as a low thrum pierced the thunder outside. That led to a sudden burst of momentum which planted Taylor's skull even deeper into his headrest. *Don't hurl! Don't hurl! Don't hurl!*

The whole experience felt like it lasted for an eternity. In reality, the *Osyrys* had barely been off the ground five minutes when the battering of nerves and steel subsided, and the smooth, even glide of null gravity flight took over.

"Earth orbit achieved, Chief," Frank announced. "Proceeding to the stargate."

That was so *not a shuttle ride.* Taylor caught his breath and fixed his gaze on the Tri-V. Gone were digital projections of the lush greens and blues of his homeworld. They'd been replaced by an endless tapestry of stars. *I don't care how many times I do this, I ain't never gettin' tired of that.*

A series of pings chirped from Quint's display. "Looks like we've got a packed house today." He toggled the image for a better reading. "Sensors are picking up multiple ships to starboard."

"Put it on the Tri-V, will ya?" Taylor asked from his seat.

Quint swiped a set of hand gestures over his console, prompting the Tri-V unit down front to project a three-dimensional render of the space to starboard. Sure enough, there were eighteen other ships preparing for transition.

"Stargate is coming into visual range now," Quint reported.

"Confirmed," Frank said. "Hyperspatial generator is online and active."

Hyperspatial generator. Taylor could've gone the rest of his life without hearing those two words again.

Once into hyperspace, a ship's fusion plant would power its generator. That in turn received instructions from the nav system to effectively draw the ship through the void from her starting point at the stargate to a designated emergence point at her destination. That, by all rights, was where humanity's understanding of hyperspace technology ended.

Whereas many groups in the Union were fairly forthright about their tech, the Science Guild was anything but when it came to the machinations of their generators. The Guild built the drives offsite and programmed them to interface with each ship's nav atlas, the directory of planets and stargates used throughout the Union which was maintained by the Cartography Guild. The Science Guild then issued the drives with one nonnegotiable condition—*tamper with the tech and risk losing it.* Most mercs were good with that arrangement. After all, so long as one got to and from a payday on time, why should it matter if he understood the means by which that happened?

Taylor was not one of those mercs. He couldn't be.

According to the Science Guild's report, the likely cause of Terry's accident had been a faulty engine. Taylor had always found that odd, given the reputation of Terry's lead engineer, Rick Blaney, as a total efficiency hawk. If something was wrong with an Eagles ship, no matter the system, Blaney was on it. The lone exception to that came from the one system Humans were explicitly forbidden to explore.

The generator.

"Stargate is coming into range," Frank said. "Stand by for hyperspace transition on my mark."

Taylor wiped his palms on his shirt to get rid of the sweat. "ETA to transition?"

"Thirty seconds," Frank answered.

The massive ring grew larger in the Tri-V.

"Fifteen seconds…" Frank said, "ten…nine…eight."

Taylor's heartrate ticked upward as the eighteen other ships closed into formation around the *Osyrys*, the stargate's event horizon pulsing a dazzling cascade of luminescent blue ahead. *It'd be gorgeous if it weren't so damn terrifying.*

"Five…" Frank said, "four…three…two…one."

Taylor closed his eyes as a mild groan reverberated through the *Osyrys*'s hull. It was followed by the odd sense of disorientation. Then…nothing.

"Hyperspace transition successful," Frank said. "Reactors One and Two are synchronized into a shared workflow. Hyperspatial generator is online and operating well within safety parameters."

Taylor exhaled and opened his eyes. The sight in the Tri-V had shifted again, this time from a stunning starscape to the formless, colorless white of hyperspace. "Nice job, nav. Reset the clock."

"Emergence clock reset and engaged," Frank said. "One hundred seventy hours and counting until emergence in the Piquaw system."

The clock above the Tri-V flashed green with a hundred and seventy hours then began its countdown.

One transition down, four to go. Taylor reopened his all-hands channel and ordered his crew to stand down from stations.

* * *

As expected, the next hundred and seventy hours were relatively uneventful. Oddly enough, it always took that long for a ship to proceed through hyperspace, no matter her proximity to a destination. If the ship had to go too far, as was the case for the *Osyrys* to Sakall, multiple transitions would be needed. Still, each transition always took a hundred and seventy hours, no more, no less.

Just one more thing we don't understand.

On the final day of the first transition, Taylor woke and filled a bulb container with coffee then pulled on his mag boots for the trip up to the bridge.

"Mornin' y'all," he said, pushing his weightless self to the lower level then engaging his boots for footing. "How do we look?"

"Engineering reports Reactors One and Two are still purring like kittens," Billy said. "All other systems continue to show in the green."

"Good enough for government work." Taylor trudged to his command chair and buckled in, finding a slate with the morning duty report waiting for him. The next few minutes were spent reading over it while the others finished the prep work for Transition Two.

"Hyperspace emergence in three…" Frank said, "two…one… mark."

Thankfully for Taylor, emergence from hyperspace wasn't nearly as disorienting as transition. There was still a mild bout of nausea, followed by the thrum of the main engines coming back online, but that was about it. After a brief second, the Tri-V image returned to stars.

"Nicely done, y'all," Taylor said. "Now how about we—"

"Whoa!" Frank bolted upright in his seat. "Where in the hell?"

"Incoming!" Billy shouted.

* * * * *

Chapter 7: Close Encounters

"Shields up!" No sooner had Taylor shouted the order than a massive blast rocked the *Osyrys*'s starboard hull. The ship shook, but Frank managed to control her as the shields came online.

"What the hell was that?" Taylor asked as the bridge lights turned red.

"Solar-powered laser defense satellite," Billy answered. "At least, that's my guess."

"We got any plans to shoot back?" Taylor asked.

"Gimme a second to track the firing vector back to the source." Billy swiped furiously at his console. "Target acquired."

"Blow that bushwhackin' bastard outta the stars!" Taylor snarled.

The Tri-V image pinged with Billy's acquisition of the satellite. A split-second later, the dot vanished from the projection in a plume of light. All went quiet.

"Target destroyed," Billy said. "We are clear."

Taylor relaxed from his belts and straightened in his chair. "Smitty, I need you to pull double duty at damage control and tell me how bad we're hit."

"No worries." The Aussie swiped up a fresh screen on her console and ran down the data. "All things considered, I'd say it's not bad."

"Explain," Taylor said.

"That first barrage laid quite the wallop to Sections Five through Nine," Smitty said. "Nevertheless, hull integrity in those areas remains solid. All damage suffered after the shields came up seems relatively negligible."

Billy exhaled through his nostrils. "I'll say this for the *Ryley Osyrys*. She can take a sucker punch all right."

Taylor glanced to the Tri-V. A large sphere lay several thousand kilometers off the port bow, its surface covered in swirling shades of brown intertwined with the occasional swath of blue. To the planet's left from this vantage point hung two moons. To its right lay a broken chain of asteroids. "Correct me if I'm wrong, Frank, but Piquaw ain't exactly known for its sprawlin' deserts."

"No, sir," the Buma said.

"So what am I lookin' at?" Taylor asked.

Frank finished his task then spun his seat to face his CO. "I wish I could answer that, Chief, but I've got nada. I've rerun the nav record twice to see if I entered something wrong, but everything checks out. By all rights, we should be orbiting Piquaw. Only, the *Osyrys* brought us here instead."

Billy furrowed his eyebrows. "Straying off course in hyperspace is impossible. You enter through the stargate. Your generator steers the transition. You exit at the emergence point for the destination selected from the nav computer. That's it."

Taylor turned to astrometrics. "Quint, you got any thoughts here?"

The commander ran a palm over his bald head. "Sorry, Chief, but I'm just as clueless as the probie. Piquaw resides in a binary star system containing two white dwarves. This system, per my early analysis, seems more akin to Earth's solar system with a single yellow dwarf at its center."

"This system got a name?" Smitty asked.

"Not one that's on record, no," Quint said.

Taylor did a double-take. "Are you sayin' this star system ain't in the Union nav atlas?"

"That's exactly what I'm saying." Quint pointed to the system rendered on the Tri-V. "Wherever this is, it doesn't exist as far as the Cartography Guild is concerned, nor ostensibly does the route that brought us here. All I can say for sure is that, wherever we are, we must still be in the Tolo Arm since we've only transitioned once from Earth."

An uneasy silence descended onto the bridge.

"What in the bloody hell have we stumbled onto here?" Smitty asked.

An alert yelped from Billy's station. "That's a discussion we'll have to table for another time. Right now, we've got company."

"Report," Taylor said.

"Sensors are tracking two bogies inbound to our position," Billy said.

"Make and model?" Taylor asked.

Billy ran a check. "Both vessels appear Maki in origin. Looks like a cruiser and a frigate. Sensors are also tracking a *Behemoth*-class cargo carrier halfway around the planet, but she's holding position."

Taylor wasn't sweating the *Behemoth* as those ships weren't built for combat. The cruiser and the frigate, on the other hand, were issues. "Time to intercept?"

"The cruiser is coming from a geosynch orbit," Billy said. "That puts her here in roughly ten minutes at current speed. The frigate is coming from the far moon, which makes it more like thirty."

Two red blips representing the Maki ships flickered onto the Tri-V.

"Somebody please tell me we've got a stargate around here someplace," Taylor said.

Quint swiped at his screen. "We do. It's just past that asteroid field from our current location, but it's there."

"Helm, can we make it?" Taylor asked.

Frank tilted his beak. "If we take a wide arc past that belt, we could probably bypass the frigate. Even still, that cruiser is close enough now that we're gonna dance with her, whether we want to or not."

Taylor hoped like crazy that this system's gate master proved less of a jerk than Earth's. "Okay, let's do this. Frank, lay in a course for the stargate by way of the asteroid belt. Steady as she goes."

"Ayew," the Buma said.

"Billy." Taylor glanced back to tactical. "Gimme a tac rundown on the Maki cruiser."

The XO called up the ship's schematics on his console then mirrored to a side panel on the Tri-V. "Typically, Maki warships of this class are equipped with multiple fixed missile batteries, plus two dozen tubes, give or take, spinal-mounted lasers, and anti-ship lasers near most of their key sections."

Hold it together, T. Taylor felt a spike of adrenaline. "Keep our defenses up for a fight, but don't power weapons until they power theirs."

"Sir?" Billy wrinkled his nose.

"Nothin' says these folks were behind that satellite," Taylor said. "If there's even a snowball's chance they'll give us some insight into where we are, I don't wanna blow that by comin' off as a hothead. We stay cool until we've got reason not to."

The XO nodded and went back to his screen.

Please don't give us that reason. Taylor returned his focus to comm station. "Smitty, hail that cruiser and let's see if she's feelin' chatty."

The Aussie worked her terminal. "Preparing to broadcast on all channels. You're on."

"Unidentified Maki vessel," Taylor said. "This is the EMS *Ryley Osyrys*. We have inadvertently wandered into this system and mean you no harm. We wish to talk. Please acknowledge."

Everyone waited for a reply.

"Unidentified vessel," Taylor repeated. "This is the EMS *Ryley Osyrys*. We do not desire a conflict. Please state your intentions or we will be forced to declare you as hostile."

Again, no answer.

"So much for friendly conversation" Frank grumbled.

Taylor inhaled for a final attempt. "Unidentified Maki vessel. This is—"

"Inbound cruiser is powering weapons!" Billy announced.

"All crews, prepare for combat." Taylor reset his intercom from ship-wide to engineering. "Tactical, reset condition red and arm weapons—shields forward. Keeto, I'm gonna need full power to the reactor. Helm, adjust our course to match the cruiser's approach."

The low moan of engines rolled through the ship as the group sprang into action.

"Sixty seconds to contact," Frank said.

"Tactical, what's our status?" Taylor asked.

"Forward laser batteries are charged and online," Billy said. "Missile tubes one through four are spun hot with thirteen through sixteen on deck packing anti-missile countermeasures."

Taylor fought to recall his studies in search of a strategy. "Do those ships have any vulnerabilities that we know of? Somethin' we could exploit?"

Billy considered then shook his head. "Sorry, Chief, but no. Pound-for-pound, that cruiser is our equal in almost every way."

"Enemy contact in thirty seconds," Frank added.

Pound-for-pound. Taylor's thoughts turned to some of the old match-fight footage he'd seen as a kid. During one specific bout, the victor had won the contest by focusing a rapid, multi-shot attack on his opponent's left-face. That, in turn, had forced the latter to cover, thereby exposing his jaw to a full-force uppercut from down low. The result had been a knockout.

Here's hopin' this cruiser fights like Glass Joe. Taylor cleared his throat. "Billy, I want you to concentrate the brunt of our assault on the portside bow of that cruiser—lasers only, repeated bursts."

The XO looked up. "We'll get more punch out of missiles."

"I know," Taylor said. "I also know that we've got one helluva journey yet to travel when this is over, and I don't wanna do that sans most of our munitions. We open with lasers then upshift to missiles when they roll to evade. At the very least, that should back them off long enough for us to run."

The XO nodded and worked his controls. "Specified systems online and ready."

Taylor cinched up his harness.

"Ten seconds to contact," Frank said. "Five…four…three…"

A volley of red dots poured from the enemy ship on the Tri-V and rocketed toward the green blip, representing the *Osyrys.*

"Enemy ship has fired missiles," Billy said. "Deploying countermeasures."

A chain of thumps reverberated through the hull as the *Osyrys* launched her anti-missiles. Back on the Tri-V, a second volley poured into space, these dots also green, and sped toward their red counterparts. The two shades clashed at center-image, sending a wash of light sweeping across the projection.

"Enemy birds are off the board," Billy announced. "Preparing to fire lasers…now."

Multiple trails of green streaked from the *Osyrys*'s bow in the Tri-V and streamed toward the opposing blip. The latter countered with a hard roll to port.

"There's our window!" Taylor shouted. "Target their fusion torch with one through four and fire!"

A fresh plume of dots bristled from the *Osyrys*'s forward missile tubes and raced toward the Maki, which countered at once with anti-missiles.

Taylor had anticipated this. Still, the hope was that at least a couple of his own birds would skirt the cruiser's defenses to make his point.

Not one *Osyrys* warhead struck pay dirt.

"Damnit!" Taylor snarled.

Warning klaxons rang, and lights flashed dim across the bridge as enemy lasers pelted the *Osyrys*'s shields.

"What's our play, Chief?" Quint asked.

Taylor rubbed his temples.

"Chief?" Frank's voice ticked upward with alarm. "I don't mean to rush you here, but we're about to land smack in the crosshairs of that cruiser's spinal mount. Whatever we're doing, we need to get on it, fast."

Taylor fought frantically for perspective as the scene around him continued to unravel. He couldn't find it. "I'm out of my depth here, Billy. I need help, and I need it now."

Billy chewed his lip. "Okay, Frank, listen up. On my signal, skew turn ninety degrees off axis to port. Once that happens, these guys are gonna turn to match us, at which time I plan to kick them in the nuts with everything on our starboard side plus two ship killers. Best case scenario, one or both SKs make contact. Worst case, both detonate prior to impact and maybe blind their scopes in the blast. Either way, get ready to haul ass for that stargate."

"Lock and load," Frank said.

Taylor re-keyed his intercom to ship-wide. "All crews. Brace for radical acceleration!"

Billy fixed his gaze on his Tri-V. "Steady…Steady…And, *turn!*"

The *Osyrys*'s engines surged to life, sending Taylor's entire body wrenching into his harness with the sudden force of extreme gravity. For a moment, he feared he might swallow his own tongue—teeth clenched and skull buried into his chair's headrest—but he hung in. Eventually, the pressure subsided when the *Osyrys* reoriented.

"Enemy ship is coming about!" Frank announced.

"Damn right you are," Billy murmured with a grin. "Try this on for size."

A fusillade of missile fire sprayed the void between the Eagles' flagship and her aggressor, forcing the latter to lurch hard. To her credit, the Maki warship managed to neutralize most of Billy's assault before impact.

But not all of it.

A column of ship-killer-green detonated in the center of the cruiser.

"Booyah!" Quint howled. "Enemy ship is off the board! Way to swing that fargin axe, Captain!"

Taylor sighed with relief then braced through another wave of G forces as his helmsman accelerated toward the stargate. "Smitty, how bad are we hit?"

The Aussie skimmed through her data. "We've got minor breaches on A and B Decks, but emergency bulkheads are holding,"

"Casualties?" Taylor asked.

"None reported so far, but responders are still en route." Smitty faced her CO. "I'll keep you updated."

A chime from the intercom interrupted the exchange.

"Engineering to bridge!" Keeto growled.

"Bridge here," Taylor answered.

"Chief, we cannot take another pounding like that," Keeto said. "That last volley came within twenty feet of cutting clean through to Reactor One."

Taylor's heart jumped into his throat. "Containment?"

"Steady, but not for long if we're hit like that again," Keeto said. "My teams are starting their repairs now."

Billy perked up. "Whoa, hang on."

Crap, what now? "Keeto, I gotta go." Taylor thumbed off the intercom and turned back to tactical. "What is it?"

"So as it turns out," Billy said, "that little party of ours with the cruiser opened the door for her frigate friend to close the gap on us."

"ETA?" Taylor asked.

"Two minutes," Frank said.

Taylor was really starting to dislike this day "Can we avoid her?"

"Not anymore, no," Billy said.

Taylor rubbed his chin as the first few clusters of asteroids passed his ship in the Tri-V. "Spin up tubes six through twelve and prep to fire when that frigate's in range. Frank, keep your foot on the gas until we reach that stargate. Smitty, get ready to hail the gate master. Tell them whatever their fee is for an unscheduled openin', we'll pay it."

"Ayew," the group said in unison.

Taylor shifted in his seat, eyes fixed on the Tri-V, as the red dot representing the frigate closed on their position. "Helm, status?"

"Contact in thirty seconds," Frank said.

"Smitty, any word from the master?" Taylor asked.

The Aussie shook her head. "None yet."

C'mon, Dumbo. Open up already so I can pay you all my peanuts. Taylor clutched at his chair arm.

"Enemy contact in five..." Frank said, "four...three—"

"New ship!" Billy cut in. "Repeat, we've got a new ship on the board!"

Taylor searched the projection but saw nothing. "Is it the *Behemoth*?"

"No, it's..." Billy broke off, eyes darting left to right, right to left across his screen. "I swear, it was just right there!"

Frank stabbed out a finger. "There!"

The smallest of red blips pinged the Tri-V image, appearing from seemingly out of nowhere, and throttled up into a straight-line burn toward the frigate.

"What is that?" Quint asked.

"No idea," Billy said. "Whatever it is, it must've been hiding behind one of those asteroids. I'll tell you this, though, it's coming fast."

"How fast?" Taylor asked.

"Right now, it's pulling upwards of ten Gs."

Taylor watched in amazement as the unknown vessel screamed toward the frigate's aft section. There, it unloaded a thick surge of particle fire onto the latter's torch housing.

"Direct hit!" Billy yelled. "Maki frigate is breaking off!"

A chorus of whoops bellowed across the bridge.

I don't know who's flyin' that thing, but I owe 'em a drink. Taylor had barely caught his breath when Smitty turned to face him. "Chief, we're being hailed."

"Put it to speakers." Taylor waited for her to give him the *you're on* signal. "Unidentified vessel, we're much obliged for the—"

A stream of incoherent syllables poured through the intercom speakers, filling the room with a garbled ball of noise. Eventually, the syllables formed into words once Taylor's pinplants could iron out the phonetics and syntax.

"Identify yourself and state your business immediately," the male voice demanded.

Taken aback by the alien's tone, Taylor glanced to Billy, who shrugged. "This is the EMS *Ryley Osyrys*. And who might you be?"

A long pause preceded the alien's reply. "What company do you represent?"

"Pardon?" Taylor asked.

"You began your vessel's identification with the letters EMS," the alien said. "That stands for Earth Mercenary Ship, does it not? I will therefore ask again. What company do you represent?"

Taylor narrowed his gaze. "Swamp Eagle Security out of Jacksonville, North Florida. Why?"

Something that sounded an awful lot like gasps filled the line.

Oh, that can't be good. Taylor's eyes bulged at the alien's next question.

"Where's Terry Van Zant?"

*****

Part Two

Chapter 8: Ruined

Taylor sat in stunned silence as the only reply he could muster inched its way to his lips. "Excuse me?"

"Terry Van Zant," the voice repeated. "Where is he? I must speak with him at once."

Incredulous looks bounced across the bridge like ricochets.

"Ahem." Billy motioned for Smitty to mute the channel. "What's going on here?"

No one had a clue, least of all Taylor. He reopened the comm. "I'm sorry, but Terry ain't here."

"Why not?" the alien asked. "Where is he? And who are you?"

Taylor exhaled and gave his name. "I'm the Eagles' commander and chief executive officer. Have been for about a year now."

Another pause.

"The frigate you encountered is doubtless in the process of repairing her systems," the alien said. "She'll return soon. We should leave, immediately."

Taylor tried in vain to stifle a chuckle. "Listen, whoever you are. I appreciate the help just now, but I ain't in the habit of takin' my crew anywhere, much less deeper into unknown space with folks I don't know. Why should I trust you?"

The alien heaved a sigh. "Because once, long ago, your brother did."

Taylor had deliberately not mentioned his relationship to Terry. *Who are you?* It was then that he got his first real look at the alien ship's appearance on the Tri-V. The vessel was tiny, maybe the size of a school bus, with a sleek armored frame, dual laser turrets, and a square-shaped nose that, oddly enough, reminded Taylor of a shark. *Hammerhead.*

"Hey Chief?" Billy glanced up from his station. "I hate to press you here, but the alien's right. That frigate just re-fired her main reactor. She's preparing to come around."

"If you're thinking of making a run at the stargate, don't," the alien said. "The Krulig control it. They'll never let you through."

"What the hell's a Krulig?" Taylor asked.

"They're the beings who operate this system," the alien said. "I'll explain later, but for now we must get to the surface. My people can offer your ship and crew safe harbor on Rukoria, but we must hurry."

Rukoria? Taylor glanced back to Billy who spoke his next words via pinplants for privacy.

"If these people wanted us dead, they'd have never intervened on our behalf," the XO said. "They'd have let that frigate fight it out with us. I say we hear them out, at least until we can find a viable way to transition out of here."

Taylor muttered a curse. "Alien vessel, we are inclined to comply with your request. Lead the way. My ship will follow you down."

"Acknowledged," the alien said.

The trek to the planet took about an hour, at which time the *Osyrys* encountered the same atmospheric turbulence as it had leaving Earth. Oddly enough, Taylor didn't think twice about it this time. He was too wrapped up in his own thoughts to notice. *Who are these people, and what's their connection to Terry? Why don't they know he's dead? Do they know who may've been responsible for the accident?* Taylor had spent six long years pondering these questions. Now, it seemed he was finally poised to get some answers.

Once the *Osyrys* had crossed through Rukoria's stratosphere, she began her descent through the clear, blue sky toward a massive expanse of desert below.

"Sensors are detecting something on the surface," Frank said.

"Can you be a little more specific?" Billy asked.

Frank gave another pass of his screen. "Sorry, sir, but I can't. It's not giving off any sort of readings, electromagnetic or otherwise. Whatever it is, though, it's big."

"How big?" The words had barely left Taylor's lips when the mass in question came into view via the ship's ventral cameras on the Tri-V.

Boasting a jagged skyline that went on for miles in all directions, the sprawling metropolis ahead looked more like a junkyard than an actual city. Its buildings—what remained of them anyhow—resembled towering hulks of twisted metal, whereas the smaller ancillary structures favored scorched mounds of steel and ash.

There was also, best as Taylor could tell, no detectable movement on the ground. Just an empty maze of abandoned streets lined with trash and debris. *What happened here?*

Static crackled the intercom.

"Your sensors should be reading a nav beacon roughly five degrees to port," the alien said. "Have your pilot shift your vector toward it. There, you'll find an open docking bay, waiting to receive you."

Taylor wrinkled his nose. "Is this bay below ground?"

"It is," the alien said. "Our Sanctuary possesses a jamming system that will mask your ship's EM signature, but it must reside underground. It's how we keep our own ships hidden from the Krulig. As I said, safe harbor."

Taylor was anything but comforted by that explanation. He motioned Frank to make the adjustment. "We're headed there now."

"Excellent," the alien said. "We'll see you shortly."

Feeling the *Osyrys* shift her descent, Taylor continued his survey of the devastation below. In many respects, it reminded him of the pictures he'd seen of Iran last century after the Galactic Union had bombed that country following the ISIS attack at first contact.

"We've got activity ahead," Billy said.

The Tri-V toggled onto a large, rectangular hole which was situated between two of the larger buildings.

"Is that thing big enough for us?" Smitty asked. Meanwhile, the gunboat descended into a smaller aperture nearby.

"Yeah, but it's gonna be tight," Frank said. "No offense to the Powers That Be, but I need everyone in this room to shut their mouths for a minute and let me work."

"Do your thing, Brother," Taylor said.

The Buma's hands were a blur of feathery digits at his station. "Touchdown in ten…nine…"

The scene in the Tri-V turned from blue skies and scorched earth to the slate-gray confines of a docking hangar as the *Osyrys*'s thrusters fired outside.

"Five," Frank said. "Four…three…"

A mild thump reverberated through the hull—the landing struts touching ground—followed by the whir of the engines' deceleration sequence.

"And we're down," Billy announced.

Taylor felt his nerves relax. "Way to thread the needle, Frank. You're as skilled as advertised."

The Buma exhaled and disconnected his pinplants.

Now free to move, Taylor unbuckled from his seat and headed for the bridge lockers to get an oxygen kit.

"I don't think you're gonna need that." Quint pointed to his screen. "It looks like this world's atmosphere is close to Earth's. We oughta be fine."

Taylor took a kit anyway then closed the locker. "Smitty, touch base with the platoon sergeants to see how our troopers are doin'. After that, meet me and Billy at the debarkation hatch on E deck. Quint, you have the con."

Billy opened his mouth to speak, but Taylor was already in motion.

"You sure you wanna do this?" Billy asked once they'd reached the hatch. "You're the commanding officer of this entire outfit. It makes sense that you'd stay on the bridge and leave the site work to me."

The indicator above the door flashed red to green.

"It's like you said before," Taylor replied. "If these folks wanted us dead, they'd have never gotten involved with that frigate."

"Who says they want us dead?" Billy cocked his head. "Trust me, there's a ton of bad stuff you can do to an enemy that doesn't involve a flatline. I agreed with your decision to come down here, but let's slow our roll here and be smart about this."

Taylor stared at the deck. "These guys referenced my brother by name, Billy. You can spout protocol to me all you want. I can't *not* be a part of this."

Footfalls sounded from the adjacent corridor.

"Hey, Smitty," Billy said once the Aussie had rounded the corner. "How are the troopers?"

"The probies are a bit shaken, which is to be expected," Smitty said. "Still, the veterans are holding things together."

"Jack and Stan?" Taylor asked.

"Surprisingly on the ball," Smitty said to her boss. "I'll admit it. The farts were a good hire. Your reporter friend, on the other hand, needed the threat of house arrest before she'd follow my order to stay in her cabin."

Taylor nodded his thanks then started for the hatch, only to be met by a hand in his chest.

"Let me and Smitty clear the area before you debark," Billy said. "We'll let you know when you're good."

"That up for debate?" Taylor asked.

"Not even a fargin little," Billy said. "Now step aside."

Taylor frowned and stepped back while Billy pulled his Firestorm and placed his finger along the trigger guard. A beat later, the hatch swung open, and both officers rushed through it.

"Clear," Billy called.

"Clear," Smitty followed.

Taylor emerged from the *Osyrys* to join them.

As it turned out, the hangar bay which housed them was far larger than its entrance, spanning several hundred yards in every direction. Most of the space was illuminated from above by artificial lights, which became apparent when the aperture above the *Osyrys* sealed shut, choking off the last bits of sunlight.

No, that ain't disconcertin' at all. Taylor looked around but only saw his officers.

"Check it out," Smitty said.

Taylor followed her gesture past a dark console and a matted wad of exposed wiring to the hangar's back wall. There, slumbering on a platform beside two more of its kind, was the alien gunboat. *Where's your crew?*

The hiss of hydraulics reverberated through the chamber, sending all three Humans stepping back with weapons up. Next, the gunboat's side hatch opened, and three figures, two males and a female, emerged from the craft wearing ratty brown trousers and matching tunics. Of average height and lean, the aliens were surprisingly humanoid with deep, charcoal gray skin, snow white hair, and luminescent gold eyes which seemed to glimmer in the dim lights overhead.

"You may lower your firearms," the center alien said. He was shorter than the other male with a slender frame and close-cropped white hair.

Taylor recognized his voice from earlier.

"I can assure you that you are among friends here," the alien said.

Taylor motioned his people to stand down. "Who are you?"

"My name is Yakano Valawn." The alien bowed his head. "I am commander of the Rukori Freedom Corps, or RFC, and head of this facility. These are my first officers, Sergeants Douron and Balar."

The brawnier male with dreadlocks bowed, then the female.

Taylor gave the only response he knew. "Mornin', y'all."

Valawn chuckled. "Indeed, you are from North Florida."

Taylor wasn't sure how to take that. "This is Commander Dinah Smith, head of Riverside Company. The other is Captain William Dawson, my executive officer."

Both officers nodded.

"William Dawson?" Valawn all but ignored Smitty. "As in, Billy Dawson?"

"That's right," Billy said awkwardly.

"Terry used to speak quite highly of you." Valawn extended a hand. "It's a pleasure to make your acquaintance."

Billy studied the stranger's palm before shaking it. "Yeah, sure. You, too."

"You mentioned before that your brother is no longer in charge of the Eagles," Valawn said. "May I inquire as to why that is, and why he did not come with you?"

Taylor didn't answer.

"Is he…back on Earth?" the alien pressed.

Taylor wasn't sure how to respond, or if he even wanted to. Ultimately, he opted to stick with the *honesty is the best policy* approach. "My brother passed away six years ago."

"Six years." Valawn's voice trailed off, his expression turning abruptly pensive. "Please forgive me if this is out of line, but may I ask how it happened?"

Taylor did his best to abridge the story for time. Once he'd finished, the alien commander took a few moments before speaking again.

"I, um." Valawn swallowed. "I'm terribly sorry for your loss, Colonel Van Zant. Truly, I am."

"It's just Chief," Taylor said. "Terry was the colonel of this outfit, not me. Now, can I ask you some questions?"

Valawn managed the slightest of nods.

"Who in the hell are you people," Taylor asked, "and what was your connection to my brother?"

Billy cleared his throat. "While you're at it, you can explain how and why it is our flagship brought us here."

Valawn wrinkled his gray-skinned nose. "Am I to understand that you've never heard of us?"

Taylor shook his head.

"And you've never heard of the Krulig, nor their presence on Rukoria?"

All three Humans gave blank stares.

"Well then." Valawn straightened and turned for a nearby exit. "We have much to discuss, indeed. Come with me, and I'll endeavor to answer all of your questions."

Taylor fell in line with the others as the name *Keeto* flashed in his lower-right field of vision. "Yeah, Keeto. What's up?"

"I've completed my preliminary analysis of the *Osyrys*'s damage from engineering," the Athal said. "Now I'd like to inspect the hull from the outside, if it's safe."

Taylor relayed his lead engineer's request to Valawn who nodded is okay. "You're clear, Keeto. Come on out."

The sound of fluttering wings bristled from inside the *Osyrys*'s debarkation hatch as Keeto darkened the doorway. "Ah, Chief. There you are. I need—" The Athal's globular eyes bulged. "This cannot be."

"It can't be what?" Billy asked, renewed alarm in his voice.

Keeto floated down to the gunboats. "This is First Republic technology."

"First Republic?" Taylor blinked. "As in, the society of folks that existed before the Galactic Union?"

Keeto nodded but didn't reply. He hovered there, staring in awe at the tiny ships.

"We call them bandilaroes," Valawn said. "Our ancestors left them to us many thousands of years ago. Now come. I'll explain everything."

*****

Chapter 9: Time in a Bottle

Taylor saw to his engineer's need, then followed their host out of the bay with Billy and Smitty.

In stark contrast to the open hangar, the rest of Valawn's Sanctuary seemed cramped and uncomfortable. A bi-leveled complex of scarred steel and pitted concrete, the place was little more than a collection of spartan living spaces interconnected by a series of dimly lit corridors.

The group paused when two other aliens passed them in the hall. Both wore the same tattered garments as their comrades and regarded the Humans with curious gold eyes.

"How many people live down here?" Billy asked when the aliens had gone.

"A hundred six, as of last count," Valawn said. "We have other cells scattered topside about the badlands. However, this facility serves as the hub for all RFC operations in the region."

Badlands. Taylor wondered if that meant the desert or the city inside it. "As fallout shelters go, it's an impressive place. Did you build it yourselves?"

"No." Valawn shook his head. "It belonged to one of the regents who presided over this district before it fell. As it happened, he was also something of a collector, with the bandilaros you saw in our hangar being his most prized possessions."

Taylor gathered from his host's use of the past tense that the regent wasn't around anymore to claim his possessions.

Rounding their fifth corner into a new corridor, the group entered a stairwell which took them down to a makeshift briefing room on Level Two. A meager space with grime-stained walls and a scuffed floor, the room housed a rectangular table with stool chairs and a viewscreen on the back partition. There was, however, an odd swirl painting by the door, which gave the room its only color.

"Please, make yourselves comfortable," Valawn said.

Taylor nabbed a stool across the table so as to put his back to the wall then watched their host vanish into a corner. When the alien returned, he did so holding a tray of glasses with an all-too-familiar bottle—or rather, a jar.

River City Blond Whiskey. Taylor recognized the riverboat on the label.

"Your brother gave this to me at our last meeting," Valawn said.

"That don't surprise me." Taylor watched his host tip the jar over a glass, then hand the drink over. "River City was always Terry's brand, especially the single stock. He had to become a merc to afford the stuff, but once he could, he rarely drank much else."

Valawn filled glasses for the others, then himself. "It was our intention to drink this together once the Krulig had been vanquished from my homeworld."

"The Krulig," Taylor said. "Those are the guys you mentioned before. The ones who attacked us at the emergence point."

"Indeed," Valawn said. "They were doubtless taken aback by your arrival in Rukori space. As you can imagine, we don't get many visitors here."

"And why is that?" Taylor asked. "Hell, while we're on the subject, how come we've never heard of these Krulig, or you people, for that matter?"

Valawn sat down and sipped his whiskey. "To understand the Krulig is to understand greed and cowardice. To understand the Rukori is to understand the impact the Ancient War had on the galaxy."

Billy arched an eyebrow. "You mean *the* Ancient War? As in, the one eons ago that saw much of the First Republic wiped out by the Canavar?"

"That is correct." Valawn aimed a pensive stare at his glass. "Magnificent creations, the Canavar. I've only read of them in what remains of our archives, of course. But, as I understand it, they were the stuff of nightmares, genetically engineered by the Kahraman to be the perfect weapons of mass destruction."

"'Perfect monsters' is more like it," Smitty scoffed. "We learned of the Canavar during Union history in grade school. They devastated hundreds of worlds before their reign of terror was ended by the Raknar."

Raknar. There was a term Taylor recognized. The Raknar were giant armored robots built millennia ago by a race of aliens called the Dusman for specialized combat with the Canavar. They were piloted by flesh and blood beings, a lot like the CASPers of present day, only a lot bigger.

"What does the Ancient War have to do with you folks?" Taylor asked. "Or my brother?"

Valawn shifted on his stool. "As is well chronicled, the number of species which comprised the First Republic was legion, with my people, the Rukori, being one of the eldest. This gave our citizens a modicum of status back then." The alien frowned. "It also made our homeworld, Rukorilyn Prime, a target for the Canavar."

Taylor noted his host's naming of a different homeworld, not the current one, called Rukoria. "I take it Rukorilyn Prime was one of the worlds lost to the Canavar."

Valawn nodded. "The Rukori fought valiantly, as one would expect, forsaking nothing in the name of the cause. In the end, however, our efforts proved as futile versus the Canavar as those of our comrades. By the time the Raknar arrived, little remained on Rukorilyn Prime worth returning to."

"So that put your ancestors in the market for a new home," Smitty said.

"Correct," Valawn said. "As fate would have it, this all transpired as the Galactic Union was taking root. The new government, made of independent guilds rather than a centralized authority, would—in theory—bring with it a new way of life for its constituents—one of a more libertarian nature, where citizens were free to do as they pleased with little interference from the government itself."

"And the Rukori weren't fans of that?" Billy asked.

"The Rukori have always supported liberty," Valawn said. "Always. At the same time, our elders recognized from the start that conflict, be it on a small scale with tribe versus tribe or a larger one with world versus world, was destined to be an inherent part of life in the new order. They wanted no part of that. Thus, given all that our people had endured, it was decided that the Rukori would look outside the galactic core for a place to rebuild in peace."

Smitty made a face. "You certainly achieved that out here. As Union space goes, it doesn't get much more out in the boonies than the Cresht region of the Tolo Arm."

"That was the idea," Valawn said.

"But how have you managed to stay hidden all this time?" Taylor asked. "Again, no one back in the Union has ever even heard of you folks."

Valawn sipped his drink. "Unfortunately, I do not have an answer for that. The archives speak only of an arrangement with the Vergola Council prior to the Rukori exodus."

"The who?" Smitty looked up.

"The Vergola Council," Valawn said. "The Vergola were a race of engineers and ship builders during Republic times. They were also, like the Rukori, among the Republic's older members. As such, when the time came for the newly formed Cartography Guild to assume oversight of the stargate system, it was widely known that the Vergola would be involved."

"I don't suppose your archives tell who formed the guilds?" Smitty asked. "Cartography or otherwise?"

Valawn shook his head. "I'm sorry, but they do not."

Taylor drummed his fingers. "What about this arrangement you mentioned? Do your archives speak to that?"

"Not beyond the obvious, no," Valawn said. "They tell only of my ancestors' desire to remain undisturbed in exile. To that end, a deal was struck with the Vergola to have Rukoria and her stargate expunged from the Union's new planet atlas. The Council complied, and the rest, as your people say, is history."

Taylor bolted upright. "Hold on. The Vergola actually did it? They removed an entire world from the atlas? Coordinates and all?"

"According to our records, yes," Valawn said. "That was the agreement."

Taylor glanced across the table to find looks of equal shock on the faces of his colleagues.

"I'll be damned," Billy murmured. "Half the mercs I've ever worked with suspected there were worlds out there that the Cartography Guild either A, didn't know about or B, wasn't sharing. If what you're saying about these Vergola is true, you essentially just confirmed that at least the former is true."

"Which begs the question," Smitty said. "What else is out there that no one's aware of?"

Taylor's mind raced with the ramifications of this development. *Hidden worlds off the grid with operable stargates?* The knowledge was a gamechanger.

A nasty looking gash on a nearby wall sent Taylor's mind in a new direction. "This happened, what? Fifteen, twenty thousand years ago?"

"That's right," Valawn said.

"And all because Rukorilyn Prime was sacked in the War?" Taylor continued.

"Yes," Valawn said.

Taylor proceeded cautiously with his next words. "So…what happened to your second homeworld?"

The alien commander dropped his gaze. "You're referring to the ruins."

"Yeah," Taylor said. "Did one of the other races find you and attack or what?"

Valawn took in a long breath then let it out. "No. We were not attacked. Rukoria's fate was regrettably forged by her own people's hands."

Taylor held quiet as revelation set in. "You did this to yourselves."

Valawn took a long pull of his whiskey. "In the centuries that followed our arrival here, my people built cities to the sky that threatened the borders of the gods. We grew our understanding of science and technology, not to mention ourselves." He paused, staring at his hands. "Then one day, about thirty years ago, a young boy living in a remote village on the edge of the southern continent ventured into the wilderness, and it all went away."

Taylor watched his host's demeanor darken with each syllable. Before, Valawn had been speaking in academic terms, as someone who'd learned of his people's history through study. Now he was speaking from experience.

"The boy came home early from the forest," Valawn said in a low voice. "He claimed to have been bitten by something, an insect. The boy's parents monitored his health for several days, then went on about their lives when all seemed fine. Only, it wasn't fine."

Taylor felt a chill. "The boy was a carrier for somethin'."

Valawn nodded. "His symptoms didn't present for more than a week, and when they did, they were barely noticeable. A mild fever, a light rash. Nothing to raise alarm. In time, the boy's condition progressed, first to skin lesions and fatigue, then to internal hemorrhaging and organ failure. Eventually, the sickness claimed his life."

"What was it?" Billy asked. "The sickness?"

"Our scientists called it the Winter Death," Valawn said. "Put simply, it was a virus that ravaged the Rukori immune system, thereby turning even the smallest illnesses into a death sentence. It was also highly contagious, as evidenced by the inferno-like speed with which it spread through the population."

"How bad did it get?" Smitty asked.

Valawn stared into his glass. "Terry's medical officer asked that same question. I believe the term he used after I'd answered was 'global pandemic.'"

Taylor looked away, his thoughts swirling with visions of Earth's Dark Ages or the Jyntu outbreak that swept through Nigeria in the early-twenty-second century. "So, after all that time and sacrifice to build their new world, the Rukori civilization was done in by a bug, compliments of Mother Nature."

"If only that were it," Valawn murmured.

Taylor wrinkled his nose.

"The Winter Death was indeed the catalyst for my people's undoing," Valawn said, "but it did not bring about the apocalypse you witnessed above. That came ten years into the crisis when our people began turning on each other."

Billy's tone was low and even with his next question. "Bombs?"

Valawn nodded, golden eyes downcast. "We called it the Cleansing. Ironic, isn't it? For all our championing of peace as the cornerstone of noble society, in our darkest hour we became the very monsters our ancestors sought to escape when they fled the Union. It began when the residents of one district attacked another in a quarantine dispute. That escalated to a conflict between cities, then regions, before eventually devolving into a war of nations. By the time the bombings ended, everything we'd built—everything we stood for—was little more than sand and ash." Valawn slumped back on his stool. "And that, my Human friends, is when our hallowed saviors, the Krulig, swooped in from the heavens to save us all."

Smitty raised an eyebrow. "So the Krulig brought a cure then."

"The Krulig brought the *makings* of a cure, based on a similar pathogen they'd encountered on another world," Valawn said. "Our healers took it from there, using Krulig resources. By that point, more than eighty percent of the global population had been eradicated, either by the Death itself or the bombs meant to snuff it out. The remaining Rukori sought refuge in the old quarantine zones which still serve today as our primary urban centers."

"Who are they?" Billy asked. "These Krulig. Moreover, how did they find you in isolation after all this time?"

Valawn shrugged. "We honestly don't know how they found us. They simply emerged one day from hyperspace and made contact. As for whom they are?" He considered. "They are no one."

"Come again?" Taylor perked up.

"The Krulig are no one," Valawn repeated. "At least, that's who the archives say they were at the time of our ancestors' exodus. The Krulig were a minor race under the dominion of the Vergola, used mostly for labor and other menial jobs. That's it. They didn't even hold a seat in the old government."

"What do they want in the here and now?" Smitty asked.

"Perhaps the better question is, what don't they want?" Valawn snorted. "When the Krulig arrived twelve years ago, they were content lending their aid free of charge as we frankly had nothing to offer in return. As time wore on, however, and the Rukori recovered, that ceased being the case. Now, the Krulig take everything we have of value, from the crops in our fields to the power amassed by our makeshift solar capacitors. They leave us only what we need to survive. The rest they ship off-world for sale to the highest bidder."

"So why not run them out?" Billy scratched his head. "I mean, clearly that's the point of your insurgency, right?"

"Were the Rukori a united people, then that might be possible," Valawn said. "Alas, we are nothing if not divided. Say what you will for the Krulig's intentions, they still put food in the bellies of many Rukori children. Couple this with their role in retrieving our society from the brink, and there are many among us—especially survivors of the Cleansing—who have resigned their loyalty to the status quo."

Taylor's thoughts returned to his original question. "How did Terry get mixed up in all this?"

"While the Krulig are powerful, they are not, best as we can tell, many in number," Valawn said. "At present, we estimate that there are no more than three hundred spread across the planet. Thus, in order to preserve their stronghold on Rukoria, they require help."

"Ah." Billy crossed his arms. "The Krulig contracted with Union mercenaries to serve as an occupation force."

"Precisely," Valawn said.

"But why Humans?" Taylor asked. "The Mercenary Guild is littered with species more qualified than us, any one of whom would've been more than happy to take this gig for a proper payday."

"That may be," Valawn said. "However, as Terry explained to me, Earth has been quite the hotbed for mercenary activity since their induction into the Union last century. You're also a young world, which is to say there are many among you searching for fame and fortune in the stars."

Smitty shook her head. "Why Swamp Eagle Security, though? Why not bring in a legit heavy hitter for this? Someone like Asbaran Solutions or the Golden Horde?"

"Because the hiring of a Horseman would've been far too high profile in Union merc circles," Billy said. "A redneck outfit out of Jacksonville, North Florida, on the other hand, would've barely made news on Earth much less around the galaxy. That presumably would've made them easier to manipulate."

"Only the Krulig didn't count on Terry bein' a turncoat," Taylor said.

The XO answered with a *you got it* gesture.

"Terry's people had only been planetside a few weeks when my operatives first encountered them," Valawn said. 'It happened during a food raid outside of Nyo Colony. He had us dead to rights, your brother did. Then he saw that our prize that evening was a trove of fruit to feed our families. He let us go. We began working together shortly thereafter."

Terry. Taylor thumbed the edge of his glass. "I take it you liked my brother from the start, then."

"Oh, lords no." Valawn laughed. "At the risk of offending, I thought Terry Van Zant was a loud-mouthed arrogant braggart at first, sent here by the gods to get us all killed."

"Sounds like Terry, all right." Billy smirked.

"But then I got to know the man," Valawn said. "I saw the good he was capable of, and the results he could deliver in the field. Terry was a born fighter, through and through. He went to great lengths, at significant risk to himself and his company, to help the Rukori, be it through illicit supply runs for weapons or an extra cache of food when we needed it. Terry was a good man. He will be sorely missed."

A momentary silence fell on the room, causing Taylor to risk a glance at his XO from the corner of his eye. Billy was just sitting there, eyes on the table and thoughts clearly someplace a lot further away than that. *I'm sorry, man.*

Smitty cleared her throat. "Forgive me, Valawn, but none of this explains how our crew came to be here today."

"Ah, yes." Valawn shifted. "Terry and I realized after about a year that for my people to truly be free, we needed two things: a legitimate fighting force of our own, equipped with real weapons and ships, and a way to bring that force here to Rukoria."

"Why not aboard the Eagles' old flagship, *Bogrider*?" Taylor asked. "She'd have offered more than enough space to haul a force of that size, plus her navigator would've known the way back after the initial drop."

"You presume that your comrades arrived here of their own volition," Valawn said. "They did not. No non-Krulig ship, mercenary or otherwise, has ever emerged directly into our system, not even the Krulig themselves twelve years ago. Rather, they did so by way of the *Behemoth* you saw in orbit, and it's on that ship that they've shuttled in aid for their cause ever since."

Billy scratched his head. "That's actually pretty smart. Why compromise the location of your cash cow when you can ferry in the help and be done with it?"

"Exactly," Valawn said. "The Eagles were no different. So, Terry and I devised a plan to sneak our RFC operatives onto the *Behemoth* for the purposes of cloning its nav data. That information would then be returned to Earth for download into a ship of our own."

Taylor's grip tightened on his chair. *Osyrys.*

A nearby wall terminal chirped out an alert.

"Excuse me, Commander," a low voice called through the speaker.

Valawn rose from his seat and tapped a button on the console. "What is it, Douron?"

"We just received a communique from one of our contacts," the Rukori sergeant said. "She asked to speak with you at once."

"Pass it to Balar," Valawn said. "She's cleared to handle this."

"Sir," Douron added. "The communique came from Flower of the Sands."

Valawn's golden eyes widened. "I'll take the call in my office. Valawn out." He spun to face his guests. "Please excuse me for a moment."

The group watched from their seats as the RFC commander took his leave.

"You buyin' all this?" Billy asked.

Taylor pointed to the mason jar on the table. "Seems to me the evidence is pretty irrefutable at this point."

Billy heaved a sigh. "Well, I guess now we finally know what Operation Hammerhead was."

"Looks like," Taylor agreed.

"Any clue on how we plan to get out of this mess?" Smitty asked. "From the sound of it, these Krulig bastards rule the roost around here, and Colonel Van Zant screwed them hard. Even if we were to take up arms against the Rukori—and I'm not suggesting we do—I'd wager there's no way the Krulig will deal with us."

Taylor chewed his lip. "One thing at a time, Smitty. One thing at a time."

"My sincerest apologies, Chief Van Zant, but I must cut our time here short," Valawn said as he rushed back into the room. "My soldiers and I have urgent business in Nyo Colony that cannot be delayed."

"What's going on?" Billy asked.

"One of our cell contacts has reached out to us with some critical information," Valawn said. "I must meet with her at once."

Taylor considered before posing his next question. "How can we help?"

Billy all but jumped out of his seat.

"I couldn't possibly," Valawn said.

"It's done." Taylor rose to his feet. "Now tell me what you need."

*****

Chapter 10: Out of the Badlands

"You sure you wanna do this?" Billy asked on their way out of the briefing room.

Part of Taylor wanted to be honest and say no, that the whole idea of everything he'd just heard scared the hell out of him. But he knew better. "Terry was here, Billy. That much is clear. All these years, my family thought the Science Guild was at fault for the *Bogrider*'s accident. If Terry turned on these Krulig as Valawn suggests, then that changes everything. Either way, I've gotta follow this rabbit hole to see where it goes."

Billy gave a reluctant nod as the group re-entered the hangar. "I'll make the arrangements with Quint, then meet you back here for launch."

"Sounds good," Taylor said. "Do me a favor and have Paul tag along. By the sound of it, things up top ain't so grand for livin' conditions, and there could be folks in need of medical assistance. I'd like to offer them whatever we can."

"Paul's never dealt with Rukori anatomy," Billy said.

"No, but Terry's doc had," Taylor said. "Have Paul check the *Osyrys*'s med directory to see what he can find."

"Ayew," the XO said.

Taylor turned to Smitty. "Me, Billy, and Paul are gonna take this mission. I need you to hang back and oversee repairs while Quint works astrometrics to find us a way out of here."

The Aussie arched a blonde eyebrow. "You sure? By the sound of things, you gents could use a hand."

"We'll be fine," Taylor said. "Quint, on the other hand, is gonna need all the time he can get at his post. Believe me. You're a bigger help to the crew down here than topside."

"You're the Chief." Smitty tipped a half salute, then trotted after Billy as Valawn emerged through the bay door.

"Interesting fellow, your XO," the Rukori said. "He's not what I expected."

Taylor faced his host. "What exactly is it that you know?"

"I understand enough about Captain Dawson's split from the Eagles to know he's the last one I'd have expected to see here today, wearing your colors." Valawn's expression turned rueful. "It tore your brother up, you know, the way he and Dawson ended things. It was the biggest regret of Terry's life."

Taylor grunted and pocketed his hands. "He told you about that, huh?"

"Over quite a bit of River City Blond, yes." One of Valawn's corporals motioned him over. "Excuse me for a moment, Chief."

Taylor nodded, and the alien took his leave.

"Hey Chief, you got a minute?" a voice called.

Taylor turned to see Frank crossing the hangar floor with Keeto in tow. "Hey, boys. What's up?"

Frank looked around before speaking. "While you and the others were up there talking to the Rukori CO, I took the opportunity to dig through the *Osyrys*'s nav system to figure out what happened after our stargate transition from Earth."

Taylor shared Valawn's story about the Vergola Council, the stolen *Behemoth* nav data, and Terry's mission to download that information into the Eagles' new flagship.

"That's how we ended up here at Rukoria," Taylor concluded.

Frank swallowed and kept his voice low. "With respect to our alien friend, sir, what Keeto and I found goes way beyond one hidden world."

Taylor cocked his head.

"Frank and I found dozens," Keeto said, "maybe even hundreds of worlds in the *Osyrys*'s archives that, as far as we know, no one in the Union has ever heard of."

"And all of these worlds show up in our nav atlas?" Taylor asked.

"They're in the system, but not in the atlas," Keeto said. "The information for these worlds is stored on a standalone ghost drive, which is isolated from the main nav computer. That's why we're just now finding it."

"Clearly, the colonel's engineers wanted to keep this info a secret," Frank said, "as they should've. If they'd dropped this data straight into the *Osyrys*'s nav atlas, it's likely the Cartography Guild would've learned about it and taken action. By keeping the data isolated on a ghost drive, the crew could keep it free of prying eyes but still accessible when they needed it."

Keeto scratched his head with a pincer. "I should apologize, Chief. My team must've triggered the drive during our pre-launch inspections. When we engaged the hyperspatial generator, the ghost drive interfaced with our nav computer and overrode Sakall to bring us here instead."

Taylor considered the implications of what he'd just heard. "Well hot damn, fellas, that's the best news I've heard all day. It sounds like Swamp Eagle Security just hit the fargin jackpot for future contracts."

"Yeah, about that." Frank frowned. "Our shiny new jackpot may or may not have a shiny new grenade attached to it."

Taylor furrowed his eyebrows.

"What my feathery colleague here means to say," Keeto added, "is that there is no end to the number of parties who would seek to acquire this information. Once word gets out that the Eagles have access to these worlds, people will come for us, be they rival mercs, pirates, and most especially the Cartography Guild. We must be prepared for that when we transition home."

Thoughts of Terry's accident flooded back into Taylor's mind like a tidal wave. *Is this what got you killed?*

"Hey Chief, I need a signature over here," one of the engineers said from the jetway.

Taylor stayed the woman with a finger. "Thanks for the update, guys. Y'all keep diggin' and let me know what you find. Just keep this on the quiet. Senior staff only."

"You got it, boss." Frank fired off a salute, then hurried off with Keeto.

"Chief Van Zant," Valawn called from a nearby lift. He was joined there by Sergeant Douron and the corporal he'd been speaking with. "We can depart whenever you're ready."

* * *

Once topside, Valawn led the group three blocks south through the city to where they were supposed to pick up a ground transport that would take them on their journey.

Up close, Taylor found the devastation even more striking than he had from the air. There was seemingly no end to it. He shook his head as he thought about what the district had looked like in its heyday, or the number of occupants who'd called it home. *What a loss.*

Eventually, the group halted outside of an abandoned warehouse, which hosted two vehicles under covers in the forward bay. Long and rectangular, with scarred metal frames and roller balls underneath for motion, they reminded Taylor of the flatbed cargo haulers he'd seen running about Jax Startown. He sniffed the air. "Does this thing run on fossil fuels?"

"The Krulig seize most of the power we generate, so we make do with what we can. Here." Valawn handed each Human a set of work clothes. "Put these on over your uniforms, lest you stand out in the crowd."

Taylor inspected the garments before pulling them on. "How long until we reach this Nyo Colony place?"

"It'll take us roughly ninety minutes after leaving the district to clear the badlands," Valawn said. "After that, we'll head north into the mountains then exit into the piedmont on the other side by the colony. Total transit time is about four hours."

"Seems like a lot of bobbing and weaving," Billy said. "Isn't there a more direct route?"

"The run through the mountains can be quite treacherous for those who don't know the terrain," Douron said. "That's how we keep the Krulig from tracking us back to the Sanctuary."

Smart. Taylor boarded the hauler's back bench seat with Billy and Paul, while Valawn, Douron, and the corporal named Retay took the seats up front. A minute later, the hauler's engines glugged to life, and they were off.

"So," Taylor said once they'd cleared the mountains, "who's this Sand Flower person we're goin' to meet?"

"Flower of the Sands," Valawn corrected over his shoulder. "That's her handle for comm purposes. Her real name is Kalil Padona. She serves as centress over all of Nyo Colony."

Taylor took the term 'centress' to mean some sort of governor. "She sounds pretty important."

"She is," Valawn said. "In addition to her status as one of the foremost officials in the region, she's also one of our oldest tenured cell members."

"I guess that makes her pretty integral to your movement," Taylor said.

"Indeed," Valawn said. "I've known Kalil since the birth of the Rukori Freedom Corps. She's the antithesis of a risk-taker. This tells me that whatever she's called us there to say, it's important. Were she to be discovered, the Krulig's minions would almost certainly have her executed."

"Yeah, about those minions," Billy added. "Do the Krulig still outsource their garrison work to Humans? If so, that could get complicated."

Valawn shook his head. "No. To the best of our knowledge, the Krulig haven't contracted with another Earth outfit since the Eagles."

"Did they find out about Terry?" Taylor asked.

"I wish I knew," Valawn said. "If the Krulig did learn of Terry's duality while under their employ, they never spoke of it to any of our contacts."

"Who do they contract with then, if not Humans?" Paul asked.

Douron snorted, his long, white dreadlocks fluttering in the wind. "A nasty race of four-legged monsters, that's who. Hairy little beasts that also walk on two legs."

"They arrived on Rukoria just after the Eagles left and immediately began wreaking havoc on the population," Valawn said. "They've served as the Krulig's right hands ever since."

"These four-legged monsters got a name?" Billy asked.

Douron growled another curse. "The Zuul."

Taylor traded uneasy looks with Billy.

"Well, now we know why we were facing off against Maki warships earlier," the latter said. "The Zuul have used them for years."

"That's not all we know," Paul added. "We know an Athal engineer who's gonna be pissed as hell when we get back to the *Osyrys*."

Taylor frowned under his hood. *Ain't that the truth?* "You said a while back that the Krulig can't track you through the mountains."

Valawn nodded.

"What's to stop them from sendin' the Zuul straight into the badlands to search for you?" Taylor asked. "I mean, were I in charge, I'd think a ruined city would be tops on my list of places to look for an RFC installation."

"Oh, rest assured, Chief Van Zant," Valawn said, "we get more than our fair share of Zuul search parties in the badlands. Thankfully, our cities are vast, thus giving us plenty of space to hide."

"It helps that the Zuul never bring Rukori to flesh out their numbers," Douron added.

Billy looked up. "Why not?"

"Radiation levels in the districts were dangerously high, and in most instances fatal after the Cleansing," Valawn said. "That led most Rukori to avoid them at all costs. In the years since, those levels have returned to normal. However, the Krulig have gone to great lengths to keep that information from my people."

"I'll bet they have," Paul said. "Rule number one for managing an occupation: keep your subjects confined in tight spaces. It makes them easier to manage."

"Exactly," Valawn said.

The group talked for a while longer as the hauler made its way through the mountains and down into the piedmont, at one point passing a sizable mesa to the west that looked oddly out of place. Not long afterward, the Nyo Colony skyline appeared on the horizon.

In stark contrast to the metropolitan hulk Taylor had left behind, the compound ahead looked more like a decaying prison camp than a colony. Spanning six square miles, the compound was comprised of around eighty structures, all clustered into a sort of loose grid with dirt paths separating each row. Some of the buildings were small, ramshackle huts made of wood and stone. Others were taller structures made of deep-scarred steel, most likely used for storage or cargo. There was also a twelve-foot-tall fence that framed the entire complex.

Old quarantine zones. That's how Valawn had described these installations earlier.

Now, Taylor understood why.

"Please, gentlemen. Let me do the talking." Valawn motioned Retay to slow their approach when a security checkpoint came into view.

The corporal did as ordered, slowing the hauler's speed then halting it at the fence.

"Credentials," said a Rukori male in a black uniform.

Valawn reached into his tunic and came back with a set of papers, which he handed over.

"State your business," the Rukori guard said.

"My crew and I hail from the mining operation outside of Bartahl Colony," Valawn said. "Our foreman deployed us here to fetch supplies for our dig."

A rustling sound inside the checkpoint station caused Taylor to peek out from under his cowl.

Short, squat, and grotesquely muscular, the Zuul guard bounded out on all fours and cleared the space between them in three even strides. There, the alien rose onto its haunches beside its Rukori counterpart and sniffed the air.

Stay cool, T. Taylor retreated under his hood as a mild breeze kissed his skin. *You're downwind for now, so just stay cool.*

"What's the expected duration of your stay?" the Rukori guard asked.

"Only a day," Valawn said. "Our people require us back first thing on the morrow."

The Rukori perused their documents, while the Zuul aimed its furry nostrils skyward.

C'mon, c'mon. Let's go!

The former returned the papers. "Very good, then. Be sure you stick to that schedule. Move along."

Valawn conveyed their thanks and tucked away their credentials.

Once Retay had moved them through the gate, Taylor quickly observed just how far the Krulig's reach over Valawn's people went. There were Zuul everywhere, be it the guards at the gates or those inside, patrolling the streets. They were all armed, too, a fact clearly not lost on the locals, most of whom seemed content to keep their distance.

Speakin' of locals. Taylor searched his surroundings, spotting only a few. "Where is everybody?"

"At home, most likely," Valawn grumbled. "The next tribute ceremony is less than two weeks away. There are preparations to be made."

"Tribute?" Taylor leaned left as Retay steered them onto a side road.

"Yes," Valawn said flatly. "Each season, the residents of every colony meet in their respective town squares to pay homage to our Krulig masters with a bounty of gifts."

"Why do they need gifts?" Billy asked. "I thought these guys took what they wanted."

"Oh, rest assured, Captain," Valawn said. "What isn't taken in tribute is taken by force. By complying with the pageantry, however, my people at least stand a chance of keeping what they need rather than having to beg for it later."

Douron grunted. "And these thugs have the audacity to call themselves our benefactors."

Taylor was beginning to understand his brother's motives for getting involved with these people. It was then that he got his first glimpse of Rukoria's elusive overlords.

Tall and menacing, the Krulig sported a stocky humanoid frame under its black-armored uniform, but with the features of a reptilian species. Its skin, which shone dark green in the sun, was covered in scales, while its head, round and bald, carried adult-male dimensions with spiked horns and deep-set crimson eyes. The alien turned on its boot heels and stared at the oncoming hauler.

"He doesn't look friendly at all," Paul noted.

"No, Doc, he does not," Billy agreed.

Taylor ducked his head, mindful to cover his face, as the hauler zoomed past the Krulig en route to their destination, an aging shack on the outskirts of town.

"I'll take the hauler to the refueling depot and top off the tank then load up on supplies," Retay said once the craft had come to a stop. "Any requests?"

Taylor hopped off with the others.

"Our water recyclers are running dangerously low on filtration fluid," Valawn said. "Make sure you get two extra containers of that, plus extra fynar seed for our hydroponics bay."

"Understood." Retay waited for them to step clear, then eased on the accelerator and rolled out of sight.

"Gettin' supplies after all, huh?" Taylor asked.

"Just because we're here on mission doesn't mean we can't take advantage of the time," Valawn said. "Besides, if we return to the gate without supplies after telling the guard that's our objective, it'll cause problems."

Taylor stood aside while Billy and Douron headed inside to clear the shack.

"Excuse me, Commander Valawn, but what's that over there?" Paul pointed to a group of buildings outside the fence between the colony and the mesa they'd seen coming in. Unlike the structures of Nyo, however, which had seen better days, these structures were far more modern, boasting round corners, smooth steel, and fresh pavement all around. They were also extremely well-guarded.

"That, doctor, is the Krulig operations compound," Valawn said. "It houses the Zuul barracks, along with their training areas, armory, and a landing field on the facility's backside. The compound also houses the gaudy monstrosity that is the lord prefect's primary residence."

"Lord prefect?" Taylor didn't recognize the term.

"Each colony is presided over by a Krulig prefect," Valawn said. "These beings serve as both the head of the local government and the ultimate authority over the Zuul garrison stationed on their soil. The lord prefect is the supreme head."

"And he presides over Nyo Colony," Taylor surmised.

"Correct," Valawn said. "His name is Yolik Sadeed, and by all rights, his is the face of the entire Krulig occupation. All the prefects from the other colonies answer directly to him. They always have."

A shuttle passed by overhead. It circled wide and put down near the far-side guard tower.

"This lord prefect sounds like a real peach," Taylor said.

"You have no idea," Valawn muttered.

The shack's front door swung open as Billy and Douron reemerged into the street.

"Looks like we're clear," Billy said. "There's nobody inside."

Taylor started for the shack with the others while Douron stood watch outside. The place was completely empty, save for a smattering of broken pottery on the floor and some old equipment that looked like it hadn't been used in years. There was also, Taylor noticed, very little natural light coming in. That made much of his surroundings hard to see.

Wonderful. Taylor followed Valawn through the front common area, nostrils filling with the scents of dust, ancient wood, and animal droppings, then into a small room near the back. Again, there was nothing. Just more empty space, with a skylight overhead and a second door on the far wall.

And there'll be nobody home. Taylor was about to say something when unseen footfalls preceded the second door's opening.

"Centress Padona." Valawn gave a bow. "Welcome."

Two figures emerged from the shadows. The first was a tall Rukori male, wearing the same tattered work clothes as Valawn. The other was a small Rukori female whose lined face and shriveled hands told the story of her age.

"Greetings, Valawn," the centress said in a warm tone. "As always, it does me good to see you."

"And I you, Centress." Valawn straightened and clasped his hands. "To what do we owe the honor of your presence?"

"The information I possess was too important for a comm transmission. Before we start down that path, however…" The centress turned a curious eye to the Humans. "Perhaps we might discuss the presence of your companions."

Valawn gestured with a hand. "Centress Padona, please allow me to introduce Chief Van Zant, Captain Dawson, and Dr. Wright of the Earth Mercenary Ship *Ryley Osyrys.*"

"Van Zant." The woman's golden gaze widened. "You're with Swamp Eagle Security."

"Yes ma'am," Taylor said. "It was our ship that happened upon your planet earlier today."

The centress brightened. "Well, this is outstanding news. If you are here, that means Colonel Van Zant fulfilled his promise to bring help. Tell me, how many ships are with your convoy? How many fighters?"

Taylor pursed his lips. "I'm sorry, ma'am, but it's just us. The crew of the *Osyrys.*"

The centress' snowy eyebrows knit. "I don't understand. According to our plan, the colonel was supposed to—"

"Terry Van Zant passed way, Centress," Valawn said cutting to the chase. "This is his younger brother, Taylor."

The Rukori woman held her tongue, and Taylor wondered if he looked as awkward as he felt.

"Please forgive me, Chief Taylor," the centress said. "I'm terribly sorry for your loss."

"It's okay." Taylor tried to sound reassuring. "There was no way for you to know."

The centress shifted, as if pondering her next words. "If I may…how is it that you've returned to Rukoria if Terry's mission was a failure?"

"My brother didn't fail," Taylor said. "He got your nav data back to Earth as planned, and even got it uploaded into a ship. He just didn't get the chance to finish the job."

"And is that why you are here?" the centress asked. "To finish the job?"

Billy shifted beside the doctor and cleared his throat.

"With respect, ma'am," Taylor said. "I didn't even know you folks existed six hours ago. Right now, my primary focus is on findin' a way home for my ship and her crew."

The centress nodded, seeming to understand.

"So," Valawn said, "this information you spoke of. What's so important that you'd risk exposing yourself to present it to us?"

The centress reached into her robe and came back with a small device the size of a matchbox. She then placed the device onto the floor and pressed a button, sending a cascade of light spiraling from its top into the open. There, the light hovered at the center of the room before it converged into a holographic map of the open desert.

"What are we looking at?" Paul asked.

The centress waved her fingers, causing the image to tighten on a specific plot of sand which was lined with plants.

"This is a bulsina field roughly thirty miles south of Nyo Colony," the centress said. "At almost eighty acres in size, it's by far the largest in this region and a major food source for our people. Tomorrow, our workers will exit the gate at sunup to go harvest the field's crop."

Valawn crossed his arms. "I don't see the problem. We always harvest the bulsina field during this time of the season."

"Indeed, we do." The centress faced the RFC commander. "I was just informed by Lord Prefect Sadeed that the Krulig intend to seize a sizable portion of the crop as this month's tribute."

"How sizable?" Valawn asked.

The centress exhaled. "Three-fourths of the haul."

"That godsdamn alien swine!" Valawn flared his nostrils. "That's more than twice their normal demand!"

"Yes, it is," the centress said. "The lord prefect says the extra take is to benefit a Krulig mercy mission off-world."

Valawn snorted in disgust. "Please. Sadeed intends to sell the bulsina crop to a buyer, just like he does with everything else he seizes. That's the way this works."

Taylor put up a hand. "At the risk of askin' a stupid question, what's so special about this desert plant that the Krulig would jeopardize your food supply? Ain't there somethin' else you can offer as a compromise?"

"Finding a compromise would require these monsters to have a modicum of conscience." Valawn grunted. "Believe me; they do not."

The centress shifted the holo image with another wave of her fingers. This time when the light reconfigured, it did so on the form of a fruit with the shape and coloring of a pear.

"The bulsina fruit is one of the few sources of produce we've been able to cultivate in these conditions," the centress said. "It grows wild in the desert and, when peeled, yields a pink flesh-like substance which is extremely sweet and rich in nutrients."

Paul snapped his fingers. "Do bulsina plants showcase yellow flowers when they're in bloom?"

"They do, actually," the centress said.

Paul turned to his peers. "I've seen this fruit before in Jax Startown. One of Pete Harvick's guys had scored some from a XenSha on Karma Station and was passing it around. The aliens call it kenso fruit. It's considered a real delicacy."

"I take it then that the XenSha pay for that delicacy," Billy noted.

"Like you wouldn't believe," Paul said. "Pete's guy won his in a bet. Ordinarily, though, he says kenso fruit goes for roughly ten credits a bushel."

Taylor ran the math in his head. Ten Galactic Union credits equated to roughly a thousand dollars in US currency. He returned his focus to the hologram. *Damn, there's gotta be an eight-figure payday there, minimum.*

"We cannot allow the Krulig to take that crop," Valawn said. "We simply can't. We'll offer tribute another way."

"I'm open to suggestions," the centress said.

Valawn stared at the floor, clearly deep in thought. When nothing came, he exhaled and turned to Taylor. "Chief Van Zant, I understand that the Rukori people are strangers to you. You have no history with us, and thus no stake in our plight. Even still, the Rukori aren't strangers to Swamp Eagle Security. It is with that thread in mind that I would humbly request your company's assistance, if you'll allow it."

Taylor turned aside and rubbed his temples. *Really, T, how did you think this was gonna end when you came down here?* Billy and Paul were anxiously waiting for Taylor's reply when he opened his eyes.

"The frigate in orbit I know about." Taylor caught a sideways look from the XO. "Talk to me about ground numbers."

"On average, each colony is occupied by four to five hundred Zuul, plus twenty to thirty Krulig," Valawn said. "Most of them stay confined to their barracks; however, there are anywhere from two to three dozen Zuul patrolling the streets at any given time."

"How about ships and battle mecha?" Billy asked. "Is there anything beyond what's in orbit?"

Valawn shook his head. "The cruiser and the frigate were all that I knew of, and the *Osyrys* destroyed the former. There are, however, two to three shuttles posted at every colony for cross-desert transit and use during personnel changes on the ships."

"Has that *Behemoth* ever posed a problem?" Paul asked. "I mean, I know they're typically only used for cargo, but still."

"The *Behemoth* won't be an issue," the centress said. "The Krulig dispatched it back through the stargate after your ship vanished from their scopes."

"Shit," Billy snapped.

"Does this mean what I think it does?" Paul's eyes darted from man to man through his glasses.

"The Krulig are makin' a dash for reinforcements." Taylor excused himself from the group and fixed his stare on the hologram. He hated a bully—always had—and that's exactly what they Krulig were. At the same time, he couldn't afford not to think of his own people. The *Osyrys* had taken a beating versus the Maki warships, and that'd been with her weapons and shields at full capacity.

Then there was the ground situation. Even if Nyo Colony were at the low end of Valawn's projections with three hundred Zuul, they'd still outnumber the Eagles' personnel by almost four to one.

There's gotta be somethin' we can do. Taylor allowed himself another second to think, then rejoined the others. "Let me get back to my senior staff and see what we can work up."

"Bless you, Chief Van Zant," the centress said with relief. "Truly, you are a gift from the gods."

"Yeah, well, don't go grantin' me sainthood yet." Taylor shot her a sobering look. "I said I'd meet with my staff to evaluate the situation. For now, that's it. If my advisors tell me this is a fool's errand, I can assure you that all bets will be off. I will not—repeat, not—commit my people to a fight we can't win. I just won't. Are we clear on that?"

Valawn exchanged looks with the centress. "That's perfectly fair. How might we be of assistance?"

The clatter of footsteps outside interrupted the discussion.

"Excuse me, Commander," Douron said as he burst into the room. "We have a problem."

"What is it?" Valawn asked.

"There's a squad of Zuul headed this way."

Valawn spun to the centress. "You must go, now."

The little Rukori turned for the door with her aide, though not before imparting a final word to Taylor. "Regardless of your decision, I thank you for coming here today to hear us out. Safe travels to you and your crew, and I hope to speak with you again in the days ahead."

Taylor would've tipped his cap were he wearing one. "Ma'am."

The centress offered a parting smile, golden eyes gleaming above deep gray cheeks, then vanished from sight.

"Come," Valawn said. "We, too, must be going."

Exiting through their original door, Taylor ran down the hall behind Billy and Paul while Valawn and Douron brought up the rear. Once to the common area, the group bolted through the exit into the open, where six Zuul locked eyes on them from fifty yards up the street.

"You!" The lead Zuul snatched a weapon off its back.

The air between the two groups ignited in a staccato of laser fire as Billy and Douron staked out each side of the street.

"*Go!*" the XO shouted past the butt of his rifle.

Valawn grabbed Taylor's arm and led him with Paul to safety behind the shack.

"What's the status on our ride?" Taylor asked.

"I was just wondering the same thing." Valawn drew his comm device and put it to his mouth. "Retay, where are you?"

A crackle of static preceded the corporal's reply. "I'm loading the final supplies now. Why, what's happening?"

"We're pinned down outside the meeting point and taking fire from six Zuul," Valawn said.

"Acknowledged," Retay said. "I'm on my way."

"Negative." Valawn shook his head. "There's no way you'll reach us without being caught yourself, or worse. Stand by while I find an alternate rally point."

"We're about to be overrun here!" Billy yelled from his crouch on the corner.

Taylor rounded the shack with his rifle and tapped off two quick shots. Both struck a Zuul square in the chest, collapsing it to the dirt. "Valawn, we got an exit strategy or what?"

The RFC commander reached under his tunic and fished out a small cylinder with an access panel atop its casing.

"What is that?" Paul asked.

"It's an old Rukori reconnaissance drone," Valawn said. "We found three of them on the bandilaros when we discovered the Sanctuary."

Taylor jerked back when a laser bolt exploded the wall near his face. "Yeah, well. Whatever it is, I suggest you get it airborne before we all become dog food out here."

Valawn laid the device on the ground, then stepped back and pulled a palm-sized controller from his pocket. The drone was in the air shortly thereafter.

"Retay," Valawn said, searching the data. "Proceed to the harvest barns four blocks east of our original pickup point. The Eagles and I will meet you there."

"Understood," the corporal said.

Taylor whistled, then flashed a *fall back* hand signal to the others.

Billy acknowledged, then motioned Douron to go first.

The Rukori sergeant nodded and took off running, only to face-plant in the dirt mid-stride when a laser bolt slammed his back.

"Douron!" Valawn yelped.

"Got it!" Paul answered.

Before Taylor could think, the Eagles' doctor had sprinted into the open, weapons fire spiking the sand at his feet, and scampered to the big Rukori's side.

"Billy!" Taylor shouted.

The XO was already on it. He threw up his rifle, and together with the others, held the Zuul at bay while Paul got Douron to safety.

"Let's roll!" Billy said.

The group took off through the district, cutting back and forth through a maze of alleyways, with Valawn leading the way. Not long after, they emerged from between two harvest barns onto a side street like the one they'd left.

"Where's Retay?" Billy searched for the hauler as sounds of an angry horde trailed them from behind.

A loud v*room* answered, followed by a billowing cloud of dust on fast approach from the north.

"Coming in!" Paul pointed up the street.

Retay slammed the hauler to a stop, sending several crates toppling over in the bed. "Get on!"

Taylor bounded over the sidewall and took a defensive post near the back. Billy did the same on the bed's other side, while Valawn took the seat beside Retay.

"Paul, you got Douron?" Taylor asked.

"As best I can, yeah." The doctor pulled a dressing from his bag and put it to the Rukori's wound. "I have no idea how his body will react to nanites, so I've gotta do this old school until we get him back to Sanctuary."

"Go!" Valawn ordered.

Retay gunned the engine, sending a spray of debris flying into the faces of a group of Zuul that rounded the corner in pursuit, and were immediately driven back by Human laser fire. From there, the hauler tore off down the road, then hooked left toward the southern checkpoint.

"How far to the gate?" Taylor called.

"Two minutes," Retay said. "Just stay down, try not to get shot, and we'll handle the rest."

"Check that." Valawn inspected the drone feed on his slate. "The Krulig are redeploying their forces to block our egress."

"We got other options?" Billy asked.

Valawn swiped at his screen to shift the drone's trajectory. "As it stands, most of the redirected Zuul are coming from the Krulig compound, which is all the way to the east. The remainder are coming from the town square at the colony's heart."

"What's your point?" Taylor asked.

"Our current heading takes us straight through the Zuul reinforcements to get to the south gate," Valawn said. "By contrast, it will take them a while to get to the west gate."

"Can we make it?" Paul asked.

"If we hurry, yes," Valawn said.

Taylor was about to give a thumbs-up when the blaring cacophony of engines, live firearms, and screaming aliens roared onto the scene.

"Heads up!" Billy yelled.

Retay pulled the yoke hard right as an armored Zuul transport sliced in behind them.

"Retay, if you've got a gas pedal on this tub, I highly suggest you step on it." Taylor pushed over a stack of crates for cover as the exchange of fire resumed.

"I can assure you, sir, that is my intention," the corporal answered.

The hauler bucked hard as an enemy laser bolt tagged its right-rear quarter panel.

"They're gaining on us!" Billy yelled.

Valawn pointed to an A-frame building ahead. "There's a cut-through on the far side of that storage shed. If memory services, it'll bypass the central stretch and put us out a half-mile from the west gate. Take it, now."

Every head in the hauler rocked left as Retay swung the yoke hard to the right, eliciting a mechanical howl of protest from the hauler's stabilizers. The craft bucked and fishtailed, but soon recovered to resume its heading.

"They're still with us!" Billy yelled.

Taylor slapped a fresh chem mag into his rifle and tapped off a series of rounds, only to see them ping wide off the transport's nose plating. "Our rifles ain't worth jack against that thing's armor. We need somethin' else."

"Chief Van Zant!" Retay called. "There's a crate with an orange label just behind my seat. Can you reach it?"

Taylor slid down behind his post while Billy covered and crawled to the box. "I'm here."

"Open the crate and reach inside," Retay said. "You'll find a bundle of silver canisters. Pull one out and get ready to throw it at the Zuul."

"We're throwing supplies now?" Billy recoiled as enemy fire pelted the crates in front of him.

Taylor examined the canister in his hand. "What's in this?"

"Trinolium," Retay said. "We use it to fuel our lamps and cookstoves while hunting in the badlands."

Nice. Taylor clutched the canister in his palm and swiveled onto his knees. "Billy, on my signal."

The XO nodded and readied his rifle.

Taylor reared back and let fly. "*Now!*"

The silver container toppled end over end as it soared through the air. It struck the ground in the middle of the street and rolled to a stop just as the Zuul transport roared over top of it.

"Smile, you son of a bitch." Billy tapped his trigger.

A wash of orange blossomed under the transport, which reeled to evade. Instead, the pilot lost all control, sending himself, his craft, and his crew careening into a storehouse, which burst into flames.

"*Yeah!*" Taylor pumped his fist.

"*Duck!*" Valawn screamed.

A smattering of laser fire pelted the hauler's frame. Unlike before, however, when the fire had come from behind, now it was coming from up ahead.

Taylor peered past the top of his crate. Three Zuul guards were camped out in front of the gate with weapons drawn.

"Everyone hang on." Retay snatched back on his shifter. "These three are mine."

Taylor and Billy didn't argue.

A final rev crooned from the hauler's engine as Retay hammered the throttle. The next sounds heard were the thumps of three skulls smashing the front end and the crash of gate metal as the vehicle tore free into the open desert.

*****

Chapter 11:
Old Debts

No one said a word during the ride back to the badlands, least of all Taylor. In truth, he was happy for the reprieve as it gave him time to think.

Once the group had reached the district, they stashed their hauler as before, then returned to the Sanctuary where the RFC and Eagle crews were waiting.

"Thank you all for your assistance in the colony," Valawn said in the hangar. "Centress Padona and I are grateful, as is Douron for you saving his life. We are in your debt."

The big Rukori nodded.

"Forget about it," Taylor said. "I'm just glad everybody came home alive."

"That makes two of us," Valawn said. "Now if you'll excuse me, I must accompany the sergeant to medical, then debrief my staff regarding the bulsina crisis. I expect I'll hear from you soon?"

Taylor shook the commander's hand. "You will."

"Captain Dawson, Dr. Wright." Valawn bowed goodbye, then departed with Douron and Retay.

"I think I'm gonna follow suit and take off, guys." Paul gestured to the blood on his shirt. "A hot shower and a fresh change of clothes sounds pretty good right now, plus I haven't eaten anything save a power bar since breakfast."

"Go." Taylor shooed the doctor out. "We'll catch up with you later aboard ship."

Paul started for the *Osyrys*'s boarding hatch, only to sidestep Smitty who hurried out into the hangar.

"You blokes okay?" the Aussie asked.

"Fine, Smitty, thanks," Taylor said. "Things just got a little hotter upstairs than we'd anticipated."

"I know," Smitty said. "Sergeant Balar patched the bridge crew in on Valawn's comm feed after you left Nyo Colony."

"So you know about the Zuul then?" Taylor asked.

Smitty nodded. "I'm not alone, either. Frank and Quint were on the bridge with me, as was Keeto, who'd come up from engineering."

Taylor winced. "How'd Keeto take it?"

"About as well as you'd expect from someone who lost his entire family in a Zuul massacre." Smitty pocketed her hands. "He's pissed as hell. As an aside, he's also extremely motivated now to get max potential out of our remaining weapons systems."

"I'll bet he is," Billy murmured.

"How go the other repairs?" Taylor asked.

Smitty produced a slate and handed it over. "You'll find the details in my report. In summation, all of our primary systems—life support, propulsion, etcetera—are online with minimal issue. Our weapons systems, shields, and parts of the outer hull, however, will have the engineering guys working overtime a while before they're back up to speed."

Taylor skimmed the report's highlights then put it away. "Billy, let's reconvene for church in ten minutes, bridge conference room. Pass the word. Smitty, I want you to coordinate—"

"Smitty, will you give me a second with the Chief?" Billy asked.

The Aussie's gaze cut from the XO to the chief, then back to the XO. "No worries. Take your time. I'll be on the bridge if you need me."

Billy waited for her to leave before speaking. "Permission to speak freely?"

"Always," Taylor said. "You know that."

"This crew has been running on the ragged edge for eighteen hours straight," Billy said. "They've been shot at, forced to land in a nuked city, allied with an alien species no one's ever heard of before, and oh by the way, none of us has a clue how we're getting home."

Taylor dropped his eyes.

"Listen, Chief, I get where your head's at here," Billy said. "Really, I do. Terry's fingerprints are all over this situation. That haunts the hell out of me, so I can only imagine what it's like for you. I also understand why you'd want to help these people. The Krulig swooped in at a time when the Rukori were vulnerable and have been exploiting the hell out of them ever since. That's a rotten deal for anyone, much less a race of people with their legacy."

Taylor bit his lip.

"We're gonna find a way to help the Rukori," Billy said. "But we can't do that if the whole crew is running on fumes. Let's slow our roll, get some rest, and come at this thing fresh tomorrow, when we've all got some perspective."

Taylor exhaled, and keyed his comm via pinplants. "Change of plans, Smitty. Tell Keeto and the others to stop what they're doin' and pack it up for night. Same goes for you. We'll reconvene for church at oh-eight-hundred tomorrow."

"Ayew." Smitty said. "I'll relay the order."

"Good choice," Billy said once the call had ended.

"Thanks," Taylor said. "I guess for all those sessions in Cortes's trainin' room, I've still got a tendency to jump the gun at times, huh?"

Billy put a hand on Taylor's shoulder. "Don't sweat it. This would be a tough spot for anybody, much less someone with your personal ties to it. And for what it's worth, I'd take you into battle over a lot of the colonels I know with ten times your experience."

Taylor rolled his eyes. "Whatever."

"No, it's not whatever," Billy said. "You've got a good head, Taylor, and good instincts in a fight. You've come a long way in the last year, as evidenced by your performance at the colony. You didn't freak out, and you didn't freeze. You just did your job."

Taylor grunted. "I sure as hell froze in the fight with the warships, though."

"You didn't freeze," Billy said. "You hesitated out of a lack of butt time in a command chair. That's natural. What isn't natural for a lot of commanders is the ability to set aside one's ego to ask for help. You did that when it mattered, and we got through it. The rest will come in time."

Taylor hoped his XO was right. "What's on your docket for the rest of the night?"

"Eh, not much." Billy raised a shoulder. "First, I figure I'll grab a shower, then a bite. After that, maybe I'll treat myself to a bourbon or two before I hit the rack."

"You flyin' that bourbon solo?" Taylor asked.

"That's usually my preference, yeah."

For the briefest of moments, Taylor considered offering some sage wisdom of his own. *The man's got his reasons, T. Let him be.* "Night, Billy."

"Night, Chief," Billy said. "Get some rest. I'll see you tomorrow before church."

* * *

Taylor genuinely tried to follow his XO's advice to get some sleep that evening. Alas, the hamster wheel that was his mind had other ideas. All night he tossed and turned, thoughts swirling with events from both the last twenty-four hours and the last six years. The Rukori, the Krulig, Terry, the *Osyrys*. It was all so much to process. Yet as big as the situation was—fraught with insurrection, conspiracy, maybe even murder—Taylor couldn't believe how connected it all felt, or for that matter how connected one little family from Jacksonville, North Florida was to the entire thing. *My family.*

Taylor rose the next morning and fixed himself a coffee on the miniature pot he'd brought from the Clubhouse, then sat down to think. *They're all lookin' to me for direction on what to do next. How in the hell do I answer that?* Unable to find clarity alone, he tabled the conundrum long enough to get dressed, then headed for the lift to meet Billy before church.

"Morning, Chief," Quint said as Taylor entered the conference room with the XO.

"Quint," Taylor greeted. "How'd you sleep?"

"About as well as you, apparently." The bald officer pointed to the bags under his CO's eyes. "I'd say we're all gonna be in need of some high-quality R&R when this is over."

"Amen to that." Taylor patted Quint's arm then headed for his seat at the end of the table, making eye contact with everyone in attendance along the way. As expected, the senior staff was there—Billy, Quint, Smitty, Keeto, and Frank—as were Jack Bowyer and Jed Stan, both of whom wore sergeant stripes in keeping with their contracts. Valawn was also there, representing the RFC.

"Chief." Sergeant Bowyer rose and extended a hand.

"Good to see ya, Jack." Taylor shook it. "I appreciate you boys comin' up today."

"Weren't no trouble at all," Jack said. "To the contrary, we were a little surprised you'd want a couple of old grunts like us in attendance for somethin' like this."

Taylor snorted. "Are you kiddin'? Given all that's in front of me right now, I need every bit of insight I can get."

Jack chuckled as Stan rose to join them.

"You'll get our best, Chief," the latter said in his Mississippi drawl. "On that, you can bet your heard-earned credits."

Taylor thanked them both, then sat to begin the briefing. "Before we kick this off, I wanna start by givin' credit to every single person in this room for the exemplary conduct you've shown thus far. These ain't exactly been ideal circumstances for a first contact, but we've gotten through it."

The group nodded.

"Now." Taylor clasped his fingers. "Best I can tell, everybody here has a problem. For the Rukori, that's a bully problem. Did everyone get a chance to read Billy's report from yesterday's site mission?"

More nods.

"Good," Taylor said. "Long story short, the Krulig are about to take food from the mouths of a whole bunch of people, many of them women and children. I ain't about that. Not one damn bit."

Valawn brightened across the table. "So that's it then. You'll help us."

"I'll get to that," Taylor said. "The other problem we have pertains to us, the crew of the *Osyrys*. By all rights, we're trapped here on Rukoria until we can find a way past that last frigate through the stargate. Now I've been rackin' my brain all night for ways to have our cake and eat it, too. By that, I mean a plan where we get to go home, and the Rukori don't lose the lion's share of their winter food supply."

"And what did you find?" Valawn asked.

Taylor chewed his lip. "Sadly, not much. I'm sorry, Valawn. I just don't see an end where we pull this off. Not in orbit versus the warship given our current state, nor on the ground versus the Zuul."

Valawn ran a gray-skinned palm through his snow-white hair. "I don't understand. Surely there must be something you can do." He snapped his fingers. "What about those armored suits of yours? What was it Terry called them? Oh yes. Combat Assault System, Personal. You do have those, do you not?"

"We do have CASPERS, yeah," Billy said, "but not nearly enough to contend with that many Zuul. Our people would be outnumbered five to one, at least. Plus, the CASPers we do have are two, sometimes even three generations old because that's all we can afford."

"You've gotta understand, Valawn," Taylor said. "Swamp Eagle Security ain't the outfit it was when Terry was in charge. We're a lot smaller now, with a lot less resources at our disposal."

The RFC leader slumped back in his seat. "So, there it is, then. Once again, my people and I are left to fend for ourselves."

"I didn't say that." Taylor raised a palm. "Swamp Eagle Security may not be able to stop the Krulig from takin' this crop. But if we play our cards right, maybe we can make it the last crop they ever put their money-grubbin' claws on."

Valawn wrinkled his nose. "What are you suggesting?"

"Help me get the *Osyrys* back through the gate to Earth," Taylor said. "From there, we can recruit the aid my brother promised, then come back here in force with the requisite numbers to rid Rukoria of the Krulig for good."

Valawn didn't answer at first. He just sat there, mulling his host's proposal.

Taylor didn't envy the alien's position. Throughout their history, the Rukori had been put through the ringer, first by the Canavar on their native homeworld, then by the Winter Death on their adopted one, and at present by the Krulig on the decimated remains of the latter. Now here they were again, being asked to pin their hopes for salvation on a Human, and another Van Zant at that.

Hang with me, brother. We'll get through this. Taylor wondered if he'd believe that, were their roles reversed.

"Very well," Valawn said. "Tell me your plan."

Taylor sat up straight. "First things first, let's start with the situation in orbit. On any given Sunday, a Navarro cruiser should be able to hold her own versus a Maki frigate. Problem is, our weapons and shields were seriously degraded in the skirmish with the cruiser, and frankly I'd rather my flagship avoid another conflict if possible."

"What do you recommend?" Valawn asked.

"We need a way to draw that frigate off our backs long enough for the *Osyrys* to break atmo," Taylor said.

"Like a decoy," Billy said.

"Correct," Taylor said. "It don't have to stay up forever, just long enough to give the *Osyrys* a head start toward the stargate."

Valawn rubbed his chin. "I suppose we could use a bandilaro. I hate to forfeit one, as we only have two. However, it is the most logical choice."

"How do you propose we fly it?" Billy asked.

"Clearly, we'll need someone aboard to man the controls." Valawn's expression dropped as soon as he'd uttered the suggestion.

Taylor knew why. For the plan to work, the bandilaro would have to burn her engines until the last possible moment to keep the frigate at bay. That meant no killing her reactor to go dark as she'd done in the asteroid field.

Somebody's takin' a one-way trip.

"Excuse me, gentlemen." Keeto cleared his throat. "Did I not read in Billy's report that the RFC possesses some sort of drone technology?"

Valawn nodded. "You did, and we do."

"It may be possible to modify the bandilaro's nav system to function via a similar form of automation," Keeto said. "Granted, we'll most likely lose our connection as soon as the ship crosses the thermosphere. However, as long as she's placed on the proper trajectory, she should be fine to operate independently past that point."

"Like an old windup toy," Quint said. "Set her on her way then let the frigate follow her out. No steering required."

"Precisely," Keeto said.

Taylor faced the engineer. "Do you think you could rig the system to work that way?"

"I'll need access to a drone to be certain," Keeto said. "But yes. I do believe I could."

Visible relief washed over Valawn's face. "You shall have it."

"Yo, I got a question." Frank put up a hand. "All this bait-and-switch stuff sounds fine and good, but it's all for crap if we can't open that stargate to transition outta here. Last time I checked, that can't happen by remote. We got any thoughts on that?"

Billy exhaled. "We'll have to physically put somebody on the admin station, probably a group of somebodies. As for how we do that, I'm open to options."

Valawn considered. "The Krulig ferry supplies from the surface to their stargate crews once per day via the shuttles in their compound. If we could infiltrate one of those shipments, we could use it as cover to smuggle ourselves aboard the stargate. Thoughts?"

Billy rocked his head from side to side. "Sounds plausible enough."

"Pardon me, sirs, but doesn't this raise a whole new batch of issues?" Smitty leaned forward. "According to astrometrics, the *Osyrys*'s projected transit time from surface launch to the stargate is three hours at best possible speed. That means the Krulig will see us coming, a revelation which I'm sure will prompt them to suspend all inbound traffic."

"She's right," Taylor said. "In order for this to work, the strike team will have to be docked and inside the admin station before *Osyrys* clears the Sanctuary."

Frank grimaced. "Three hours is a long time to be holed up in quarters as cramped as a stargate admin station."

"Indeed." Valawn reclined in his seat. "But I may know someone who can help us."

Taylor raised an eyebrow.

"Her name is Natona," Valawn said. "She's an RFC operative who works in the Krulig compound outside of Lyndu Colony. She routinely travels with their crews to the stargate."

"How exactly does she pull off that bit of magic?" Quint asked.

"As was observed outside the checkpoint," Valawn said, "the Krulig employ Rukori citizens for a number of menial tasks. That includes things like janitorial and servant duties on the stargate. It's one less thing our masters must outsource to the Zuul."

"And you're sure this person will help us?" Smitty asked, a note of skepticism in her voice.

"Natona is one of my most trusted allies," Valawn said. "If anyone can get a team aboard the stargate, it's her. She will assist us. I guarantee it."

Taylor sat forward. "All right, then. Let's run down the timeline. First, we launch a bandilaro from the surface and use it to draw the frigate out of range. While that's happenin', our strike team will infiltrate the Krulig compound outside of Nyo Colony and hop a shuttle to the stargate. Once aboard, the team will signal the *Osyrys* to launch, at which time this whole deal becomes a sprint to the finish whereby our strike team seizes the control room, the *Osyrys* returns to hyperspace, and chaos reigns supreme on the admin station, allowin' our people to slip out to safety. That about sum things up?"

Everyone nodded.

"Excellent," Taylor said. "Questions?"

Smitty raised a hand. "Once we're aboard the stargate, we'll have to seize the command codes for the *Osyrys* to escape."

"Typically, the Krulig in charge has those," Valawn said. "We'll find him in the control room once we're aboard. The trick, therefore, will be to seize said room before the Krulig can lock out the computers."

"Leave that to us," Taylor said. "What else?"

The RFC commander shifted awkwardly in his seat. "I have one. Alas, I'd rather not ask it, but regrettably I fear I must."

Taylor would've bet a paycheck he knew what was coming.

"What assurances do my people have that the Eagles will return once you've escaped through the stargate?"

"You wanna know if we intend to bolt and leave the Rukori high and dry," Billy said.

Valawn nodded. "I only raise this because, as you noted earlier, Chief Van Zant, this incarnation of Swamp Eagle Security is not the one that agreed to help us six years ago. You are in no way tied to us, and frankly that's not much to go on when it comes to putting my operatives at this much risk."

Taylor had wholly expected that question. He was just happy it'd come at the end of the briefing, so he wouldn't have to deal with the blowback from his answer. *Sorry, Billy.* "The Eagles will return as promised because they'll want to pick up their commandin' officer. I'll be leadin' the strike team, personally."

The XO rocketed forward amid a gaggle of confused looks. "Chief, I really don't—"

"The decision's made, Captain," Taylor said. "This is my call, and I've given it. Time to move on."

Jack coughed into his fist, while the XO settled down. "My apologies, sir, but we can't allow you to do that."

Taylor shot the sergeant a sideways look.

"Not alone, that is," Jack added. "I didn't know your brother, but I did know of his reputation. Terry Van Zant did a lot of good things for a lot of folks, and hear me when I say, that ain't a trait you find much in our line of work."

"Damn straight," Stan agreed.

"Me and Stan never got the chance to work for Terry," Jack said, "but we dang sure come here to work for you. As such, we'd kindly appreciate it if you'd let us watch your ass on this here operation."

Taylor studied the old men's body language, rigid as it were. *They ain't takin' no for an answer.* He was honored. "You're in."

"Deal me in, too," Smitty said.

Billy whirled. "Commander Smith, I'd rather—"

"It's done." Smitty cut him off. "Like the fart said, we all came here to fly free with the Eagles, right? Isn't that the old saying? Well, that includes me. Besides, somehow I doubt the *Osyrys* will have much need for a comms officer when she breaks orbit." The Aussie turned to her boss. "Just tell me where you need me, Chief, and I'm there."

Taylor was quickly starting to understand why Ron Carnegie had hated to lose this woman. "Okay then. We have to assume that the *Behemoth* will spend minimal time on the other side, rallyin' the troops. Per the RFC's records, a round trip for these guys typically takes two transitions. That's a hundred and seventy hours each way, minus the twelve they've already been gone. Tax, title, and all, that gives us thirteen days to prepare. Let's get this right, y'all. Dismissed."

One by one, the group filed out of the conference room en route to their respective divisions. Not surprisingly, one staffer stayed behind.

"What's on your mind, Billy?" Taylor asked.

The XO drummed his fingers on the table. "Permission to speak freely?"

"I swear, man, if you ask me that again I'm gonna dock your pay." Taylor feigned a chuckle but got a scowl in response.

"That was a fargin shitty thing you just did," Billy said, "keeping me in the dark about your plan to lead the gate team. I'm your executive officer, Taylor. I'm supposed to know these things before the crew does, so I can back you."

"And would you have backed me here if you'd known my intentions?"

"Hell, no." Billy snapped. "I'd have delayed church until we could reach a compromise."

Taylor folded his arms. "A wise man once told me that when entering a complex situation, I should always evaluate my strengths, weaknesses, opportunities, and threats, then leverage that information accordingly for best possible success."

Billy rolled his eyes.

"You know I'm right, Brother," Taylor said. "The fact is, I've got no experience leadin' a starship into battle. Not yet, anyway. You, on the other hand, do, and that was on clear display when we emerged into this system. If the *Osyrys* lands in a fight with that frigate, she stands a better chance of makin' it out with a seasoned officer in command than a twenty-three-year-old kid still learnin' the ropes. Like you said, it ain't complicated. It's just good old common sense."

Billy muttered a curse. "So you think I'm more qualified to lead the *Osyrys* into combat. Fine. You still could've remained onboard and left the gate strike to Valawn. He's got more experience than you, too, ya know."

"Sure, he does," Taylor said. "And I'll be leanin' on that from the word *go* to come home alive."

"But why go at all?" Billy threw up his hands. "You've done your job, Taylor. You've agreed to bring the Rukori help. Why hang yourself out there to be stranded with them?"

Taylor chewed his lip. "A Van Zant made these folks a promise."

"Yeah, but that Van Zant wasn't you. It was Terry, and believe me when I say that for all his strengths, your brother was no stranger to writing checks with his mouth that his ass couldn't cash."

Taylor heaved a sigh. "One man's word is his family's bond. That's the way our daddy raised us—all of us. I can't break from that now. I *won't* break from that now. I also won't put the crew of this ship in jeopardy to honor my upbringin'. All I ask is that you follow my orders, and if things go sideways, you tell my family what happened. Start with Rita. She's tough. She'll handle the others."

"I'd prefer to not have to tell her anything at all," Billy said.

"Same here," Taylor said. "Hence why I want you to get home, recruit the meanest pack of redneck SOBs on the block, then high tail it back here to bail my ass out of the fire."

Billy didn't bite on his CO's attempt at levity.

Taylor didn't blame him. Billy had never spoken of it, but Taylor had always known of his XO's lasting unease over the way his first stint with the Eagles had ended. It wasn't fair what had happened, and no one who'd understood the situation had blamed Billy for leaving. That still didn't change the fact that, in doing so, the XO had walked out on a lot of folks who'd called him friend, most of whom weren't around anymore to mend fences.

That ain't on you, Brother, and neither is this. Taylor debated saying something, but decided it best that he stay quiet.

"Friggin' Van Zants," Billy grumbled. "I swear, man. Never in all my days have I ever met a more stubborn tribe of people."

Taylor grinned. "It's all part of our charm. We good?"

Billy exhaled. "Yeah, Chief. We're good."

"Fantastic." Taylor got to his feet "Now that that's settled, what do you say we head down to mess hall. I skipped breakfast earlier, and honestly I could go for a topper on coffee."

*****

Chapter 12: Let's Make a Deal

The next ten days were a whirlwind of planning as every member of the *Osyrys* crew went about preparing for the operation to come. For Taylor, that meant teaming with Valawn to pick the rest of their team, then assemble their strategy for reaching the stargate control room undetected.

On the eve of the operation's launch, Taylor wrapped his final repairs meeting with Keeto then returned to his cabin to clean up for supper. Ordinarily, that wouldn't have been a big deal, since most of their meals were pretty basic. That night, however, Frank had taken over the galley to create some sort of gourmet concoction, the likes of which Taylor couldn't begin to pronounce. He just knew it was French, and the Buma had even gone so far as to set a dress code for the occasion.

Dress code, my ass. If there was anything Taylor despised more than being shot at, it was wearing a tie. As such, he'd planned to exercise his right as CO and compromise with jeans without any holes and a Swamp Eagle Security golf shirt. He did, however, plan to tuck in said shirt, which, by his standards, was a big damn deal.

Now where did I put that belt? Taylor had just slipped on his boots when someone knocked at the entrance to his cabin. "Just a second."

Another knock.

Damn, persistent much? Taylor got to his feet and pulled his hair into a ponytail en route to the door.

"Hi," Lisa said from the corridor outside.

"Hey." Taylor could've sworn he'd meant to speak actual words beyond that one, but it never happened.

Lisa blinked. "Can I come in or what?"

Still speechless, Taylor stepped back and motioned her inside.

Gone were the frayed jeans, worn sneakers, and all-around casual attire that typically defined the Jax reporter's appearance. Per Frank's mandate, those had been replaced by stylish heels, a sleek silver pendent, and an elegant blue evening dress that would've killed in Cocktail Junction.

I, um…. Taylor snapped to his senses and cleared his throat. "What can I do for you, Lisa?"

"We need to talk," Lisa said.

"About what?" Taylor asked.

Lisa brushed back a strand of her autumn-brown hair and examined the room's décor. They included a framed portrait of Taylor's family and a signed poster of the Generals' first World Series team. She smiled at the latter. "I remember that squad. Game Seven fell on the night of my eleventh birthday party. My mom got pissed with me and my dad because we kept ducking out on my guests to check the score."

Taylor pocketed his hands. "It almost sounds like you were a Generals fan."

"Are you kidding?" Lisa scoffed. "They were playing the Cardinals, I'd have rooted for scurvy that night if I'd had to."

Taylor chuckled.

"Say…" Lisa returned to face him, "you got anything to drink around here?"

Taylor found himself puzzled by that request, but he rolled with it. "I've got water and beer."

"What kind of beer?"

"The free kind."

Lisa seemed to consider that. "Ah, why not? Gimme the beer."

Taylor crossed the floor to the small refrigerator by his nightstand and came back with two bottles of ice-cold beer. He popped the tops on both and handed one over.

"Long Branch Light." Lisa frowned at the label. "You are a local."

"There's always the water," Taylor said.

"Some might say that's exactly what you just gave me."

Taylor cocked his head. "Does this little courtesy call come with actual questions, or did you just stop by to dump on my taste in alcohol?"

Lisa took a pull off her Long Branch and winced. "I think we can both agree that, prior to now, I've respected your position and given you your space to work, right?"

Taylor pondered her point. Aside from a brief spat with Smitty on day one, Lisa hadn't been a hindrance. Sure, she'd asked for some access here and there, plus the occasional interview, but nothing of real consequence. "Yeah, I think we're in agreement there."

"Good," Lisa said. "Now I need you to recognize something. I've got a job to do, too, and I can't well do that if I'm confined to the *Osyrys* for the entirety of our time here."

Taylor scratched his whiskers. "That's a fair point. I'll talk to Valawn and see if I can get you some extra access to the RFC station."

"I don't want more access to the RFC," Lisa said. "I want to join the stargate mission."

Taylor almost choked on his beer. "I'm sorry?"

"You heard me. By this time tomorrow, there's gonna be a lot going on. I want to be there, in the trenches, watching it all happen so I can record it for my story."

Taylor wiped his mouth. "You do realize there'll be plenty to document from right here on the ship, right? When Billy calls the ball to bring the *Osyrys* out of the Sanctuary, there's gonna be plenty of fireworks."

"Maybe," Lisa said. "Or there could be none at all after we launch. That's the point of your little decoy trick, isn't it? To pull the Zuul warship out of position so the *Osyrys* can break for the gate?"

Taylor grunted and glugged at his beer. *Somebody's been talkin' after church.*

"So, what do ya say?" Lisa asked. "Can you do me a solid and grant me this one request or what?"

Taylor shook his head. "Out of the question."

"Ah, come on, Taylor," Lisa protested. "Read my file. This isn't my first rodeo in a hot situation. I know what it's like to be shot at."

"Do you also know what it's like to be marooned on an alien world millions of light years from home?" Taylor's look turned sideways. "Because that's a very real possibility for everyone on this team if the *Osyrys* don't make it back to pick us up."

Lisa stepped forward. "I'm prepared to take that risk."

Of course you are. Taylor rubbed his forehead. "Why are you so hellbent on makin' this happen?"

"You do understand I'm a reporter, right? This is kinda what we do?"

Taylor smirked a reply.

"Fine." Lisa pled her case by recounting all that had transpired, along with the revelation that other worlds existed besides those made public by the Cartography Guild. She then concluded with her best point yet. "Don't tell me your brother's accident hasn't been on your mind lately."

Don't answer that.

"I can get you those answers, Taylor," Lisa said. "With everything I've learned here, I guarantee you my editor will sign off on an investigative piece. Once that happens, we'll blow this thing wide open. I promise."

Taylor scoffed aloud, his first instinct being to tell the reporter how utterly full of crap she was. But then he caught himself staring at her, or rather her body language. *Squared shoulders, stuff lip, tight fists.* He considered. *This is personal for her somehow.* "Why do you want this so badly?"

Lisa furrowed her eyebrows. "I thought I was pretty clear on that. This is a huge story, and I'm—"

"I understand why the *Times* wants the story," Taylor said. "I want to know why *you* want this story, so much so that you're willin' to put your life on the line to get it."

Lisa collapsed onto the bedside and ran her fingers through her hair. "I wasn't entirely honest with you about how I came to Jax. I didn't leave Houston because of a transfer. I left because the *Chronicle* fired me."

Taylor held quiet while she explained.

"I'd been working a story for the better part of two months about a rogue element inside Astro Industries that was working both sides of the Zuparti conflict in the Jesc Arm. On the record, Astro was under contract with the Zuparti to lend aid where needed. Off the record, my source said they were arming the Zuparti's enemy to force a rider onto their contract and jack up their earnings."

Taylor vaguely recalled the events. "I take it you published the story."

Lisa nodded. "Turns out my source wasn't as reliable as she'd let on. Astro wasn't double-dipping at all. To the contrary, they were following the terms of their contract to the letter."

"I'm guessin' that didn't jibe with the Zuparti," Taylor said.

Lisa shook her head. "They filed a grievance with the Mercenary Guild as soon as my story hit the GalNet and requested that their contract be terminated. The Guild complied, of course, thus prompting Astro to file suit against the *Chronicle*, seeking millions in damages for lost revenue. By the time the saga ended, the paper had settled out of court, and I'd been booted out on my ass with a newfound understanding of the word blacklisted."

"Ouch," Taylor said. "How'd you come to end up in Jax then? Why not head back to Chicago, or someplace closer to home?"

"Two things you've gotta know about me, Taylor. I love what I do, and I never back down from a fight. As for Jax, my editor at the *Times* is an old friend from college. He found out what happened and landed me a freelance spot in their bullpen until I got back on my feet. I've been in Duval County ever since."

"How do you like it so far?" Taylor asked.

Lisa took another pull off her beer. "Truthfully, I came here expecting to hate the place. Per my understanding, North Florida was nothing but a state full of backwoods hicks with enough religion, fried food, and guns to populate a small moon. But then I got to know the area. I got to know the culture and the people." She looked up. "Folks around Jax genuinely care about their community, be they transplants from out of town or the natives whose families date back to the War of 1812. They look out for each other, support each other's businesses. More importantly, they'll do whatever it takes to do right by their loved ones. From where I sit, the whole Union could benefit from a little more of that. Lord knows, I did."

Taylor folded his arms. "So this is about redemption, then. A chance to clear your name."

"There's nothing to clear," Lisa said. "I chose to cut corners and rush a bogus story to press. That's on me. By contrast, this story has the potential to forever change both our understanding of Union hyperspace travel as well as the Guild who runs it. That story's gotta be told, Taylor. It's gotta be. All I need now is the ending."

Taylor put his beer down and slumped back against the wall. He empathized with Lisa's plight, truly. At the same time, granting someone access for an interview and granting them clearance for a site mission—particularly one with this much at stake—were two totally different things. Not only would such a move put Lisa's life in danger, but it would also jeopardize the lives of Taylor's fellow team members as they'd now be tasked with watching over a reporter in addition to their other responsibilities. In no scenario was that acceptable.

"Listen, Lisa," Taylor sighed. "I appreciate your position here. I really do. However, I simply cannot sign off on this."

"But—"

"But." Taylor raised a finger. "I will make you this compromise. I'll grant you bridge access from launch to transition. That way you'll be able to chronicle the *Osyrys*'s dash to the stargate, while gettin' real-time updates from the admin station via my team's comm chatter. Fair enough?"

Lisa's twisted expression said she wasn't thrilled with his deal. Still, she had to know it was the only one on the table.

The reporter fumed for another moment, then extended a palm. "Fair enough."

"Good." Taylor shook it, then accepted her empty bottle as she strolled past him to the door.

"You know," Lisa said. "That stuff ain't half bad once you get through the first few swigs. Gotta be cold, though."

Taylor touched two fingers to his ear. "Did you hear that?"

"Did I hear what?"

Taylor grinned. "Another angel in Heaven just got her redneck wings."

Lisa rolled her eyes. "See you in the mess hall, Van Zant."

*****

Chapter 13: Interception

Taylor rose the next morning and powered down three cups of coffee instead of his usual two with breakfast, hoping for an extra boost to kickstart the day. Afterward, he bypassed his usual hunter green fatigues in favor of the 231-series Nightshade BDUs. The latter's pattern, comprised mostly of black, dark blue, and gray, was designed to obscure the wearer's shape in dark environments. Thus, given that most stargate admin stations were anything but sunny inside, Taylor hoped the extra cover would give his people an edge.

Every little bit helps. Once he'd finished dressing, Taylor fastened his gunbelt and holstered his Firestorm then headed out to the Sanctuary's hangar.

"Good morning," Billy said as he emerged from the *Osyrys*. "I know it's a little late in the game, but any chance I could still talk you out of this? I'll throw in a case of Long Branch gratis to make it worth your while."

"Temptin' but no," Taylor said. "Nice try, though."

Billy shrugged as Smitty, Jack, and Stan filed out to join them, all wearing rag clothes over their Nightshades. "The four of you, come with me."

The group trailed the XO past a trio of RFC deck hands to the back of the hangar, where Keeto was waiting beside a stack of crates. Each one carried the Hemming Arms logo on its side.

"What's up, fellas?" Taylor asked.

"Just before we launched from Jax," Keeto said, "our Hemming rep stopped by for his usual delivery."

"I know." Taylor said. "I was there, remember?"

"You were there for the shipment's end. You didn't see what was loaded on first." Keeto walked over to the nearest crate, his wings fluttering, and flipped open the lid. He then reached inside and came back with a rifle.

"Well now." Jack licked his lips. "Ain't that a pretty sight to behold."

"Meet Hemming's latest creation, the JXR-14 assault rifle." Keeto presented the weapon. "It's a compact carbine variant of the JXR-10s we carry standard. Like its counterparts, the 14 is built to fire either semi or fully automatic, though its primary appeal comes by way of its universality."

Smitty wrinkled her nose. "How do you mean?"

"When Hemming set out to design a new rifle, they did so with the goal of creating a weapon that could be sustained in the field using whatever parts were available." Keeto pointed to the rifle's side. "Note the universal attachment rail on the side of the receiver. This makes the 14 compatible with every scope or optic sight Hemming manufactures, and even some from its competitors. The rifle also accepts most synthetic and metal magazines.

Taylor nodded and grabbed a rifle for study.

In addition to a streamlined frame and grip assembly, the JXR-14 presented a shorter barrel than the 10—about twelve inches—with a trimmed-down muzzle brake. It also featured a glass-filled polyamide stock which folded back along the receiver. By comparison, the 10s Taylor was used to had fixed stocks. *That'll make it easier to conceal. Nice.*

"I heard about these rifles when I was still with Steeldriver," Smitty said. "I didn't think they were expected out until the fall."

"They're not." Billy grinned. "We're just special that way."

"The partnership between Hemming Arms and Swamp Eagle Security dates back to the early years of both companies," Keeto said. "In that time, we've cultivated something of a relationship with them, so much so that when Hemming prepares to unveil new products, they'll often pass them to us for a sort of pre-release trial run. In exchange, they get our endorsement for use in promotions, and we get our first ten shipments at cost."

Taylor shouldered the 14 and peered down the sight. "Call it the perk of bein' an Eagle. We may not be able to spend with the big boys, but at least with us you get to test drive the latest toys before they do."

"Staying on that theme." Keeto reached into crate two and came back with a vest. "Hemming also provided us with a batch of their new body armor. It boasts a ten percent reduction in overall weight with a fifteen percent boost in durability versus laser and projectile weapons."

Billy grabbed one of the new helmets and flipped the visor up. "I've gotta say, Chief, I'm a little jealous. The one site mission I get benched for is the one on which Keeto decides to break out the fine china."

"Consider this extra incentive to hustle back with my ship once you're through that stargate," Taylor said.

The hangar's rear exit slid open, and Valawn entered with Retay.

"I just received word from our contact in Nyo Colony," Valawn said. "The supply shuttle is on schedule to depart for the stargate at thirteen hundred hours."

Taylor double-checked the time in his pinplants. *That's in five hours.* "Any word on our Maki friend?"

"Currently parked in a geosynchrnous orbit," Billy said. "We'll wait for your team to exit the badlands then we'll deploy the bandilaro. By the time the frigate reaches it, your shuttle should be well on its way to the gate if not already docked."

"Good deal," Taylor said. "We'll check in once we've taken the shuttle then again from the stargate. As discussed, update two is your cue to launch the *Osyrys* from the Sanctuary."

"Ayew," Billy said. "You kids had better hit the road."

Valawn turned to Retay, while Keeto returned to his hardware. "Go topside and ready the cargo hauler. We'll meet you there in a moment."

"Yes, sir." Retay saluted and took off for the lift, almost colliding with Lisa as she exited the *Osyrys.*

"Good luck," she mouthed to Taylor.

Taylor smiled and pulled a tunic over his uniform. "Smitty, Jack, Stan. Gear up with Keeto's new swag and head topside with Retay. I'll join you there in a minute."

The trio acknowledged and trotted off, as did Valawn.

"Take care of yourself up there, all right?" Billy said. "And keep Smitty close. I know Jack and Stan are solid by reputation, but I've got experience with the commander. She knows her way out of a jam should you land in one. She'll do you proud."

"I don't doubt it." Taylor patted his XO's arm. "Safe travels, brother. I'll see you back here in a few weeks."

"Bet your ass, you will," Billy said.

"Excuse me, Chief." Keeto fluttered back over. "May I ask one favor?"

"Name it," Taylor said.

The Athal looked up, nostrils flared. "If you get the chance to kill Zuul, kill them well…for me."

Taylor briefly recalled the nightmare which led to the alien's joining his crew. "Count on it, my friend. We'll even tell them you said hi."

Keeto's clicking sound said he approved.

* * *

Once topside, Taylor shouldered the rucksack containing his mag boots and other supplies for the stargate then ambled across the street to where Retay had the cargo hauler waiting to go. Smitty and the others were there, too, as were three extra Rukori who secured five oversized containers onto the flatbed. As Retay had explained, these climate-controlled bins were typically used for moving large shipments food or perishable goods between colonies. Today, however, they'd be shipping something else to the stargate.

Now I get why they told us to pack oxygen kits.

"Thank you for doing this." Valawn stepped forward. "For coming on this mission. You could've stayed behind on your ship, and no one would've blamed you."

Taylor shrugged. "I know. Fact is, though, I ain't doin' nothin' I wouldn't ask one of the others to do in my stead."

"Perhaps," Valawn said. "Nevertheless, the host in me is glad that you'll be staying with us a while when this is over. There is much about the Rukori people that's well worth knowing—things that don't involve violence or bloodshed. Your brother got to experience that firsthand. Now, so will you. That's assuming, of course, that we all make it home alive today."

Taylor chuckled darkly and tossed his ruck into one of the bins with the others. *Ri-ight.*

The ride to Nyo Colony took its usual four hours. Whereas before, however, the streets inside had been modestly populated, now they were bustling with aliens.

"Looks like you folks are gearin' up for an event of some kind," Jack said. "What's the occasion?"

"Today is Tribute Day." Valawn followed his answer by elaborating on what that meant.

"We couldn't have picked another date?" Smitty asked.

"Not in time to beat the *Behemoth*," Valawn said. "If history holds true, she should be returning through the emergence point in the next eighteen hours, and most likely with another warship in tow. If the *Ryley Osyrys* is to leave, it must be now."

Taylor pulled his cowl down low as a Krulig, flanked by a unit of Zuul, passed them on a corner.

"There." Valawn gestured to a turnoff ahead. "The shipment hauler will use that cutoff route to skirt the crowds toward the landing field. It's our best chance to take them unseen."

"Acknowledged." Retay veered off the main thoroughfare and eased the hauler down the narrow dirt strip until a cluster of empty warehouses came into view.

Valawn pointed to the middle structure. "That one."

Retay nodded and pulled the craft inside, then Valawn closed the door.

"Time." Smitty bailed over the side, grabbing her 14.

"The shipment should be here any moment," Valawn said, clutching his own 14. "We must hurry."

Jack sniffed the air. "How come I smell fuel?"

"The refueling depot for Nyo's hauler fleet isn't far from here," Retay said. "We'll pass it en route to the landing field."

The RFC corporal had barely spoken when an engine revved close by.

"Places." Taylor sprinted to the door.

"If I may," Valawn said. "There will almost certainly be Rukori on that hauler. Please don't kill them unless you absolutely must. Krulig loyalists or not, they are still my kin."

Taylor shook his head. "No promises."

"The target just entered visual range at the end of the street," Stan called from the door's other side.

"Head count?" Smitty asked.

"Looks like four Zuul guards and one Rukori driver," Stan said. "All armed."

Taylor clutched his rifle. "Eagles, take the Zuul. Valawn, the Rukori is yours. Clean and quiet, y'all. That's how I want this done."

"Ayew," the group said.

"Retay, you're up," Taylor said.

The RFC corporal threw a scorched tunic over his shoulders and ambled into the street, favoring his right leg. "Help! There's been an accident!"

The incoming hauler skidded to a standstill, shrouding the scene in a dusty haze.

"What happened?" The Rukori driver asked. "Are you—"

Pop, pop. Two laser bolts struck the Zuul to his right as another leaped to its feet.

"Intrud—"

Pop, pop. Pop, pop, pop. Pop, pop.

By the time the firing subsided, all four Zuul lay face-down in the dirt, while the lone Rukori sat motionless in his seat before the wrong end of Valawn's 14.

"Clear," Jack called through the cloud.

"Clear," Stan answered.

"Valawn," the Rukori driver snarled. "I should've known."

"Kaidon," Valawn greeted. "It's been a long time."

"The lord prefect will have your head for—"

The butt of Smitty's rifle smashed the Rukori's skull, dropping him in a heap to the ground.

"Sergeant Bowyer," she said. "Take the driver inside and make sure he can't warn his peers. Move."

Jack sprang into action, while Stan and the others grabbed the Zuul and Retay moved the second hauler into the warehouse.

Valawn shut the door once everyone was inside. "Hurry. Help me move our storage bins onto their hauler with the rest of the shipment."

Retay and Stan took the first pair of containers, while Smitty and Taylor took the second pair, and Jack took the straggler.

A thick *clang* rattled the air as Jack's bin struck the pavement.

"What in the fargin blazes of hell, man?" Stan protested.

"Don't look at me," Jack defended. "This sucker's heavier than the others."

Taylor narrowed his gaze, while Retay inspected the overturned container.

"Open it," Smitty said.

The RFC complied and entered a series of keystrokes into the bin's access panel. A second later, the seal released and a dazed Lisa Kouvaris staggered out, clutching her oxygen mask.

"Okay, so let's never do that again," she grumbled.

"Bloody hell!" Smitty erupted.

"I thought we had a deal, Lisa," Taylor said. "I lead the strike team down here. You stay on the *Osyrys* with bridge access up there. Did I miss the part where that changed?"

Lisa heaved a sigh. "Sorry, Taylor. Er, Chief. It was not my intention to mislead you."

"Ya don't say." Taylor tilted his head.

"Right." Lisa glanced around, finding angry looks everywhere. "It's like I said last night. I've got a job to do, and I can't do that from aboard a starship while the real action is happening down on the surface."

Smitty snorted. "I say we leave her here with the Rukori driver. We can pick her up on our way back to the Sanctuary when the mission is over."

"I wouldn't recommend that," Retay said. "The entire Colony is swarming with Zuul. Even in here, there's no way to ensure she won't be found."

"What about somebody else here in Nyo Colony?" Jack asked. "Ain't you got a contact or someone who could hide her a few hours?"

Valawn shook his head. "Ordinarily, I'd say yes. With today being Tribute Day, however, even our most ardent supporters will take pause at the notion of harboring a fugitive."

"Great," Lisa said. "So it's settled. I'm coming with you."

Taylor stepped in front of her. "You're to stay behind us at all times, no questions asked."

"Sure, but—"

"I ain't finished. You will speak to no one. You will act only when instructed to. Hell, it's probably best that you not even breathe without our say so. Break any of these rules, and you're liable to get yourself or somebody else on this team killed. I can't have that. Now, is anything I just said in any way, shape, or form unclear to you?"

Lisa swallowed but didn't flinch. "No, I hear you."

Jack fished a bag out of the reporter's bin and looked it over.

"Good," Taylor said. "Then help us move these bodies so we can get goin'."

The group moved quickly to pile the slain Zuul out of sight then secure the unconscious Rukori driver to the abandoned hauler. From there, they boarded the flatbed of the confiscated hauler and took positions at their respective storage bins.

"And now comes the fun part," Jack muttered past his oxygen mask from Bin One.

"Ah, stop your bitchin' and get in already," Stan said from Bin Two. "It's a tight space, not a death trap. It ain't gonna kill ya."

Smitty rolled her eyes from Bin Three and climbed in.

"You're with me," Taylor said to Lisa.

The reporter did a double-take. "Wait, I was just in that. There's no way we'll both fit."

"It'll take some creative bending on our part, but we'll make it work," Taylor said. "Now get in."

Lisa put on her oxygen mask and slid down inside the container. Once she'd gotten settled, Taylor handed his rifle to Valawn then wedged himself in beside her.

"Comfortable?" Valawn asked from overhead.

"Not even a little," Taylor said past his mask.

Valawn reached down and handed Taylor a small vial filled with a mucus-green liquid. "I must apologize in advance for this. Harmless or not, it's nothing if not effective when unleashed in the open."

Taylor snatched the vial from his host's fingers. "Yeah, yeah. Hurry up and seal us in already so we can get it over with."

Valawn nodded and looked to the other bins. "Everyone ready?"

"Ready," the others answered.

"See you on the other side." Taylor saluted the Rukori with his vial.

"Yes, my friend. You most certainly shall." With that, Valawn closed the lids and locked the seals, plunging Taylor and the others into total darkness.

* * * * *

Chapter 14: Intruders

"So," Lisa's voice said in the dark. "Do I get to ask what's in the creepy vial of green goo Valawn just handed you?"

"You'll find out soon enough," Taylor said. "Suffice it to say, it's nothin' we have to ingest, if that's what you're worried about."

"It was, actually," Lisa said.

Taylor reached into the tac vest under his tunic and produced a pin light, which he flipped on.

"What's the plan?" Lisa asked, her face illuminated from the top down.

"The landin' field we're headed to rests right outside the Krulig operations compound," Taylor said. "That means we can't seize the shuttle out in the open, or we risk bein' spotted by the watchtowers. Once we're inside the cargo hold, though, all bets are off."

"So we're taking the bins into the shuttle, then jumping out like some sort of jack-in-the-box?" Lisa's expression soured. "That's thin, Taylor. Real thin."

Taylor wasn't arguing. Still, it was the best plan they'd been able to devise, given the circumstances.

The name *Valawn* appeared in Taylor's lower-right field of vision.

"This is a comm test," the RFC leader said. "Chief Van Zant, can you hear me?"

"Yeah, Valawn, I've got you." Taylor widened the channel to bring in the others via their own pinlinks. "Smitty, Jack, Stan. This is a party line. You got a clear copy?"

"Five by five," the trio said.

The shipment hauler's engines sputtered to life, rumbling the floor under Taylor.

"We're preparing to depart," Valawn said. "I'll talk you through as much of what I see on the ride in as I can. After that, I'll leave the line open so you can listen in the rest of the way."

"Roger that," Taylor said. "We're standin' by."

The engine outside *ka-chunked* into gear as the world beyond the bin began to move.

"I won't even lie, man," Lisa grumbled. "Had I known I was gonna ride this box all the way into the lion's den, I might've opted to stay behind after all."

Now she gets it. An unseen chime interrupted Taylor's thought. "What was that?"

"Gimme a second." Lisa finagled her arm out from under Taylor's back then twisted herself to reach her bag.

"Can I help you?" Taylor winced.

"Just chill out. I'm almost there."

"Easy for you to say," Taylor growled. "You're not the one with a knee diggin' into his groin like a friggin' railroad spike."

Lisa froze. "Oh, right. Sorry."

Taylor exhaled with relief when the reporter shifted again, this time to pull a slate from her bag. "What is it?"

"I don't know," Lisa said. "According to this, we just passed in close proximity to a major power source."

"What kind of power source?" Taylor asked. "Like a generator?"

Lisa swiped through a series of screens. "No, this is way bigger, and definitely nuclear. Here. Check out these neutron readings." She showed him the device.

What the hell?

"We've just cleared the checkpoint out of Nyo," Valawn said. "We're approaching the landing field now. I have a visual on the shuttle."

"Security?" Smitty asked.

"So far, I count two Zuul standing guard at the boarding ramp with another two exiting the debarkation hatch." A pop of static crackled the line. "Check that. Make it three Zuul exiting the hatch."

Taylor rubbed his chin. "How about Krulig officers."

"None so far, but that's not surprising" Retay said. "The Krulig typically leave this sort of work to the Zuul. I do, however, expect we'll cross paths with them on the stargate, if only in the control room."

That makes sense if there's only three hundred of them.

"Coming up on the shuttle now," Valawn said. "Going silent."

The hauler's momentum slowed as the engines decelerated.

"Good day to you, sirs," They could hear Valawn's voice say.

"You're late," a feral voice snapped. "The shuttle has been prepared for nearly twenty minutes."

"My humblest apologies," Valawn said. "We got a last-second communique from the stargate crews, indicating a shortage on dako loins. As you know, that particular cut of meat takes time to process and pack. Otherwise, it goes bad almost instantly."

One of the Zuul snorted. "I care not for your excuses, Rukori. Tell me, where is the rest of your group?"

"Back in the square," Valawn said. "They were needed elsewhere for the tribute ceremonies. Thus, my partner and I agreed to deliver this shipment ourselves."

Another snort. "Stand aside."

"That's our cue to pop 'em, y'all," Taylor said to the other Humans via pinlink. He then cracked open his vial and poured out its contents.

Nothing happened.

C'mon, c'mon!

Lisa's eyes went saucer-wide.

Fargin A! Taylor buried his nose in his sleeve, bile rushing to his throat, as the foul scents of rotting meat and porta-johns invaded his nostrils. *Oh, that's just so wrong!*

Footfalls pattered the ground outside of the bin. A sniff ensued, followed by a flurry of revolted sneezes.

"Is there a problem?" Valawn asked.

The Zuul snarled back.

"Oh, dear," Retay said. "Forgive me, sirs, but I think we may have a problem."

"What is it?" Valawn asked.

"The seal on Bin One seems to be failing," Retay said. "We must hurry or we'll lose the load."

"It is the same for this one as well," another Zuul said.

Taylor's heart jumped when fingers jiggled the bin lid above his head.

"No, you idiot!" a third Zuul protested. "If you open this travesty out here, we will be forced to impound it!"

"A thousand apologies, sirs." Valawn withdrew his hand. "What, then, would you have us do? If we do not act to repair these containers now, we risk losing the entire load, thus prompting the ire of Lord Prefect Sadeed to rain down upon us all."

A scrum of alien voices chattered off to the side. When they returned, it was the initial Zuul who spoke.

"Dako meat is for Krulig, not Zuul. Let the reptiles deal with it. Take the shipment aboard and conduct your repairs in the cargo hold."

"Are you certain?" Valawn asked.

"Yes, yes," the Zuul snapped. "Now get this awfulness away from here."

Taylor relaxed against the bin wall and said a silent *thank you* as the hauler began moving again.

"You knew the Zuul would sniff the containers, so you used the vial goop to throw them off our scents." Lisa looked impressed. "Nice play."

"Thanks," Taylor said. "I use the same trick huntin' deer back home, only in that case they're the only ones who can smell the maskin' agent."

"We could only be so lucky." Lisa frowned and pinched her nose.

"Ain't that the truth," Taylor agreed.

Once the hauler had reached the edge of the boarding ramp, the entire bin tilted upward as the vehicle climbed into the hold. From there, a series of mechanized whines ensued, followed by a pair of *ka-chunks* as something grabbed hold of the container to shift it into the bay.

"We're almost there," Valawn murmured. "We'll launch as soon as Retay returns from debarking the hauler. Then we'll spring the trap."

"Acknowledged." Taylor whispered the update to Lisa, whose smirk implied a less than thrilled attitude about enduring an atmo breech in these conditions.

Hey, you're the one who snuck off ship to be here. Taylor probably shouldn't have taken pleasure in that, but he did. As it turned out, the launch experience was nothing short of misery for both of them—the racket and pounding of limbs, to say nothing of the stench. By the time it ended, Taylor's head was ringing like a bell tower, and his muscles felt like pounded hamburger.

"You okay?" Lisa asked, breathless.

"Sure," Taylor muttered, his face pressed to hers as both Humans hung suspended in zero G against the bin lid. "I'm all fargin aces here."

"Sarcasm doesn't become you, Chief."

"Yeah, well. You'll have to forgive me. I get a little testy when I've chewed off most of my teeth enamel."

Lisa gulped and rubbed her head. "Touché."

As the shuttle broke free of Rukoria's orbit, Taylor listened through the open comm as Valawn bantered with Retay while continually engaging the Zuul who'd been assigned to them. None of the beasts obliged, of course, but that was okay. The exchange told Taylor's team how many aliens were present in the passenger cabin, which had been Valawn's intention the whole time.

"Pardon me, sirs," Retay said. "My partner and I should check the bin seals to ensure our patches are holding properly. I presume one of you will need to accompany us into the hold?"

One Zuul gave a cursory grunt, but multiple mag-booted footfalls followed.

"Steady, y'all," Taylor said via pinlink. "Once this happens, it's gonna go down fast. Listen for your signals and make every shot count."

"Ayew," the others said softly.

The footfalls continued until eventually Taylor could hear them outside of his bin. *They're in the hold.* He pulled his Firestorm and waited.

Two knocks tapped his bin lid, then a pause, then one more.

Two Zuul total, one in front of my container. Taylor listened as Valawn trudged down the row of containers, relaying similar information to the others.

"What are you doing?" one of the Zuul asked.

"Checking the volume levels for the preservation fluid," Valawn said. "Everything sounds good."

Taylor glanced to a nervous Lisa.

"Let's begin from the front," Valawn said. "Retay, if you'd be so kind as to access Bins Three and Four, I'll handle One and Two."

"Understood," Retay answered.

Now it was Taylor's turn to feel anxious. *Easy, T.*

A final beat passed as the sound of fidgeting fingers returned to Taylor's bin lid.

"Seal check in three," Valawn said, "two…one."

A rush of light swamped Taylor's vision as he pushed up from the bin, Firestorm in hand.

"*Intru—*"

Pop, pop.

The Zuul's last syllable exited the back of his head in a floating stream of skull bone and gray matter.

The other Zuul lunged to counter, but Jack cut him down. *Pop, pop, pop.*

"Runner!" Stan shouted via pinlink.

A third Zuul released its boot lock and leapt for the exit, having entered the hold at the last second.

Pop, pop, pop.

The beast tumbled into a wall, sans most of its cranium, courtesy of Smitty's Firestorm.

"Clear," the Aussie said.

"Jack, Stan." Taylor turned his head. "You're up."

The old sergeants braced against their respective bins and pushed off, soaring in a single-file line through the exit and into the corridor outside. A few seconds later, fresh screams sounded through additional gunfire.

Talk to me, fellas. Taylor exhaled when a squelch broke the comm silence.

"The cockpit's secure," Jack said. "Y'all can come on up when ready."

Taylor glanced back to his bin. "Lisa, you okay?"

The reporter waved a hand.

"Good," Taylor said. "Stay here with the Rukori until we come back. Smitty, you're with me."

Taylor took point with the Aussie behind him. Together, they pushed off and floated into the corridor then hooked right past two more Zuul corpses to the cockpit.

"Chief," Stan greeted.

"Sergeant," Taylor answered. He then turned his attention to Stan's colleague who held a brown-furred Zuul pilot at gunpoint.

"Everybody," Jack said. "I'd like you to meet Coco."

The Zuul's beady, brown-eyed glare suggested this clearly wasn't its name.

"Coco," Jack said. "Say hi to the family."

Coco hissed a response.

Thwack!

"Don't be an asshole," Stan said.

The Zuul cupped its skull as the Mississippi sergeant re-trained his pistol on the alien's head.

"Look here, friend." Jack keyed an indicator light on his own weapon. "That there is a munitions tracker. It tells me how much juice I've got left in my chem mag. Right now, it's showin' green as a mostly full load. If I eject said mag, it goes red." Jack demonstrated. "Just in case you were wonderin', this light would show that same shade of beautiful crimson were I to expend the mag's contents into your face, an act I also mean to demonstrate should you elect not to cooperate with us. Now, nod if you get me."

Coco flashed a razor-toothed snarl but nodded just the same.

"Good boy." Jack patted the alien's head. "He's all yours, Chief."

"What's our ETA to the stargate?" Taylor asked.

"About three hours," the pilot said in a male voice. "Docking will take another ten minutes once we've acquired our clearance."

"And I presume you have the codes?" Taylor asked.

The Zuul uttered a growl.

"Now Coco," Jack said. "We talked about this, remember?"

The Zuul dropped its snout. "I do. I will transmit as soon as we are hailed."

"Excellent," Taylor said. "Smitty, check the status of our supplies. I'll radio our progress back to the *Osyrys*."

*****

Chapter 15: Stealth

The shuttle was of the same Maki origin as the Zuul's warships, which meant its amenities were anything but tailored to the Human physiology. The spaces were cramped, the corridors were tight, and the seats felt more akin to that of a child's jump seat than something designed for an adult, Human or otherwise.

And here I thought straddlin' a dirt bike was awkward. Taylor shifted to get the weird lumbar hump out of his back before it could permanently damage his spine. It didn't help. *On the upshot, at least the stench of that vial crap wore off.*

"Hey, Chief," Jack called from the cockpit. "You might wanna get up here."

Thankful for the reprieve, Taylor unbuckled from his torture rack and pushed off toward the cockpit. There, he found Coco at the nav controls, while Jack and Stan guarded him from behind.

"What's our status?" Taylor asked.

Jack glanced past the Zuul's shoulder at the display. "If I'm readin' this right, we oughta be nearin' visual range of the stargate any second now."

As if on cue, all eyes turned up to see the giant ring creep into sight through the forward viewport.

It was bigger than Earth's stargate, Taylor thought. At least, that's how it appeared from a distance. "When should we expect their hail?"

A chime from the dashboard answered the question.

"How should I proceed?" Coco grumbled.

"Put it to the speakers," Taylor said. "I want to hear the conversation."

The brown-furred alien grudgingly complied.

"Inbound shuttle," a male voice hissed. "Transmit your ident credentials for stargate docking clearance."

Coco reached for the *respond* key.

"Ahem." Stan poked the alien's back with the tip of his Firestorm. "Just in case you were thinkin' of gettin' creative here, I'd advise against it. Stay cool, get us onto that admin station, and you're apt to make it through this mess alive. Cross me, though, and you'll join your pack in the Entropy afterlife."

Coco snorted. "Zuul do not believe in an afterlife."

"Well, that tracks," Jack muttered. "Remind me to tell you about Jesus later if we don't kill you first."

Coco glowered at the old sergeants.

"Go on," Stan said.

The Zuul returned to his console. "Stargate control, this is the Shuttle *Santuva.* Prepare to receive ident credentials…now."

Taylor waited anxiously to see if their new friend's desire for survival outweighed his sense of duty.

"Credentials confirmed," the comm voice said. "You may proceed to Bay Two at your leisure."

"Acknowledged. *Santuva* out." Coco disconnected the channel and sat back.

"See?" Stan grinned. "That weren't so hard, now was it?"

The stargate loomed larger in the viewport as Coco eased the shuttle toward it. From there, he locked in his approach vector to the admin station, where a circular entry point irised open.

Taylor had never seen a docking bay at a stargate before. The ones he'd encountered had all utilized docking collars. The shuttle continued onward through the hatch, then set down on a platform, where a set of mooring clamps locked it in place.

"We are down," the Zuul said.

"Coco, my boy," Stan said, patting the alien's shoulder, "it's been a real pleasure workin' with you today."

The Zuul's eyes narrowed, then widened with revelation as a surge of electricity bolted him upright.

"How long do you expect he'll stay out?" Taylor asked.

Stan put away his stun device and studied the unconscious alien. "I'm told Hemming builds these things to put a grown man down for upwards of four hours. But a Zuul?" He shrugged. "Who knows?"

"Let's not take any chances," Taylor said. "Gag him, bind him, and stuff him into a head somewhere until we get back. We'll wake him then for the return trip."

"You got it." Stan unhooked Coco's belts then grabbed the alien's shoulders and floated him out of sight.

Lisa was waiting in the cargo hold when Taylor returned. "So, what's next?"

"For you, there is no next," Taylor said. "You're stayin' here."

Lisa opened her mouth to protest, but clearly thought better of it.

"Smart girl." Smitty floated in to join them.

"Whatever." Lisa smirked. "You guys be careful out there."

"Yeah, you, too," Taylor said. "Now get and find some place hidden to hole up. There's gonna be a crew in here shortly to unload these supplies, and the last thing we need is for them to find a Human stowaway, waitin' with the merchandise."

Lisa gave the group a *good luck* wave then coasted out of sight as Valawn and Retay entered on foot in their mag boots.

"I just got our confirmation from Natona," Valawn said. "She stands ready to receive us."

"Okay then. Let's get to it." Taylor slid off his Rukori tunic, figuring disguises were useless at that point, and he was just about to lay it aside when Valawn stopped him.

"You might not want to do that just yet," the RFC leader said.

Taylor wrinkled his nose as the RFC leader reached into his tunic and fished out another vial of green goop.

"Wonderful," Jack muttered.

Taylor snatched the ampoule from the alien's grasp then floated back to his bin and climbed in, while the others did the same.

"Good?" Valawn asked.

Taylor adjusted his oxygen mask and flashed a thumbs-up.

"Now we find out how good this contact of theirs really is," Smitty said via pinlink when all had gone dark.

"Hard to argue with the RFC's results so far," Taylor answered. "Besides, it ain't like we had a plethora of options here."

The Aussie commander grumbled something else but didn't push it.

"Docking bay pressurization is confirmed," Valawn said. "As before, I'll leave the comm line open for you to listen in."

"Understood," Taylor said.

"Preparing to move out."

Taylor listened from inside his bin as a collection of gear sounds preceded the clearance chirp of the entrance indicator. Next came the *ka-chunk* of the hatch opening, followed by a series of motorized whines as the boarding ramp lowered onto a metal surface outside.

"Manifest, please," a female said.

Taylor replayed the voice in his mind. *Definitely not Zuul.* A muddle of grunts in the backdrop told a different story. *At least two.*

"What is your primary cargo?" one Zuul asked.

Valawn listed a string of items.

"Excuse me, madam?" Retay cut in. "You should know that we experienced some seal issues with Bins One through Five before leaving the surface."

"The dako meat?" The female's voice ticked upward with concern. "Were you able to salvage the load?"

"Thankfully, yes," Retay said. "I would, however, recommend that we get these bins into proper storage as soon as possible. That way if we encounter more issues, we can keep the meat cooled under optimal conditions."

The female cleared her throat. "Very good, then. Everything else seems to be in order. My crew will be along shortly to inventory the remainder of the shipment. In the meantime, I'd suggest we move Bins One through Five to Holding Zone Two ourselves. It's on this level and possesses a cooling unit."

"As you wish," Valawn said. "Could I bother your two watchers to help us shift these onto cargo sleds?"

Only two Zuul. Taylor would take those odds.

The aliens muttered in protest but clanked across the decking in their mag boots just the same.

"Crack 'em, y'all." Taylor emptied his vial then waited as Zuul claws clasped his container. A spaz of furious sneezes followed.

"This bin seal is failing," the Zuul snapped.

"Quickly then," the female said. "We must hurry, lest we all pay when the Krulig lose their delicacy."

The scratches outside Taylor's bin continued at a rushed pace as, together, the Zuul and Rukori extracted each bin from the shuttle's hold and placed them onto cargo sleds for transport. It took some effort, but eventually the job was done, and the world outside of Taylor's hiding place began moving again. In the minutes that followed, he did his best to track their caravan's movements, however, the station's null gravity made that tough to do. By the time Taylor felt like he was getting a feel for things, the caravan arrived at their designated holding zone.

"Retay, as before," Valawn said. "If you'd attend to Bins Three and Four, I'll tend to One and Two."

"Yes, sir," Retay said.

"In three," Valawn said. "Two…"

Wait, where are the—

A rush of dim light swept into the bin as Taylor pushed out, gun in hand. Nothing happened.

What? Taylor scanned the room, finding only an empty storage space along with Valawn, Retay, and a Rukori female he didn't recognize. Short and frail, the girl was the picture of petite with rags for clothes and matted white hair that hung in rings down her face. She was the antithesis of a threat, Taylor thought. It was then he spotted the two flaccid Zuul, bobbing in their boots behind her, each one sporting a visible gash to its throat amid growing globs of crimson. *Damn, Lady.*

"Natona." Valawn trudged to the girl's side.

"You cannot stay here." Natona cleaned her blade on the hide of one of her victims then sheathed it in her tunic. "The others from my crew will be here shortly with your shipment. Some are Krulig sympathizers. You must go, now."

"What about you?" Jack climbed out. "Where are your—" He paused upon seeing the Zuul. "Oh. Well, all right then."

"There's an old quarantine space three levels down," Natona said. "It hasn't been used in years. You'll be safe there."

"Three levels are a long way to move in the open," Smitty said. "I presume you have an alternate route?"

"I do," Natona said. "The space is accessible by way of an old maintenance shaft which lets out into this room." She motioned to a nearby panel. "It's why I ordered the dako meat, so I could justify bringing you here."

"Nice," Taylor said. "Let's gear up."

Now free to cast off their disguise, the group did so without preamble, then floated over to Bin Five to begin unloading their supplies. Once they'd all been fitted with the proper weapons and body armor, they attached their mag boots to the decking and prepared to move out.

"The control room is just above our current location," Natona said. "Unlike here, it is not beside a shaft access, meaning you'll have ground to cover once you're out in the open. I've prepared a map to show the way." She produced a slip of paper from her tunic and handed it over. "I've also provided the access code to get through the entrance."

"How'd you come by that?" Smitty asked.

The Rukori pursed her lips. "It's a long story."

"Thank you, ma'am." Taylor tucked the map into his pocket. "For everything."

Natona nodded.

"Take this." Valawn slipped a comm device into the girl's palm. "I'll contact you when we're close to making egress. When that happens, I want you to come with us."

"Valawn, please," Natona said. "There are others here who are loyal to the cause. I can't just—"

Valawn cut her off with a look. "The Zuul may be fools, but the Krulig are not. They'll discover it was you who helped us, and they'll kill you for it. I want you off this station, Natona. Please."

The girl considered, golden eyes downcast. "Very well."

"Thank you." Valawn squeezed her hand, then released it to rejoin the others. "Now go."

Smitty was waiting at the shaft access when Valawn trudged over. "Looks like I owe you an apology. I guess we can trust your contact after all."

"I'd certainly hope so." Valawn grinned. "I'd have been sorely disappointed with my sister had she proven otherwise."

I'll be damned. Taylor matched the Rukori's smile with one of his own then keyed his comm while the others filed into the shaft. "Corn Husker, this is Tomahawk. You got a copy?"

It took about twenty seconds for a reply to come.

"Corn Husker here," Billy said. "We read you five by five."

"What's your status?" Taylor asked.

Another twenty seconds passed.

"Patched and ready. The party invitation was sent on schedule, and our guest is outbound to collect. All we need now is the official word to kickstart the festivities."

Taylor's pulse quickened. "Consider the word given, Husker. Party on."

*****

Chapter 16: Into the Fire

The next two hours drew out like molasses on a frozen mountain morning in Taylor's mind. He hated waiting. The only times he was okay with this much inaction was during deer season, when he'd sit for hours in a tree stand waiting for an eight-pointer to stroll past.

Let's go, already! Unable to take it any longer, Taylor rose from his seat and began pacing the team's hiding place.

"Hey." Smitty pulled him aside. "I know you're anxious, but you've got to stop waiting for things to break loose. They'll happen when they happen. Until then, slow it down, take a breath, and clear your head so you're ready when they do."

Taylor dropped his gaze. "You know, for a second there, you kinda sounded like Billy."

"What can I say, mate?" Smitty shrugged. "I learned at the feet of the master."

The XO's name flashed in Taylor's field of vision. "Speak of the devil." He keyed the comm. "What's up, Husker?"

The transmission lag was only ten seconds this time because of the decreased distance between sender and receiver.

"We've got a problem," Billy said.

"What kind or problem?" Taylor asked.

Valawn walked over, having apparently heard the commotion. "What's happening?"

The XO's voice was back in Taylor's head before the latter could answer.

"We cleared orbit as planned, but we've been intercepted by another ship."

"You mean the frigate?" Taylor furrowed his eyebrows. "I thought we sent that on a wild goose chase after the bandilaro."

Tick, tick, tick.

"We did," Billy said. "This is a different ship, make unknown. It must've launched from the surface shortly after we did because it's been lock/step with us since we reached the asteroid belt. Frank's managed to put some distance on it, but not before that thing could tag our aft armor near the torch."

"Damage?" Taylor asked.

"Reactor One is offline," Billy said. "At present, we're trying to fire up Reactor Three to compensate, but the circuitry connecting them got fried in the firefight. Engineering is working on a bypass as we speak."

"What are the odds they'll have that up by the time you transition?"

Tick, tick, tick.

"Fifty-fifty. Until then, Reactor Two's a solo act."

Taylor felt his stomach clench. The *Osyrys* could manage well enough in normal space on one reactor. In hyperspace, though, she'd need the lion's share of a full unit just to power her generator. That left very little energy for the ship's other key systems, like life support.

Time to work your magic, Keeto. Taylor rubbed his temples. "What do you need from us?"

"Stick to the plan," Billy said off the lag. "Get to that control room and have that gate open so we can transition straight through when we arrive. I don't wanna give this, whatever it is, another crack at us if I can avoid it."

"Ayew," Taylor said. "I'll check in when it's done. Tomahawk out."

Smitty waited while her CO disconnected the channel. "Everything all right?"

"Not exactly." Taylor recounted the conversation. "We need to take that control room, now."

The ascent back up the maintenance shaft took an extra flight than before, though the trek was easy due to the station's lack of gravity. Once the group had coasted up to the desired level, they found their footing near the access hatch then reengaged their mag boots to move out.

"Rukori personnel are not permitted past this point," Valawn said in a low voice. "It's restricted to Zuul and Krulig only, and the former aren't allowed inside the control room. We should expect resistance from this point forward."

"Okay, farts," Smitty murmured. "You're up."

Jack smirked and took the point, while Stan faced the hatch and toggled the visor settings on his helmet.

"Thermal shows three Zuul headed this way," the latter said. "Stand by."

"The Krulig in charge will be wearing a blue sash on his uniform," Valawn said. "It might be prudent to keep him alive until our objective here has been accomplished."

"Agreed," Taylor said.

"All right, we're clear," Stan said, after a few moments.

"Retay, you're on lasso duty," Taylor said. "Let's go."

The team filed through the opening with Jack out front, then fell at once into a diamond formation with Taylor at center-group, motioning directions. From there, they moved with all the swiftness they could muster in mag boots, each person working with head up, rifle raised, and finger at the trigger guard should the need to pull arise.

It did, quickly.

Pop, pop.

A single Zuul blew backward upon rounding a corner.

Pop, pop. Pop, pop, pop.

Two more followed.

"Go, go, go!" Taylor signaled.

The group advanced another forty yards, picking off aggressors as they went, and leaving the bodies to Retay for fastening onto tow lines. Eventually, the team halted at the final turn to the target.

"Looks like four Zuul guardin' the entrance," Jack whispered via throat mic. "That's two left and two right."

"How about inside?" Taylor asked.

Stan adjusted his visor view. "I've got nada on thermals."

"Krulig are cold-blooded," Valawn said. "Their bodies do not emit heat signatures."

Taylor swore under his breath. *Looks like we're doin' this blind.* "Jack and Stan, you're on the Zuul out front to set up our run. Once we're in, Smitty and me will sweep left while Valawn and Retay sweep right. Y'all clear on your jobs?"

Everyone nodded.

"Good," Taylor said. "Call the play, fellas."

The two sergeants gave each other a three count, then slid past the corner.

Pop, pop. Pop, pop. Pop, pop, pop, pop.

A beat passed before Jack's voice came back on comms. "Clear."

Two Zuul were listing in their boots by the door when Taylor approached the entrance. The others tumbled weightless down the corridor amid swirling globs of red.

"You set?" Stan asked. Meanwhile, Jack fetched their victims.

"Yeah." Taylor clutched his rifle. "Do it."

The Mississippi sergeant entered their stolen code into the access panel. A second later, the indicator light flashed green and the door swooshed open.

"Intruders!" a Krulig shouted.

Pop, pop. Smitty answered with dual trigger taps.

Pop, pop, pop. Taylor followed.

The entire scene devolved into chaos as the others glided in, shots bristling the air as, one by one, the officers fell prey to the Eagles' assault. From an execution standpoint, the op was almost flawless. By the time the firing ceased, four of the five Krulig floated motionless through the chamber as laser-charred heaps of flesh. The fifth, wearing a blue sash, was held frozen at gunpoint, thanks to Smitty's 14.

"Don't even think about it," the Aussie warned.

"Clear," Stan called.

"Clear," Jack echoed, a trail of dead Zuul flowing behind him on lines. Once all were inside, the old men secured the entrance with a mag lock then stepped back to survey their surroundings.

"Everybody good?" Taylor asked.

"Ayew," the others agreed.

"Valawn." Taylor turned to the FRC leader. "What's our status?"

Valawn trudged to the nearest console, which was backed by a large, oval viewport, and checked the display. "All systems remain in the green. We have access."

Nice. Taylor keyed his comm. "Husker, this is Tomahawk. We're—"

"Gun!" Jack shouted.

A blast of light turned Krulig leader's head into a stump. It fell away, fingers tickling the butt of Retay's sidearm, and offered no further resistance.

"Well now, that's a bloody problem." Smitty sidestepped the corpse and trudged to Valawn's console.

"What are you doin'?" Taylor asked.

"Seeing if I can salvage this mess," Smitty said. "I spent some time on a stargate once while working with Steeldriver. Mind you, I never got anywhere close to the ops room. However, I did get to observe the gate master working with similar equipment."

"Do you think you can figure it out?" Jack asked.

"Maybe," Smitty said. "I'll need some time, though."

Blam, blam, blam!

A chorus of fists pounded the door, joined by a klaxon.

"What was that about needin' time?" Jack asked.

Smitty went to work at her console. "I could use some help at Station Two."

"On it." Stan demagnetized his boots then pushed off to the console beside Smitty and buckled in. "What do you need?"

Taylor keyed his comm as the two began talking. "Husker, this is Tomahawk. We've taken the target, but we've got issues."

Tick, tick, tick.

"Ah, hell," Billy grumbled after hearing the situation.

Yep, that was pretty much my thought, too.

"Whatever Smitty's doing, tell her to double-time it," Billy continued. "As things stand, we're thirteen minutes out, but that extra ship is about to close the gap on us. I think we can hold out, but it's gonna be fargin tight."

Taylor spotted a Tri-V below the viewport. "Can somebody get me access to this station's sensor grid?"

Stan swiped at his screen. "I think so."

It took a moment, but eventually the Tri-V flickered alive to render a 3D projection for all to see. Sure enough, the blip representing the *Ryley Osyrys* was on its way with a second blip charging right in its tracks.

If the Osyrys misses her transition, she'll be a sittin' duck. Taylor ran a palm through his hair. "Hold your course, Husker. One way or another, we'll get this done. Tomahawk out."

Minutes drew out like hours as the chaos around them continued to unravel. Soon, dozens of fists joined the chorus outside.

"Hey, Chief?" Smitty asked. "I think I've got something."

Taylor trudged to her side. "Please tell me it's good news."

Smitty's fingers blew through keystrokes on her display. "I think…it could be…*yes!*"

A massive thrum rumbled the deck as the capacitors powering the stargate jolted online. A second later, the space outside the viewport erupted in light as a dazzling blast of energy burst forth into the void.

"Way to go, Little Lady!" Jack whooped.

Smitty was too into her work to respond. She tapped a final command into her console and the light wave outside retracted back inward, forming the barrier, or event horizon, into hyperspace. "The stargate is open, sir."

"Husker, this is Tomahawk. You are cleared for—"

A shower of sparks sprayed their air in front of the door.

"That's a cuttin' torch!" Jack announced.

"Damnit!" Taylor snarled. "How long do we have?"

Jack studied the device he'd fixed to the entrance. "That's an LR-series mag lock, which is one of the best in the business. I'd expect it'll hold a good seven, maybe eight minutes in these conditions."

That ain't enough time. Taylor spun back to the Aussie. "Can you lock out the computers to keep the Krulig from shuttin' down the gate?"

Smitty chewed her lip. "I could, but I wouldn't advise it. They might break the system and we wouldn't be able to leave when we wanted to."

Taylor barked a curse.

"I'll do it," Retay said.

All eyes turned to the corporal as the commotion outside continued.

"I'm sorry?" Taylor asked.

"You need someone to stay behind and keep the Krulig at bay while your ship escapes through the stargate." Retay patted his own chest. "I'll take care of it."

Valawn's jaw hung open. "Retay, you can't."

"I beg your pardon, sir, but I can, and I shall," the corporal said.

"Everyone just bugger off a minute and let me think." Smitty rubbed her temples. "I may have another solution."

A glimmer of hope flickered as Taylor faced the commander. "Explain."

"Stargates require an enormous amount of power to function, right?" Smitty asked. "Well, big power means a big possibility for overload, which typically leads to a power regulation system of some kind."

Taylor shook his head. "You're losin' me."

"I propose we flood the capacitors with all the solar energy in their reserves," Smitty said, "then let the safety protocols kill the transfer before the system goes critical. If my math is correct, there's no way the Krulig will be able to come in and simply shut off the gate. Not at first, anyway. They'll have to let some of that excess energy bleed off, or they'll risk blowing the gate's powerplant."

Jack snapped his fingers. "It's like muscle after extreme exertion. If you don't give it a proper cool down, you could rip the whole thing."

"Well done, fart," Smitty said. "In theory, that should buy the captain the time he needs to get the *Osyrys* through the stargate."

"How long will it take you to rev up the capacitors?" Taylor asked.

Smitty considered. "Five, maybe six minutes."

Taylor gave her a *go* motion.

"That still leaves us with another problem," Jack said. "How do we get ourselves out of here given that Door Number One ain't an option?"

"I may have an answer there," Stan said, "as I think I've managed to dig out a schematic of our location. As it stands, we're right here." He pointed to a block near the screen's upper-right quadrant. "If I'm readin' this right, there should be nothin' but empty corridor space on the level beneath us. A few jigs and jog once we're down to it, and we oughta be able to work our way back to the dockin' bay."

"That's all fine and well, Stan, but how do we drop to it?" Taylor asked.

"Easy." The old sergeant reached into his vest and fished out a device the size of a matchbox.

Micro-explosive.

"If Door Number One won't work," Stan said, "then we make ourselves a Door Number Two that does."

"Do it," Taylor said.

*****

Chapter 17:
Enemy at the Gate

Taylor relayed the new update to Billy, then took cover across the chamber while Stan set his charge on the floor. After that, the sergeant grabbed the slate into which he'd cloned the station's map data and floated over.

"You ready?" Stan asked.

Blam, blam, blam! The protests at the door answered on Taylor's behalf.

"Right." Stan ducked his head. "Fire in the hole!"

Click…KABOOM!

A thick haze filled the control room as the wretched smell of fried electronics and seared steel saturated Taylor's nostrils.

"Hurry it up, farts! Let's go," Smitty called through the fog from the new exit.

"I'm really gettin' sick of her," Jack muttered.

Taylor pushed himself upright and plodded to the hole with the others. From there, he pulled himself down with help from Valawn, then shouldered his rifle to move out.

"Which way?" Retay asked.

Stan checked his slate. "Accordin' to this, we've got a junction about twenty yards up on the right. After that, we pass through an interchange, then cut over three sections to our shuttle bay."

The group fell into formation beneath the red glow of the emergency lights and began to move. They cut left at the first junction then right into one of the smaller corridors.

Pop, pop.

Two laser bolts sizzled the wall ahead.

Shit. Taylor dipped low, rifle up, as Smitty aimed over his shoulder. Both returned fire on the squad of attacking Zuul, as did Jack, Retay, and Valawn on the other side of the passageway.

"We've gotta get past this narrow stretch!" Stan yelled over the staccato of weapons fire "We're fish in a dadgum barrel down here!"

"Cover me!" Jack announced.

Stan and Retay complied, while the Oklahoma sergeant put aside his rifle long enough to reach into his ruck and dig out a telescopic device the size of a cardboard tube. Next came a flashbang grenade, which he fitted to the end of the launcher. He then keyed the rig active and propped it atop his shoulder. "Y'all hang on to your britches."

Everyone covered their eyes and ears.

Funk…BOOM!

When Taylor looked up, all five Zuul were writhing in agony.

Pop, pop. Pop, pop, pop. Pop, pop.

All went calm save for the klaxon.

"Stan, what's next?" Taylor asked.

The sergeant checked his slate. "This way."

The group trudged onward, this time with Retay on point while Jack and Stan took turns crisscrossing from hall to hall, picking off any Zuul they encountered. An interchange down and three sections later, the team arrived at the entrance to their hangar as an audible *boom* shook the decking from above.

"The Krulig just breached the control room," Smitty said.

"And not a moment too soon," Taylor said. "Everyone set?"

Everyone nodded, while Valawn relayed a "fall back" message to Natona via comm.

Taylor tapped the *enter* key on the access panel, causing the entrance to slide open. Once inside, the group coasted over through the bay toward their shuttle, which still slumbered with its ramp down on the far-side docking pad.

"Y'all get in and get set to fly," Stan said on his way up. "I'll check on our alien navigator, then meet you in the cabin."

Taylor didn't argue. He raced up the ramp behind the sergeant and up toward the cockpit where Jack was already waiting in the pilot's seat.

"Can you fly this thing?" Taylor asked.

"I'll muddle through," Jack said, flipping switches. "Get back to the passenger cabin and buckle in. We'll launch as soon as I fire the engines."

"Copy that," Taylor said.

Just then, Valawn entered the cockpit in a visible panic. "I can't find Natona."

"What?" Taylor turned to face him.

"She's not responding to my calls," Valawn said. "I've tried multiple times, but to no avail."

"That's not our only problem," Stan said as he coasted in to join them. "Coco's gone."

"Dammit!" Jack snapped.

Taylor was just about to posit another question when a new thought dawned. "Where's Lisa?"

Static crackled the dashboard comm speaker.

"Attention, crew of the Shuttle *Santuva*," a male voice said in a calm, even tone.

Definitely Krulig. Taylor palmed his face as Smitty floated in.

"I must warn your pilot that he'd be ill-advised to attempt a launch," the voice said. "My people have locked out his credentials to open the bay. As a result, all he'll succeed in doing by firing his thrusters is killing everyone aboard."

Taylor faced his pilot. "That true?"

Jack checked his screen and frowned. "Yeah, it's true. That scaly bastard has nixed our access."

Taylor turned to Valawn. "Ideas?"

The RFC leader considered but offered no reply.

"Tomahawk, this is Husker! You copy?"

What now? Taylor opened his pinlink comm and cringed at what he heard. Billy's voice was almost inaudible through the roaring crescendo of laser batteries, hull explosions, and yelling personnel in the background. *That can't be good.* "Go for Tomahawk."

"We're setting up for our gate approach, but that other ship has caught up with us. We're taking heavy fire."

Another squelch popped the shuttle comm.

"Attention, shuttle crew," the cool voice repeated. "Please acknowledge."

"What's our play?" Smitty asked.

"Stand by, Husker." Taylor had barely spoken the words when the bay entrance opened beyond the shuttle's viewport, and five Zuul stepped out, accompanied by a lone Krulig officer.

Taylor studied the reptile for a long pause, then turned his focus to the Zuul, specifically the last one in line with the chocolate-colored fur and beady, brown eyes. *Coco.*

"Y'all mark my words." Jack scowled. "If I do nothin' else today, I mean to kill that sombitch."

"Get in line," Stan agreed. "I don't suppose we got any weapons on this tub, do we?"

The Krulig officer motioned back to the bay entrance. This time when the door opened, two familiar figures were shoved to the forefront.

"Bugger me," Smitty grumbled.

Lisa offered a small wave beside an expressionless Natona from the platform.

"You have twenty seconds to disarm and debark." The Krulig took a rifle from Coco and aimed it at the women. "Twenty."

Taylor grimaced.

"Nineteen."

Stan leaned past a distraught Valawn and kept his voice low. "What are we doin' here, Chief?"

"Eighteen."

Taylor rubbed his temples.

"Seventeen."

Think, dammit, think! Unable to find a solution, Taylor gritted his teeth and keyed his pinlink comm. "Transition when ready, Husker. We've seen to it that the door stays open."

The lag this time was almost nonexistent.

"Godspeed, Tomahawk," Billy said. "We'll see you on the flipside."

Taylor dropped his head. *I sure hope so, brother.* "Ayew. Tomahawk out."

The Krulig outside continued his countdown.

"Ten."

Taylor glanced to Jack. "Lower the ramp."

"You sure?" Jack asked.

Taylor exhaled and set aside his 14. "We've been lucky in that we haven't lost anybody today. That ain't a streak I care to break if I can help it. Now do it."

Prodding out with the others, Taylor made sure to keep his hands in clear view while descending the boarding ramp. As expected, the Krulig was waiting on the platform twenty yards away, as we were the Zuul who held the girls at gunpoint.

"Very good," the Krulig said. "You may stop right there."

Taylor halted next to Smitty at the foot of the ramp and faced his inquisitor. This Krulig looked different than the others. For one, he was smaller in stature, with a lean physique, shorter horns, and a sharp jaw. His attire was also different, boasting gold trim along the shoulders and an elegant black cloak that reached his ankles.

"Thank you for your cooperation," the Krulig said with an easy smile. "Hear me when I say, it was truly not my wish to see you and your compatriots dead."

Taylor glowered at his captor. *Smug and pompous. Nice.*

The Krulig shifted his crimson gaze to the RFC leader. "Hello, Valawn. It's good to see you again."

Valawn's lip curled as he spoke. "Lord Prefect."

Taylor raised an eyebrow. *Yolik Sadeed, I presume.*

"I must commend you," Sadeed said. "This mission of yours to seize control of the stargate. It was ambitious—far more so than the RFC's normal tactics."

"Continue to underestimate us" Valawn bit back. "It will be your undoing someday."

"Perhaps. Alas, that day is not today." Sadeed clicked his tongue. "When will you learn, Valawn? There is no changing what is. Many of your kind have accepted that, and as a result, now reap the rewards of my benevolence. Why can't you?"

Valawn was practically seething as his golden eyes flicked to Natona.

"So," Taylor said. "Where do we go from here?"

"Now we take you into custody for interrogation," Sadeed said cheerfully. "That way we can all get to know one another."

A tinge of blue light from a nearby viewport caught Taylor's attention. It was the stargate's event horizon outside. The doorway to hyperspace was still open. *Come on, Osyrys. Kick it in the ass.*

The lord prefect followed Taylor's gaze. "Ah. You're doubtless waiting for your ship to transition. I can assure you, it will not."

"We'll just see about that," Smitty grumbled.

A lone dot blipped in the black as the *Ryley Osyrys* crept into visual range, her aft section doused in weapons fire from her pursuer.

"Oh, very well." Sadeed flopped out a green-scaled hand to Coco, who filled it with a comm device. "Sadeed to Tulipza, please acknowledge."

The crackle of static preceded Zuul's response. "Yes, Lord Prefect."

"As soon as that Navarro is in range, I want it blown from the stars," Sadeed said. "Use whatever means you deem necessary. Understood?"

"Yes, Lord Prefect," the Zuul said. "It shall be done."

Taylor's fists clenched as the Krulig put down the device. Meanwhile, outside the viewport, the second dot continued its assault on the first as each ship ripped into the other with every projectile, laser, and battery she had. Even at this distance, the scene was pure carnage.

C'mon, hurry! Taylor could almost make out the *Osyrys*'s shape. *Just a few seconds more.*

The comm in Sadeed's palm crackled a final time. "Firing solution acquired."

"Execute."

A colossal blast exploded from the alien ship's bow, then rippled the space between its owner and the *Osyrys*. There, it struck the latter's hull with the violence and ferocity of a lightning bolt from Zeus himself.

"Billy!" Taylor screamed.

A plume of fire sprayed from the *Osyrys*'s hull, only to be swallowed up in the void. Still, the ship recovered, coughing debris from its damaged sections, and lumbered forward.

Taylor briefly considered closing his eyes but couldn't do it.

"Hey, Chief?" a familiar voice called.

Taylor glanced back to the platform.

"Do me a favor." Lisa reached into her tunic. "Keep an eye on my Cubbies this season, will ya? Especially our new pitcher…Flash."

Taylor's eyes went wide. *Please don't.*

Everyone covered when the stun grenade appeared in Lisa's hand.

Boom!

All five Zuul reeled in anguish, as did Sadeed. This gave Lisa the window she needed to push herself free, while Natona thrust a hand at a nearby console. A split-second later, orange lighting strobed the hangar and a new klaxon sounded.

"She's triggered a manual release!" Jack yelled. "We've got sixty seconds until our shuttle is ejected from the bay!"

Natona looked up from the platform. "Valawn, go!"

"I will not!" Valawn shouted. "Not without you!"

Seeing the aliens recover, Stan pulled a Firestorm compact he'd hidden in his shirt and opened fire, while Jack retreated into the shuttle's cargo hold. When the latter returned, he did so with weapons for the others.

"Cover!" Taylor caught a Firestorm in mid-float then turned it on a Zuul who'd taken aim on Lisa.

"Thanks," she said on her way by him.

"The reporter is in!" Valawn called from the shuttle. "Natona, come on!"

Still battling her captors, the Rukori female pulled free of one Zuul and shoved another, only to have her wrist grabbed by Coco.

A single laser bolt deprived the Zuul pilot of his arm. The next one deprived him of his head.

"Never let it be said I ain't a man of my word," Jack muttered with his 14.

Everyone else turned their fire on the remaining Zuul as Natona made her escape. The Rukori had just cleared the platform and was coasting to the pad toward the shuttle when a lone sound eclipsed the chaos.

Pop.

Natona froze, mouth open, and her golden eyes bulged.

"*No!*" Valawn screamed. "Natona!"

His sister never heard him. Instead, she rolled backward, clutching the hole in her chest, and floated away. Meanwhile, Sadeed lowered his rifle and left through the exit.

"Get him inside!" Taylor shouted. "Quick!"

Jack grabbed the maddened Rukori and thrust him back as Taylor, Smitty, and Retay fended off the last two Zuul.

"Time to go, Chief!" Stan yelled, laser bolts pelting the wall behind him.

Taylor peppered off a volley of return fire then started to backpedal. He'd almost reached the ramp when an earth-shaking *kaboom* rocked the stargate.

What in the hell?

A titanic flash across the viewport, and a lone ship with a trim profile rocketed free of the blast. It wasn't the *Osyrys.*

God in Heaven, what have I done?

"Chief, look out!" Retay yelped.

A lone laser bolt sheered through Smitty's shoulder as she thrust herself in front of her CO. The Aussie screamed.

"Heads up!" Stan barked.

Taylor dove forward to catch Smitty, but in doing so, he opened a gap for a Zuul to block his path to the shuttle.

"Go!" Taylor ordered.

"But—"

"I said fargin go, Stan. *Now!*"

The sergeant's expression paled, but he followed the command and retracted the ramp. A moment later, the divider wall between the platform and the docking pad sealed shut, and the shuttle was blown out into space.

*****

Part Three

Chapter 18: Confined

Taylor jolted awake to the sensation of something hard and cold under his skin. He recoiled, pain shooting through his head like an icepick, and fought through the fogy haze of his mind to recall his final moments of consciousness. He'd been stranded in the stargate's docking bay with Smitty when the shuttle carrying Jack, Stan, Lisa, and Valawn had been ejected into space. The Krulig had then taken him and Smitty into custody, at which time something solid had struck the back of his skull. Then, blackness.

Smitty! Taylor staggered to his feet, the rank odors of dust and mold thick in his nose, and squinted through the dim light cast from overhead at his surroundings. He was in a confinement cell. That much was evident. The cold thing from earlier had been the concrete floor under his chest, a decor that, by all appearances, seemed to be the norm throughout the chamber. The only break in the otherwise rock-solid scene came via the iron bars separating Taylor from the stone walk space that led out to the exit.

"Hey, Smitty." Taylor listened but heard only the clamor of voices in the distance. "Smitty, you in here?"

Again, no response.

"Commander Smith," Taylor repeated. "Are you present?"

An audible groan came from one cell over.

"Smitty, is that you?" Taylor asked.

"Yu-yeah." Her voice was groggy and low. Apparently, she'd been knocked out, too. "Where are we?"

Taylor peered around the grime-covered walls. "Looks like some sort of holdin' area."

"On the stargate?" Smitty asked.

Taylor spotted sand tracks on the floor and realized there was gravity. "No, I'm thinkin' they brought us back to Rukoria."

Smitty gave another groan, seeming to regain her wits. "How long do you suppose we've been here? Hours? Days?"

Hinges creaked from down the hall, interrupting Taylor's reply. A few seconds later, two Zuul emerged from the shadows, carrying batons that glowed blue at the ends.

Yeah, that can't be good. Taylor stepped back as Zuul one put its hand to the access panel then swung open the cell door. From there, the Zuul entered to face the Human inside.

"Top of the mornin', fellas." Taylor wasn't sure of the time, but he didn't figure it mattered. "What can I do for—"

A jolt of searing pain ripped through Taylor's side as the baton crackled to life against his ribs. He screamed.

"Chief!" Smitty pounded her own cell bars. "Come to me, you four-legged sons of bitches! I'll kill the whole bloody lot of ya!"

Taylor crumpled to his knees as the baton silenced, his muscles twitching and completely unresponsive. The next sensation he felt was that of the Zuul grabbing him by the shoulders to drag him out, while Smitty continued her protests.

*****

Chapter 19: Confessions

The ensuing three hours were a blur as Taylor faded in and out of consciousness. There was water and heat, followed by ice and freezing cold. There were more baton shocks, followed by the beating from a good old-fashioned blunt-force instrument.

Such was Taylor's life for the next five days. At least, that's how long he thought it'd been. He couldn't be sure. Even more confusing was the fact that never once in all that time had the Zuul presented him with a question.

Not even one. Taylor awoke one morning to the cool comfort of his cell floor pressing against his cheek. A week earlier, the same sensation had startled the daylights out of him. Now, it meant solitude, and solitude meant safety.

Taylor was good with solitude. He shoved himself upright, wiped his matted hair from his face, and found a fresh bathroom bucket waiting beside his cell bars. *Small pleasures.*

"Hey Chief?" Smitty's voice called from the next space over. "You awake over there?"

Taylor swallowed. "Yeah, Smitty. I'm here."

"You all right? From the sound of it, that last walloping you took was a dandy."

The aching in Taylor's extremities said the Aussie was right. "I'm okay. What about you? How's your shoulder?"

"You asked me that yesterday," Smitty said, "and the day before, and the day before that. The shoulder's fine."

Taylor blinked. "Smitty, how long have we been down here?"

"Today marks day ten, plus or minus a wakeup."

Taylor laid his head against the wall to his right. *Fargin A, son.* "Have the Zuul been comin' for you, too?"

"No," Smitty said. "For whatever reason, you're the only one they seem to be interested in."

Taylor rubbed his face. *Lucky me.*

"Do you think Valawn and the others made it back to the badlands?" Smitty asked.

"Man, I sure hope so. I wonder if—" Taylor's eyes bulged as visions of the *Osyrys* enveloped in light swept through his mind. "Billy!"

Smitty's voice was barely a whisper. "They didn't make it."

"We can't know that," Taylor said. "They beat that second warship to the gate. That much we know."

Smitty heaved a sigh. "You saw the blast, Chief, just like I did. Trust me, I don't want to believe it either. The fact is, though, that a flash of that magnitude could only have been generated by a nuclear explosion. That means a reactor. No ship walks away from something like that, not even the *Osyrys*."

Taylor stared at the floor. Most days he liked it when his senior staff could provide perspectives contrary to his own. It helped the decision-making process. Today, however, wasn't one of those times.

I don't want to believe it, either. Taylor considered the undercurrent in Smitty's tone when she'd said that. *Not your business, T. Skip it and move on.* "So, how does a nice girl from northeast Australia end up stateside as a sailor in the navy?"

"That's quite a long story," Smitty said.

"It would appear as if we've got time," Taylor answered.

Smitty exhaled in her cell. "The short version is my parents were researchers—marine biologists, actually. As kids, we traveled all over the world, until one day my father took a grant from Duke University to study migratory shark patterns off the Carolina coast. I was eleven when we moved to Durham, and had even planned to study marine biology myself. Problem was, in all that moving about, my folks never thought to sock anything aside for their own kids' education. The navy offered a solution to that."

"But you never went to college." Taylor knew that much from her personnel file.

"No," Smitty said. "My mum got sick toward the end of my second tour, and my dad couldn't afford the nanite treatments. By then, I'd already been approached by Ron Carnegie about joining Steeldriver when I got out. So I took the gig, paid my mum's med expenses in cash, then ran off into the cosmos to 'kill aliens, get paid,' as the expression goes. That's been my career since."

Taylor recalled his own family's bout with past-due medical bills, as well as his decision to go merc. *We all do what we have to, don't we?*

"Hey, Chief?" Smitty piped up. "Can I ask you something?"

"Sure, shoot."

"Why did Captain Dawson leave the Eagles all those years ago?"

Taylor's gaze returned to the floor. *Guess we're goin' there after all.* "I take it Billy never told you that story, huh?"

"No, sir," Smitty said. "He did not."

The conversation paused when two Rukori females entered the chamber carrying food trays with bread and water. One of them made eye contact with Taylor on her way in.

"Hi," he said.

The girl didn't answer, nor did she continue looking at him. She put down his tray, slid it through the bars, and scurried out with her companion as quickly as she'd appeared.

"So, what'll it be, sir?" Smitty asked once the block door had slammed shut. "You gonna 'fess up with the story or what?"

Taylor weighed his options. On one hand, he understood why Billy probably wouldn't have spoken of these events. It wasn't anything personal against Smitty. Silence had just been Billy's way, always.

At the same time, Taylor also couldn't forget the laser bolt that Smitty had taken on his behalf. *Sorry, brother, but she's earned it.* He cleared his throat. "What do you know about Billy's life before the navy?"

Smitty thought about it. "Not much, really. I know he and his family moved to Jax from Lincoln when he was fifteen. After that, he began attending Lee High, which is where he met your brother on the baseball team. The two became friends, and the rest is history."

Taylor scratched the beginnings of a full beard on his chin. "I don't suppose Billy ever mentioned the name Marla McBride, did he?"

"Can't say as he did. Why? Was she his girlfriend or something?"

"Try fiancé."

The cell block went quiet.

"Billy was engaged?" Smitty's voice trailed up with the question.

"Is that so hard to believe?"

"No, it's just…I guess the captain always struck me as the 'duty first' sort. In my experience, guys like that typically don't have room in their lives for much else, no matter if they're military, merc, or otherwise."

Taylor crossed his legs. "That's a fair point. Lord knows Billy ain't what you'd call the sharin' type."

"So, who was she?" Smitty asked. "This would-be Mrs. Dawson?"

Taylor sighed to the ceiling. "Marla was a local girl, born, bred, and raised in Duval County. She and Billy met during sophomore year at Lee, when her family moved across town into the old Avondale neighborhood. She was smitten with Billy from the jump, almost as much as he was with her."

"How did Colonel Van Zant like her?" Smitty asked.

"Oh, Terry loved her," Taylor said. "Everybody did. Marla was sweet and fun-lovin', plus she genuinely seemed to care for Billy. Together, the three of them made for one helluva crew throughout high school, then they kept in touch after Billy and Terry joined the navy. Tick forward another three years or so, and Billy decided the time had come to make things official with a ring."

"How long were they engaged?" Smitty asked.

"Almost five years," Taylor frowned, "which was part of the problem."

A hint of reservation entered Smitty's tone. "How do you mean?"

"Had the choice been Marla's, they'd have been married a month after the proposal," Taylor said. "By that point, she and Billy had been together almost seven years, and she was ready to settle down. She wanted the house, the dog, and the picket fence. Mostly, though, she wanted a family."

"Huh." Smitty seemed to consider that. "In all the time I've known him, the captain never struck me as the anti-kids type."

"That's because he's not," Taylor said. "He wasn't back then, either. He just wanted to change his circumstances a bit before they took that step. You see, Billy's family didn't have much growin' up. His dad was a mechanic, his mom was a waitress, and, while they both loved their kids immensely, neither earned enough in their paychecks to make things like Christmas an event. Billy didn't want that life for his children or his wife. He wanted them to have nice things, live in a nice house, attend a good school. The Eagles represented his best shot at makin' those dreams a reality. So he poured everything he had into the company, especially his time."

Smitty grunted. "Let me guess. The little missus got tired of sleeping in an empty bed, so she found others to fill it when the captain was away."

"Nah, nothin' like that," Taylor said. "Marla loved Billy. She always had. At the same time, she was also very Human and extremely lonely."

"All right then," Smitty said. "What happened?"

Taylor folded his arms. "The Eagles had just come back from fulfillin' a bigtime contract with the Lumar over in the Jesc Arm. That called for a celebration. So, everybody went out to Cocktail Junction to tie one on and blow off some steam. Everybody, that was, except for Billy."

"Where was he?" Smitty asked.

"He was where Billy always was back then," Taylor said, "on a transport headed for Karma Station to lock down the company's next gig. Anyway, Marla got wind that the gang was out, so she got dressed, packed her things, and headed over to Startown to meet up. She had a lot to drink that night. Everyone did."

Smitty hesitated with her next question. "Who was it? One of the senior staff?"

Taylor's gaze plummeted. "No…It was Terry."

"Bloody hell!" Smitty blurted.

"Yeah," was all Taylor would say.

Smitty stewed in silence for a long moment before speaking again. "I don't get it. Everyone knew of Terry Van Zant's reputation with women. But his best friend's girl? What kind of scumbag does that to someone he's known since high school?"

"You'll get no argument here," Taylor said. "All I can say is Terry was blackout drunk and stressed as hell when it happened. Same went for Marla. That's two people with a ton of pent-up issues, a whole lot of history, and a full fifth of River City Blond to pass the night. One thing led to another, and by the time it was over, both parties knew they'd made the biggest mistake of their lives."

Smitty grumbled something under her breath. "Please don't take offense to this, Chief, but if what you've said is true, your brother was an evil bastard."

Taylor exhaled and reclined against the wall. "Honestly, Smitty? Were Terry still alive to tell this story in person, I'm pretty sure he'd agree with you. But it is what it is."

The creak of metal hinges ended the discussion.

Break time's over. Taylor got to his feet as the two Zuul from earlier re-entered the cell block. "Time for a fresh round, huh fellas?"

Zuul one put its hand to the access panel while Zuul two swung open Taylor's cell door like normal. What happened next, however, wasn't normal.

"Lord Prefect Sadeed would like a word with you," the lead Zuul said. "Move."

*****

Chapter 20: Inquisition

Once out of his cell, Taylor was escorted down the corridor to a changing area, where he was actually allowed to bathe. After that, he was given new clothes—Rukori rags with makeshift cloth sandals—then shown out into the open, where a blast of pain assaulted his eyes.

"Let's go," the nearest of the two Zuul said.

Taylor paused long enough to blink through the effects of his first sunlight exposure in ten days then trudged forward in his restraints. He was inside the Krulig compound outside Nyo Colony he'd seen during his first trip down with Billy. The place was bigger than he remembered. At least, that's the way it felt on the inside. The accommodations were also noticeably better, with larger buildings, spacious quarters, and updated tech throughout. Everything about it was neat, clean, and modern—a stark contrast to the dilapidated filth of the colonies.

Welcome to the high life, T. The clamor of footfalls caused Taylor to stop as two units of Zuul hurried past him. By the look of things, he'd come about fifty yards from the holding area, with another hundred to cross were he to break for the perimeter. Problem was, he hadn't a clue where to go from there. His only two options were southeast back to Nyo Colony, in which case he'd likely be gunned down, or west toward that big mesa he'd seen coming in.

"I said move," a Zuul barked.

A static-charged *pop* ripped through Taylor's back as the Zuul baton touched Human skin. He yelped and shuffled forward. *Son of a bitch! I'm sick of those things.*

The group continued their march through the compound, turning left at the barracks, then right at a multipurpose space—again, all modern construction—before eventually halting outside a building that, even by Krulig standards, couldn't have been more out of place. Defined by its towering columns, pointed spires, and rib-vaulted exterior, the tri-level structure looked more akin to a gothic cathedral than something one would find in a military installation.

Now that's what I'd call a gaudy monstrosity, all right. Taylor peered upward and recalled Valawn's description of Sadeed's primary residence.

"This way," a Zuul said.

Taylor trudged to the entrance, where a third guard waited, palm over an access panel to grant them passage through security. Once inside, Taylor was herded down an elaborate stone corridor into what appeared to be a stateroom.

"The lord prefect will see you shortly." One of the Zuul shoved Taylor into a seat beside a table and sparked his baton for emphasis.

Taylor jingled his restraints to indicate he understood. He was about to offer a witty retort when something in the corner caught his attention. It was a Rukori swirl painting like the one he'd seen in Valawn's briefing room back in the Sanctuary. There was another like it across the room, plus a variety of other artifacts scattered around the chamber, some of them Rukori and others not.

Looks like the lord prefect's a collector.

Both Zuul snapped alert when footfalls sounded from outside. Shortly thereafter, Sadeed entered alongside a third Zuul, the latter wearing an ornate gold ring in its left nostril.

If Taylor remembered his Zuul anthropology lessons right, the ring identified this particular alien as being the drewga, or alpha in charge.

"Leave us," Sadeed told the guards.

The two Zuul bowed and vanished from sight.

"So," Sadeed said. "You're the one who led the infiltration of my stargate."

Taylor wasn't obliged to answer that.

"It's all right, Chief Van Zant. We're well aware of your identity, and that of your company." Sadeed strode toward the table, his black cloak flowing behind him, and took a seat. "Ah, where are my manners. We haven't yet been formally introduced. My name is Yolik Sadeed. I am the lord prefect of this region." He gestured to the Zuul. "This is my associate, Drewga Vyxe Tulipza."

Tulipza nodded and folded his arms.

So, you're the bastard who shot at my flagship. Taylor glowered at the alien. *Henceforth, you shall be called Tulips.* "Nice place you got here. I'm guessin' it's of Krulig design?"

Sadeed chortled out a laugh. "Oh, so he does speak. Excellent. I was beginning to wonder if I was dealing with a mute."

Taylor made a face.

"Yes," Sadeed said. "My residence is of Krulig origin. This particular building was modeled after an ancient Suvari Clan temple circa the fourth ruling dynasty of my homeworld. Naturally, our taste for architecture has evolved since then. However, the period you see reflected here remains among my favorites."

Taylor motioned at the painting. "Interestin' décor choice."

"Indeed," Sadeed said. "The furnishings were my idea. This job requires that I interact on a regular basis with numerous Rukori officials. It was my hope that by dressing this chamber with certain items reflecting their culture, I'd foster an environment where everyone could feel comfortable."

"How thoughtful." Taylor said. "For a dictator."

"Oh, come now, Chief Van Zant." Sadeed flashed a wry smile. "You speak as if our presence on Rukoria is unanimously unwanted. I can assure you, not all Rukori share the RFC's belief that we are evil. To the contrary, there are many among the colonies who view us as allies, if not even friends. We did save them from extinction, after all."

"Funny." Taylor grunted. "You sure weren't that friendly to Valawn's sister when you put a laser bolt through her."

Sadeed lowered his crimson gaze to the table. "We've suspected for some time that the RFC had a plant on the stargate. Alas, we didn't know until then who that person was. I regret that the situation unfolded as it did. However, you must understand that I had no choice."

"There's always a choice," Taylor said.

"Is there?" Sadeed tilted his head. "Tell me then. How do you respond when someone encroaches upon your company's interests? After all, is Swamp Eagle Security not the means through which you care for your loved ones? What happens when an adversary threatens those means, and by extension, them? Do you reserve reaction in hopes of finding a compromise, or do you defend what's rightfully yours?"

Taylor rankled at the analogy. "This may come as a shock, but Rukoria ain't yours to defend. It belongs to Valawn and his people."

"And I'd never argue otherwise," Sadeed said. "I would, however, posit that my people went to great lengths at significant cost of our own resources to aid the Rukori's fight against the Winter Death, then again during their reconstruction. Are we not, therefore, entitled to a slice of the pie, as your people say?"

Taylor rolled his eyes and changed the subject. "You mentioned your homeworld earlier. How come nobody in the Union has ever heard of it, or you for that matter? Are the Krulig a race of recluses or what?"

"Recluse is a harsh term, but not an entirely inaccurate one," Sadeed said. "Many eons ago, my race was quite active in the greater galactic community. We explored the cosmos, conducted commerce with other species. We even played a part in founding the galaxy's political landscape. Regrettably, though, a series of unfortunate events saw us driven from our space five thousand years ago and scattered among the stars. There we've remained ever since."

"What sort of events?" Taylor asked.

"It's complicated." Sadeed dismissed the topic with a wave of his green-scaled palm. "Enough talk of ancient histories and conflicts long past. That is not why I summoned you here."

"And why did you summon me here?"

"To talk about you, of course."

Taylor feigned a yawn. "I hate to disappoint, Mr. Sadeed, but there ain't much to tell. When you get right down to it, I'm just another hillbilly Human from North Florida, lookin' to make a credit wherever he can. Hell, to be honest, I still don't even know how I got here."

"That makes two of us," Sadeed said. "I was under the impression, per the reports, that Swamp Eagle Security had perished with its leader six years ago."

A flash of heat popped in Taylor's cheeks. "Yeah, well, there's your first mistake. Don't believe everything you read on the GalNet."

"So I'm told," Sadeed said. "Nevertheless, you can imagine my surprise four weeks ago when a Navarro cruiser bearing the Eagles' colors arrived on my doorstep, causing trouble. That's an interesting vessel, by the way. An interesting vessel with an interesting name."

"Thanks. We like her."

"Pity you'll never see her again."

Taylor narrowed his gaze. "Oh, I don't know. It's like you said. Swamp Eagle Security has a pesky way of showin' up when folks least expect. Hell, I wouldn't be surprised if the *Osyrys* emerged from hyperspace right now to wreak all kinds of havoc on the status quo."

Sadeed heaved a sigh and extended a hand to Tulips, who filled it with a slate. From there, the lord prefect swiped up a screen then faced the device toward his guest. "As you can plainly see, most of the explosion was absorbed by the stargate. Even still, the radiation fallout in the surrounding space is clearly consistent with that of a detonated nuclear reactor. Wouldn't you agree?"

Taylor glanced at the data then back at his host. "How do I know you didn't fabricate these numbers?"

"Please." Sadeed huffed. "We both saw the blast, as did your colleague in Cell Block One. She said as much in her last conversation with you."

Smitty. Taylor had suspected they'd had an eavesdropper.

"I must say." Sadeed put away the slate. "As streaks of misfortune go, yours with hyperspace seems to be never-ending. First your brother, now your friends. One wonders if perhaps the Van Zant clan shouldn't avoid interstellar travel altogether moving forward."

Taylor snorted. "What do you know about my brother?"

"Quite a lot, actually," Sadeed said. "I'm the one who tendered the garrison contract that brought his company to Rukoria. Coincidentally, I'm also the one who had him killed."

Taylor lunged from his seat—teeth bared, and hands clenched to fists—only to be snatched back down by his restraints.

The Zuul drewga laughed at him from the corner.

"I can see by your response that this vexes you," Sadeed said in a cool tone. "I do not begrudge you that. Were it my kin who'd been lost, I'd likely have reacted in a similar fashion. Take your time. We'll resume our conversation when you're ready."

Taylor closed his eyes and took in a few breaths, letting them all out in long, even drags.

"For what it's worth," Sadeed said, "I took no satisfaction in ordering the colonel's execution. To the contrary, few decisions in my career have weighed upon me with such gravity."

"Is that so?" Taylor asked.

"It is," Sadeed said. "Every day, in every corner of the Union, countless beings are born through no fault of their own into unspeakable circumstances. Some are born into poverty, as your brother was. Others are born into lives of slavery, or worse. It's been my experience that most of these beings inevitably succumb their fates. But then there are some—the chosen few—who defy the universe's will for their existence and forge ahead to seize destinies of their own. Terry Van Zant was among those chosen few. As a Krulig, I admire that more than you could possibly know."

Taylor wasn't sure how to take that last statement. "So, you were a fan then."

"Oh, I was," Sadeed said. "I spent months vetting suitors for the Rukoria contract, many of whom boasted portfolios far more impressive than Swamp Eagle's. Once I'd done my due diligence on Terry, though, I knew I'd found my candidate. We met aboard a Maki cruiser just off Karma, as I didn't want to be seen on the station. There, the documents were signed, and a date set to bring the Eagles' forces onto my *Behemoth*." The Krulig trailed off, his emerald expression visibly crestfallen. "Never in my wildest of dreams could I have imagined upon leaving that meeting that one day Terry would betray me."

Taylor looked up. "So you knew. You knew of Terry's alliance with the RFC."

Sadeed gave a somber nod. "It cut me to the core to give that order."

"So why do it?" Taylor snapped. "If you were such a Terry fanboy, why not just fire him, file a grievance with the Merc Guild for breach of contract, and walk away?"

Sadeed reclined in his seat. "As you've doubtless surmised, Rukoria's existence is a secret to the rest of Union. For a great many reasons—some obvious, some not—I wish to keep it that way. Terry's betrayal threatened to jeopardize that secrecy, so he was dealt with."

"How?" Taylor asked.

"That is a topic which unfortunately requires me to keep a modicum of confidentiality out of respect for the other parties involved."

Taylor's lips formed a line as understanding set in. "You put a hit out on my brother with a rival company."

"Not a hit, per se." Sadeed raised a finger. "More like a request for information in exchange for payment. You see, when the colonel returned to Earth for the purposes of RFC recruiting, it was decided that the best place to neutralize those efforts was on Karma Station, where he'd be most vulnerable. By the same token, my Krulig brothers and I did not want a public conflict that would expose us all in the process. So, a plan was devised to board the Eagles' flagship while she was docked and siphon the F11 from her reactor system while rigging the gauges to show it was full. Hyperspace would then take care of the rest."

Taylor shook his head. "There's no way you could've accessed to the *Bogrider*'s engineerin' section without her security codes. I take it that's the information you bought?"

"Correct."

"I'll give you every credit in my account right now if you'll tell me who took that contract."

Sadeed drummed his fingers. "While that *is* a tempting offer, I'm afraid I must decline. What I can tell you is that the party in question was extremely desperate and therefore eager to cooperate without many questions. The rest I must keep to myself as per our agreement."

Taylor's thoughts churned with possibilities. While it was true that Terry had made a lot of friends during his tenure as a merc, he'd also accrued more than his fair share of enemies. The Zuul. The Oogar. The Tortantula. Terry had clashed with all of these and then some over the years. *So who in the fargin blazes of hell was it?*

Patience, a new voice answered in Taylor mind. It belonged to Billy. *Stay cool, be patient, and allow the situation to come to you.*

Taylor took in another breath and fought to collect himself.

"Let us advance the discussion a bit, shall we?" Sadeed said. "I think we can both agree that I've been as candid and forthright with you as I can. I've answered your questions about the Rukori, told you the truth of your brother's fate, and even acknowledged my own hand in the latter's deliverance. I've hidden nothing from you save for those details I'm bound by guild law to uphold. Are we in agreement on this?"

Taylor gritted his teeth but nodded.

"Good," Sadeed said. "Now it's time for you to reciprocate. The RFC has been little more than a thorn in my side for years. Nevertheless, it has become clear to me of late that Valawn and his band of insurgents mean to escalate their campaign against our presence on Rukoria. The attack on the stargate is proof of this."

Taylor chuckled. "And here I thought you appreciated an overachiever."

"Indeed, I do," Sadeed said. "At the same time, if you've learned anything prior to now, it's that I do not take threats to my affairs lightly. Now, what was the RFC's intention for the *Ryley Osyrys* once she'd transitioned through the stargate?"

Taylor answered with his best *eat shit and die* look.

"Come now, Chief Van Zant," Sadeed said. "Clearly, you're a man of reason, yes? Let us consider two facts at play here. Fact one: there's no one coming for you. Your ship. Your crew. They're all gone, as is the last of Terry's legacy. It doesn't have to be so for you or your companion. Lest we forget, I possess the means to send you both safely home when my *Behemoth* returns from hyperspace."

The family man in Taylor winced. *Haven't they been through enough? They've already lost Dad and Terry. It'll kill them to lose you, too.* Then there was Smitty, not to mention Lisa, Jack, and Stan, wherever they were. *Maybe you can cut a deal for everyone.* "How do I know you won't just kill us in transition like you did with Terry?"

"You don't," Sadeed said flatly. "This leads me to fact two, which is that in choosing not to cooperate you'll deprive me of any possible motive to keep you alive. Let me be clear. Such an end is not my wish. As far as I'm concerned, your last two weeks in my care are penance enough for your actions against us."

Taylor grimaced.

"Push me, though, and I will not hesitate to end you." Sadeed leaned in. "Now, I will ask you again. What was Valawn's plan for the *Osyrys*? Where was she going? What was her mission?"

Taylor dropped his eyes. *Allow the situation to come to you.*

"Move aside, Lord Prefect." Tulips strode forward and drew a battle blade from his hip sheath. "I will garner the information you seek."

Sadeed waved off the assault then exhaled through his nostrils. "Why must Humans insist on making everything difficult? Is such behavior merely engrained in your species?"

"Not at all," Taylor said. "Contrary to popular opinion, we're actually pretty rational. You're just a dick."

The Zuul sneered but was stayed again by the Krulig.

"I understand, given all that's been said, that you might need time to process." Sadeed rose and pushed in his chair. "In the interest of civility, and out of respect for Terry, I'll allow you that. Know this, though, Human. On the morrow, you and I shall speak again, and when we do, things stand to go quite differently should your demeanor fail to change."

"I'll bring the beer." Taylor grinned.

Tulips approached his boss as the latter began to leave. "Shall I return the prisoner to his cell?"

"No," Sadeed said. "Our guest needs some time to think. Leave the woman where she is and put him into Cell Block Two. That way he can be alone with his thoughts."

That don't sound fun.

The drewga nodded. "As you wish."

Taylor watched from his seat as the lord prefect took his leave. After that, Tulips came along and hoisted Taylor up by the restraints.

"You do realize he's gonna kill us both, right?" Taylor asked. "Sadeed has no intention of lettin' me leave this planet alive, nor will he do so for the Zuul when your contract here is up."

The drewga snorted. "My troops and I live like kings in this facility while our kin want for nothing back in Union space. Why would we ever want to leave such an arrangement?"

Taylor lacked a comeback for that.

"You should know that your brother and I were acquainted," Tulips said.

"Is that a fact?" Taylor frowned. "Somehow I don't see you two bein' pals."

"We met only once in passing. Sadly, he did not know at the time who I was, nor did he know of my connection to the lord prefect."

"Ya don't say?" Taylor quipped. "And where exactly did this chance encounter happen?"

The Zuul's lips pealed back into a wicked smile. "Karma Station."

Patience! Billy repeated.

Taylor loosened his fists and unclenched his jaw, then squared himself to face his captor. "You oughta know something, too, Drewga."

Tulips waited.

"Before this is all over, I aim to kill you. It ain't gonna be today, and it probably won't be tomorrow. But someday I'm gonna best you, and when I do, your blood is gonna flow down through my fingers like the juices of a Georgia peach."

The drewga snarled and snatched out his blade.

"Easy," Taylor warned. "The lord prefect wants another chat, remember? That means you and me don't get to dance today. But soon. Real soon."

The Zuul huffed with indignance but clearly understood. He returned his blade to its sheath.

"Good doggie," Taylor said. Now, take me to my new suite."

*****

Chapter 21: Conversations in the Dark

Taylor staggered back to keep from tripping on his chains when his Zuul escort shoved him down the stairwell into Cell Block Two. Once inside, Taylor quickly observed Sadeed's meaning about the lack of accommodations. The place was a pit, literally and figuratively. Boasting jagged rock walls and an uneven floor riddled with holes, the space was dark as pitch-black night, with stale, wet air and zero visibility save for that allowed by torches in the corners.

We must be deeper underground this time. Taylor ducked to avoid a stalactite when entering his cell only to step in a puddle. *Awesome.*

The Zuul escort barked a *stay back* command then slammed the door to the cage.

"What are the odds I can get some room service down here?" Taylor asked from the bars. "I'll take a cheeseburger all the way with fries and a beer. Feel free to toss in a little bacon, too, if you've got it."

The Zuul said nothing as it bounded up the stairs out of earshot.

Mangy mutt. Taylor kicked the gunk from his toes and gave his eyes a chance to adjust in the dark. He still couldn't see much. "Hello?"

Dripping water kissed the cavern's floor somewhere in the distance.

"Is there anybody else in here?"

The crackling of the torches was all that answered.

Fantastic. Taylor felt his way to the cell's rear and collapsed with his back to the wall. "Well, T. You've really gone and stepped in it this time, ain't cha?"

A low groan rolled through the darkness.

Taylor snapped alert. "Hello?"

"Would it be too much to ask that you keep your voice down?" The voice featured the deepest baritone Taylor had ever heard. "Between the filth of this chamber, the discomfort of these restraints, and the stench of your natural odor, I believe my senses have endured enough abuse for one day, to say nothing of my sanity."

Taylor debated whether to tell the voice's owner that he'd actually bathed earlier. He opted instead for, "Sorry to offend."

"I neither need nor want your apology," the voice said. "My only wish is to be left alone."

Taylor peered into the black, hoping for a glimpse of his cellmate. "You got a name?"

"None that I wish to provide."

"Mine's Taylor. Taylor Van Zant."

"How lovely for you."

Taylor frowned and blew a hair strand from his face. "Fine, have it your way. If you're not gonna tell me your name, can you at least tell me where we are?"

"In a holding area."

"Gee, ya think?"

The unseen stranger heaved a mammoth sigh. "We are in Holding Area Two, if you must know, located eighty yards north of the lord prefect's main residence, between the entrance to Cell Block

One and the north gate. Now, my chatty friend, is that enough to quell your overdeveloped sense of curiosity so that you can leave me be?"

Taylor shrugged. "I reckon that depends."

"On what?"

"On the degree to which I get bored," Taylor said. "Too much silence makes me anxious. After a while, I'm inclined to break into show tunes to pass the time. For the record, I do a mean Andrew Lloyd Webber."

"Oh, dear gods."

"Hey, Hoss, you asked." Taylor hunched forward and hugged his knees, briefly wondering if their conversation was being monitored. *Not that it mattered.* "How long you been stuck down here?"

"Far longer than I care to recall."

"Is that so?" Taylor cocked his head. "Who'd you piss off to land down here, anyway? The Zuul or the lord prefect?"

"Both, it would seem," the voice said. "The latter gave the order which resulted in my abduction and subsequent relocation to this quaint little sand pit of a world. The former was tasked with carrying that order to fruition."

Taylor arched an eyebrow. "So you're not a Rukori then?"

"I'm awestruck by your skills of deduction, Mr. Van Zant. Tell me. How long have you worked in investigations?"

Taylor flipped him the bird through the dark. "Most folks I know don't go through the trouble of kidnappin' somebody unless they've got reasons for doin' so."

"Indeed."

"I don't suppose you'd care to expound on what those reasons are?"

"Indeed, I would not."

Taylor heaved a sigh. "Are you always this combative with your cellmates, or am I just special?"

"I couldn't say."

"Why not?"

"Because you're the only cellmate I've ever had."

Taylor wrinkled his nose. *Seriously?*

The conversation halted when new footfalls bounded down the steps toward them. They belonged to the Zuul who'd brought him not ten minutes earlier.

"Back so soon?" Taylor asked. "I didn't think Sadeed wanted to meet again until tomorrow."

"That is still the order," the Zuul said.

"What brings you down then?" Taylor asked. "You come to stare at all the zoo animals?"

The Zuul grinned and put its hand to the cell's access panel. "Drewga Tulipza felt that you would benefit from a refresher on our treatment of unruly guests."

"I'm unruly now, huh? Way to go, me."

The alien produced a baton and sparked open the tip. "Move."

Taylor sighed and stepped out into the corridor, casing a cursory glance to the other cell. "Looks like we'll have to pick this up later."

"If I curry any remaining favor with the gods," the voice huffed, "I'll be spared that experience by way of the fact that you'll be unconscious or dead when you return."

"Nice to know you care," Taylor muttered.

"Don't take it personally, Van Zant. I just don't like people very much."

"Ya know, I never would've pegged that about you." Taylor paused when something metallic stirred in the other cell. It was rough and muted, like chains being dragged over concrete, and accompanied by the thick, heavy footfalls one might expect from a giant.

What are you?

Slowly, a massive figure eased into view by the torchlight.

Taylor blinked, opened his mouth, closed it, and blinked again. *Well, that explains a lot.*

As was indicative of its species, the alien across the hall resembled in many ways a small elephant that walked erect on its hind legs. Same wrinkled features. Same pitch-black eyes. Same mountainous gray frame, but with two trunks instead of one.

"You're a Sumatozou," Taylor said. "A gate master."

The big alien nodded in reply. "And you're a Human. Aren't we the perceptive pair?"

* * * * *

Chapter 22: Officially Non-Official

As it turned out, Taylor's quality time alone with the Zuul interrogators wasn't over now that he'd met with Sadeed. Once he was done with the guard that had taken him from Cell Block Two, he was dragged back to his hole and allowed to sleep things off until the next morning, when he was taken for a second meeting with the lord prefect.

True to his word, Taylor said nothing. And true to *his* word, Sadeed reacted in kind.

"Very well, then," the lord prefect said. "If you won't listen to reason, and the drewga's tactics aren't working, then perhaps it's time we try a different approach."

Ding, ding.

Sadly, the beating that came next was only the warmup for the main event. Once the Zuul were done working Taylor over with their batons, he was dragged out into the compound and deposited in the open sand where he was pitted against an opponent. The first go-round saw him facing a massive Rukori the size of Valawn's sergeant, Douron. The alien was mean, too, swinging and hammering Taylor's body with the might of a sledgehammer. Of course, Taylor was never just fighting an opponent. Not on even ground, anyway. Most of his adversaries brought weapons, whereas he had only his fists. Others came with comrades, often making the contest two or even three on one. In one instance, Taylor squared off against three Zuul and a Rukori, all of whom were armed.

Taylor had been lucky to survive that one.

Hang in there, little buddies, he thought to his nanites. *Please, just a little while longer.*

The microbots in his bloodstream gave no answer. They just kept working, repairing his bones and tissues as best they could from the damage wrought by the aliens.

Taylor awoke on fight day five to the slimy sensation of something wet and slick on the side of his face. *Ugh, gross.* He rolled out of the scum puddle, gagging.

"Fascinating," the Sumatozou said from across the hall. "I was almost certain they'd killed you this time."

"You sound disappointed," Taylor grumbled.

"Not at all," the gate master said. "To the contrary, I couldn't care less whether you live or die. I am the picture of indifference."

Taylor wasn't sure how to take that. He pushed himself upright, brushed his hair from his face, and spit something hard and gooplike onto the floor. *I don't even wanna know what that is.*

"I must admit, Human," the Sumatozou said. "Through all my time in captivity, I've never once seen another prisoner take the sort of punishment you've endured. You are to be commended for your resilience."

Taylor's bruised expression turned sideways. "I thought I was your only cellmate."

"For this location, you are. That doesn't mean I haven't encountered other inmates in prisons prior to this one. As you know, the Zuul are nothing if not fond of their interrogations, be they fruitful or not."

Taylor's aching ribs echoed the truth of that statement.

"You mentioned at the outset of our meeting that your name is Van Zant," the Sumatozou said. "I've been wondering. Are you related to Terry Van Zant?"

Taylor rolled his eyes. "Is it just me or did everyone and their grandma know my brother?"

"Only by reputation," the big alien said. "I served the Cartography Guild for eight years as master of the Piquaw Stargate here in the Tolo Arm. During that time, I dealt with numerous merc companies from Earth. Asbaran Solutions, the Iron Conquistadors, the Emerald Stormriders. I even crossed paths with Swamp Eagle Security once, if only by comm exchange."

"Well ain't you the social butterfly?"

"I beg your pardon?" The Sumatozou sounded put off by the comparison.

"Relax, Hoss. It's just a figure of speech. While we're on the topic of names, I didn't catch yours."

The gate master wrinkled his nose. "I already told you that."

"You do recall that I've had the holy hell kicked out of me for the better part of two fargin weeks now, right? You'll have to excuse the lapse in memory."

The Sumatozou grunted. "Humans. Why the Mercenary Guild ever saw fit to allow a backward species like yours into its ranks, I'll never know."

"Rumor has it they thought we were scrappy. Now are you gonna fess up with that name or am I gonna be stuck callin' you Gray Ass for the rest of our stay together?"

The alien folded his arms. "My name is Japhara Hylune. I am…or at least I was, a grand latura with the Galactic Union's Cartography Guild."

Grand Latura? Taylor didn't recognize the term. "I thought you said you were a gate master."

"I was," Japhara said, "for nearly thirty years, in fact. It was the same for my father before me and his before him. Such has been the noble calling of the Hylune line for more than a dozen generations."

Taylor couldn't help but notice how the Sumatozou radiated pride when speaking of his profession. It was like sharing a cell with a cult follower. *What I wouldn't give for a nice Jehovah's Witness right about now.* Taylor kept that to himself as the alien continued.

"Halfway through my thirtieth year of master service, I was reassigned to the Guild's atlas division as a cartography fellow. There I studied for three years at the feet of our curators before graduating to the rank of latura, then grand latura before my abduction."

"Sounds like bein' a latura is a pretty big deal."

"Even you, Human, can't fathom the depths of that understatement." Japhara turned up his chin. "Of the thousands of Sumatozou who serve the Cartography Guild across the galaxy, less than one percent will even be considered for latura status. It's the highest possible honor a member of my species could ever hope to attain."

Taylor yawned. "I'm still waitin' to hear why that is exactly."

"Latura is the Sumatozou word for envoy," Japhara said. "It is we who represent the Guild's interests throughout the Union, as it pertains to the usage of our transit atlas."

"Ah, right. The atlas."

"Yes, the atlas. It's the repository of worlds within every ship's nav system that is ubiquitous throughout—"

"I know what the damn thing is, Japhara."

If the alien rankled at being cut off, he didn't protest. "Whenever changes are made to the atlas, be they minor adjustments for natural phenomena or major alterations for things like wars, the Guild relays these changes in the form of update patches throughout the stargate network. Ships then dock with their respective stargates, download the patch, and go on about their business. Whenever something goes awry with the process, a latura is dispatched to the gate in question to troubleshoot the issue."

"Congratulations," Taylor said. "You're an interstellar IT guy."

"That's a gross oversimplification, but yes."

Taylor shook his head. "I don't get it. Why would the Cartography Guild need to commission a special group of Sumatozou for that? Why not just use the in-system gate masters? They're already present on-site and could solve the problem when it arises."

"If a hyperspatial generator is the engine by which interstellar travel is possible," Japhara said, "then our transit atlas is its guide. Maintaining the integrity of that guide, therefore, is of the utmost priority to my superiors. By keeping the circle of those who understand the atlas' inner workings small, the Guild Heads minimize the chances of its contents being manipulated, or worse, corrupted with false data. That ensures hyperspace travel remains safe for everyone."

Taylor snapped his fingers. "So the Cartography Guild is all about safety, then. That's good to know. Silly me, I was under the impression, based on the fees you a-holes charge us for stargate usage, that you were in it for the credits."

Japhara bristled at his cellmate's sarcasm. "You do realize what a massive undertaking it is to operate an apparatus as expansive as the stargate network, yes? There's hardware to maintain, routes to track, and an endless litany of charts to curate. Such endeavors require time and resources, neither of which come free."

Taylor shrugged. "Whatever, man. I can't speak to rest of it, but from where I sit, I think we can both agree that your curators suck at their jobs."

"Excuse me?"

"Look around, genius. We're stranded on a world that's nowhere to be found in your stupid atlas. I'd wager it ain't the only one, either. That means your beloved Guild Heads either don't know these worlds exist, in which case they're incompetent, or they do know and want to keep the rest of us in the dark about them. Regardless, it's safe to say your employers stand to take one helluva credibility hit if word of Rukoria's existence gets out around the Union."

The Sumatozou turned his back to his cage bars.

"So which is it?" Taylor asked.

The alien didn't answer.

"Come on, Japhara. The cat's out of the bag. We both know it. Right here and right now, drop the charade and tell me the truth. Hell, it ain't like either one of us is gonna leave here alive to tattle on the other." Taylor didn't believe that, but it served his purposes to say otherwise.

Japhara paced in his cell for several moments, muttering. After about the fifth circuit, he paused, faced his counterpart, and heaved a sigh that could've blown down a mountain. "The worlds you speak of are known among the latura as Non-Official Planets, or NOP worlds. They are housed in a secure directory within the atlas's core architecture, accessible only by grand latura and the Guild Heads themselves. Not even the gate masters know of their existence."

I knew it! Taylor whirled in disgust. "Why would the Cartography Guild keep that kind of knowledge from the public? What does it serve? Moreover, what right do they have to do so?"

"It is not our place to question the Guild's wisdom," Japhara said. "Ours is only to trust and follow."

Taylor tossed up his hands. "And here I thought the Zuul were the lap dogs in this equation."

"Watch your tone, Van Zant." Japhara rose to his full height, nostrils flared. "You hail from a world whose affiliation with the Galactic Union spans, what? A century? You couldn't begin to understand what came before, or the sacrifices that have been made to safeguard the freedoms mankind now enjoys. My people were there. For thousands of years, we've served the Cartography Guild as faithful stewards of the atlas. It's because of that trust—because of that bond—that the Guild Heads saw fit to bestow upon us an insight into the universe that few beings, much less a primitive race of apes like yours, could ever begin to grasp."

Taylor waved off the explanation. "Whatever helps you sleep at night, Hoss."

Japhara crowded against his bars, his expression grim. "You ask why the Cartography Guild would keep the NOP worlds from you. Well hear this, Human, and hear it well. There are things in the galaxy that neither you, nor the Rukori, nor anyone else in the Union are prepared to face. Old things, dark things. Things that would tear your civilizations to shreds if unleashed on your soil, and it's my people—*my Guild*—who fill the gap between those unspeakable horrors and your families. Remember that the next time you care to cast condemnation on things you do not understand."

Taylor opened his mouth to hurl another insult, but fought back a chill instead. *He ain't playin' around.*

"Insolent fool." Japhara snorted. "One day, you'll learn."

Taylor watched in silence as the Sumatozou stalked to the back of his cell and sat down. Ordinarily, he would've been fine with the quiet. This time, however, it left him far too much space to ponder Japhara's warning.

Like it or not, the alien had been right when he'd spoken of humanity's relative inexperience with the galaxy at large. They'd only been traveling out of their own solar system for a century, and if history was any indication, many of those exploits hadn't gone well.

Case in point, the all-out slaughter that had been the Alpha Contracts.

If there were truly monsters in the unseen regions of the galaxy, then mankind was the last species in the Union that needed to face them.

We're not ready. Taylor shuddered when a related thought occurred to him. As things stood, his ship, the *Ryley Osyrys*—assuming she was still out there—represented the only Human vessel in existence with the ability to enter that realm.

We got lucky with the Rukori, but what do we encounter next time? Taylor cleared his throat and thought of something else. "You mentioned you were abducted earlier."

"Correct."

"That sucks, no matter how you slice it. How long have you been trapped here? Six months? A year?"

Japhara exhaled. "Next month will mark my fourteenth year in Krulig custody."

Taylor's jaw fell open. "And you're still alive?"

"Such is the burden for one carrying the mark of asset." Japhara huffed. "I was taken by two Krulig officers from my post on the planet Kash-Kah and brought aboard a Maki cruiser. There, I was interrogated for weeks on end about the atlas, specifically my knowledge of the NOP worlds."

"I thought only grand latura knew of those."

"As did I prior to that meeting. Nevertheless, Sadeed learned of the worlds somehow, and he saw me as a means of procuring that information."

"What did he want with it?" Taylor asked.

"The same thing all Krulig want." Japhara snorted. "Wealth and power. Unlike most of his kind, however, Sadeed was smart enough to realize that he needed to accrue these things in secret lest they be taken from him."

"Taken by who?"

Japhara started to speak but seemed to think better of it. He settled for, "Anyone in the Union who would seek to acquire such luxuries for themselves."

Taylor found that response interesting. Still, he decided not to push his luck. "So when Sadeed figured out he couldn't get the NOP list on his own, he snatched a grand latura and forced him to hack the atlas and extract the list on the Krulig's behalf."

"Not hardly," Japhara said. "The foundation for the transit atlas is woven directly into the fabric of the stargate network. There is no hacking it, not even by the Guild Heads. The system is far too ancient and complex, with measures of encoding even we do not understand. This is why my Guild can only hide worlds from public viewing rather than deleting them outright. The system won't allow for the latter."

"Okay; fine," Taylor said. "If hackin' the gate network was off the table, then how'd you score the NOP list?"

Japhara shifted his legs. "What do you know of the GalNet and its machinations?"

Taylor considered the question. "About as much as the next guy, I'd reckon. When a ship is licensed for stargate usage, its owner signs a mandatory agreement with the Information Guild to transport GalNet data—be it government messages, guild info, personal mail, or what have you—to and from their various destinations. It's how the Union moves data between star systems in lieu of hyperspace communications, kinda like the old Pony Express."

"Very good," Japhara said. "Once a starship emerges from hyperspace, it transmits its inbound data to that system's stargate, which receives the packets, then sends the vessel the data meant for its next destination. Regardless of stargate or ship, every exchange requires the establishment, albeit briefly, of a two-way data stream between sources."

Taylor raised an eyebrow. "Are you sayin' you used the data stream as a bridge into the gate system so you could extract the NOP list?"

"Not at all," Japhara said. "Such an intrusion would almost certainly trigger alarms and alert the Guild Heads to my presence. What I did was capture a one-time image of their data stores from my side of the stream."

Taylor didn't follow.

"Answer me this," Japhara said. "Let's imagine that I was ordered to extract elements of a one-page report from the desk in your office. Which would be the more prudent course of action: to breach your campus and remove the information physically, or use a drone from afar to snap a picture of the entire report via the window behind your chair?"

Taylor pursed his lips. "You used the data stream as a sight line to copy the full transit atlas, NOP list and all. That allowed you to get away clean then vet the data later."

"That is correct."

"But…how?"

"I'm a grand latura, remember? I possess an understanding of stargate technology rivaled by few in the Union. That includes the system's windows, although in this case, it was more like the universe's smallest keyhole."

Taylor wished like hell his lead engineer could've been present to hear all this. "So Sadeed got his scaly mitts on the NOP list. Then what?"

"In keeping with his desire to stay hidden, Sadeed and I began combing the list for potential worlds where he could build his new empire. Several were explored. Ultimately, though, it was Rukoria that caught Sadeed's eye."

"How come?"

"You'd have to ask him," Japhara said. "I'm a grand latura, and even I had never heard of the Rukori people. In the end, I suppose it didn't matter. Once Rukoria had been targeted, Sadeed ordered me to load the NOP list onto a slave drive to his *Behemoth's* nav system then again to an old Krulig frigate which now serves as his primary personal vessel." The alien paused. "I must confess. I'd very much like to know where he procured the latter. Krulig ships haven't been seen in Union space for over four millennia. Most in the guilds thought them all destroyed."

Taylor didn't care about the ship's history as much as its design. "Let me guess. Small vessel with a trim profile? Looks like a bullet in space?"

"You've seen it then."

Taylor muttered a curse. *That's the ship that attacked the Osyrys.* He climbed to his feet. "We need to get outta here. Now."

"I'm open to suggestions," Japhara said. "I'd be remiss, however, if I didn't point out that no one has ever escaped this facility."

"Yeah, well." Taylor grunted. "Mama always said I was the go-getter of the family."

"Why do I sense she was correct in that assessment?"

Taylor glanced up. "Was that a compliment?"

"Not even close," Japhara said. "It was merely an observation, based solely on my knowledge of your idiot brother."

Dick.

New footfalls from above caused both beings to turn.

"Ah, give it a rest already, fellas." To Taylor's surprise, it wasn't a Zuul that entered the chamber but rather a Rukori servant girl dressed in the usual rags.

She approached the cell alone and put a tray of food and water in front of Taylor's cage. "Not exactly the Sawgrass Resort and Spa down here, is it?" the girl asked quietly.

Taylor jumped. *Who the…*Then, slowly—through the gray paint, the white wig, and the makeshift alien features—the girl peered up from under her cowl to reveal Human eyes as green as the sea. "Li-sa?"

The reporter grinned. "Hey, Taylor."

*****

Chapter 23: Uplink

"What the hell are you doin' here?" Taylor asked.

Lisa looked wounded. "Do I seriously have to answer that?"

"Yeah, ya kinda do."

"I'm here to help get you out."

Taylor glanced up the stairwell, expecting a Zuul guard to appear at any moment. It didn't happen. "How'd you manage to get down here without an escort?"

"Oh, I've got an escort," Lisa said. "He's perched upstairs with a rifle and one of those wicked-ass blades, waiting on me to come out."

"And he didn't follow you down here why?"

"Apparently, he can't stand being around me." Lisa made a face. "Come to think of it, that's been the theme with the last three guys I've dated. Maybe it's me."

Taylor smirked.

"Fine," Lisa said. "Valawn gave me another vial of that green goop along with this getup I'm wearing. It's worn off enough for our noses, but apparently it's still pretty gnarly smelling to the Zuul."

Taylor pursed his lips. "Lisa, I seriously don't know what to—"

"Then don't." She dropped her eyes. "Let's not mince words on this, okay? It's my fault you're down here. If I'd have just listened to you and stayed on the *Osyrys*, I'd be…" She trailed off.

"You'd be precisely wherever they are right now," Taylor said. "Any word on that, by way?"

Lisa shook her head. "As of when I left a few hours ago, there'd still been no word from Billy or the others. Valawn's people are continuing to search for signs they made it through the stargate, but to be honest, it's not looking good."

The block door creaked open and Lisa's Zuul guard eased down the stairwell, mindful to keep its distance. "No talk, Rukori. Only serve. Time to go."

Lisa nodded then lowered her voice to a whisper. "See you soon, Chief. Oh, and enjoy the bread. The baker made it special." With that, she shot him a parting wink, pulled her cowl down low, and took her leave.

Taylor watched, helpless in his cage, as the reporter vanished from sight, then up the stairwell out of earshot. It had taken a lot of guts to walk in here like that. *And her a civilian, no less.* Whatever sins Lisa Kouvaris had committed prior, Taylor was pretty sure they were square moving forward.

"Intriguing woman," Japhara said once quiet returned to the block. "And resourceful, for a Rukori."

Taylor didn't bother with a correction. "They've kinda had to be that way from the start to survive here."

"Ah," Japhara said. "The RFC leader spoke of his people's origins then. What all did he tell you?"

"Not much," Taylor said. "Just that his ancestors were tired of war after seein' a huge chunk of their population wiped out by the

Canavar. So, they petitioned the Vergola Council to let them skate without a trail once the guilds were up and runnin'. They've stayed off the grid ever since."

Japhara's eyes widened slightly. "Valawn told you of the Council?"

"Briefly, yeah. He said back in the day, they were—" Taylor broke off when Lisa's last words replayed in his mind.

"Enjoy the bread," she'd said. "The baker made it special."

Please be what I think you are. Taylor scooped up his food tray and hurried to the back of his cage. There, he sat down and began picking apart the loaf in question.

"Playing with our food to pass the time now, are we?" Japhara quipped.

Taylor didn't answer. He just kept picking through the bread. Eventually, his fingers touched something solid and familiar. *Jackpot!* Taylor extracted the pinlink from his dinner and applied it to the port behind his right ear. "This is Chief Taylor Van Zant of the Earth mercenary group, Swamp Eagle Security," he said via thought. "Does anyone copy on this channel?"

No response.

"Attention, anyone on this line. This is Taylor Van Zant of Swamp Eagle Security. Do you read?"

A pop of static crackled the line, followed by a squelch from the other end.

"We gotcha five by five, Chief," a voice answered in Taylor's head.

Man, I love those guys. Taylor exhaled. "It's good to hear your voice, Jack."

"Likewise," the Oklahoma sergeant said. "I see Ms. Kouvaris was able to deliver our little present in her bread basket."

"You got eyes on her?" Taylor rushed to ask.

"I surely do," Jack said. "She just exited the Krulig compound and is about to meet up with Stan…now. We've got her."

Taylor closed his eyes. *Thank you.* "So, what have I missed?"

Jack outlined how he, Stan, and the others had fled back to the surface after being ejected from the stargate, then hid out in Nyo Colony until it was safe to return to the badlands.

"You oughta know, sir, that it was Ms. Kouvaris who insisted we come back," Jack concluded. "Don't get me wrong, me and Stan would've found a way to do that anyway. However, ain't neither one of us pretty enough to pull off that little masquerade you just witnessed. One of Valawn's people tried to step in, but Lisa insisted it be her."

"That right?" Taylor asked.

"Oh, yeah," Jack said. "She's got lady stones the size of church bells, you ask me. She ain't afraid to swing 'em around like wreckin' balls, neither, when it suits her."

Taylor chuckled.

"How are you holdin' up?" Jack asked.

Taylor recounted his experiences of the last several days, namely his meeting with Sadeed and his numerous sessions with the Zuul.

"Sombitch," Jack murmured in awe.

"Tell me about it," Taylor agreed. "You talked to Smitty?"

"No, but Valawn's contacts say she's alive," Jack said. "The commander is bein' retained in Cell Block One where you last saw her."

"We got a plan on how to get us out of this hole?"

"Yes and no," Jack said. "Even if we committed the entire RFC fightin' force to your extraction, there's no way we'd make it through all those Zuul to get both of you out. One, maybe, but not the two of you." The old merc trailed off. "You know, Chief, given your current position in relation to the commander's, there's a better than fair chance we could extract you, then come back for her. I don't like it, but you're the head of this outfit. That makes you the priority."

"Not an option," Taylor said. "Not even close. We go together or not at all, period. Understood?"

"Yes, sir."

Taylor could hear the relief in the sergeant's voice. "How do things look outside?"

"By my count, we've got no less than three hundred Zuul holed up in that compound with another two or so back in town."

"And the watchtowers?" Taylor asked.

"Two Zuul per tower on six-hour shifts around the clock."

Taylor tugged at his whiskers. "What sort of numbers have we got to counter?"

"Valawn has roughly four dozen RFC soldiers ready to roll," Jack said. "He thinks he can recruit another two dozen or so from Nyo, but he'll have to reach out to cell heads from the other colonies for anything more."

"How long will that take?"

"A day, at least. Maybe two."

Taylor stifled a curse. "Any chance we could get help from civilians?" He hated asking that, but it was what it was.

"Believe it or not, I put that very question to Valawn as soon as we got back to the Sanctuary," Jack said.

"And?"

"And he's hesitant to go that route," Jack said. "For one, many of the Rukori are too afraid of Krulig reprisals should something go wrong. Those who ain't afraid of the damn lizards are the ones still loyal to their cause."

"Which could create a security risk," Taylor said.

"You got it," Jack said. "By the looks of things, we get our choice of numbers or surprise in this situation. We don't get both."

Taylor slumped back against a wall as part of him lamented ever getting involved with the Rukori to begin with. *We're fightin' for your freedom, you cowards,* he wanted to say. *Get off your asses and help!* At the same time, the other parts of him—the rational parts—understood the natives' hesitance. Their people had endured more tragedy than most could imagine, from the grizzly fate of their ancestors at the hands of the Canavar to the one suffered by this generation at the hands of the Winter Death. Krulig occupation or not, most Rukori were just happy to be alive.

Still, something else gnawed at Taylor, some unseen detail that, for whatever reason, loomed just out of understanding's reach.

The Winter Death…The Krulig…

The darkest of thoughts crept through Taylor's mind.

"Chief, you there?" Jack asked.

"Yeah, Jack, sorry." Taylor sat up straight. "Did Keeto leave behind any of that Hemming hardware we brought?"

"He did, actually. It ain't much, but it's stowed in Valawn's hangar."

"What do we have?"

"Two crates of Firestorms, three of the JXR-14 assault rifles, a small case of micro-explosives, and a half dozen Hemming long guns."

Taylor considered that last one. "You know your way around a sniper rifle?"

"Does a bear shit in the woods?"

Taylor took that as a *yes.* "How about Stan? How's he at long distances?"

"Not as good as me, but better than most," Jack said. "Why? What are you thinkin'?"

Taylor recalled the lack of distance between the Nyo refueling depot and the Krulig landing field. After that, his thoughts turned to a stunt he'd seen in one of those old movies they'd shown during throwback night at the Hell House. *Oh, that's so very thin.* He thought hard for alternatives. None came. "Get Valawn on the line. Tell him I'm gonna need to make some arrangements."

* * * * *

Chapter 24: The Runaround

"You can't be serious," Valawn said once Taylor had explained his plan.

"I know it ain't perfect," Taylor said, "and there's plenty that can go wrong. However, given the resources we have as weighed against those we don't, I still say it's our best option."

Valawn paused, doubtless considering. "Many of our people in Nyo Colony won't be pleased with this. Setting aside that it'll completely destroy one of our biggest assets, it'll also put them squarely in conflict with the Krulig. They won't like that."

Taylor briefly considered sharing his thought from earlier. *It's just a theory until you've got proof.* He decided to stick with the facts. "I know a lot of Rukori don't want to jeopardize their standin' with Sadeed. That makes sense. Look at it this way, though. If my plan works, your people will have regained their freedom. If it don't, they can always pin the mess on a handful of renegade kin and a pack of dumbass rednecks from Earth. That ain't an insurrection. It's a nuisance. The Krulig won't sacrifice their investment here over a nuisance, not with all they can still milk from it goin' forward."

Valawn went off comm to think, then returned a second later with his answer. "Very well. What will you require of me?"

The call ended with Taylor relaying his condolences to Valawn for the loss of his sister. After that, Taylor pulled the pinlink from behind his ear and hid it away under a rock near the back of his cage. *One way or another, this whole thing ends in twelve hours.*

"Van Zant," Japhara called from across the hall. "You sound very busy over there."

"Nothin' you need to concern yourself with, Hoss. Just sit back, relax, and know that, soon enough, you'll have your solitude back."

The Sumatozou stepped forward and clasped his cell bars. "You have a plan to escape."

"Nope. Just thinkin' about the future is all."

Japhara's expression twisted. "Don't lie to me, Human. I know such behavior is commonplace among your people, but it's both offensive and dishonorable to mine. You can at least show me that most basic of respects."

Taylor stretched out in the corner and cradled his head on his arm. "Take it easy, Japhara. I didn't mean to ruffle your feathers."

"I have no feathers."

"Thanks for clearin' that up," Taylor said. "Now get some rest. Tomorrow's gonna be a busy day."

* * *

Much to Taylor's delight, his captors never came for him that evening. This left him to sleep a whole four hours—by far the most he'd gotten in one sitting since his confinement. All of that changed, of course, when his friends with the batons returned the next day and took him away for a refresher course on Zuul interrogations. As it happened, that morning's session proved particularly vicious, so much so that Taylor feared he might not have been able to hold out had he not known what was coming. He screamed through vice-clenched teeth as wave after wave of electricity tore through his body, igniting his nerve endings as if on fire, and reducing his muscles to useless jelly. It was an agony transcendent of any Taylor could've imagined. Even still, he held it together by filling his thoughts with anything he could to pass the time. He thought of his sisters, Rita and Jo, and how much he missed them—how much he missed all of his family, even his mom, who'd never forgiven him for going merc. He thought of his best friend, Rex, and their arguments over baseball. He thought of Billy and the other Eagles, and how much they'd come to mean to him in the last year.

Mostly, though, Taylor thought of the man responsible for setting this entire thing in motion six years ago—the man whose shadow Taylor Joseph Van Zant had spent most of his life trying to outrun.

Hang in there, little brother. The voice was as crisp and clear in Taylor's mind as the last time he'd heard it in person. What a spectacular day that had been, filled with sunshine and surf, ice-cold beer, blackened mahi sandwiches grilled to perfection, and throngs of beautiful girls wearing bikinis deemed illegal in some countries. *Just hang in a little while longer. Help is on the way.*

Terry…

A splash of muck water in Taylor's face jolted him awake. He sat up, every inch of him throbbing like hell, and looked around. "Where the—"

"You're back in your cell," Japhara said. "You've been there, lying sideways in that filth, for almost three hours."

Three hours? Taylor fought to recall the sun's position in the sky when the Zuul had dragged him back. *Just slightly west.* Tack on three more hours, and—

"Shit!" Taylor jumped to his feet, muscles quaking in protest, and stumbled to retrieve his pinlink. "Jack, it's me. You there?"

"Right here, Chief. I was startin' to get worried. You all right?"

"I'll manage," Taylor said via thought. "Valawn fill you in on the op?"

"He sure did," Jack said. "I've gotta hand it to you. This plan of yours? It's bold; real bold. Your brother would've been proud."

Taylor's eyes flicked skyward. "Thanks. What's our status?"

"Locked and loaded across the board," Jack said. "Valawn and his people are holed up in Nyo Colony, waitin' on our signal. Me, Stan, and the others are roughly two miles west of your position near the foot of the mesa."

Taylor nodded.

"Chief, can I put forth one suggestion?"

"Go ahead."

"Let me and Stan go after Commander Smith. You're gonna have your hands full as it is gettin' out of that hornet's nest you're about to kick up. We can get to Smitty."

Taylor shook his head. "Negative. I need the two of you on those long guns, layin' down cover fire while we egress."

Jack exhaled over the line. "Copy that. What else?"

"What's the status on our mouse trap?" Taylor asked.

"Laid down last night while it was dark. We lucked out, too, in that we got no sandstorms to screw up the work. We can light her up when ready."

"Good deal." Taylor retraced the route to Cell Block One in his head. If Valawn's people did their job, the majority of the Zuul would head southeast back into Nyo Colony. With any luck, that would leave a skeleton crew at the compound, which Taylor could evade long enough to grab Smitty, then head west toward the mesa. That just left one last issue, the lone Zuul guard that always stood watch over Cell Block Two from the stairwell.

Shift's over, pooch. Taylor keyed his comm. "Tell the others to get ready. This party's about to get started."

Jack's response was as singular as it was resolute. "Ayew."

"Van Zant!" Japhara called. "Talk to me! What's happening?"

Taylor didn't answer. Instead, he scooped up the stone he'd been filing down for just this occasion, palmed it in his right hand, and marched to his cell bars. "Hey, room service! Get your bitch-ass down here! I'm hungry!"

A feral snarl preceded the *wham* of a slamming door, followed by the pitter-patter of quadruped footfalls down the stairs.

"What did you call me?" The angry Zuul stalked into the torchlight.

"You heard me," Taylor said. "I want some food. Let's go with pizza this time—extra cheese with everything on it, but skip the green peppers. Those things ruin a pie."

The guard peeled back its lips for another growl.

"You gonna snap to it or do I have to say fetch?" Taylor stood back smiling as the enraged alien lunged for his cell. *Come get some, shorty.*

The access panel glared green, and the Zuul bounded in. It was the last move the alien would ever make.

Thwack!

The wet crunch of rock meeting bone pierced the air when Taylor's arm slammed down onto the Zuul's head, splitting its skull and pushing straight through to the brain. The alien twitched, blood and gray matter spewing from its wound, then it collapsed dead to the cavern floor.

Happy trails, asshole.

"Van Zant!" Japhara said. "Please! Take me with you!"

Taylor rifled through the Zuul's hip pouch, taking its stun baton and battle blade for good measure, then used the latter to slice off the alien's hand.

"Van Zant!" Japhara persisted. "Don't be a fool! I can be of use to you! I can help you retrieve your comrade!"

His pillaging complete, Taylor whirled to face the Sumatozou. "I'll make you a deal. I'll let you out of this cell and get you free of this compound in exchange for one favor."

"Name it," Japhara said.

"No."

The Sumatozou did a double-take. "What? Why not?"

"Because I don't know what that favor is yet," Taylor said. "I just don't see any way that havin' a free marker with a grand latura can be a bad thing. Hell, I might not live long enough to call the damn thing in. But if I do, you *will* pay it, no questions asked. Those are my terms. Take 'em or leave 'em."

The alien began pacing his cell.

"Tick tock, Japhara."

The Sumatozou barked a curse. "Fine. I'll pay your marker when the time comes."

"I've got your word on that, right?"

"Yes, yes. Just let me out already so we can get moving."

*****

Chapter 25: Squeeze Play

Once outside the cavern, Taylor and Japhara moved quietly through a series of stone corridors before arriving at the security junction just down from the main entrance. They were in luck. There were only two Zuul working the section.

Taylor raised his baton but thought better of the noise. He pulled his battle blade instead and turned to Japhara, whispering, "I can't do this alone. You with me?"

The Sumatozou nodded.

I sure hope so. Taylor watched the Zuul come closer, then raised his hand to signal the move. *Take 'em!*

In a single, fluid motion, Taylor slipped from his corner, caught Zuul one by the head, and slid the blade past its throat. The alien never made a sound.

The same couldn't be said for its companion.

Snap!

Taylor spun to see the other Zuul drop like a ragdoll to the floor, its head having been twisted 270 degrees.

"Don't look so surprised." Japhara wiped his hands. "The Sumatozou are among the mercenary races, you know. Just because we choose not to fight at times doesn't mean we aren't capable of doing so."

Taylor was impressed. "Good on ya."

The coast momentarily clear, the duo proceeded onward up another set of corridors, halting every few corners to bypass the other guards. From there, they worked their way to the structure's main entrance, where they halted at a patch of sunlight being cast onto the floor from the outside.

"How does it look?" Japhara mumbled.

Taylor peered forward onto the open ground. "Sadeed's residence is roughly twenty yards straight ahead. The entrance to Cell Block One is on the far side of that."

"How about security?" Japhara asked.

"Way more than we can take with a blade and a stun baton." Taylor was just about to lead them back in search of an alternate route when Japhara caught his arm.

"Wait," the alien said. "Look there."

A hauler approached from the main barracks and eased to a stop directly in their path to Cell Block One. It was piloted by two Krulig and met by several Zuul, who began boarding the cargo bed with supplies.

"Let us be patient," the Sumatozou said.

Taylor bit his lip. "Ya know, Japhara, between my childhood and my tenure with the Eagles, I've been at this merc thing for most of my life. In all that time, I still can't believe I've never once heard of these guys."

"The Krulig?" Japhara asked. "That's not surprising. Their species has been circling the proverbial void of extinction for millennia."

"Yeah, Sadeed mentioned that in our first meetin'," Taylor said. "He told me a series of unfortunate events about five thousand years ago that led to his race's banishment from their solar system. They've been nomads ever since."

"A series of unfortunate events." Japhara scoffed. "Take my word on this, Van Zant. The Krulig have no one to blame but themselves for what happened to their people. My lords, the Guild Heads, had little choice but to act as they did."

Taylor snapped back to his companion. "Wait. It was the Cartography Guild who drove the Krulig out? Why?"

"Plainly put," Japhara said, "the Krulig stole from us and were caught."

Taylor hadn't a clue what that meant.

"As should be clear by now, the Krulig are an exceptionally resilient race," Japhara said. "They are also, coincidentally, among the greediest beings to ever step foot in Union territory. Their treachery started small, when a handful of their officers began siphoning funds from our daily stargate transactions. In time, that betrayal grew to the full-fledged theft of Guild property for sale on the underground markets. When my lords learned of this, it was decided that a message needed to be sent, and sent it was. Such began the Krulig species' march toward oblivion."

Taylor narrowed his gaze. "How would the Krulig have access to Cartography Guild funds and property?"

"Simple." Japhara shrugged. "The Krulig are the original gate masters."

Taylor's jaw dropped. "Bull shit."

"Such crude language." Japhara pointed back outside. "Look."

The final few Zuul climbed onto the hauler with their crates. The craft then re-fired its engines and took off across the compound.

"I believe now would be an opportune time to summon your friends," Japhara said.

Taylor applied his pinlink and keyed his comm. "Jack, you all set?"

"Ready when you are, Chief," the old merc said. "Just say the word."

Taylor didn't miss a beat. "The word is given, Sergeant."

A booming thunderclap shook the earth, sending a thick pillar of black smoke billowing skyward to the south. A high-pitched klaxon responded.

"All squads!" a Zuul voice barked through speakers across the compound. "Proceed at once to the Nyo Colony fuel depot! Transports are standing by!"

The swarm of Zuul who'd filled the compound scattered on cue, many heading south on foot while others scrambled to the transport haulers waiting to take them to the explosion site.

Thanks, Valawn. Taylor clutched his baton. "Let's roll."

Sticking to the perimeter, which offered the most cover, Taylor and Japhara weaved their way across the facility, pausing briefly to scoop up real weapons, until they reached the stairwell down to Cell Block One. There, Taylor cut across right to clear the opening, while Japhara button-hooked left to do the same. Once inside, the duo proceeded down to the confinement area.

Pop, pop.

One Zuul fell at the first junction.

Pop, pop. Pop, pop, pop.

Three more followed around the bend.

Spotting the entrance to Smitty's cell ahead, Taylor picked off a final Zuul, then produced his confiscated hand for use on the access panel.

"Chief?" Smitty blurted in surprise. Her eyes went even wider upon seeing the Sumatozou. "Where in the bloody hell did he come from?"

"Long story," Taylor said. "I'll explain later. For now, we gotta go."

Smitty stepped back as Taylor opened her cage.

"Can you move?" Taylor asked.

"Are you kidding? I've been waiting two weeks for someone to ask me that." Smitty snatched a rifle from one of the dead Zuul and ran through its operations. "You're on point. I've got your six. Call the play."

Together, the group slipped out of the cell block and back up toward the entrance. They'd just cleared the exit into daylight when a voice shouted from behind, "*Intruders!*"

Ah, hell.

Taylor's rifle rocketed to his shoulder as Smitty did the same from a knee. A spray of laser fire erupted from their weapons, scattering the Zuul brood before it could advance.

"Run!" Smitty shouted.

Taylor chattered off another barrage while Japhara sprinted for cover behind a nearby warehouse. Next went Smitty, then Taylor once the others had taken position to lay down covering fire.

"Please tell me you've got a plan for getting us back to the Sanctuary," Smitty said, panting.

A laser bolt smashed the corner near their position, causing all three beings to lunge backward.

"We don't have to make it back that far," Taylor said through a shower of debris. "We just have to make it past the fence and back out into the open."

"Then what?" Smitty asked.

"Then we hitch a ride." Taylor keyed his comm while the others kept the Zuul pinned down across the yard. "Jack, it's Taylor. We've got Smitty and are headed for the western gate."

"Copy that," Jack answered. "Your limo's inbound!"

Another laser blast pelted their location, prompting Smitty to return fire. She pulled back a second later when her chem mag went dark. "I'm out."

"We cannot stay here," Japhara said.

"Agreed." Taylor replaced the Aussie at the corner and blistered off a laser shower of his own. "Both of y'all get ready to run for the fence. We break on my signal."

"What about the guards in the watchtower?" Smitty asked.

"I'll handle it," Taylor said. "Now get ready."

Japhara presented his weapon. "Take this. By my count, it's got 10 more rounds in the mag than yours."

Taylor accepted the alien's offer. "Much obliged."

Japhara nodded and took his mark beside the Aussie commander.

"*Go!*" Taylor barked.

Smitty and Japhara launched into a dead sprint for the fence while Taylor laid down covering fire from the warehouse. Once he'd effectively pushed the ground Zuul back, he turned his barrel on the two manning the watchtower and let loose with a tight three-second spray of laser fire. After that, he took off running behind the others.

Pop, pop.

One gate guard fell.

Pop, pop, pop. Pop, pop.

The other two followed.

Smitty was the first to cross the barrier and skid to a halt outside. "Where's our bloody ride?"

Japhara met her in the sand, stabbing a finger to the southeast. "There!"

A lone cargo hauler roared into view, carrying three Rukori passengers. Two of them, Taylor didn't recognize. The third, however, he most certainly did. "It's Douron!"

"Ah!" Japhara stumbled back as smoke trailed from a fresh scorch wound in his shoulder.

Taylor threw up his rifle and fired back on the Zuul, only to see his mag go dark. *Oh, no.*

Hearing the lack of fire, the watchtower guards returned to their posts and took aim.

A thick bolt of energy sliced the southern sky and slammed the platform, exploding the entire tower to bits in a sudden wash of flames.

"Hell yeah!" Smitty decried.

Taylor stood back as the hauler ground to a stop ahead and Douron put away his K-bomb launcher.

"Get on!" the big Rukori ordered.

Taylor jumped over the side of the truck and into the bed, while Japhara and Smitty did the same.

"What is that?" one of the Rukori asked of the Sumatozou.

"He's with us!" Taylor ducked as new fire pelted the sand nearby. "Now get us out of here!"

The pilot selected maximum acceleration, and the craft sped off west toward the mesa.

"We've got incoming," Smitty announced.

Of course we do. Spotting a case of JXR-14s near the front of the bed, Taylor snatched one out and racked the slide. After that, he slid two more to Smitty and Japhara, then assumed a shooter's crouch beside Douron as six Zuul sprinted on all fours in pursuit.

Round after round the group let fly with their weapons, as wave after wave of Zuul kept coming. Soon six Zuul became a dozen, then two dozen, then three dozen. Eventually, the group looked up to see a full-blown horde chasing them.

"These little wankers are like locusts!" Smitty snarled. "How far to—"

"Chief Van Zant!" Japhara shouted.

Taylor followed the alien's motion to see a lone Zuul emerge from the pack, clutching a launcher like Douron's.

"Get down," Jack said in Taylor's head.

"*Everybody down!*" Taylor screamed, watching the Zuul as he dove.

No sooner had he hit the deck than the Zuul's head evaporated in a puff of red. A split-second later, the puff was followed by a distant *pop-pow* rolling in from the west.

"Tell that Rukori slacker to step on it," Jack growled. "Me and Stan can't take 'em all."

Another Zuul head stained the sand red, followed by two more. Over and over the long guns did their job, while Taylor and the others continued firing from the hauler.

"We're not gonna make it!" Japhara called.

"Yes we are!" Taylor answered. "Just a few more yards!"

"But the mesa is still—" Smitty broke off when the pungent scent of hauler fuel hit her nostrils. "Oh, shit!"

A final surge of thrust shoved the transport forward as the frenzied Zuul drew in tightly on the vehicle's tail.

You bastards never could mind your surroundings. "Jack, we clear?"

A pause preceded the sergeant's reply. "Yes, sir!"

"Good," Taylor said. "Show these fargin pricks how we party on the Fourth of July!"

A colossal *woof* rolled across the desert, accompanied by a blast of heat that caused everyone to shield their faces. Soon the pungent smell of fuel was replaced by the repugnant scent of seared flesh, and a chorus of howls swirled skyward as the ground behind the hauler ignited.

Interrogate that, assholes. Taylor climbed to a knee as the transport eased to a stop at the foot of the mesa. Jack, Stan, and Lisa were already there waiting, as were Retay and a dozen RFC troops, who picked off the remaining Zuul.

"Glad you could make it," Jack said.

"You and me both," Taylor agreed, hopping out.

"And you brought friends." Stan nodded to Japhara.

Taylor gave a quick round of introductions. "What's the story on our evac?"

"Valawn and his people are inbound now from Nyo Colony," Lisa said. "They've called in a bandilaro to take everyone back to the Sanctuary."

"ETA to dustoff?" Taylor asked.

"Five minutes, per the last check in," Jack said.

Taylor turned to Smitty. "This little reprieve of ours ain't gonna last long. Sadeed *will* circle the wagons, and when he does, all those Zuul who deployed to the depot blast are gonna redirect here."

"Say no more," the Aussie said. "I'll shore things up as best I can with Retay and the RFC until our cab arrives."

"Thanks, Smitty." Taylor handed her a pair of extra magazines he'd taken from the hauler, then watched her trot off to her new post.

"Sir, if I may?" Stan asked. "What's our plan after this?"

"Come again?" Taylor asked.

The Mississippi sergeant shifted with visible unease. "I hate to be the bearer of bad news here, Chief, but all signs point to the *Osyrys* bein' blown away at the stargate. That leaves us marooned here. Don't get me wrong, I ain't pissed about that. As mercs, we know the risks when we sign on for these contracts. I would, however, like to know what life for us looks like henceforth once we're back at the Sanctuary."

Taylor hadn't had time to think that far ahead, so he wasn't sure how to answer. He glanced to Jack. The old merc's body language said he'd been wondering the same thing.

"One thing at a time, gentlemen," Taylor said. "I know that ain't the ideal response, but it's all I got for now. You got my word, though, we'll figure this out together."

Both men seemed good with that.

"Coming in!" someone called from the lookout cliffs overhead.

Another hauler was inbound, this one carrying Valawn and a handful of other Rukori. The vehicle eased to rest alongside the mesa, and the RFC leader hopped out.

"It's good to see you, Chief," Valawn said. "Jack told me about what happened to you at the hands of the Zuul. I'm sorry you had to experience that."

"I appreciate that," Taylor said. "Thankfully, all that's over, and we're here now."

"Indeed," Valawn said warmly.

"Excuse me, Commander?" Retay trotted over to join them. "Bandilaro Two just radioed in. They're on approach, but they say there are three platoons of Zuul circling the fire zone toward our position."

Valawn nodded, then returned to the Humans. "I've instructed my pilot to land in the clearing behind the mesa. Come, we must hurry."

Taylor fell in beside Lisa toward the landing zone, then whistled for Smitty and Japhara to follow.

"I've got a visual!" the lookout Rukori said.

Taylor bladed his hand over his eyes as the hammer-headed craft circled in over their position, then fired its thrusters to land. The ship was halfway through its descent when it vanished in a fireball of light.

* * * * *

Chapter 26: Dropped

Taylor wheeled backward as the object that had just been a bandilaro careened into the desert as a hulk of mangled steel.

"Damnit!" Jack snarled into his sleeve.

"What in the hell?" Stan murmured.

A Maki shuttle soared by overhead and peppered the ground where the group was standing.

"You didn't honestly believe your paltry little ships could evade us forever, did you?" Sadeed gloated through the ship's external speakers.

"Go!" Valawn shouted. "Everyone, back to the mesa! Now!"

Taylor sprinted for a row of boulders near the foot of the mesa as the ravaged remains of their former ride smoldered in a heap not fifty yards away. The entire scene devolved into chaos.

"What now?" Lisa called from the next boulder over.

Taylor racked his brain for ideas.

"Whatever we mean to do, we should do so now." Japhara peered through his rifle scope. "A large contingent of Zuul have broken off from Nyo Colony and are approaching our position. Time is of the essence."

Taylor turned to Valawn. "That hauler of yours. Is it fast enough to get us out of here, maybe to Nyo?"

"It is," Valawn said, "but we just destroyed one of the colony's largest assets without permission from its citizens. There are many there who don't like us right now."

"What about one of the other colonies?" Taylor asked. "Bartahl, maybe. Ain't that the next closest settlement?"

Valawn shook his head. "Not with the hauler's current fuel load. We'd lose power halfway through the trek, then be stranded in some of the roughest desert Rukoria has to offer."

Sadeed's shuttle screamed by for another pass, unleashing a volley of laser fire into the rock field. That sent everyone below diving for cover as calls for their surrender showered them from above.

"Ladies and gents, we cain't stay here." Stan coughed into his sleeve. "These rocks make us fish in a damn barrel for the Zuul."

"I'm open to suggestions, Sergeant," Valawn said.

No one had a response. They held there, pinned down by the shuttle, as more and more Zuul swarmed toward the mesa. Soon the Rukori began to panic.

"Chief?" Smitty's tone trailed up in confusion. "Don't hold me to this, but I think we've got another ship incoming."

What? Taylor slid around the side of his boulder and followed her direction. Sure enough, a lone gray dot descended from the western sky. It was quickly joined by another dot, then another and another, until there were eighteen total, looming larger by the second.

"Is that what I think it is?" Lisa asked.

Taylor didn't dare respond. Instead, he watched from behind his rock as the dots on the horizon gradually took on shapes.

Come on, baby. Taylor all but jumped from his skin when a new voice blared from the lead ship's speakers. Unlike Sadeed, however, its owner didn't call for surrender. Rather, it let loose with the fabled twentieth century battle cry of one Charlie Daniels.

"*What this world needs is a few more rednecks!*"

"Hell yeah!" Smitty erupted.

The Maki shuttle was already in retreat when the lead dropships roared onto the scene. It lurched to get free, but still took a hard cannon shot to its stern armor in the process of bugging out.

"Tomahawk, this is Corn Husker," Billy said via comm. "Sorry we're late."

Taylor exhaled, then spoke aloud for the others to hear. "Better late than never, Husker. It's *damn* good to hear your voice."

Smitty blew out an exhale of her own.

"Likewise," Billy said. "As promised, I took the liberty of inviting some friends to our little soirée. I hope you approve of my guest list."

Taylor watched as the hulls of each dropship came into view. All told, there were three insignias between them, representing three different outfits. They were Swamp Eagle Security, the Steeldriver Defense Group, and the Iron Conquistadores.

Hometown heroes, united again. A wayward laser bolt smashed the rock near Taylor's head, snapping him backward. "Billy, we sure could use some ground support down here if you've got it to spare."

"Bulldog's way ahead of you," the XO said, referencing Quint's callsign.

As if on cue, one of the Eagles' dropships broke formation and unleashed a spray of weapons fire on the forming Zuul horde, scattering the aliens like ants. The beasts ran for cover, but were quickly cut down as streams of Human troops began dropping from the sky.

"Tell Bulldog thanks for that," Taylor said.

"You can tell him yourself once this is over," Billy said. "Now, if you're done playing with those pea shooters down there, how about you grab Blue Devil and meet me behind that mesa for an upgrade."

"What kind of upgrade?" Taylor asked.

Billy held coy. "You'll have to come see for yourself. Husker out."

Taylor leapt to his feet and tagged Smitty, callsign Blue Devil, on the shoulder. From there, the duo took off across the sand as the lead Eagles' dropship fired its thrusters to land. After the vessel was down, she lowered her boarding ramp and Billy Dawson strode out, piloting a shiny new Mk 8 CASPer.

"Nice digs, Husker," Taylor pointed to the arsenal covering the suit's eight-foot-tall exterior. "Assault class, gen three?"

"Good eye," Billy said. "Ron Carnegie felt we needed some better gear for this mission, so he spotted us a few Mk 8s from the Steeldriver reserve stash. His only request was that we return them in some semblance of working order when we're done."

Taylor cocked his head. "And you responded how?"

"I told him we'd do our best." Billy aimed a thumb past his steel-armored shoulder. "You gonna stand there gawking all day, or are you gonna suit up?"

Taylor needed no further promoting. He scrambled up the ramp into the drop bay with Smitty, the latter catching a quick nod from Billy as she ran.

Once inside, Taylor shimmied out of his rags and into a haptic suit, which was required for CASPer operations. He then tied his hair back and changed out his pinlink before bounding into the cockpit. The clamshell canopy sealed shut around him.

"CASPer systems are active and online," the canopy Tri-V read as he connected the leads to his haptic suit. "Welcome, Chief Van Zant."

Thank ya, ma'am. I am damn glad to be here. Taylor flexed his arms and legs, then peered around his cocoon at the state-of-the-art tech at his fingertips. Like most everyone of his generation, he'd grown up idolizing these machines. He'd colored pictures of them as a kid, owned their action figures as a tween, then studied their actual specs while in the Duval MST program at Lee High School. Now here he was about to walk off this ship, piloting the number one model on the market.

Oh, yeah. Taylor keyed his comm. "From the top, Husker, gimme a situation report. Orbital first."

"Orbit began a bit tricky, but I think we've got things in hand," Billy said. "We brought five ships—EMS *Stargell* and *Bradshaw* of Steeldriver, the EMS *Valiente* and *Desafío* of the Conquistadors, and the *Ryley Osyrys* leading the way. We'd hoped that would give us the numbers edge once we emerged from hyperspace. Trouble is, the Krulig brought back four more ships of their own with that *Behemoth*."

"Class?" Taylor asked.

"All frigates," Billy said. "Pair those with the one already here, and that made it an even fight at five on five."

"Any sign of the ship that attacked y'all at the stargate?"

"None so far."

Neither Taylor nor his gut appreciated that assessment. He was about to ask something else but stopped short. "Wait, if you're down here with Quint, then who's in command of the *Osyrys*?"

Billy's response carried a tinge of a smile. "Frank."

"You're kiddin' me," Taylor said. "You left a Yankee Buma chef in charge of my flagship?"

"What can I say?" Billy chuckled. "The birdman stepped up when called upon."

Taylor couldn't lie. The thought of a four-foot-tall Buma from Brooklyn perched high in the *Osyrys*'s captain's chair was a funny one. "Okay, so Frank's got orbit under wraps. What's the story on our ground forces?"

"We've still got Zuul stragglers trying to advance on the mesa, but most of the horde fell back to either their compound or Nyo Colony when our people arrived. Where they go from there is anybody's guess at this point."

"I take it you've got a plan," Taylor said.

"Part of one, anyway," Billy said. "Steeldriver has deployed their forces to the far side of Nyo in case the Zuul try to flee east. The Conquistadors are doing the same from the north."

"You aim to squeeze the Zuul south into the open desert to minimize collateral damage in the colony."

"That's the notion," Billy said. "I've redirected Quint east with Atlantic Company to shore up Carnegie's line. Lieutenant Bishop, meanwhile, is holding down the fort beyond the ridge with Riverside Company until Smitty can resume command."

The Aussie stepped forward in a CASPer of her own, this one a scout class. "Speaking of Bishop, he just radioed in. We've got a secondary pack of Zuul trying to bypass the RFC front. With permission, I'd like to rejoin my company and handle it."

"Permission granted." Taylor stood aside. "Happy huntin', Blue Devil. We'll see ya on the bus ride home."

"Ayew." Smitty bounded down the ramp, fired her suit's jumpjets, and was gone.

"I really do like her," Taylor mused aloud.

"Yeah," Billy said. "I do, too."

Taylor paused as the last of his weapons systems came online. "Billy, I think it's high time we switch things up and play some offense for a change. What do you say?"

"I'd say I'll bring the bats." Billy grinned. "After you, Chief."

*****

Chapter 27: Lockdown

Taylor descended the ramp with Billy and was met at the bottom by three more troopers in CASPers, waiting to accompany them out.

"Sirs, we just got a communique from Commander Furlong over in sector four," the first trooper said in a thick New England accent.

For a second, Taylor thought he was hearing Rex. "And what did Quint have to say—" He glanced to the trooper's name placard. "Chowdahead?"

"He says the majority of the Zuul have been forced out of the colony, but a mob of the mongrels have dug in hard at the compound." Chowdahead grunted. "Apparently, they don't wanna vacate the preemies."

"Shocker," Billy muttered.

"Radio back and tell the commander we're en route to assist," Taylor said. "After that, coordinate with Riverside Company to get us another CASPer squad for support, then meet us back here to roll out."

"You got it." Chowdahead flashed a quick salute, then trotted off with his comrades.

"Looking good there, Chief," Lisa remarked from a nearby boulder.

Taylor turned the reporter's way as she approached. "If I ask you to stay with the ship, will you actually do it this time?"

"Scout's honor." Lisa raised her left palm.

"Wrong hand," Taylor corrected.

Lisa shot him a smirk. "Give 'em hell out there. We'll see you when you get back."

Taylor glanced past her shoulder to see Japhara standing a few feet away. "Same goes for you, Hoss. My people will comp you a ride home when this is over. Until then, stay put here and try not to get shot."

The Sumatozou gave an exaggerated bow. "Believe me, Van Zant, I wouldn't dream of doing otherwise."

Taylor hoped that wasn't sarcasm. He still saw Japhara as a pompous ass, but he didn't wish the alien ill, either.

Chowdahead returned, joined by his two squad mates and five more CASPers.

Lock and load. Taylor spaced out from the crowd with his team in tow. He then checked his HUD controls via pinlink and exploded across the desert in an adrenaline-charged burst of mechanized speed. *Woo!*

"Not bad, eh?" Billy said via comm after a few seconds. "I keep telling you we need to splurge for once and score a few of these for the command staff."

"You know my policy, Husker," Taylor said. "We make the buy with cash or not at all."

"Buzzkill," Billy grumbled.

Taylor throttled up his capacitors to max out his foot speed. The sensation was downright exhilarating—all that power, all that ability—churning in perfect harmony with his body and mind. Granted, this was far from Taylor's first experience with a CASPer. It was, however, his first time in a Mk 8, and if the silky-smooth ease and flawless fluidity with which this model handled was any indication, it was a far cut above the Sevens he was accustomed to piloting.

"Hey, Husker," Taylor called. "You still with me back there?"

A blur of alloy steel blazed past Taylor's flank, fired its jumpjets, and soared eighty feet past a dune, where it landed in perfect stride toward the target.

Damn.

"Sorry, Tomahawk, I didn't catch that last question," Billy said. "Probably because I was too busy smoking your slow-poke ass."

Look at that. The XO's got jokes. Taylor cleared the dune with a thrusted hurdle of his own, then blasted forward to keep up.

"Krulig compound is a quarter mile out," Chowdahead announced with the other troopers. "And by the looks of things, it's a happening place."

Taylor tightened his Tri-V view on the scene ahead. Sure enough, the entire compound was embroiled in weapons fire. Still, neither side—Krulig/Zuul nor Rukori/Human—seemed to be gaining ground on the other.

We've got the firepower, but they've got the numbers. Taylor keyed up his CASPer's weapons systems via pinlink and selected the arm-mounted chain gun from the HUD. After that, he checked his K-bomb count and secondary munitions. "Listen up, y'all. There's no place to hide out here, which means we need to surge through their front as fast as possible before we're pinned out in the open. Watch your lines and stay sharp, then hit 'em fast and early. We'll reform with the others once we've breached the perimeter."

"Ayew," the group chorused.

The checkpoint to the western gate was just ahead. It was also crawling with twenty Zuul, who'd clearly seen the Humans coming. The aliens pulled their rifles, but no launchers.

Score one for the away team. "Husker, these pooches look a little tense to me. What do you say we toss them a few muscle relaxers to loosen them up?"

"I'm a fan," Billy said. "K-bomb launchers are online with targets acquired." Taylor did the same. "In three…two…one…*mark!*"

A concussive wash of heat and light rocked the Zuul front as Taylor and Billy fired their launchers. To their credit, several of the aliens managed to skirt the blast before it hit, but at least six did not. This left the remainder of the pack reeling to recover as all ten CASPers slammed through their line in a tempest of projectiles and laser fire.

"Chief, look out!" Billy shouted.

Taylor wheeled right as a Zuul fired at him with a rifle. He keyed his chain gun and ended the threat with a burst. The next Zuul that attacked did so from close range and down low to negate the CASPer's guns.

Deploy arm blade. Taylor pivoted on one foot and met the alien's charge with a thrust and yank of his right arm. The alien gulped, blood pouring from its chest armor, then crumpled to the sand as two halves instead of a whole form.

"Remaining bandits are bugging out," Chowda announced.

"Chief Van Zant!" a familiar voice shrieked.

Taylor spun toward the source.

Three CASPers bearing the Conquistadors colors were under heavy siege from six more Zuul, the lead mech belonging to Sergeant Fernandez.

"Husker, Chowda!" Taylor yelled. "You're with me!"

The Eagles blasted free of the checkpoint and plowed into the Zuul, decapitating some and obliterating the rest in a flurry of weapon fire. The exchange ended with a loud *shing* courtesy of Chowda's arm blade as it plunged through the final attacker's chest.

"Dez, you okay?" Billy rushed to the sergeant's side.

"Si, I think so." Dez got to his feet, breathing heavily. "It's a good thing you fellas got here when you did."

Taylor frowned at a fourth CASPer lying motionless on the ground, its shell missing a canopy and its operator missing a face. "Our timin' could've been better."

"Could've been worse, too," Dez said. "It's good to see you."

"What's the status of your people?" Billy asked.

"Per our last comm check, Commander Garcia had taken most of Brahma Company east to take out the Zuul armory," Dez said. "Everyone else headed north toward the capacitor relay station to knock out the enemy's infrastructure."

"Are those the hottest two areas?" Billy asked.

"Si, for now," Dez said.

Taylor looked around, finding nothing but Zuul corpses littering the compound. "Where are all of the Krulig?"

"You got me," Dez said. "Based on the description Captain Dawson gave us, I've yet to see one. And I've crossed this place twice already."

Taylor traded looks with his XO.

"Excuse me for a moment." Dez turned aside, as if receiving a communique through is pinlink. "Entiendo. En camino."

Taylor knew just enough Spanish to get that Dez had just received new orders. "What's up?"

"Brahma got lit up pretty bad off the drop and is taking heavy fire," Dez said. "My squad and I are being rerouted to assist."

Taylor studied the armor of Dez and his people, tattered as it was. He then turned to one of his own troopers. "Lady Jade."

The Eagle CASPer stepped forward.

"Me and Husker are gonna head north for that power station.," Taylor said. "Take five of our people and go east with Dez to help out Brahma Company. I'll put in a call to Blue Devil about gettin' you some extra hands."

"Aye, sir." Jade flashed a salute.

"Gracious, Amigo," Dez said. "Really."

Taylor scoffed. "You're the one who left behind a stack of Union contract cash to come here and bail me out of the pot, remember? This is the least I can do. Now go."

Dez and Jade took off across the yard with five of the Eagles' CASPers. That left Taylor, Billy, Chowda, and a trooper called Razorback to press onward. Slowly, the group worked their way north, each CASPer covering a partner as the quartet crisscrossed their way from strip to strip and corner to corner. As expected, the Zuul were everywhere. They came from the streets. They bounded off catwalks and out of buildings, attacking with teeth bared and weapons primed, but never once alone. They fought with the same ferocious pack mentality that had come to define the species. Still, the CASPers pressed on.

A K-bomb detonated on a building ahead of them, stopping the group in their tracks.

"What have we got?" Chowda called.

Engines revved in the distance as Taylor stuck his head out. "One armed transport, inbound."

"This one's mine." Razorback strode forward to the center of the street. There, he squared himself and presented the heavy Magnetic Accelerator Cannon, or MAC, which was mounted to his left shoulder. "This here's how we get shit done in Pine Country."

The MAC fired, slamming the hauler and its occupants fireballing into an adjacent wall. No one survived.

"Tomahawk, this is Bulldog," Quint called via comm. "I need a copy, and I need it right away."

"Go for Tomahawk and Husker." Taylor re-opened his party line.

"What's your position?" Quint asked.

"Just down from the northern checkpoint, headed for the Krulig capacitor station," Taylor said. "You?"

"Over by the lord prefect's residence," Quint said.

Taylor clenched his teeth. "Bulldog, please tell me you've got eyes on Sadeed."

"Negative, Tomahawk," Quint said. "In fact, we've yet to see a single Krulig anywhere on the premises."

Taylor couldn't get past that.

"What we *do* have," Quint continued, "is a horde of new Zuul piling in from the southeast by way of Bartahl Colony."

"The Zuul called in the cavalry," Billy surmised.

"Looks like it, yeah," Quint said. "They've paired up the Zuul remnants of Nyo and are preparing to surge back toward the urban population."

Taylor barked a curse.

"Oh, it gets better," Quint said. "We just detected a major power spike somewhere near the landing field south of the compound."

Taylor snapped his head up. "Let me guess. Your neutron readin' is off the charts."

"How'd you know?" Quint asked.

Taylor faced his XO. "The ship that attacked you at the stargate, it's a Krulig frigate. Sadeed keeps it stashed in an old Rukori catacomb beneath his compound."

"That scaly prick's looking to run for it," Billy said.

"And he's takin' his prick brothers with him," Taylor finished.

"I don't get it," Chowda said. "If this creep bails, he's leaving a ton of his own people behind."

"Don't matter," Taylor said. "Sadeed knows the Rukori can't defend themselves after we leave. Not in their current state, anyway. He also knows we don't have the resources to garrison this place long-term."

Billy muttered a curse. "Run today, live to occupy another day."

"Bingo," Taylor said.

"What do you want us to do, Boss?" Quint asked.

Taylor chewed his lip. "Rally everybody you can—Eagles, Conquistadors, whoever—then head south of Nyo and do what you can to stifle that Zuul surge. Husker and me will stop the frigate."

"Ayew," Quint said. "Good hunting, Tomahawk."

"Same to you, Bulldog. Tomahawk out." Taylor signaled his team out by way of a nearby alley, then shifted comm channels as he fell in behind them. "*Ryley Osyrys*, this is Tomahawk. You copy?"

A beat passed before Frank answered the call. "*Osyrys* copies, Tomahawk. We're glad to hear your voice."

"Likewise," Taylor said. "What's our situation in orbit?"

"As of five minutes ago, we've whittled the enemy force down to two frigates," Frank said. "The *Bradshaw* and the *Valiente* have both on the run as we speak. Everything else, including that *Behemoth*, now comprises a new scrapyard out here in the black."

"What's your position?" Taylor asked.

"Just parked in geosync orbit," Frank said. "Why?"

"I need a sensor sweep of the area just south of my current location," Taylor said. "There's a ship about to launch from there, and I need an access point to get down to her so we can keep her grounded."

"Stand by," Frank said.

Taylor charged onward as Billy and Chowda closed ranks ahead. Three Zuul had leapt out of nowhere and took aim on the CASPers with their rifles. The latter answered with a quick *zip* from their chain guns, reducing the aliens to puddles in their path.

"Okay, I'm back," Frank said. "I got good news and bad news. The good news is you no longer need to worry about that access point."

"And the bad news?" Billy asked.

"The entrance to that catacomb just spiraled open," Frank said. "Based off the readings I've got here, I expect that ship to be airborne in the next five minutes."

Taylor was really beginning to dislike this day. "Fine, we'll make do as best we can. In the meantime, take the *Osyrys* back to the stargate and be ready to head Sadeed off at the pass if he gets by us."

"Ayew," Frank said. "We'll check back later to pick you fellas up. *Osyrys* out."

Taylor accelerated toward the southern checkpoint, the high-pitched hum of maxed-out RPMs singing in his ears. There were eight Zuul guarding the gate. *Key HUD, access munitions.* His chain gun ammo was running low, same for his K-bomb inventory. He also didn't want to burn the power needed to discharge his MAC, as he'd doubtless need the juice once they intercepted the Krulig frigate. That left two options: his arm blade and the laser carbine that was clamped to his CASPer's leg.

Old school it is. Taylor pulled the latter.

Once through the checkpoint, the group tore off through the open terrain and reached the edge of the landing field to find its center spiraled open, exposing a gaping pit below.

"That's him!" Taylor pointed to the vessel on the docking pad.

Sporting a smallish stature at roughly ninety yards long by seven high, the vessel featured a bullet-like shape with its cigar-tube fuselage, pointed nose, and trimmed-out torch section.

"Payback time." Billy took aim at once.

Shelling out round after round, the four CASPers unloaded on the frigate's outer hull with a barrage of weapons fire, but to no avail.

A series of mechanized *clack*s rang out when the vessel's mooring clamps released.

Ah, screw this. Taylor keyed up his MAC and sighted in.

A mushroom of sand and fire rocked the ground at Taylor's feet, blowing him forward and flipping him head-first into the pit.

"*Chief!*" Billy scrambled down after his CO, shoulder weapons primed and carbine drawn. Chowda went next, followed closely by Razorback. The CASPers met immediate resistance upon touching down as wave after wave of Zuul poured from the connecting tunnels into the chamber.

"I thought we'd run most of these things out of town!" Chowda shouted past the butt of his carbine.

"That makes two of us!" Razor agreed. The duo popped a pair of their K-bombs and hurled them down the nearest opening. A colossal *boom* ensued, but the Zuul kept coming.

"Chowda, look out!" Razor yelled.

Before the New Englander could react, three Zuul rammed his shins, while two more hammered him in the back, toppling him over. A cascade of sparks ensued when two Zuul teed off on Chowda with their rifles. "Hang on!" Razor pinged one with a headshot, while Billy ran the other off with a hit to its chest armor. The latter yelped and darted for cover in the tunnel.

"Thanks, gentlemen," Chowda said, panting, as all save the ship went quiet.

"Don't mention it," Billy said. "For a minute there, I thought we were—"

A round exploded on the XO's chest, blowing him across the pit amid a plume of smoke and fire.

"Billy!" Taylor screamed.

A new horde of Zuul poured from the north corridor and leapt at the XO.

Taylor shouldered his carbine but couldn't get a shot. A loud *thump* shoved him forward from behind. It was followed by another and another until eventually he, too, and been knocked off balance. He struggled to a knee, but was met again with weapon fire from three more Zuul. They hit him again, and again, and again.

"Armor integrity at thirty-two percent," the HUD read. "Thirty percent."

A chorus of screaming aliens, shrieking instruments, and raging weapons fire filled Taylor's ears, turning the world to madness. "*Billy!*"

A massive explosion rocked the scene, catching the Zuul off guard.

That was Taylor's cue. He surged to his feet, ripped the remaining aliens from his back, and smashed them skull-first into the closest rock wall he could find.

"Hell yeah!" Chowda whooped.

Five CASPers leapt down from the ledge and tore into the horde, led by someone in a scout suit.

Smitty.

The Aussie's sword blade cut left as she touched own, sheering a Zuul in half, then she unloaded on three more with her carbine.

A gust of wind swept the chamber. The Krulig frigate was lifting off.

"Stop that bloody ship!" Smitty yelled.

Taylor was all too happy to oblige. He strode forward, keyed his HUD, and went straight for the big gun.

"MAC controls online," the HUD read. "Firing solution acquired."

The charge indicator flashed from red to orange, then a second later, to the world's most glorious shade of green.

"Hey, Asshole!" Taylor shouted. "If you're gonna crash a party, *crash* a party!"

A bone-jarring thunderclap erupted from the cannon's barrel, sending the Mach 8 round slamming with a vengeance through the vessel's portside armor. The frigate bucked hard, exhaust vents billowing smoke and debris.

Taylor waited for the system to reload, but, before he could fire again, the Krulig ship throttled down its thrusters and settled back onto its platform.

Suddenly, all went silent.

Taylor didn't have to look behind him to know what that meant. *Busted.* He turned slowly to see no less than a hundred Zuul surrounding his people, all armed and poised to fire at the first command. *Damnit.*

A flurry of electronic gears whined into motion from the ship, followed by the eerie hiss of decompressing air.

Taylor knew what that meant, also. *Time for another chat with the man.*

The frigate's boarding ramp lowered, and Yolik Sadeed stepped out. "Chief Van Zant."

"Lord Prefect," Taylor answered. "Fancy meetin' you here."

The Krulig smirked then glanced to his minions. "Take them."

*****

Chapter 28: Birthright

Taylor dropped his carbine and powered down his CASPer's weapons as the Zuul horde parted, clearing a path to the others. Billy was there, trashed armor and all. It was the same for Chowda, Smitty, and the rest of the commander's crew from Riverside Company. There was, however, one notable absence.

Razorback. Taylor peered around the chamber but found no sign of the trooper. Then, slowly, another pack of Zuul parted near the back of the cavern. A ravaged CASPer lay face-up in the dirt, its canopy torn open and its cockpit stained bright red. Nothing moved, not the mech itself, nor the operator inside—what remained of him, anyway. *Damn.*

"I must say, Chief Van Zant," Sadeed announced. "I didn't expect we'd meet again, you and I."

"I'm happy to disappoint." Taylor keyed his comm, then issued what he hoped wouldn't be his last mental command as an Eagle. "Keep your ears on, y'all."

New footfalls sounded from up the ramp when Tulips emerged to join his boss on the ground.

"Drewga," Taylor said. "Just so you know, I ain't forgot about that promise I made you back in the residence."

The Zuul offered a razor-toothed grin. "I welcome your attempt to keep it."

"All in good time." Taylor glanced back to the ship as dozens of Krulig filed into view. "So that's it then. You and your fellow iguana pals were just gonna light out and leave the Zuul to fend for themselves."

"Not at all," Sadeed said. "I had every intention of returning to Rukoria once your Human friends had transitioned back to Earth. In the interim, the Zuul were to maintain my interests here in keeping with the rider I just negotiated on their contract."

Taylor whistled. "Man, I'd hate to know what that set you back."

"Funding wasn't an issue," Sadeed said.

"See, that's what I don't get." Taylor said. "Why put yourself through all this hassle for a payday when it's clear you've already got money? Cut bait and go."

"Humans. Always so short-sighted." Sadeed turned to the drewga. "I must see about our repairs. Kill them and let's be on our way."

"Hang on." Taylor raised a palm. "Ain't you gonna answer my question?"

Sadeed exhaled. "Why would I ever care to do such a thing?"

"Easy. You're all about bein' candid and forthright, remember? Or was that just a line of crap you fed me durin' my interrogation?" Taylor waved off his previous statement. "You know what? Never mind. Something just occurred to me. It's the new gate masters who hold honor in high regard, not the flunkies they replaced."

Billy raised an eyebrow.

"Tell ya later," Taylor noted via pinlink.

"Interesting," Sadeed said quizzically. "For all his years in custody, Japhara has never once spoken to another being, let alone a Human. And yet obviously he opened up to you. Why?"

"Reckon I'm just personable that way," Taylor said.

Sadeed's crimson gaze narrowed. "Fine. Seeing as how I have time while our crews tend to my frigate, I shall indulge your curiosities."

Atta boy. Taylor checked his HUD for new surface movement.

"The Heads of the Cartography Guild are among the richest beings in the Galactic Union," Sadeed said, "far more than most know. Their wealth and power exceed that of even the Union's oldest citizens. And yet they keep it all to themselves, offering little more than table scraps to their constituents. They are as greedy as they are arrogant."

"Clearly my brother never told you the one about the pot and the kettle," Taylor said.

"Make your jokes, Human," Sadeed said. "Neither you nor the Rukori can fathom what my people sacrificed in the name of societal progress. In the aftermath of the Great War, peace returned to the galaxy, but it was an empty peace. Everyone knew the challenges facing them with life under the new government, and so began the arms race to see which of the surviving species could thrive in the new system. Our lords, the new gate keepers, were at the forefront of that struggle. Many sought their knowledge of hyperspace, yet for all their would-be allies, it was my ancestors who stood at their sides until order could rise from chaos."

"Order in the form of the Guilds," Taylor said.

"Correct," Sadeed said. "The Cartography Guild as we know it today would not exist without the Krulig. We stood with the Guild

Heads after its formation. We forged its alliances, spilled blood for its causes. We kept our lords' secrets in ways no one else could, and for what? So the fruits of our labors could be handed off to those self-righteous sycophants, the Sumatozou?" He snorted. "The thought repulses me."

"To hear Japhara tell it, the Krulig had no one to blame for their downfall but themselves," Taylor said. "You preach about greed and corruption, but it was your people, not his, who stole from the Guild and got caught."

Sadeed scoffed. "What you call theft others would call justice."

"Potato, potahto," Taylor replied.

"The ancient Krulig never expected equality with the Guild Heads," Sadeed said. "They only wanted what was due them for their service. When our lords wouldn't give that, they opted to take what was rightfully theirs."

Taylor cocked his head. "This all seems pretty personal. If I didn't know better, I'd say you were there for these events."

"Don't be stupid." Sadeed huffed. "It was my generation who paid the price for the Guild's betrayal, as did the one before ours and the hundreds before them. We are the offspring of our forefathers' death sentence, destined to roam the cosmos like animals for the last five thousand years, while our rivals, the Sumatozou, suckle at the teat of our birthright."

Taylor rolled his eyes. "Oh, cry me a river."

"Excuse me?"

"Your ancestors crossed the Guild and got run off their soil." Taylor flipped up a hand. "Shit happens, man. Nut up already and go settle a new homeworld like the Rukori did."

Sadeed's gaze became a glower. "The Guild Heads weren't content to merely strip us of our homeworld. They continued hunting us, pushing us deeper and deeper into the furthest reaches of space until there were scarcely enough of us left to populate a moon." He gestured to his kin. "Look around. The community you see here represents the largest gathering of Krulig in one place in more than a thousand years. *I* made that community a reality, Human, and I alone bear the responsibility of preserving it."

Taylor checked his HUD. *Still nothin'.* "So tell me then, Alien Moses. Why build your promised land here? Surely there were other worlds you could've chosen."

"Who says we aren't exploiting those as well?" Sadeed asked slyly.

Taylor gnawed his lip. "Question stands. Why Rukoria?"

"As you observed in my office, I am quite fond of antiquities," Sadeed said, "especially those which provide insights into my enemies. One such item is an ancient Krulig data archive I acquired during my travels to find the others. It's a journal, really, kept by one of the first gate masters. It chronicles life from his perspective into the burgeoning Union as the Guilds were taking root."

"I take it Valawn's people were referenced in this journal," Taylor said.

Sadeed nodded. "The Rukori were traitors. They fought and died versus the Canavar, sure, but so did scores of other species, my own included. Everyone gave, only when the time came to rebuild, the Rukori leveraged their ties to the past and left the other races to pick up the pieces."

"Hadn't they earned that?" Taylor asked. "I mean, they were among the Republic's oldest members. That implies they paid a lot of dues that others didn't have to."

"Some might agree with that logic," Sadeed said. "I, however, would not. The Rukori abandoned the Union when it needed them most. Thus, you can imagine my delight when, of all the worlds the NOP list could've yielded, the Rukori's lost homeworld was among them."

Taylor leaned in. "Then why not come down here and face them yourself? Why puss out like a fargin coward and send a plague to do your dirty work?"

Sadeed's scaly expression turned sideways. "Well now. That is intriguing. Japhara knows nothing of our work with the Winter Death. How is it that you do?"

"Honestly?" Taylor stood back. "I didn't until just now. Thanks for the confirmation."

Sadeed's lips formed a line.

"So, how'd you do it?" Taylor asked.

"The Rukori immune system is quite resilient," Sadeed said. "Still, like those of most other species, it can only defend against those agents it recognizes from its natural environment. Introduce something foreign to that environment—a common virus from another world, for instance—and the potential exists to completely upset the balance."

"You mean bring the Rukori to their knees," Taylor added.

"Potato, potahto." Sadeed replied with a grin.

"That still doesn't explain how you deployed this virus," Smitty said. "You'd have had to come here via hyperspace like the rest of us, yeah? That means the Rukori should've spotted you at the emergence point."

Sadeed clicked his tongue. "You forget your hyperspace physics, Commander. Spectrally speaking, there is no advanced warning given when a starship emerges from hyperspace. There is only the signature of one's engines to denote his presence—engines which, if rendered inactive, leave nothing to detect this far out from the sensor source."

Billy stepped forward. "You entered hyperspace at full thrust through a stargate, then killed your engines upon emergence and coasted in dark."

Sadeed's smile widened. "Who says we used a stargate?"

Taylor's eyes went straight to the frigate. *That ship has a hyperspace shunt.*

"Pardon me, Lord Prefect," a Krulig called from the interior of the ship. "Engineering reports that repairs are almost finished. We should be ready to depart shortly."

"Excellent." Sadeed turned back to his hostages. "Now, if you'll excuse me, I really do have places to leave. Drewga Tulipza."

"Yes, Lord Prefect."

"Kill these Humans immediately, then meet me on the bridge."

Taylor's pulse began to race as the legion of armed Zuul closed ranks on the CASPers.

"Make ready!" Tulips raised his arm. "Aim!"

"Howdy, folks!" someone called from above.

All eyes including Sadeed's turned skyward.

"Can somebody direct me to the Maître D'?" Jack asked from the ledge. "Me and my friends here are outta towels, and frankly this place is kind of a shithole."

The friends in question were Stan, Quint, Valawn, and a crapload of Rukori—all armed. The crazy thing was, of all the aliens in attendance, only a handful were RFC. The rest were civilians.

"Hey, Valawn." Taylor keyed off his comm, ending the broadcast. "I take it Jack patched you in to my call like I asked."

"He did," Valawn said. "As you can see, there were many among my countrymen who found the prefect's words…illuminating."

Tulips dropped onto all fours. "Kill them all!"

A torrent of weapon fire filled the chamber, sending Taylor lunging for cover as Sadeed and Tulips broke for an adjacent corridor.

"Where you headed?" Billy shouted.

"After Sadeed," Taylor yelled back. "This ends today."

Billy opened a party line via pinlink. "Chowda, stay here with Riverside and batten down the hatches versus the Zuul. Blue Devil, you're with me and Tomahawk."

"Ayew!" the troopers said.

Once through the exit, Taylor sprinted down the corridor and arrived at a junction with passages to the left and right. *Which way?* He keyed his HUD and switched to thermal. Several heat signatures were active around him, but one in particular was headed away at a high rate of speed. *Tulips.*

Taylor darted left in pursuit, then took off down the tunnel with the others hot on his heels. Two Zuul leapt out to block them, but Taylor cut them down with his carbine. The next pair met the same fate, as did the pair after that, the pair after that, and finally the trio that tried to block their exit from the catacombs.

Almost there. Taylor bounded up the ramp into open daylight and skidded to a halt outside. "Where is he?"

Billy looked around. "There!"

A Maki shuttle was just landing to the east of their position. Tulips was almost to the hatch, as was Sadeed.

Oh, hell no. Taylor keyed his MAC and took aim.

"Firing solution acquired," the HUD read.

The round exploded from the cannon and tore into the shuttle. The craft pitched forward and nose-dived into the desert, where it burst into flames.

"Stay!" Taylor shouted to the aliens.

Sadeed followed the order and froze.

Tulips, however, in keeping with his hotheaded nature, did not. The Zuul spun on his haunches, teeth bared, then charged forward with a rifle in one hand and a K-bomb in the other.

"I said, *stay!*"

This time, the drewga obeyed, not because he meant to, but rather because the round from Taylor's carbine sheared off half of his face.

The Zuul toppled over, surprisingly still conscious, and lay sprawled in the sand like a pretzel.

Taylor marched over and deployed his arm blade, its stainless-steel edge glinting in the sunlight. "Terry Van Zant sends his regards."

The alien choked and gurgled a protest. They were the last sounds of his life.

"So," Sadeed said snidely. "Where then do we ever go from here?"

Taylor was done talking. He keyed up his chain guns, squared his shoulders, and took aim.

"Wait!" a new voice shouted.

*****

Chapter 29: Showdown

Taylor turned to see Japhara Hylune walking toward them, holding the corpse of a slain Zuul in his right hand. "I thought you couldn't dream of leavin' the dropship."

"Dreaming of something and physically doing it are two entirely different things." Japhara tossed the thing aside and glared at the Krulig prefect. "Van Zant, I realize it is I who am in debt to you. That gives me no right to ask for anything. Nevertheless, you now know what it means to avenge your family's honor. I would humbly ask, therefore, that you allow me this chance to avenge mine."

Taylor studied the alien for a long moment. He didn't like Sumatozou. He never had. As Union species went, they were arrogant, prejudiced, and as self-righteous as it got. Even still, in that instant, and given everything that had transpired, he felt obliged to honor the request of this one. "Billy, Smitty. Stand down."

"Sir?" Billy's voice trailed upward. "You sure about that?"

"Yeah, I am." Taylor faced his cellmate and stepped back. "Do what you have to. We'll hold the area and make sure he doesn't try to weasel out."

Japhara bowed his head. "Thank you."

"Good luck, Hoss." Taylor took his place at a corner of the battlefield while Billy and Smitty did the same, creating a loose triangle.

At the space's center, both aliens took their marks in preparation for a species' conflict more than five thousand years in the making.

"I must commend you, Japhara." Sadeed began to circle. "I would've never believed in all the time we've known each other that you had this kind of spine. It's certainly not commonplace among your kind."

"There is much about the Sumatozou that you do not understand, Krulig," Japhara said. "You never did. Now you never will."

With that, the pair charged to center ground.

"Kick his ass, Japhara!" Taylor shouted.

The Sumatozou fired in with a punch, but the blow sailed wide when Sadeed ducked clear of the shot. Japhara followed with a right, a left, then another right, each fist pummeling the air like a bomb, only to fly astray as the nimble Krulig shifted and whirled away. As the exchange wore on, the Sumatozou's breathing turned increasingly laborious.

"What's the matter, Slave," Sadeed taunted. "Has fourteen years in captivity deprived you of your skills to fight? Where's that spirit of yours?"

Japhara leapt upright and roared toward his adversary.

"Don't let him bait you!" Taylor's warning came too late.

In a swift, even motion that was as fluid as it was easy, Sadeed sidestepped the Sumatozou's charge, then pirouetted on a heel to land a brutal, claws-out slash to Japhara's face.

The big alien screamed though a crimson mist.

"Pathetic." Seizing on the window, Sadeed closed in tight and unloaded a ferocious volley of claws-out strikes to his opponent's head and shoulders.

Japhara threw up his hands to block, but all that did was open his abdomen to attack. Over and over, Sadeed tore into the Sumatozou's flesh, all the while staying as close as possible to neutralize the Sumatozou's size advantage. Soon, Japhara's midsection began to resemble raw hamburger meat, but the Krulig kept at it.

"Say the word, and we'll end this!" Taylor shouldered his carbine.

"You will not," Japhara barked. "This is *my* fight. I will decide its ending." With that, the Sumatozou bowed up and slammed a bone-jarring smash to the Krulig's ribcage.

The latter shrieked and backpedaled, visibly shaken.

"You were saying about my spirit?" Japhara growled.

Sadeed answered with a sneer, then reacquired his stance.

Back and forth the two aliens battered each other, the Sumatozou relying on brute strength and blunt-force power to deliver his punishment, while the Krulig leaned on elusiveness and cunning. Each fighter did his fair share of damage as the bout continued. However, it was the Krulig who eventually regained the upper hand.

Leveraging his superior footwork, Sadeed slipped right past a hook, then left past a cross, then lunged forward as a breathless Japhara wheeled awkwardly to recover. It wasn't enough.

A howl of agony pierced the air amid a geyser of red from Japhara's side. The Sumatozou crumpled to the ground, unable to move.

"Your species was always inferior to ours," Sadeed said, panting. "That's why we were chosen for the mantle of gate master, while you were merely appointed. The Sumatozou should never have been held that status. *Never.* You're not worthy. The fact that you were serves only to demonstrate the truth."

"And what truth is that?" Japhara scoffed from his back.

Sadeed flashed a twisted grin. "That the Vergola, for all their supposed knowledge and wisdom, are no more capable of running hyperspace today than they were twenty thousand years ago."

What? Taylor had barely thought the word when Sadeed kicked a toe into the sand, launching a Zuul battle blade into his scaly palm.

"The hour has come for you to meet your afterlife, Sumatozou." Sadeed squeezed the weapon's hilt and charged. "Goodbye."

"Japhara!" Taylor disconnected his arm blade and lobbed it to the Sumatozou.

Japhara caught the weapon and spun.

"I..." Sadeed staggered back, eyes bulging in disbelief. He gulped, gulped again, then gradually turned his focus to the steel object protruding from his gut.

"Now, Lord Prefect, allow me to impress upon you a *new* truth." Japhara relinquished his hold on the weapon and eased to his feet. "The Krulig are done for. When the Guild Heads learn of your treachery here, they will hunt down the last of your wretched kind and finish what they started. None of you will survive. Is that clear? Not one. I will see to that personally. By the time we're done, neither you nor your legacy will merit even a footnote in the annals of Union history."

Sadeed half smiled, his words coming in a dull rasp through blood-stained lips. "Remember this moment, Humans. Remember it well. For the next time the Council targets a race for extinction, it may well be yours."

"Newsflash, Asshat," Taylor said. "Things have changed since your time in exile. There is no Council anymore, Vergola or otherwise. Those factions died out eons ago with the rise of the Guilds, which are run by the collective. That includes the Cartography Guild."

Sadeed managed a laugh before fluids from his mouth caused him to choke. "You ignorant ape. The Vergola Council *is* the Cartography Guild! They always have been! Don't you see? They never—"

Japhara snatched the arm blade from Sadeed's body and, in a single, fluid stroke, sheared off the prefect's head with it.

No one said a word.

"Did I just hear that right?" Billy asked via pinlink. "The entire Cartography Guild—and with it every tie the Union has to hyperspace—rests squarely under the control of one ancient species?"

Taylor was still too stunned to answer.

"The whole point of the Guilds was ostensibly to create a balance of powers rather than one all-powerful centralized group as it was with the First Republic," Smitty said. "If what Sadeed said is true, this violates everything the Galactic Union stands for."

"I know you're speaking to each other via pinlink." Japhara spiked the blade into the ground and faced the CASPers. "I can assure you, it is not necessary."

Taylor swallowed. "So it's true then. The Vergola Council is still alive and in control of the Cartography Guild."

The Sumatozou peered out at the horizon.

"Answer me, Japhara," Taylor pressed.

The alien bellowed a sigh. "The Vergola Council has presided over hyperspace since the dawn of our civilization. Lest we forget, it was they who discovered the stargates to begin with, and thus it is they who have fostered an understanding of that realm unmatched by anyone else in society."

"That still don't make this right," Taylor said.

"Perhaps," Japhara said. "But ask yourselves two simple questions. One: what species throughout history has ever willingly relinquished that kind of power? Two: if they did, who among us is honestly more qualified than the Council to wield it? Humans? Sumatozou? Krulig?" He leaned in. "The Zuul?"

Taylor shuddered, his thoughts returning to Japhara's warning from their cell.

"There are things in the galaxy that no one in the Union is prepared for," Japhara had said. "Old things, dark things. Things that would tear your civilizations to shreds if unleashed on your soil."

Is he right?

Japhara straightened to face the others. "Hear me, all of you. If you value the lives of your friends, your crew, and your families—to say nothing of your own—you will forget what was said here today and never speak of it again."

"Is that a threat?" Billy asked.

"No." Japhara glanced to Taylor. "It is merely a word of advice from one captive who does not wish to see harm befall another."

The group nodded as footfalls sounded behind them.

"Is everyone all right?" Valawn trotted out of the catacombs to join them.

"We're fine," Taylor said. "What's the status on the Rukori?"

"A bit confused given the revelations of your transmission, but I expect we'll manage in time." Valawn halted next to Smitty. "Word of Sadeed's betrayal is already spreading through the other colonies. Our people now know beyond any shadow of a doubt that the Krulig were responsible for the Winter Death. That's all because of you."

Taylor shook his head. "We told you we'd bring help, no more no less. Captain Dawson here did that. You folks did the rest."

"Indeed," Valawn said. "You're a man of your word, Chief Van Zant, just like your brother. Rukoria owes the Eagles a great debt of gratitude."

Billy stepped aside as if fielding a call. "Copy that, Jack. Round up the prisoners and have them escorted into the Krulig holding areas. We'll figure out what to do with them from there. Husker out." He turned to Taylor. "The last of the Zuul are laying down their arms, as are the Krulig from Sadeed's ship."

"What about those last two frigates in orbit?" Taylor asked.

"Surrendered five minutes ago," Billy said. "Same for the stargate crews. Carnegie and Cortes are on their way down now to discuss the return trip home."

"I presume you can help us with that?" Smitty asked Japhara.

The Sumatozou grinned. "I wouldn't dream of doing otherwise."

Now free to do so, Taylor blew out a sigh for the ages and turned his attention to the magnificent western sky. *It's over.*

*****

Chapter 30: Beer Snobs

The Humans remained on Rukoria for the next three days to repair their ships and divvy up the spoils, including the two Maki frigates and Sadeed's frigate.

Like everyone else, Taylor's focus had been on the Krulig ship for its hyperspace shunt. What he couldn't have known prior to signing over the frigates as payment to the other companies was that Sadeed had apparently anticipated this and rigged his frigate to blow when a non-Krulig tried to access its systems. It had detonated spectacularly.

Taylor drank a lot of Long Branch Light that evening.

By the time the fourth day arrived, Taylor couldn't wait to get on the road. He said his final goodbyes to Valawn and the Rukori, then boarded his dropship for the *Osyrys* to set sail for the stargate. He'd just settled into a book and a cold beer when a knock came from outside his cabin. "Come in."

The door slid open, and the XO coasted in.

"Hey, Billy, what's up?" Taylor asked from his bunk.

"Not much." Billy handed over a slate. "I figured you'd wanna know that we've cleared transition without issue, and Keeto's got us firing on all cylinders toward home."

"Good deal." Taylor paused before continuing. Historically, he'd dreaded hyperspace transitions. This time, he'd practically slept through it. *Huh, I'll be damned.* "Did Carnegie and Cortes make it offworld okay?"

"Yeah, they transitioned just ahead of us," Billy said. "Hey, did Carnegie seem a little off to you?"

"How do you mean?" Taylor asked.

"I don't know." Billy scratched his head. "He's just typically a lot more personable than that. He came. He did his job. He took his ships and left. The end."

Taylor considered the XO's point. "Ron's been retired for what, almost a decade? I won't begrudge the man a little rust on his first return trip to the black. Besides, I'm just glad he came."

"Amen to that," Billy said.

Taylor gestured at his mini-fridge. "What are the odds I can tempt you with a drink while you're here?"

"Of that swill?" Billy pointed to Taylor's bulb, filled with Long Branch. "No way in hell."

"Beer snob," Taylor muttered.

"Redneck," Billy answered.

Taylor grinned and straightened. "So, what's on your docket for the night?"

"Eh, not much," Billy said. "I've got a few odds and ends yet to finish on the bridge. After that, I figured I'd head down to the mess for chow. Rumor has it Frank's cooking up some Spanish paella for dinner."

"Have I thanked you lately for hirin' that guy?" Taylor asked. "Buma or not, it really is cool to have a proper cook around here."

"And he can fly a spaceship, too," Billy noted. "You up for a bite later?"

"Nah, I ate a late lunch," Taylor said. "I know somebody who might be, though."

Billy smirked, then pivoted for the exit. "And on that note, I'll leave you to—"

"Park it, Captain." Taylor pointed to the chair beside his table.

Billy exhaled and pulled himself down onto a seat. "So now we come to it, huh? The conversation?"

"Seemed like a good idea a second ago," Taylor said.

"With all due respect, Chief, Smitty and I are just—"

"If the next word out of your pie hole is friends, I swear on the ghost of Osceola I'll punch you straight in your Nebraskan junk."

The XO blinked. "Wow. Subtle."

"Listen, Billy, I get it. You and Smitty are ex-navy, and the military tends to frown on two people from the same command staff gettin' involved. It makes sense." Taylor leaned in. "There's just one issue. You ain't in the navy anymore."

"Yeah, but—"

"Not done." Taylor raised a finger. "Smitty's a great girl. She's loyal, honest, and a straight-up badass under fire. More than that, though, she *gets* you. She gets your nature. She gets your history. She even gets your dry-ass sense of humor on those rarest of occasions when you bother to let it out."

The XO dropped his gaze.

"Billy, if I've learned anything in the last half-decade, it's that tomorrow ain't promised to anybody, especially folks in our line of work. If you find somebody you can do life with, you do not, under any circumstances, pass on that. You seize it with both hands and run like the wind. Problem for you is, that requires trust." Taylor hunched forward and put his elbows on his knees. "I get why that don't come easy for you, Brother, probably better than most. Hell, I'd likely be the same way had my engagement ended the way yours did. Still, there comes a time when a man's gotta decide whether to live his life through the windshield or the rearview mirror, because when all is said and done, those are the only two options he's got. Now what's it gonna be?"

Billy sat there for a long moment, staring off into nothing. Eventually, his silence gave way to a chuckle. "When did you get to be so wise?"

Taylor shrugged. "What can I say? Zuul interrogations have a way of bringin' a man clarity."

"Looks like it." Billy pushed himself airborne from the chair.

"So are you gonna make a play or not?" Taylor asked.

"I'll think about it." Billy drummed his fingers on the seat back. "You know, there's still one aspect of all this that I can't seem to wrap my brain around."

"Yeah? What's that?"

"Terry."

Taylor cocked his head. "What about him?"

"Why would he do all this? Don't get me wrong. For all his faults, your brother was a good guy at heart. His work back home in the Jax community speaks to that. At the end of the day, though, Terry Van Zant was merc, which is to say he sought the same two things as the rest of us—to kill aliens and get paid."

Taylor scratched his chin. "What's your point?"

"Why would Terry jeopardize everything we built with the Eagles to join an insurrection with no chance of a payday? Conscience or not, it doesn't add up."

Taylor chewed his lip and looked his XO straight in the eye. "If I had to guess…I'd say Terry felt like he needed to make amends for something."

Billy wrinkled his nose. Then, slowly, realization set in.

"Well, would you look at that?" Taylor opened his fridge and peered inside. "I'm almost out of beer. That's downright criminal, if you ask me. Reckon I'll head to the galley for a reload."

"You want some company?" Billy asked.

"Nah, that's okay," Taylor said. "I've gotta pit stop past guest quarters on my way down anyway."

"Guest quarters?" Billy arched an eyebrow. "Who do you need to see down there?"

Taylor pushed off for the door. "Somebody who owes me a favor."

*****

Chapter 31: Behind the Curtain

This time when the Eagles reemerged from hyperspace, they did so at the precise coordinates they'd meant to upon entering the Rukoria stargate.

"EMS *Ryley Osyrys*, this is Earth Control," a voice said through the bridge speakers. "Please proceed on your current heading, and welcome home."

A chorus of whoops went out around the crew as everyone was understandably thrilled to see their journey end—everyone, that was, except for Taylor. His journey had a ways to go yet.

For the next six weeks, Taylor did everything he could to keep his mind preoccupied and away from the encounter that lay ahead. He conducted CASPer drills on the Eagles' firing range with Billy. He went to Happy Hour with Jack and Stan at the Hell House. He even re-read his entire collection of old Louis L'Amour books, short stories included.

Eventually, the time for waiting came to a close, and Taylor, for one, couldn't have been happier—or more nervous.

"I still cannot believe I'm doing this," Japhara muttered as Taylor crossed the tarmac toward their shuttle on the Eagles' campus.

"A deal's a deal, Hoss," Taylor said. "Look on the bright side. At least you didn't have to spend a decade in suspense before I called in that marker. Now we can both move on after today and forget we ever even met."

"You do realize how this move will likely end, yes?" the Sumatozou asked. "With both of us lined up in front of an air lock?"

Taylor shrugged. "I'll risk it."

"He'll risk it, he says," said Japhara with a huff. "Damned Humans."

Billy emerged from the shuttle and met them in front of the boarding ramp. "Our ride's prepped and ready. We can launch whenever the two of you are set."

Taylor needed no further promoting. He strode up the ramp behind the XO and headed straight for the passenger cabin to buckle in. Several minutes later, the shuttle broke through Earth's orbit and laid in its vector toward the stargate.

"You sure you wanna do this?" Billy asked once they'd docked with the admin station. "You've gotta know you can't un-ring this bell once it's done."

Taylor considered as he locked in his mag boots. "I understand. Still, what other choice do we have?"

The XO gave a slow nod. "I'll be here when you get back, engines running."

"Appreciate that." Taylor motioned Japhara to the hatch. "After you."

Once outside, the two were met by the same robotic host Taylor had encountered before leaving. The roller bot offered its usual greeting, then led the duo back down the path to the gate master's office.

"Grand Latura Hylune." Haju bowed. "It's an honor to have you aboard this facility."

"Master Haju," Japhara answered in kind. "Has he arrived?"

"He has," Haju said. "He is waiting for you in the council chamber. Everything is prepared, and you may enter when ready."

Japhara nodded then started for the stone doors across the lobby.

"Sir, if I may." Haju halted his superior by the arm then glanced uneasily at Taylor. "Am I to understand that you mean to have this Human accompany you into the chamber?"

Surprise!

Japhara remained straight-faced as he turned to his subordinate. "That was my intention, yes. Is this a problem for you, Master Haju?"

The lower-ranked alien gulped. "No, Grand Latura, there is no problem. Forgive me for asking."

"You are forgiven," Japhara said. "You may now return to your duties."

Haju aimed a parting glare at Taylor then vanished into his office.

Maybe there's hope for this day yet. Taylor waited while Japhara opened the stone doors across the lobby. Afterward, the duo passed through the opening into the dimly lit room on the other side.

At least we know they ain't afraid of the dark. Taylor gave it a beat while his eyes adjusted then looked around.

The council chamber was unlike anything Taylor had ever seen, though he guessed there were a lot of them around the galaxy. Comprised mostly of steel and glass, the room began in the foyer then tapered outward into a three-story hall, whose transparent rear wall cast the entire space in starlight.

"Communications offline," read the words in Taylor's vision. The gate master's dampening field had severed his comm link to the outside world. *Right on schedule.*

Taylor approached the main floor and spied a collection of tapestries lining the walls around him. Some of these depicted historical events like the door carving outside. Others showcased an array of styles and designs Taylor didn't recognize. All he knew was, whatever this place was, it existed for someone very important. *Like royalty.*

"Do not touch anything," Japhara whispered.

Taylor opened his mouth to respond but was cut off by a low voice, coming from the shadows.

"Grand Latura Hylune," it said in a regal tone. "Welcome home."

Japhara dropped instantly to one knee, head down. "Good day, my lord. It pleases me to come once more into your presence."

"As it pleases me to have you," the voice said. "The Council was most delighted to learn of your survival after all these years. It shall be good to have you back."

"Thank you, my lord," Japhara said. "Has the Council reviewed my report?"

"We have," the voice said. "Its contents were quite enlightening, especially those details which pertained to the Krulig scourge. It shall be dealt with, immediately."

"Very good, my lord," Japhara said.

The sounds of footfalls and swooshing fabric emanated from the shadows as, slowly, a lone figure appeared. Tall and bean-pole thin, the lanky, bipedal alien rivaled a CASPer in height, with a long neck, a small, oblong head, and vibrant blue eyes which shimmered in the darkness. Its robes were a shade of magenta, while its skin, pale and alabaster, carried a tinge of blue in the starlight.

Vergola.

"Why have you summon—" The alien's cool expression twisted upon seeing Taylor. "What is the meaning of this?"

"I can explain, my lord," Japhara rushed out. "Allow me to introduce Chief Taylor—"

"I know who he is, Hylune," the Vergola snapped. "Why have you brought him into our inner sanctum?"

Japhara stammered to respond.

"He didn't have a choice," Taylor said. "I'm the one who broke your grand latura out of confinement on Rukoria. In exchange, I made him promise to arrange a meeting between me and the Vergola Council once we got back. I presume that's you."

The Vergola answered with a sneer. "And why would you require such an audience?"

"To give you this." Taylor eased a hand into his vest and pulled out a data drive. "This device contains every last byte of your NOP list. I had Japhara extract it from my Navarro's nav system durin' our transition back to Earth."

The Vergola's demeanor cooled. "Possessing the information on the NOP list would give your company a sizable advantage over your Mercenary Guild competitors. Why would you forgo such an asset so willingly?"

"Cut the crap, man," Taylor said, drawing a cringe from Japhara. "We both know the Council or the Cartography Guild or whatever you wanna call yourselves would never allow one group, much less a Human merc outfit, to keep somethin' this vital to your operation. You *would* come for us, and believe it or not, part of me understands why."

The Vergola seemed perplexed by that statement. "Explain."

"Japhara's right," Taylor said. "Humanity ain't ready for the knowledge on this drive. Even after a century in the stars, we're just not. Couple that with the fact that I've got no desire to paint a Texas-sized target on my company's back, and returnin' this intel to its rightful owners seemed like the smartest play for everyone involved."

"The Council has your word that you've not copied Sadeed's data?" the Vergola asked.

"I extracted the NOP list myself," Japhara said. "I can therefore attest that the information contained within is intact, as the Human claims. His only request was that we allow him to keep the Rukoria route."

"And what of the Rukori?" the Vergola asked. "Now that their existence has been revealed, do they wish to come forward and rejoin the Union?"

Taylor shook his head. "Valawn and his people have problems of their own to deal with. Maybe one day they'll return to civilization, but right now their wish is to stay out of it. They did, however, ask to keep an open dialogue with Swamp Eagle Security. I'd like to honor that if I could."

The Vergola motioned to Japhara, who accepted the drive from Taylor.

"You are a credit to your species, Chief Van Zant," the Vergola said. "Most among your kind would never have taken the path you've chosen, but you did. For that, you should be commended."

"Funny you should mention that." Taylor scratched his whiskers. "Now, I'd like to discuss my terms."

Both aliens frowned.

"You said nothing of terms when you requested this meeting, Van Zant," Japhara grumbled.

"Sorry, Hoss. I was afraid if I spoke up it'd kill my shot at a meet, and frankly I didn't wanna blow that. Call it a forgiveness versus permission thing."

Japhara muttered a curse.

"What do you want?" the Vergola asked.

"Two things." Taylor flashed a pair of fingers. "First, as of this day forward, Swamp Eagle Security will never pay another credit in gate fees, ever. From now on, we'll go where we want, when we want, how we want, and neither you nor the gate masters will say a word otherwise."

The Vergola licked its lips. "Were we to grant this request, it would prove quite the windfall for your organization."

"Rule number one of business is if profits ain't where you want 'em to be, cut expenses. By my count, this is the biggest one we've got."

"Indeed," the Vergola said. "What else?"

"Next, I want a name," Taylor said.

"A name?" Japhara looked up. "A name for whom?"

Taylor kept his focus on the Vergola. "My brother's death wasn't an accident. He and his crew were murdered. Sadeed's lap dog, a Zuul drewga named Tulipza, confessed as much durin' our time together in their compound. He said his pack snuck aboard the *Bogrider* and tampered with Terry's F11 supply to prompt an engine failure durin' transition."

"If the Zuul were responsible for your brother's fate, then what name do you require from us?" the Vergola asked.

"The Zuul couldn't have boarded the *Bogrider* without access," Taylor said. "They got help from someone on the inside via contract."

The Vergola cocked its head. "And you want the name of the accepting party."

"One point to the stick man," Taylor said.

"The agreement of which you speak falls under the purview of the Mercenary Guild," Japhara said, "not the Cartography Guild. As such, the Council has no authority to—"

"Ah, give it a fargin rest, Japhara," Taylor interrupted. "We both know that one call from your boss here gets the info I need in no time. Hell, probably by lunch. Now is he gonna make it or not?"

The Vergola clasped its fingers and smiled. "Tell me, Human. Why would the Council agree to these demands, especially given that you've already forfeited your only piece of leverage?"

Taylor shrugged. "Who says the NOP list was my only leverage?"

The thin alien's glower returned.

"Let's lay our cards on the table here, fellas. Half the Union already suspects that the Cartography Guild is holdin' out on them with the current atlas. That's a given. Prior to now, though, nobody's been able to prove it. But." Taylor raised a finger. "What if word of the NOP list got out? Furthermore, what would happen if folks outside these walls got wind that one all-powerful race had coopted said Guild from the shadows and was usin' it to line their own pockets? I'd say that sort of news is likely to buzz some GalNet headlines, wouldn't you?"

Japhara pursed his lips. "But you just gave us the NOP list."

"I did. I just didn't do it alone." Taylor reached back into his vest. This time when his hand returned, it did so holding a palm-sized device made of plastic. "This here is what folks used to listen to music on back in the late-twentieth century. They called it a cassette player, or tape deck for short. Oddly enough, it's got a record feature."

Both aliens looked on, mortified, as Taylor replayed the last few seconds of their conversation.

"See?" Taylor ejected the cassette and admired one of the jewels of his collection. "Yep, these were hot little commodities back in their heyday. Granted, their sound quality pales in comparison to modern-day tech, but I still think they hold up pretty well. Wouldn't y'all agree?"

The last of the Vergola's calm began to falter. It flared its nostrils and leaned in close. "You have asked many questions of me this day, Human. Now allow me to posit one of my own. What would stop us from killing you where you stand and taking that recording before it leaves this chamber?"

'Oh, it's already left the chamber," Taylor flipped over the tape and returned it to the player. "See, another cool thing about these little gizmos is their broadcast feature."

Japhara did a double-take. "Am I to believe that you've been transmitting our discussion this whole time?"

"That was the implication, yeah," Taylor said.

"Impossible," the Vergola snapped. "Hylune, scan the chamber for signals."

Japhara hurried across the floor to an access panel near the back and swiped open its controls. "All signals, including the chief's comm link, have been disabled. No one outside this room is hearing us."

"You sure about that?" Taylor put the tape deck to his lips. "Corn Husker, this is Tomahawk. Do you copy?"

Static crackled the line.

"Go for Husker," Billy's voice said. "What's your status, Tomahawk?"

"Still down here in the council chamber, chattin' with our new friends," Taylor said. "Speakin' of, did you get all that?"

Another pop of static.

"Every word," Billy said. "The Council, the NOP list. We got it all."

"Nice work," Taylor said. "Download the recordin' file into the shuttle's data core, then carbon out to the eight independent sources we discussed. I want to make sure we're covered in case somebody here gets squirrely. Oh, and make sure Japhara gets named in the file. Call it the air lock clause."

The Sumatozou winced, but the relief in his face was undeniable.

"Copy that," Billy said. "I'll handle it now. Husker out."

Taylor thumbed off his player and tucked it back into his vest. "Now…about my terms."

* * *

Taylor paced the lobby outside the Council chamber for what felt like an eternity. In truth, it took about an hour for Japhara to reappear with a decision.

"The Council has agreed to your demands," Japhara said. "Swamp Eagle Security will never pay gate fees again so long as you are in command."

"And the name?" Taylor asked.

Japhara produced another data drive but held it back. "Might I offer a word of advice?"

Taylor folded his arms and waited.

"Revenge isn't all it's cracked up to be. It does close the wound, and there is certainly something to be said for that. However, wounds this deep leave scars. You must be prepared for that."

Taylor shot the alien a smirk. "So says the guy who lopped off his enemy's head with my arm blade. Now are you gonna gimme the data or not?"

Japhara relinquished the drive. "For what it's worth, I'm glad I did not have to kill you back there. That would have been…unfortunate."

"You'll get no argument here." Taylor turned for the exit.

"Van Zant," Japhara said.

"Yeah?"

The Sumatozou exhaled beneath his trunks. "Be safe out there. Ayew?"

Taylor glanced past his shoulder and gave his cellmate a half smile. "Ayew. See ya around, Hoss."

Billy was waiting outside the jetway when Taylor rounded the corner. "There you are. I was starting to get worried."

Taylor shooed his robot escort away, then boarded the tube to their shuttle.

"I take it our little ruse worked?" Billy asked.

Taylor produced his tape deck and gave a quick tap of the *play* button. "I'll dub copies as soon as we're back at the Clubhouse. That's our insurance policy should the Council try to renege on our deal."

Billy shook his head and smiled. "Man, please. Remind me to never again try to bluff you in poker."

"Bet you'll never make fun of my hobbies again, either," Taylor said.

Once inside the shuttle, the pair coasted to the passenger cabin, where Taylor deposited his cassette player, complete with its pre-recorded comments from Billy and picked up a slate.

"You want me to stick around?" Billy asked.

"Nah, that's okay," Taylor said. "Head on up to the cockpit and get us underway. I don't know about you, but I'm ready to put my boots down in some real gravity again."

"Amen to that, Chief."

Taylor put his head back and sighed as the XO vanished from sight. After that, he fished out Japhara's data drive and plugged it into his slate.

"The following document is the property of the Galactic Union Mercenary Guild," the screen read. "Contract Status: Confidential."

Taylor scrolled down the page in search of the answers he'd waited six long years to find. Until that moment, he could've never known the pain his heart would feel upon learning them. *Son of a bitch.*

*****

Chapter 32: Confessions of a Ghost

Taylor didn't sleep a wink that night after returning to Jacksonville. Heaven knew his body wanted it—needed it, even. Still, his addled mind refused to let his consciousness fade. He rose the next morning, fatigued and stressed out, then downed a shot of whiskey with his coffee in preparation for the day ahead.

A crack of thunder rolled through the slate-gray sky over 295 South as Taylor steered his Harley toward the last place on Earth he wanted to be. In all the times he'd made this drive—and that had been a lot over the years—he'd never once felt that way. Now, he'd have given anything to have it so again.

"Most wounds this deep leave scars," Japhara had said. "You must be prepared for that."

Taylor cursed the blacktop below. Meanwhile, the same question played over and over like a turntable in his mind. *Why?*

Spotting the exit for Tebow Drive as the first rain drops touched his skin, Taylor hooked right off the interstate and headed north up Coughlin Avenue toward the gate to his destination.

"Go on in, Chief," the guard said. "He's expecting you."

Taylor had figured as much. He waved his thanks, then leaned on the bike's accelerator to enter the compound. Shortly thereafter, he was parked and up the steps of the command center, knocking on the door to an audience with a ghost.

"Come in," said a familiar voice from the other side.

Taylor pushed open the door and entered the office. "Hey, Ron."

If Ron Carnegie's face was any indication, he hadn't slept much the night before, either. His skin was eerie pale, and his eyes were framed by bags the size of Goodyear tires. He leaned forward and put his elbows on his desk. "Morning, kid. How are you?"

"Tired," Taylor said.

Ron gave a weak smile. "Yeah, me, too. Can I offer you a drink?"

Taylor nodded and sat down while his host retrieved a jar of River City Blond from the corner shelf and tipped it over two glasses.

Ron handed a whiskey to Taylor and kept one for himself. "Salute."

Taylor waited for his host to drink first.

"Right." Ron frowned. He fired back his glass and sat down. "So, what can I do for you this fine, stormy morning?"

Taylor glared a response.

"Yeah, I was afraid of that," Ron said. "I take it you pulled some strings with that Sumatozou pal of yours to get the contract."

Taylor thumbed the rim of his glass, avoiding eye contact. "Why'd you do it?"

The old man's specter-like features faded to an even sicker shade of pale. "It's so much more complicated than you know."

"No, it's not," Taylor growled. "For the record, you oughta know that I didn't just take all this on faith from Japhara. I did some diggin' of my own when I got home last night. Imagine my surprise when personnel sent me a file showin' Samuel A. Carnegie's name on the engineerin' team that serviced Terry's ship before Karma." He sat forward, eyes narrowed to slits. "Now, I'll ask you again, Ron. Why'd you do it? Why'd you cover for your son after he effectively signed a death warrant on my brother?"

The old man hung his head and sighed. "The Eagles and Steeldriver shared something of an exchange program back then. It was a way to help our people expand their skills, be they troopers or engineers, by showing them how others across the street did business. It was mostly low-level stuff, of course, but it allowed us to help our people get better at their jobs."

"How'd Sammy get involved?" Taylor asked.

Ron ran a palm through his disheveled silver hair. "Sammy came to me about two weeks before Terry shipped out and asked if he could join the program. He knew no one would hire him after Houston, so he saw this as a way to start fresh and rebuild his reputation. He really wanted it, Taylor, more than I'd seen him want anything in a long time."

"So, what?" Taylor snorted. "Your junkie kid fed you a sob story about how bad his life was, so you put in a call to Terry and had him assigned to the *Bogrider?*"

Ron grimaced, and for a second, part of Taylor hated that he'd gone that far.

"Sammy had been clean for a while by then," Ron said in a small voice. "He was also never supposed to have that kind of clearance. He was just there to work with the programming team and upgrade efficiency on a handful of minor systems around campus. That's it."

"How did he gain access then?" Taylor asked.

"If I had to guess?" Ron shrugged. "He played the 'my dad's a Carnegie' angle to get through security, then leveraged his skills as a coder to get what he needed from there."

Taylor muttered a curse.

"I swear to you, kid," Ron said, almost pleading. "I had no idea when I signed Sammy up for the exchange program that things would go down this way. And for what it's worth? He didn't, either."

Taylor raised an eyebrow. "What does that mean?"

Ron eased up a hand, as if asking permission to move it.

Taylor nodded, then watched the old man reach into his desk and come back with a slip of paper. Tattered and worn, it resembled an old-style letter.

"What's that?" Taylor asked.

Ron stared at the document for a long moment, then slid it across the desk. "Sammy's death in New Orleans wasn't due to an accidental overdose at a party. It was a suicide."

Never in Taylor's life had he felt so blindsided. He allowed himself a moment to process, then picked up the letter and began reading.

Dear Dad, the opening line read. *I know you and I have had our differences over the years. A lot of that was the result of my poor decisions. I wholly accept that. As God is my witness, though, you must believe me when I say I didn't know what was happening until it was too late to stop it.*

Taylor continued down the page, taking in every last agonizing word of a nineteen-year-old boy's confession. Once he'd passed the final sentence—*I am so, so sorry*—he refolded the paper and returned it to its owner. "Sammy thought the Zuul meant to raid Terry's data core, chasin' dirt on a contract. He had no clue they'd go after the engines."

The old man shook his head and looked away.

"My family had a right to know this stuff, Ron," Taylor said with all the calm he could muster. "You should've come forward with what you knew."

"And what would that have changed?" Ron flipped up a palm. "Seriously, Taylor. I mean no disrespect, but what would my telling you any of this really have changed?"

Taylor stabbed out a finger to answer, but Carnegie continued.

"Not a day went by that I didn't want to tell you Sammy's secret. I'd have done anything to bring Terry back, but that wasn't in the cards. All I'd have achieved by outing my son's mistake would've been to drag my family's name even deeper into the mud, while simultaneously showing the galaxy what a shitty father I'd been." Fresh tears welled in the old man's eyes, so he wiped them away with the back of his hand. "Don't you see? That's my fault, kid." He pointed to the letter. "Every last bit of it. Sammy's mistakes? His lifestyle choices? Even his end in New Orleans. It's all my fault. If I'd just been there for him earlier on in life, I might've been able to..."

Taylor settled back into his seat as the last of the old man's strength gave way to a deluge of grief and regret. "Sammy made his own decisions, Ron. He said as much right there in his note. You can't pin everything that went wrong in his life on yourself."

"You're not a dad, Taylor, so I don't expect you to understand." Ron sniffled. "A man oughta always—always—put his family first, no matter what. I didn't do that. Instead, I gave everything I had to Steeldriver. My time, my energy, my soul. And for what? So my kids could grow up in a nice house with gobs of money and a fleet of toys they were bored with within a month?" He scoffed. "Trust me when I say, kid, that material stuff adds up to squat in the end. What my family needed—what Sammy needed—was his father. What he got was a handful of leave days from a ghost who spent most of his life off-world, chasing the next contract. I've had to live with that for almost seven years now, and for the sake of my wife and our other children, I'll go on living with it until the day they put me in the ground. That's *my* cross to bear, but I'll carry it as best I can...for them."

Silence filled the air as both men sat speechless. Meanwhile, the patter of rain escalated against the office window outside.

"So," Ron finally said. "Now that you know the truth, where do you intend to go with this?"

Taylor stroked his whiskers and weighed the myriad answers to that question. As much as he wanted to hate this man for his lack of an admission, the fact remained that Ron's point was valid. Revealing Sammy's betrayal would've succeeded only in trashing the Carnegie line, none of whom had done anything to deserve it. Steeldriver would've also been finished, since few organizations—and no one on Earth—would likely have ever worked with them again.

Did Ron Carnegie have an obligation to tell the truth? *Yes.* However, he also had an obligation to protect his surviving family and dismantling his livelihood wouldn't have done that. At the same time, it wasn't fair that the Van Zants had been forced back to the poorhouse because of the elder's Carnegie's silence.

That ain't entirely the case, T, and you know it. Taylor winced at that reality.

Sam Carnegie's role in Terry's death couldn't be argued. What also couldn't be argued was that the boy's decision to deal with the Zuul hadn't been the only driver behind the Van Zants' return to poverty after the accident. That had come via Terry's decisions, specifically those pertaining to his finances. Because of that one misstep, not even a testimony from Ron would've stopped the banks from taking everything. What the old man had done, though, was intercede on the Van Zants' behalf wherever they'd let him afterward. He'd paid their bills when they couldn't afford to, put food on their table when tips were scarce at the Hell House. He'd even offered to pay for their mom's nanite treatments when she'd gotten sick, but by then the MCA deal had materialized, which had allowed Taylor to cover those on his own.

In many respects, Ron Carnegie had been the father Taylor had never known, since his own dad passed of a heart attack prior to seventh grade. Now he understood why. "You know I've gotta tell my mom and the others, right? They deserve to know the truth about what happened."

Ron cleared his throat. "I know. Who else?"

Lisa Kouvaris comes to mind. Taylor knew the malicious origins of that thought, so he put it aside. He then rose from his seat and extended a hand. "Ron, I want to thank you for everything you've ever done for my sisters and me. You've been a real friend to us, and I want you to know nothin' will ever change that history in my book."

"History." Ron studied his guest's palm, seeming to chew on the word. "And what about the future?"

"There is no future," Taylor said. "On behalf of my family and everyone at Swamp Eagle Security, I'd like to wish you and Steeldriver well with your future endeavors. This, however, will be the last time we exchange pleasantries as anything other than colleagues. Is that clear?"

Ron nodded somberly. "Yeah."

Taylor polished off his whisky and started for the door.

"Hey, Taylor?"

"What?"

Ron swallowed. "Take care of yourself, okay kid?"

Taylor had looked back to address Japhara the day before on the stargate. He couldn't bring himself to do that here, no matter how much part of him wanted to. "You, too, old man. Goodbye."

*****

Chapter 33:
A New Dawn

Taylor purposefully avoided the news for the rest of that day. He didn't think Ron would do anything rash, but he couldn't know for sure, and he didn't want to hear about it on the Tri-V if he'd been wrong. He'd just topped off his second cup of coffee the next morning when his comm link rang.

"Go for Van Zant," Taylor said via pinlink.

"Hey, it's me," Billy said. "You need to get upstairs right now."

Oh no. Taylor closed his eyes and braced for the worst. "What's goin' on?"

"Lisa Kouvaris is here," Billy said. "She's got some news you're gonna wanna hear. Trust me, it's important."

The tenor in the XO's voice wasn't dark at all. If anything, he sounded intrigued.

So not bad news then? Taylor certainly hoped so. "On my way."

Polishing off the last of his java, Taylor shimmied into a t-shirt and jeans, then pulled his ponytail through the back of his Generals cap on his way out the door. A minute later, he was up the stairs and crossing the Clubhouse's second floor to the conference room.

"Morning, Taylor," Lisa said. "Good to see you again."

"Likewise." Taylor halted next to Billy. "What brings you back out here to swamp country?"

Lisa reached into her bag and fished out a slate. "You're gonna wanna take a seat for this."

Taylor's earlier sense of dread returned. He glanced uneasily at his XO, then proceeded to his chair at the head of the table as Smitty, Quint, Frank, and Keeto entered the room.

"Captain," Smitty said to Billy.

"Commander," the XO answered.

Taylor couldn't help but notice the faintest of smiles shared between the two officers as they crossed paths. *It's about damn time.*

"Not to be an a-hole here, Billy, but I had to cancel leave for this meeting." Quint yawned into a fist. "Can somebody please tell me why that is?"

"Ms. Kouvaris here was just about to get to that," Billy said.

Quint offered his usual indignant look to the reporter. "Oh. Well then. Do carry on."

Lisa swiped open her slate. "My editor called me just after six this morning in a total panic."

"What about?" Taylor asked.

"According to a source of his over at Steeldriver," Lisa said, "Ron Carnegie held an emergency meeting late last night with his senior staff. Shortly thereafter, all missions were cancelled, all ships were grounded, and all company operations were suspended indefinitely."

Taylor looked to Billy, who raised a shoulder.

"I was just as surprised as you were," the XO said.

"Why has Steeldriver shuttered its doors?" Taylor asked.

Lisa shook her head. "Your guess is as good as ours. We've heard nothing from the head office save for a brief press advisory, letting us know that an official word of some kind is forthcoming."

"Any clue what that word could be?" Smitty asked.

"Nope," Lisa said. "Some are saying Steeldriver may be put up for sale. Others are speculating that this is the prelude to some sort of major organizational shakeup. Until Carnegie's people make their announcement, we can't know for certain."

A knock at the door prompted everyone to turn.

"Sorry for the interruption, Chief." Paul cracked an opening and peered inside. "We just took a delivery at the front gate. It's for you."

"Can it wait?" Taylor asked.

"I guess." The doctor adjusted his glasses. "I'd be remiss, though, if I didn't mention that the package was marked as urgent."

Taylor motioned for Paul to enter.

Once to the table, Paul reached into his breast pocket and came back with an old-style mailing envelope.

"Haven't seen one of those in a while," Quint said. "Who's it from?"

Taylor gave the doctor his leave, then tore open the envelope's seal. Inside, he found a letter like the one he'd seen in Ron's office.

Hey, kid, the message began. *There are no words of apology strong enough to convey just how truly sorry I am for the harm my family has done to yours. I know you said it wasn't my fault, but blood is blood, and Sammy was ours. That makes his mistakes ours, too. My son's debt to you is one I could never repay in a thousand lifetimes, so I won't even try. What I would offer, humbly so, is the closest thing I have to a conciliation.*

Taylor blinked in disbelief at the next line.

"What is it, Chief?" Frank asked.

Taylor had to read it twice to make sure he wasn't seeing things.

The time has come for me to leave the mercenary business, the letter continued. *I've run my course with it, just as you're beginning yours as owner of the*

Eagles. I've taken what I need of my assets to live out the rest of my retirement in peace, and I hereby relinquish the rest to you. Do with them what you will. All I ask is that you never forget what I told you back in my office. Always, always put your family first, no matter what. Remember that, and you'll do just fine. Good luck, kid. I'm here if you need me. Your friend, Ron.

Taylor refolded the paper and stared blankly out the window to his right.

"Enough with the suspense already," Billy said. "Are you gonna tell us what it says or not?"

Taylor gulped. "As of last night, every acre of the Steeldriver Defense Group campus, along with every asset that goes with it—equipment, personnel, CASPers, everything—is henceforth the sole property of Swamp Eagle Security."

Quint's jaw all but smashed the table on its way down. "You're kidding."

Taylor pulled a second document from the envelope—this one a legal affidavit confirming everything he'd just said—and showed it to the group.

"Well now." Smitty folded her arms. "That bloody well changes things, doesn't it?"

"Why would Carnegie do this?" Lisa asked. "Come on, Taylor. I know you went to see him yesterday. What did he say?"

Taylor shook his head. "I promise you, Lisa. Ron never breathed a word of any of this. We talked business and family. That's it."

That was true enough, Taylor thought.

"Hot damn, I can't wait to see my new digs!" Quint jumped up and sprinted for the exit, halting awkwardly at the door. "That's assuming, of course, that we're dismissed…sir."

"Go." Taylor chuckled.

Quint bolted out the door in a blur of denim and tattoos.

"Am to presume, based off this development, that we'll be expanding the senior staff in the days ahead?" Smitty asked.

"I'd call that a safe assumption," Taylor said. "More bodies typically translate to more companies, meanin' more company commanders. I'll have to check the Steeldriver personnel files to see whose comin' over, but I've got some ideas about a few internal candidates."

Smitty tilted her head. "The farts?"

"The farts," Taylor agreed.

Smitty laughed and rose from her chair. "Well, all right, then. If you gents will excuse me, I think I'll go make sure our favorite ex-slugger doesn't do something stupid like shoot out the lights of our old house before we make it into our new one."

"I'd be mighty grateful if you did," Taylor said.

"Yo, I got a question." Frank raised a hand once the Aussie had gone. "Are we also takin' on new ships with this deal?"

"Looks like it, yeah," Taylor said.

"And will those ships be requiring new pilots?" Frank asked.

"Possibly," Taylor said. "Again, I won't know what we're workin' with until I get the Steeldriver personnel files for review."

Frank's expression was surprisingly serious. "None of them touches the *Osyrys*. That's my one request. After everything that Navarro and I have been through, she's my girl, and nobody's taking her from me without a fight."

"I would echo that sentiment for engineering," Keeto said. "Steeldriver's ships are impressive, yes. However, the *Ryley Osyrys* is one of a kind. It would be my honor to keep her spaceworthy."

"Relax, fellas," Taylor said. "The *Osyrys* ain't goin' anywhere, and neither is her crew. She's yours as long as you're a part of this outfit."

Both aliens seemed good with that answer. They said their good-byes, then left to join the makings of party outside.

"Speakin' of the *Osyrys*." Taylor turned to his XO. "I've been doin' some thinkin'. How does the title EMS *Bowden* sound to you?"

Billy wrinkled his nose. "You considering a moniker change?"

"I am," Taylor said. "The joke's over. I've had my fun with the name as is, and frankly it ain't fair to keep somethin' like that around, given the dubious history one of my officers has with its origins. It's time for a change."

Billy propped his chin on his fist, considering. "You know, I don't think it is."

Taylor furrowed his eyebrows. "Really?"

"Colonel Terry Van Zant gave the *Ryley Osyrys* her name," Billy said, "and while I wholeheartedly realize the Eagles are no longer under his command, I think it's important for a company to remember where it came from. I say keep the name as is."

Taylor couldn't have hidden his astonishment if he'd wanted to. "Okay, it's settled. The Eagles' flagship is now, and forever will be, the EMS *Ryley Osyrys*."

"May God have mercy on our souls." Billy laughed, then departed to rejoin the others.

This left Taylor and Lisa as the room's final two occupants.

"So," the reporter said. "It looks like Swamp Eagle Security is poised to become a big deal around town again. What do you plan on doing next?"

Taylor weighed how best to answer that. "Honestly? I was contemplatin' a trip to the bar to ponder that very thing. You interested?"

Lisa checked the time on her slate. "It's nine in the morning."

"Yep." Taylor grinned. "And it just so happens, I know a place that's open."

# # # # #

ABOUT THE AUTHOR

A graduate of Florida State University, sci-fi author Ian J. Malone has written in a variety of arenas ranging from public health to news and sports. When it comes to his scifi work, however, he's a firm believer that nothing shapes a person's writing like experience. That's why he credits his tenures in radio, law enforcement, and military contracting for much of his inspiration, plus the legion of family and friends who've stood with him along the way.

Beyond writing, Malone is an avid fan of audiobooks (he's legally blind) and the outdoors. It's also not uncommon to find him at a ballgame, a concert, or somewhere out by a grill.

Malone is an active member of the Science Fiction & Fantasy Writers of America and a resident of Durham, North Carolina — but he'll always be a "Florida boy" at heart.

For more on Ian J. Malone and his books (and how the EMS *Ryley Osyrys* got her name), visit him online at www.ianjmalone.net. You can also follow him on Twitter, Facebook, or Goodreads.

* * * * *

Connect with Seventh Seal Press

Get the **free** prelude story "**Shattered Crucible,**"

join the mailing list, and discover other titles at:

http://chriskennedypublishing.com/

Facebook: https://www.facebook.com/chriskennedypublishing.biz

* * * * *

Do you have what it takes to be a Merc?

Take your VOWs and join the Merc Guild on Facebook!

Meet us at: https://www.facebook.com/groups/536506813392912/

* * * * *

The following is an

Excerpt from Book 1 of the Four Horsemen:

Cartwright's Cavaliers

Mark Wandrey

Available from Seventh Seal Press

December, 2016

eBook, Paperback, and Audio Book

The last two operational tanks were trapped on their chosen path. Faced with destroyed vehicles front and back, they cut sideways to the edge of the dry river bed they'd been moving along and found several large boulders to maneuver around that allowed them to present a hull-down defensive position. Their troopers rallied on that position. It was starting to look like they'd dig in when Phoenix 1 screamed over and strafed them with dual streams of railgun rounds. A split second later, Phoenix 2 followed on a parallel path. Jim was just cheering the air attack when he saw it. The sixth damned tank, and it was a heavy.

"I got that last tank," Jim said over the command net.

"Observe and stand by," Murdock said.

"We'll have these in hand shortly," Buddha agreed, his transmission interspersed with the thudding of his CASPer firing its magnet accelerator. "We can be there in a few minutes."

Jim examined his battlespace. The tank was massive. It had to be one of the fusion-powered beasts he'd read about. Which meant shields and energy weapons. It was heading down the same gap the APC had taken, so it was heading right towards that APC and Second Squad, and fast.

"Shit," he said.

"Jim," Hargrave said, "we're in position. What are you doing?"

"Leading," Jim said as he jumped out from the rock wall.

*****

*****

The following is an

Excerpt from Book One of In Revolution Born:

The Mutineer's Daughter

Chris Kennedy & Thomas A. Mays

Available Now from Seventh Seal Press

eBook, Paperback, and Audio Book

Excerpt from "The Mutineer's Daughter:"

Kenny dozed at his console again.

There he sat—as brazen as ever—strapped down, suited up, jacked in…and completely checked out. One might make allowances for an overworked man falling asleep during a dull routine, watching gauges that didn't move or indicators that rarely indicated anything of consequence, perhaps even during a quiet moment during their ship's long, long deployment.

But Fire Control Tech Third Class Ken Burnside was doing it—yet again—while the ship stood at General Quarters, in an unfriendly star system, while other parts of the fleet engaged the forces of the Terran Union.

Chief Warrant Officer Grade 2 (Combat Systems) Benjamin "Benno" Sanchez shook his helmeted head and narrowed his eyes at the sailor strapped in to his right. He had spoken to the young weapons engineer a number of times before, through countless drills and mock skirmishes, but the youthful idiot never retained the lesson for long.

"Benno, Bosso," Kenny would plead, "you shouldn't yell at me. You should have me teach others my wisdom!"

Benno would invariably frown and give his unflattering opinion of Kenny's wisdom.

"Get it, ya?" Kenny would reply. "I'm a math guy. Probability, right Warrant? The *Puller's* just a little ship, on the edge of the formation. We scan, we snipe, we mop up, we patrol. We don't go in the middle, tube's blazing, ya? We no tussle with the big Terrans, ya? No damage! No battle! So, something goes wrong, back-ups kick in, buzzer goes off, we mark for fix later. And when's the only time you or the officers don't let a man walk 'round and don't ask for this, don't ask for that? When's the only time a man can catch up on the z's, eh? One and the same time! So I doze. Buzzer goes off, I wake, make a note, doze again till I can work, ya? Such wisdom!"

Benno usually lectured him about complacency. He asked what would happen if they *were* hit, if the shot was hot enough, deep enough, destructive enough to burn through the backup of the backup of the backup. What if they did have to face the Great Test, to rise and work and save the *Puller* themselves?

Kenny would always smile, relieved. "Well, then I be dead, ya? No more maintenance either way. Good enough reason to doze right there!"

Benno could have reported him any number of times, but he never had. Putting it on paper and sending it above them was a two-edged sword. It would solve Kenny's sleepy disdain for order, of that Benno had no doubt, but he also knew he would lose Kenny's trust and the vigorous drive the young ALS plebeian applied to every other task. Plus, it would signal to the officers above that Benno couldn't handle a minor discipline problem on his own. And it would indicate to the ranks below that Benno was no longer one of their own—when he had gone from Chief to Chief Warrant Officer, he had changed his ties, forever.

So Benno growled, but he let it slide, content only he would know about Kenny's acts of passive rebellion. No one else would ever know why the young tech kept getting extra punishment duties. Besides, it wasn't as if Kenny was actually *wrong*, in the fullness of things.

Then, before Benno could check his own side of the console to verify whether things were indeed alright, his internal debate was blown away by the unforgiving, indiscriminate lance of an x-ray laser blast.

The single beam struck the *Puller* a glancing blow, centered on a space just beneath the outer hull and aimed outboard. Armor plate, radiation shielding, piping, wireways, conduit, decking, internal honeycombed structure, atmosphere, and people all ionized and ablated into a dense, mixed plasma. This plasma exploded outward, crushing the spaces surrounding the hit and dealing further physical and thermal damage. Combat Systems Maintenance Central, or CSMC, lay deep within the *Puller's* battle hull—three spaces inward from where the x-ray laser struck—but that meant little next to the awesome destructive power of a Dauphine capital-class xaser warhead.

The forward and port bulkheads in front of them flashed white hot with near-instantaneous thermal energy transfer and peeled away, blown out by the twin shocks of the outward-expanding plasma and the snapping counterforce of explosive decompression. The double blast battered Benno in his seat and threw him against his straps to the left. As the bulkheads vanished, their departure also carried away the CSMC monitoring console the two watch standers shared with them into the black, along with Kenny's seat, and Ken Burnside, himself.

The young engineer disappeared in an instant, lost without ever waking. Benno stared, dumbfounded, at the blank spot where he had been, and of all the possible panicked thoughts that could have come to him, only one rose to the forefront:

Does this validate Kenny's wisdom?

Benno shook his head, dazed and in shock, knowing he had to engage his brain. Looking beyond, he could see the glowing edges of bulkheads and decks gouged out by the fast, hot knife of the nuclear-pumped xaser. Only vaguely could he recall the sudden buffeting of explosive decompression that had nearly wrenched him through the straps of his acceleration couch.

He knew he had things to do. He had to check his suit's integrity. Was he leaking? Was he injured? And what about Kenny? Was he gone, unrecoverable? Or was he waiting for his poor, shocked-stupid boss Benno to reach out and save him?

And there was something else, something important he needed to be doing. He wasn't supposed to just sit here and think of himself or unlucky, lazy Kenny. *Oh no,* thought Benno, still trying to marshal his thoughts back together, *Mio is going to be so angry with me, sitting here like a fool…*

"CSMC, report!"

Benno shook his head against the ringing he hadn't realized filled his ears. He reached out for the comms key on his console, swore at how futile that was, then keyed his suit mic. "Last station calling, this is CSMC. We've taken a hit. I lost my technician, console is…down, hard. Over."

"CSMC, TAO," the *Puller's* Tactical Action Officer said through the suit channel, "pull it together! We just had a near miss by a capital class Dauphine warhead. The battle with the Terrans has spread out of the main body. I have missiles up but zero point-defense. I need guns and beams back, *now!*"

*****

*****

Made in the USA
Middletown, DE
10 May 2025

75348651R00215